Susan Elliot Wright grew up in Lewisham in south-east London, left school at sixteen and married unwisely at eighteen. She didn't begin to pursue her childhood dream of writing until she left her unhappy marriage and went to university at the age of thirty. After gaining a degree in English, she decided to choose a new name, and began flicking through the phonebook for ideas. She settled on Elliot and changed her name by deed poll. Then she met 'Mr Right' (actually, Mr Wright) to whom she is now happily married. She has an MA in Writing from Sheffield Hallam University, where she is now an Associate Lecturer. Several of her short stories have won or been shortlisted for awards, and one of these, 'Day Tripper', was broadcast on BBC Radio 4. To find out more, visit her website http://www.susanelliotwright.co.uk/ or follow her on twitter @sewelliot

Praise for *The Things We Never Said*:

'Passionate, intriguing and beautifully written, *The Things We Never Said* deserves to stand on the shelf next to Maggie O'Farrell's books. A powerful and talented new voice' Rachel Hore, bestselling author of *A Gathering Storm* and *A Place of Secrets*

'This is a staggeringly accomplished first novel, perfectly paced. It sweeps you up from the very first page and doesn't let you go until the end. The hauntingly nostalgic tale of the trauma of an unwanted pregnancy in the sixties, it has echoes of Lynn Reid Banks and Margaret Forster. You can almost smell the boarding house and feel the cold of an unforgiving winter as aspiring actress Maggie faces up to some brutal choices that will affect her for the rest of her life. The ensuing trauma is entwined with a very modern tale of marriage, impending fatherhood and the perils of the workplace in twenty-first-century Britain. The two stories dovetail to perfection. It's both deeply moving and uplifting – an emotional rollercoaster.

If you love Maggie O'Farrell, you will love this' Veronica Henry, bestselling author of *The Long Weekend*

'A brave and moving story about how much can be lost and what happens next. A compelling and impressive debut' Alison Moore, author of the Booker-shortlisted *The Lighthouse*

'Two intertwined stories explore a past filled with terror and grief, and a heart-breaking present, in writing as smooth and bittersweet as fine dark chocolate' Jane Rogers, author of the Booker-longlisted *The Testament of Jessie Lamb*

'Tightly-woven and tender, *The Things We Never Said* is a beautifully crafted story that explores harsh family secrets with effortless clarity. A wonderful debut' Isabel Ashdown, award-winning author of *Glasshopper*

'I was swept along by Elliot Wright's assured storytelling' Katie Ward, author of *Girl, Reading*

'Compelling and deeply moving . . . this is superb storytelling which transports the reader with ease between past and present, across a gulf of fifty years, while gradually revealing the connection between the two. I couldn't put it down' Jane Rusbridge, author of *The Devil's Music* and *Rook*

SUSAN
ELLIOT WRIGHT

The Things We Never Said

**SIMON &
SCHUSTER**

London · New York · Sydney · Toronto · New Delhi

A CBS COMPANY

First published in Great Britain by Simon & Schuster UK Ltd, 2013
A CBS COMPANY

1 3 5 7 9 10 8 6 4 2

Simon & Schuster UK Ltd
1st Floor
222 Gray's Inn Road
London WC1X 8HB

www.simonandschuster.co.uk

Simon & Schuster Australia, Sydney
Simon & Schuster India, New Delhi

A CIP catalogue record for this book is available
from the British Library

TPB ISBN 978-1-47110-231-8
Paperback ISBN 978-1-47110-232-5
Ebook ISBN 978-1-47110-233-2

Typeset by Hewer Text UK Ltd, Edinburgh
Printed and bound in Great Britain by CPI Group (UK) Ltd, Croydon, CR0 4YY

For Francis.
And in memory of Winifred Annie Wright, 1915–2011,
a dear friend and an inspiration.

PROLOGUE

February 2009

The curtains are drawn but she knows it's still raining because she can hear the cars on the coast road swishing as they pass. There was a flurry of snow last night, but the rain seems to have driven it away, thank heavens. She hates snow; shudders when she thinks about it. The overhead bulb seems dim so she switches on the standard lamp, her finger catching on the fringed trim that's coming away from the shade. She looks again at the letter, a single sheet of paper, two paragraphs of black print with a handwritten signature. Somehow, she manages to still her trembling hands enough to tuck it back into its envelope and stuff it into the pocket of her dressing gown, conscious at once of her senses tuning up. She mustn't allow herself to panic; she just needs to think. The moment crystallises and she becomes aware, all at the same time, of the faint chink of plates from the kitchen, the smell of almost-burnt toast, the clunk of the kitchen clock labouring its way to the next minute, and the bitter-orange tang of marmalade on her tongue. She hurries out of the sitting room and along the hallway to the bedroom, where it seems she's left the radio on. She sits on her side of the bed, tempted briefly to crawl back under the covers, pull the duvet over her head and pretend it's still night.

Heavy snow in parts of the south is causing major disruption to London's transport network, John Humphrys is saying. After the news, he'll be asking the chief executive of the Local Government Association whether councils should have been better prepared. The pips go; eight o'clock. She tries to focus on the news headlines: snow; schools closed; credit crunch to worsen; Nick Clegg vows to slash class sizes; sharp increase in measles cases described as 'very worrying'. She hits the *off* button, then looks around as if not quite sure where she is. Fresh air, that's what she needs; fresh sea air. Her gardening skirt is draped over the back of the chair, and there's a jumper on the floor. And she'll need underwear, of course, and a couple of socks. But as she gathers the clothes, the thought of putting them on overwhelms her. She sits back on the bed, defeated, and allows the garments to slither to the floor. She needs to get outside. Now. If she can just feel the rain on her head and the salty air on her face, she'll be able to think more clearly.

Until she climbs the steep concrete steps up to the street, she doesn't realise how heavily it's raining. The pavements are awash; water is cascading noisily from gutters and flooding out from downpipes. There is a high sea wind, and even from here, she can hear the chunky waves thudding against the sea wall. She pushes her greying hair back from her face and stands there, allowing the rain to soak her and the wind to whip around the hem of her dressing gown. The envelope crackles in her pocket; she can feel it against her hip.

It is cold, even for Hastings, even for February. Her ears begin to sting, and the rain is icy on her scalp. Whether it's the wind or the realisation that it's February, she doesn't know, but something causes the memory to fly in, sharp and cold, settling right at the front of her mind.

It is 1962; the night is cold and dark, and the wind is biting chunks from her face. 'Watch out!' he shouts, and pulls her towards him as a roof slate crashes to the ground, just missing her. Then there is another, louder crash, and what looks like part of a chimney pot smashes onto the roof of a car behind them. 'Christ, we'll be killed at this rate.' He grabs her arm and pulls her into the gennel. 'Come on, down here, out of the wind.'

Was it then that something struck her on the head? Or was that a bit later? The memory sparkles with clarity in some places, yet is vague in others. She sways slightly, puts her hand out to the metal railings to steady herself. Despite the noise of the wind and rain, she can hear the sound of her own breathing, just as she had on that night in 1962 as she'd run down the hill . . .

. . . she hears the slap slap of her feet on the pavement as she runs. The gale is at her back and seems to be aiding her flight, so she lets herself go with it. There are bangs and crashes, glass breaking, a dog barking in the distance. The street is so littered

with debris that she has to keep leaping over things. It looks as though the town has been bombed, but the war ended years ago. She is in danger: this she knows for certain. A lump of wood lands in her path; she trips and hits the ground with a smack. The palms of her hands sting as they hit the cold pavement and she grazes both knees, although she doesn't realise this until much later.

She shakes the memory away. For a moment, she struggles to think what she's doing standing out here in her dressing gown on such a filthy morning, then she remembers. She puts her hand into her pocket; the letter is still there. It's real; she didn't imagine it.

The eerie cry of a distant seagull, its familiar call mutated, shortened by the wind, causes a swell of sadness inside her so powerful it almost steals her breath. She takes the letter from the envelope, unfolds it, and holds it steady in the wind while she reads the words again. She has thought about this moment many times over the decades, and as she'd feared, it has flung open a trapdoor to her past. Now she must peer through the void, down, down into the darkness.

CHAPTER ONE

November 2008

It's a cold, damp afternoon, but at least this morning's fog has cleared. As Jonathan Robson walks across the playground, its concrete surface polka-dotted with chewing gum, his thoughts spool forward to this evening. He's planning to cook a special meal for their anniversary – confit of duck, spicy red cabbage and dauphinoise potatoes, and he's even managed to find a half-decent low-alcohol wine. He notices a new addition to the graffiti-covered wall of the science block as he heads for the parking area: *My arse smells of apples*. He smiles; at least it's original, and compared to the rest, it has a certain quaint charm. He rounds the corner and walks right into Jerome Wilson, Year 9, a bit of a pain sometimes but a nice enough kid. He'd caught the boy reading something under the desk once, and as he'd waited for him to hand it over, he'd braced himself; some of the stuff he'd confiscated in school would make a grown man blush. But it turned out to be a book about dinosaurs. He's had a soft spot for Jerome ever since.

Jerome looks startled for a moment. 'All right, Sir?' he says.

'Hello, Jerome. Put that fag out, there's a good man.'

Jerome seems about to deny it, but Jonathan stares pointedly at the pale grey wisps that are rising into the chilly air from behind the boy's back. He tries not to enjoy the delicious whiff of second-hand smoke. Jerome grins sheepishly, glances around, takes another quick drag and then stubs the cigarette out on the wall. 'Sorry, Sir.'

'Go on, Jerome, get yourself off home and I'll pretend I didn't see that.'

'Thanks, Sir. See ya.'

He's just getting into the car when his phone beeps. Fiona. *Sorry about this morning. Didn't mean to go on at U like that, especially just b4 work. Preg hormones making me moody! C U later x.* He texts straight back. *I'm sorry too. Will be home soon. x.* Predictive text suggests '*will be good soon*', which makes him think. It's true that Fiona's been a bit snappy over the last few weeks, but he hasn't been sweetness and light himself. He yawns; tiredness is making him irritable. He really needs to sleep better tonight; he can't take many more nights of lying there watching the numbers on the clock roll through the hours while his mind jabbers away at him. When, over the last few years, he's allowed himself to imagine this time in their lives, he's always pictured the pregnancy as a time of intimacy and happy anticipation, but so far, it doesn't seem to be going that way at all. If anything, it feels like the connection between them is becoming weaker rather than stronger.

The traffic on Shooter's Hill Road is a nightmare. It crawls across Blackheath and at one point comes to a standstill, so he stops worrying about it and just looks out at the trees silhouetted like black filigree against the darkening sky. Everything will be all right tonight, it has to be – he can't bear the thought of them being off with each other on their anniversary. This will be their last anniversary as a couple; next year they'll be a family. He feels the familiar creep of apprehension. They're having a baby, and he can't shake off the feeling that he should be doing more towards it but he doesn't know what. He's not even sure what he should be saying. Even though this is a first child for both of them, he feels as though it's very definitely Fiona who's the expert. He wishes he'd paid more attention when Malcolm and Cass were expecting Poppy. If he can be as good a dad as Malcolm is, he won't go far wrong.

*

The evening goes well, so well that they skip pudding and take their wine up to bed, something they used to do quite frequently before trying for a baby became so fraught with anxiety, a 'task' to be managed with temperature charts and special diets and calendars.

'Happy anniversary,' she whispers, pushing him onto

his back and sliding on top of him. 'I didn't have time to get you a present. Will this do?'

He grins. It's the first time she's instigated sex in weeks. 'Oh, go on then. I suppose so.'

Their lovemaking is brief but joyous, more like the roll-around shags they used to have before they started trying to get pregnant. After, they hold hands as they lie side by side, hip to hip, thigh to thigh, each enjoying the heat from the other's skin, reluctant to break the connection by allowing air to move between them. For once, perhaps sated by food, wine and sex, Jonathan falls asleep quickly and sleeps peacefully for a good few hours before slipping into the recurring dream that has plagued him over the last few weeks. He is up to his knees, building a snowman. Dazzling sunlight glances off the whiteness and there are deep drifts all around. He can feel the snow under his fingers, but suddenly the cold is shockingly, unbearably intense. Then he is waist-high, trying to struggle free, and that's when he sees the child, not much more than a baby, sinking down in the snow next to him. He tries and tries to pull her out, but it's hopeless; the snow has claimed her.

Although he wakes drenched in sweat, his teeth are chattering and he feels like he did in the dream, like his bones are chilled and there's iced water in his stomach. The luminous green digits on the clock say 5.58. He won't get back to sleep now. A strip of orange light from the streetlamp falls through the gap in the curtains, making Fiona's dark-blonde hair look golden. He watches her for a moment; she's lying on her back with her arms stretched above her head; her face looks smooth and almost child-like in sleep; her lashes are flickering, and when he looks closely, he can see her eyes moving back and forth rapidly beneath the fine-veined lids. He lifts the covers and slides out of bed gently so as not to disturb her. The carpet feels warm under his feet; they must have left the heating on. But despite the warmth, he shivers as the sweat cools on his skin. The dream varies sometimes, but there's always snow, and there's always a child. Sometimes, he knows the child is himself, but not always. He assumes it's due to some sort of anxiety about the baby, especially as Fiona's been having frightening baby dreams as well. The other night she dreamt she gave birth to a dead crow. She'd woken with a cry, breathing hard, her face wet with tears; he'd held her while she told him about it, her voice wavering at the horrible details. Then she'd made a joke as if to try to banish it entirely. But long after she'd gone back to sleep he could hear the slight judder in her breath-ing, as though some part of her was still crying. He ached to comfort her, but she was locked in, beyond his reach. He shivers again. He hadn't been aware of temperature in dreams before now, although he often dreams in colour, and he knows you can dream a smell, because in the nightmares where his father is pushing his head into the lavatory pan to stop him swearing, the smell of old urine and Harpic makes him wake up gagging.

Downstairs, the kitchen hums and buzzes, its noises oddly reassuring. The burnt-down candles from their anniversary meal are still on the table, surrounded by an interesting formation of wax. Without switching on the light, he walks across the tiled floor and looks out of the window. The sky is no longer black but a smudged, slate colour, blurred by an early mist. He's had about five hours' sleep; it could be worse. And it's Saturday. He has some marking to do, but at least he hasn't got to stand in front of a class and try to look wide awake. He fills the kettle and reaches for a teabag, then changes his mind. A good, strong coffee is what he needs, something to jolt him properly awake and pull him away from the icy dream, which is still lurking just behind his eyes.

He is enjoying the rich, smoky flavour of the coffee and thinking how much a cigarette would enhance it, when he senses her behind him.

'Hey.' A warm hand on his shoulder, a kiss on the back of his head. Fiona yawns and pulls out the chair opposite. One side of her face is creased with red marks and her eyes are still half-closed. 'What's up?' she says. 'Can't sleep again? Or is it another bad dream?'

He nods. 'Can't get it out of my head.'

'What was it about?'

'I don't want to put it in your head as well.' He's told her about some of the snowy dreams, the ones where he thought the child in the dream was himself, but he doesn't think telling her about babies sinking in the snow is a great idea. 'I'm not sure which is worse,' he says, 'this or the insomnia.'

Fiona doesn't say anything for a minute, then she picks

up his mug and slowly takes a mouthful of coffee. He notices that she's started biting her nails again.

'Jonno,' she says slowly. 'This insomnia, the bad dreams and so on – is it . . .' She hesitates. 'Is it because of the baby?'

'Because of the baby? How do you mean?'

'Well, this is what I was trying to say yesterday morning – I know it was a stupid time to bring it up, but there isn't a good time and . . .' She looks down at her hands. 'I've got to say it. I know we had a lovely time last night, but apart from that, you don't seem very happy, to be honest. You're stressed, you're not sleeping. And it's all since we got pregnant.'

'I'm tired, that's all; it's nothing to do with the baby.' He looks at her. Her hair has fallen across her face so he can't see her eyes. 'Listen.' He reaches for her hand. 'We both wanted this.'

'But it's taken so long to get pregnant; you could have changed your mind.' She brushes her hair out of her face, but she still won't meet his eye. 'You told me yourself that you broke up with whatserface because she wanted kids—'

'That was totally different.'

'And you're so reluctant to . . . I mean, you haven't even told your parents yet.' Now she's looking at him again. 'What am I supposed to think?' Her eyes begin to glisten.

'Fi, I'm not unhappy,' he says gently. 'And of course I want this baby. I suppose I'm a bit scared as well, but that's normal, isn't it? Scared I'll make a balls-up of it;

scared I'll turn into my father; scared Larkin had a point – that we're destined to ruin our kids' lives even if we don't mean to.' He pauses. 'Aren't you scared too? Just a bit?'

She thinks for a moment. 'I suppose so. But I still don't see why you haven't told your parents.'

'I'll tell them soon. I just need to—'

'Jonathan, why not just tell them?'

He sighs. Even thinking about his father brings on a sort of cold dread. 'I suppose . . . it's him, really. You know what he's like.' He knows with bitter certainty that his father will be unimpressed, unmoved, convinced that being a father is something Jonathan cannot possibly succeed at. And what if he's right? What if, despite all Jonathan's pronouncements about how he'll always support his child, praise every achievement, never shout unnecessarily, what if, despite his best intentions, he simply fails?

Fiona's face softens. 'Oh, Jonno. I know he's a difficult man, but surely he'll . . .' But then she appears to lose confidence in what she's about to say. She gets up, walks around the table and stands behind him, sliding her hands down his chest and nuzzling his neck. She smells of bed and his dick twitches, but then he remembers the dream, and shrugs her off without meaning to. 'No, please don't go.' He catches her arm and turns his face into the warmth of her stomach.

CHAPTER TWO

June 1964

The ceiling is high and domed, and the white-painted brick walls make the room look stark. There's a wireless on somewhere nearby; the newscaster's clear voice is familiar: ... *announced that Senator McNamara will fly to South Vietnam next week to assess the situation. Here at home, Beatles' manager Brian Epstein has confirmed that the group's summer tour will go ahead. The tour was in doubt after drummer Ringo collapsed during a photo shoot ...*

Brian Epstein; Ringo; she knows these names. She hears a woman's voice, urgent. 'Quick! Sister's coming.' ... *twenty-four-year-old Beatle is suffering from tonsill ...* then there is a click and silence. There's something heavy covering her; she lifts her head and sees it's a coarse, peat-coloured blanket with edges overstitched in red, and on top of that, a floral bedspread. She's too hot, so she kicks the covers off and just lies still for a moment, looking up at the fancy plasterwork, way, way above her head.

It's very beautiful, that ceiling; like the icing on a wedding cake. There's a fleur-de-lis pattern along the side wall, and in the centre where there should be a light, she can just make out the shapes of winged cherubs holding bunches of grapes. She drags her eyes away from the cherubs. She doesn't remember seeing them before, and yet she knows she's been here for a while because she's acutely aware that time has passed, even though she has no memory of it actually doing so. It's a bit like when you've had gas at the dentist's. She turns her head to the left. There's a huge set of doors at the end of the room, but she can't remember what's on the other side. She should get up and look, but she's too tired; so tired that even to think is too great an effort. And there's something she needs to do before . . . before what? She has thirteen . . . days? Hours? Time is going wrong.

She sinks back below the surface and dreams about two little babies, playing in the snow, but as she opens her eyes the dream fragments into a thousand pieces. Oh, why is it so hot? Perspiration prickles along her hairline and pools in the hollows of her collarbones. How can she be dreaming of snow in this heat? Even the inside of her mind is hot and scarlet and misty. She tries to think and she feels something move, something plucking at her attention, but when she tries to focus, it scuttles off into a corner and crouches there, just out of reach. This time, though, she doesn't drift back into sleep. Instead, she lies still, flicking her gaze around the room; there are other beds, and a woman standing by the window, writing something on a clipboard. A memory flits across her mind: she sees herself writing something, *sign here; and here; good girl.* Thirteen . . . thirteen what? But it slithers away. A golden evening sunlight bathes the woman's face. She has thick, sooty eyelashes and a lot of blonde hair under her white cap, and she's wearing a uniform, a blue dress with a white pinafore. The word *nurse* settles in her mind; yes, the woman is a nurse.

'Is this a . . .' she begins, but her voice is so dry and thin from lack of use that barely a sound comes out. She tries again, this time consciously mustering what strength she can. 'Am I in hospital?'

The woman's head jerks up. 'What?'

Don't say what, say pardon, she thinks, and wonders where the thought came from.

The nurse moves away and calls out to someone, and within a minute or so, there are two more people standing around the bed. 'Go on,' the nurse urges. 'Say something.'

They are all watching her. There are two nurses now; the new one is a coloured girl, with a face as smooth and shiny as melted chocolate. The man is dressed in a tweed jacket with a saffron-yellow pullover, a white shirt and a black bow tie. He must be sweltering in those clothes. He's older than the nurses, a big man with a mass of red-brown hair and a sprawling, copper-coloured beard, which takes up the lower half of his face and makes it seem even bigger.

'Margaret,' he says, his voice low and gentle, as though he's afraid he'll startle her. 'Do you know where you a

She looks from one to another of the three faces looking down at her. Margaret; is that her name then? It doesn't seem quite right. The nurse, the first one, leans down to her and smiles. 'Go on, dear. Say something. Like you did just now.'

Maggie decides to risk it. She opens her mouth, wills the sound to come. 'Have I – have I had an accident?'

There is a burst of conversation, a palpable sense of, not relief exactly, more of release, a lifting of tension. She's not sure how she has triggered this, but they seem pleased with her.

'Not an accident; no, no; not an accident,' the bearded man says, taking a pair of gold-rimmed spectacles and a white handkerchief from his breast pocket. 'But you have been very poorly.' He polishes the round lenses before putting the spectacles on, the tiny frames all but disappearing on his great bear-like face. 'Oh yes.' He peers through the lenses. 'Very poorly indeed; and for quite a little while. Now, I want you to take things slowly, just one step at a time. Get a little more rest and I'll be along to see you again in due course.'

*

It feels like hours later when the sunlight wakes her. She tries to sit up, but catches her hair, which someone has plaited, under her elbow. The plait has come almost completely undone. How did her hair get this long? She looks around her; she can see the room properly now.

Hers is one of a row of beds, mostly empty, all black-framed and with pink-and-yellow flowery bedspreads. The walls are a light-brownish colour, like weak tea. Opposite, there are tall mullioned windows, flanked by wooden shutters. Despite the heat, they're only open a few inches at the top and bottom. Dust motes dance in the scorching sunshine that penetrates the glass; a fat black bluebottle zips back and forth, crazed in the heat. At one end of the room are double doors with glass panels above, at the other, a vast fireplace with easy chairs around it. She tries to get out of bed, but a nurse hurries towards her. 'Not yet, dear,' the nurse says. 'Wait until you've seen the doctor.'

She sees the man in the tweed jacket walking down the ward. He drags a chair over and places it next to her bed, then settles himself and smiles at her. She flops back on the pillow, exhausted with the effort of trying to get herself up. 'This *is* a hospital, isn't it?' she asks.

'Well done! Yes, this is a hospital.' He takes a notebook from his inside pocket, flips it open and writes something quickly.

She looks down at the long, greyish nightdress she's wearing, but doesn't recognise it. Lying across the end of her bed, there's a sack-coloured dressing gown, and a sudden flash of memory tells her she has worn this garment; she remembers holding the edges together because it has no belt or buttons, and walking slowly along a corridor to the lavatory, a nurse either side holding her arms. There are six lavatories in a row, but no doors. Surely she would not have used a lavatory without a door? But then she has a vivid memory of sitting on the cold china in the gloom of early morning, and looking up at the row of washroom windows, of ice on the inside of the frosted glass. And seagulls; there were seagulls screeching outside.

'Are we by the sea?'

'Not far from it. Brighton's about twelve miles away. Why do you ask?' He's looking at her intently.

'I heard seagulls . . .'

'Ah! Yes, yes, indeed. They come a long way inland sometimes. Now, tell me what you thought about when you heard the seagulls.'

'I didn't think about anything, just . . .' But there is a twitch in her memory. The sea; cold, cold water. Images flash up to her left and to her right, some frozen, some shimmering with movement, but they evaporate before she can grasp their meaning. 'How long have I been here?'

'Oh, quite a little while, I believe. Not *too* long, you know, erm . . .' He turns towards the nurse who leans down and mutters something in his ear. 'Ah yes,' he nods. 'That's right. December, wasn't it? Yes, yes. Not long before Christmas.' He is still speaking to the nurse.

'You mean . . .' She looks at the nurse. 'I've been here since . . .' She shakes her head. No; that can't be right. Why can't she remember?

'Now, Margaret,' the man says. 'Can you tell me what your full name is?'

The question bats her previous thought away. 'Margaret Letitia Harrison.' It comes out by itself. 'Maggie,' she adds, remembering that too. And then another name flashes into her head, and another; the two names are linked and for a moment everything sparkles and shouts; something is coming back, there is something she needs to do, and she hasn't got long to do it. She tries to hang on so she can read the thought, but then it shrinks back and goes out like a candle.

The man smiles, nods, writes something else in the little notebook. 'Good,' he mutters. 'Oh yes. Very good.'

Maggie feels a stab of irritation. 'Are you a doctor?'

He ignores her. 'Do you know what year this is?'

'What year?' she repeats. Surprised that it doesn't come to her immediately. Her thoughts are loose and shaky, and won't hold together. The man is waiting for an answer; so is the nurse. Perhaps they think she's simple.

'It's nineteen . . .' She pauses, then it jumps into her brain. 'Nineteen sixty-three.'

He nods, writes it down. 'Sixty-four, but that's close enough. And can you tell me who the Prime Minister is?'

'Mr Macmillan,' she is certain this is right. 'Harold Macmillan.'

'Hmm.' He writes this down, too. 'Very close, but no.' He frowns. 'Macmillan resigned, you know, not long before you came to us.' The nurse leans down and speaks into his ear again. He nods and says something back. All Maggie hears is ' . . . *not have been aware . . . circumstances . . . trauma . . .*'

'What?' She knows they're talking about her, but none of it makes sense. 'What are you saying—'

'All in good time.' He snaps his notebook shut then looks up and smiles, his eyes creasing into little slits. 'Well now, it's splendid to hear you talking again, I must say. I've no doubt you're on the mend this time. No doubt at all.'

'Please tell me,' Maggie says. 'Are you a proper doctor?'

The man chortles at this. 'That depends on what you mean by "proper", I suppose. Some of my colleagues might dispute the fact but yes, I am a proper doctor.' He extends his hand and she automatically shakes it. 'I'm Dr Carver; I'm a psychiatrist.' He pauses. 'Couldn't very well have gone into surgery with a name like that, could I?' He turns, grinning to the nurse, who smiles dutifully.

'So you think I'm mad.' He doesn't answer. She looks around the room. 'Is this . . . a . . . one of those . . .'

'It's a psychiatric hospital, yes. Now you mustn't worry about that. If you'd broken your leg, you'd go to an ordinary hospital, wouldn't you? We're very modern in our approach here, you know. It's not like the old days.'

'I'm not mad,' Maggie says. 'I just can't remember . . .' She pauses, tries again, concentrates as hard as she can on the hazy images skating just outside her mind's edge. It is as though some memory is bouncing against the perimeters, trying to find a way in.

Dr Carver is watching her intently. 'Tell me,' he says, 'do you know why you're here?' His voice has gone soft again, and she senses he is being careful. 'Can you remember anything about when you were first admitted? Or before you came to us?'

Again there are glimpses as she tries to force her brain to work, but the effort almost hurts. She shakes her head. 'I can't remember anything.'

'That's perfectly normal.' Dr Carver gets to his feet, towers over her again. 'It happens now and then, but it won't last. I've a notion it's the brain's way of protecting us. Anyhow, it's early days yet, early days indeed. Try not to think too hard.' He taps his temple twice with his index finger. 'Can't force the old grey matter into action before it's ready. Does no good, you know. No good at all.' He starts to move away. 'I'll come and see you in a day or two. We'll have a little chat.'

Maggie watches him walk down the ward as the nurse straightens the bedclothes. 'I'm not mad, you know,' she says. But the phrase *not right in the head* comes out of somewhere, and it's true, something isn't quite right in her head. There are too many spaces.

CHAPTER THREE

Jonathan feels a discernable tightening in his gut as he drives across Blackheath to his parents' house. Even if his father isn't thrilled, he'll be a *bit* pleased, surely? Traffic is slow. It's late afternoon and the light is beginning to fade as the November sky prepares to draw its blanket over the day. Out on the expanse of grassland, walkers huddle deeper into their coats against the wind; dogs chase balls and sticks; a few kids run, faces turned upwards as they pull at the strings of their kites, desperate to get the last dregs out of the afternoon. At the edge of the pond where he and Alan Harper used to fish for minnows and stickle-backs, a couple of oversized crows are shrieking at each other as they worry at a discarded burger. Blackheath: as kids, he and Alan had been beguiled by the idea that it was so-named because it was the site of a massive burial ground for victims of the Black Death, and they'd been gutted to discover that the plague story was an urban myth – the name actually came from 'bleak heath'. And when you look at the balding, boggy grass, the grimy, defeated skyline and the traffic snaking down into the polluted bowl of Lewisham and Deptford, it is utterly appropriate.

The area near Greenwich Park is crowded with cars, lorries and trailers emblazoned with the words *Zippo's Circus*. A small group of boys mill around, just as he and Alan had all those years ago; it was Billy Smart's in those days. One year, he'd asked his father if he could go to the circus as a birthday treat. 'Certainly not,' Gerald had said. 'Apart from anything else, it is extremely bad manners to ask for a gift.'

But the day before his birthday, he and Alan had gone up to the heath after school to hang around the trailers in the half-light, hoping for a glimpse of a clown, an acrobat or even Magnificent Marco the Human Cannonball. Rumour had it that Magnificent Marco had been injured so often he had his own bed at the hospital.

Jonathan was sleeping at Alan's that night and he couldn't wait, partly because Mrs Harper said she had a surprise for him, but also because she made dinners he'd never get at home, like fish fingers and chips, followed by butterscotch Instant Whip with a cherry in the middle and what she called 'chocolate mousedirts' sprinkled on top. As they crept from trailer to trailer, taking turns to climb on each other's backs to peek in uncurtained windows, he thought about the cold, silent mealtimes at home, the constant smell of potatoes boiling away on the stove. Couldn't they have chips just once?

'Oh, buggery!' Alan said. 'Mum said five at the latest and it's ten to now. Better leg it.' They ran across the grass, past the church and down Lewisham Hill to Alan's flats, feet pounding the pavement and breath charging white in the chill November air. As they clattered up the pissy-smelling stairs, he wondered what the surprise could be.

The tickets were on the kitchen table, propped up against the tomato ketchup. Alan's mum was smiling. *Eat up, chop-chop, or we'll be late and we'll end up sitting where the elephants do their business.* Jonathan was weak with gratitude and so excited he couldn't swallow. Mr Harper winked and ruffled his hair. *Not hungry, Tiger? Oh well. Waste not, want not.* And he scoffed the chips three at a time and everybody laughed. Jonathan pictured his father pushing equal amounts of mince, swede and potato onto his fork. Sometimes, he wished Mr Harper was his dad. Mr Harper liked the circus; Gerald said it was 'a vulgar, gaudy spectacle full of dwarves, misfits and layabouts', and Alan was a Guttersnipe and Mr Harper was an Oaf and a Wastrel. Jonathan didn't know what a wastrel was, and he wasn't going to look it up.

At the circus, they saw a lady in a ballet dancer's dress riding a horse standing up, four men walking down a pretend staircase on their hands, and clowns with orange hair and giant bow ties turning somersaults. When some of the clowns asked for a volunteer to hold the hosepipe and help them drench the others, Jonathan stretched his hand right up so they could see him. He could hardly believe it when they picked him.

Later, after Alan's mum kissed them goodnight, he went over it in his head. The very best bit, he decided, was after the hosepipe, when the clowns gave him a huge bag of sweets and asked where his mum and dad were and Mr and Mrs Harper shouted 'over here' and waved. The clowns carried him back, holding him high up on their shoulders while everybody clapped. When they put him down, everyone was smiling and proud of him. This was the best day of his whole life.

*

'I was expecting you before now,' his mother says as she opens the door, the hall clock chiming five behind her. He'd said late afternoon, and is about to point this out when he notices how tired she looks. 'Sorry,' he kisses her proffered cheek. 'Traffic was terrible.' As always, she's fully made-up, but today her lipstick and face powder seem uncharacteristically noticeable and clumsily applied.

'Father's in the sitting room,' she says. 'I'll be in when I've made the tea.'

It's almost dusk, but Gerald hasn't switched the lights on. He can see perfectly well in the remaining light, he says, and just because Jonathan deigns to visit them, he sees no reason to be extravagant with electricity. 'Oh, for Christ's sake,' Jonathan snaps, flicking the switch.

'Blasphemy, now, is it?' Gerald makes a big deal of shielding his eyes. There's a slight tremor to his hand,

Jonathan notices. What little hair he has left seems to have yellowed even more, and there are dark, brownish crescents under his eyes. He seems particularly frail today; thinner than he was three weeks ago. 'So,' Jonathan says, sitting in the chair opposite; his eyes stray to the four different pill containers on the side table. He's sure there weren't that many last time. 'How are you feeling?'

'That's your mother's chair.' Gerald picks up his pipe, taps it on the side of the ashtray and begins to fill the bowl with tobacco.

'She's making the tea. I'll move when she comes in. I was asking how you are; you look tired.'

'Blast!' His father twists around in his chair. 'Where the devil has your mother put my cigarette lighter?' He always calls it that, even though he hasn't smoked cigarettes for years. As he turns, he knocks his copy of *The Times* off the arm of his chair. It's folded to the crossword page, and as Jonathan picks it up, he notices that Gerald has only filled in a couple of the clues, which is unusual; he usually has the whole thing finished by lunchtime.

'Hang on,' Jonathan says, 'there it is.' He can see the silver lighter poking out from under Gerald's chair. He bends down to retrieve it and then hands it to his father.

'Ah, yes.' Gerald holds out his hand. 'My thanks.' There is a clunk as he puts the stem of his pipe between his teeth, holds the flame to the bowl and then sucks and puffs until the room is filled with billowing blue-grey smoke. He turns to Jonathan with the lighter still poised. 'Well?' he says. 'Aren't you having a cigarette?'

Jonathan shakes his head. 'No, I told you last time. I've given up.'

Gerald takes his pipe from his mouth and holds it just an inch or two away as blue smoke curls out of the mouth-piece. 'Given up? Don't talk such nonsense. You're as bad as your mother.'

'I did tell you.'

'Yes, but you've given up before and you've never stuck to it, have you? Why should this time be any different?'

This is it, he thinks; the perfect opportunity to explain about the baby. But he can't come out with it now, not while his mother is still in the kitchen. 'I'm beginning to think more about the health risks, I suppose.'

Gerald shakes his head in irritation. 'I tell you, you're more likely to die from worrying about what's going to kill you than from enjoying the odd smoke.' He sucks on the pipe again and turns to look for something on the bookshelf next to him. 'Ah,' he reaches for a slender red pack that lies among a stack of papers on top of the books. 'Here we are.' He tosses the pack – Henri Winterman's Slim Panatellas – onto the coffee table. 'You'll have a cigar, though.'

Jonathan looks at the pack. It's so tempting. But he's smoked cigars before and kidded himself that it didn't count. He ended up on fifteen a day at one point. 'No,' he shakes his head. 'Thanks anyway, but I'd better not.'

'Oh, come on,' Gerald says, still looking at him. Then when Jonathan doesn't respond, he sighs heavily, picks up the pack of cigars and throws them back on top of the books.

Jonathan sighs as well. They used to smoke together; it had never been particularly companionable, but it was one ritual they'd been able to share. It hadn't occurred to him that Gerald might actually miss it. Maybe one cigar with his father wouldn't be the end of the world, but before he can speak again, Gerald's face assumes what Jonathan has come to think of as its default countenance, a mix of irritation, disdain and impatience.

'So.' Gerald's voice is stony now. 'How is your Business and Enterprise College or whatever it is they call the local comprehensive these days?'

'School's fine.' Jonathan can hear the tightness in his own voice. All right, so his school is hardly Eton, but he doubts his father would be impressed even if it were. His father had been furious that he hadn't gone into teaching straight after university, but he'd been determined to do his own thing so he'd pretended Gerald's disapproval didn't matter. It was only much later that he began to accept that it bothered him, it really, really bothered him. When he decided to become a teacher at the age of thirty-five, he hadn't expected a fanfare, but nor had he expected Gerald to simply flick his newspaper and from behind it, ask if Jonathan was sure the profession would have him.

'No problems with behaviour?'

He hesitates for a moment then shakes his head. 'Nothing major.' In fact, managing behaviour in his school is a constant battle, but Gerald would be contemptuous of any failure to control a class.

'I saw some of your pupils in Lewisham the other day. Savages, most of them. The school seems rather lax on discipline.'

Discipline. For a moment, Jonathan flips back in time; he sees his father looming over him, carefully greased hair flopping forward as he brings down the cane onto Jonathan's outstretched palm. Jonathan vows that he will never, ever, lay a finger on his own child.

His mother comes in carrying a tray, which Jonathan takes from her and sets down on the coffee table. In the interminable period it takes for Gerald to add sugar, stir, sip, and replace the cup in its saucer, Jonathan feels as he often does in this house – as though he's ten years old again. Little has changed since then; the walls are a lighter colour but the same paintings hang from the picture rail; the curtains have a different pattern, but they're still dark and heavy; the mantle clock, wall plates, vases and knick-knacks gather dust now just as they did then. Tense Sunday afternoons; crossing the room with his father's tea, gripping the saucer tightly and praying the cup wouldn't rattle; Gerald's scrutiny from over the top of his glasses. And the sounds: the gas fire, hissing and popping; the tick of the old clock; the terrifying sound of Gerald *listening*.

He puts his cup and saucer on the table. *I've got something to tell you.* Or straight out: *Fiona and I are having a baby.* He wishes Fiona had come with him. Maybe the baby *will* bring them closer. His father is looking at him.

Just say it. He clears his throat, looks at his mum, then at Gerald. 'Now that you're both here, I have some—'

Gerald clicks his tongue irritably. 'Have you run out of razor blades?' His voice is prickly. 'Or is it now acceptable for a schoolteacher to walk around looking like a vagrant?'

Jonathan stands up. 'Oh, for God's sake, does it really—'

'Gerald, please,' his mother interrupts. 'It *is* the weekend. I think you're being a little ungracious.'

'There's always something, isn't there?' Jonathan says. 'We can never just have a normal, nice afternoon without you finding something to complain about.'

'I see I've offended your delicate sensibilities.' Gerald grapples behind his chair for his stick. 'So if you'll excuse me.' He struggles to his feet, batting away his wife's attempts to help him.

CHAPTER FOUR

Maggie can feel someone shaking her gently, but opening her eyes is an effort. She recognises the nurse. 'Betty?'

'Hetty,' the nurse smiles. 'Not bad, though. This time last week you couldn't remember your own name, never mind no one else's. Up you get then; you've been asleep since breakfast and you're to see His Nibs after dinner, by all accounts.'

'Who's—?'

'Dr Carver, lord and master. He says you can get dressed today.'

Maggie thinks for a minute. 'Dr Carver,' she mutters. The name is familiar. She looks at the nurse. 'I can't remember—'

'Don't you worry about that, dear. It'll come back, you know, bit by bit.' She starts to tidy the bedcovers. 'Meself, I don't think them pills are helping, neither.' She tucks the sheet in briskly. 'But what do I know? I'm only a nurse.'

Maggie dresses in the things Hetty has brought for her. Although she vaguely remembers these clothes – navy Crimplene slacks, a white blouse and a pink Orlon cardigan – the process of putting them on feels odd and unfamiliar, and the seams feel abrasive against her skin.

'Now, come down and talk to some of the other ladies, there's a good girl.' Maggie should feel patronised, but she doesn't, because she now knows who Hetty reminds her of: it's her mother. A pang of sadness creeps through her, because at the same moment as she remembers this, she also remembers that both her parents are dead.

She follows Hetty down the ward, out through the double doors and along a dark, tiled hallway with a shiny parquet floor that smells of Johnson's furniture polish. The day room has the same high arched ceiling and tall windows as the ward. Cigarette smoke swirls in the sunlight, and Maggie remembers that she smokes. She feels four years old again, on her first day at school when she didn't know where to hang her coat or who to sit next to. Some of the women sit at the tables playing cards or doing jigsaw puzzles; one or two look up as she and Hetty pass, but mostly they don't seem to notice. There is a television set in the corner, with the word *Rediffusion* in white lettering at the bottom of the polished wooden casing. Right in front of the set, a balding, skeletally thin woman in a turquoise dressing gown is kneeling with her face inches from the screen, apparently watching the test card. More women sit in the chairs that line the walls, some rocking back and forth, others quietly weeping or just staring into the past.

As they make their way through the room, an elderly lady with crudely dyed blue-black pigtails bounces towards them. 'Cha cha cha,' she says cheerily. Her voice is high like a child's, her face beaming. 'What's going on; what's coming off.' She twirls around, holding out the hem of her ill-fitting frock, and then sinks into an expansive curtsey. 'I'm a little bit up the pole today,' she tells Maggie. 'Better than being down the pole, but Dr Carver says I've got to stay in the middle. Cha cha cha.'

'Norma, love,' Hetty lays a hand on her arm. 'Don't get too excited, now.'

Norma grins, curtseys again and with another tinkling 'cha cha cha', dances off to talk to someone else.

Maggie can feel her heart thudding. She stands a little closer to Hetty.

'Pauline!' Hetty calls out to a young woman who has just come into the room. 'Sleeping Beauty here has finally woken up. You'll look after her for me, dear, won't you?' She pats Maggie on the shoulder and nods encouragement before bustling off to attend to something else.

Pauline is about Maggie's age and looks like a model in her candy-pink summer dress with a white cardigan slung loosely around her shoulders. Her hair is lacquered into a beehive and she's freshly made-up; Maggie can see the powder on her cheeks.

'Hello, Maggie,' she says, her voice unexpectedly deep and smooth. 'Feeling better? It's nice to see you up and about again.'

'Again?' Maggie is sure she must sound like a complete

idiot. But she doesn't know this glamorous woman. Perhaps she's one of the nurses, off duty. 'I don't think we've—'

· 'Don't worry. It's the treatment; it plays havoc with your memory. Still, they'll probably ease it off a bit now you're improving. Shocking, isn't it, what shocking does to you?' She laughs heartily at her own joke.

'Shocks?' Again Maggie hears herself repeating what's being said to her like a simpleton. 'Electric shock treatment?' She has to say it aloud so that she can take it in. 'Is that what I've had?' But then a memory switches on in her mind: there's a black box with wires; cold jelly is rubbed into her temples and she feels something rubbery being shoved between her teeth. Someone is holding her arms. A hot silver pain flashes in her skull, making her gasp. She has the sensation of being flung about, her bones and teeth shaking and rattling as though they'll never stop, then she feels herself plummeting down, down, down . . .

She shudders, feels faintly nauseous at the memory.

'Most of us have it at some point,' Pauline says. 'Makes you forget why you lost your mind, helps you to find it, then makes you forget where you put it again!'

'You've had it too?'

Pauline's face darkens. 'Four or five times a week at first.' She glances left and right. 'You want to be careful; make sure you talk to the others even if you don't feel like it, especially in front of the nurses – if you're too quiet they'll say you're "morose and withdrawn". And whatever you do, don't let them catch you daydreaming or looking out of the window – that counts as "vacant and preoccupied".'

Maggie looks at the women sitting in the chairs by the wall; most of them look vacant and preoccupied.

'Didn't know what bloody day it was half the time,' Pauline is saying. 'Nor whether I was supposed to be eating breakfast, dinner or tea. Still, it usually comes back in the end, the memory.'

'Usually?'

'Well, that's what they say. You'll be all right; you're not a Chronic, and it's mainly the Chronics who have problems.' She leans towards Maggie. 'See her, over there?'

The woman standing by the window must be in her sixties, Maggie guesses. She's looking out of the window while brushing her long, seal-grey hair.

'She's waiting for her husband to come and pick her up. He's been dead twelve years, but she forgets. They used to keep telling her, hoping she'd hang on to it, but they stopped in the end because they were just putting her through the horror of it again and again, every single day.'

Maggie tries to take all this in but it is too much, and she feels her eyes fill with tears. Pauline produces a packet of Kensitas, lights one and hands it to her. She takes a deep draw on the cigarette, feeling instantly calmed as the smoke hits the back of her throat, then she sways a little, suddenly dizzy. Pauline puts a hand out to steady her, then guides her to a chair. 'Don't worry,' Pauline says gently. 'I'll keep an eye on you. I'm on a home visit this afternoon, but I'll be back by teatime.'

Home. The word starts to poke around Maggie's consciousness like all the other memories. Home. She tries to concentrate, but she can't make the word break its moorings.

'Where do you live?' she asks Pauline.

'St Leonard's-on-Sea. It's near Hastings. Do you know it?'

Hastings, Maggie thinks. It definitely . . . and then she remembers. 'Leonard!' She grabs Pauline's hand. 'That's my brother!' She can see his face. Her mother and father are dead, but she has a brother, Leonard! His features are just beginning to solidify in her mind when a loud clapping of hands slaps her thoughts shut.

'Ladies, to the dining room please!'

*

The walls in the day room and on the ward are plain and unadorned, but here there is wallpaper: orange, green and brown circles, all jumbled up on a beige background. There are lots of square, dark wood tables, all set for four and all with a small vase of red carnations in the middle. It looks . . . nice. Maggie sits at a table with Pauline and Norma. Her mind is still bubbling with the new information: she lives in Hastings, and she has a big brother. Little snapshots of memory: Leonard combing Brylcreem through his hair and looking anxious as he prepares for a date; his broad grin as he twirled her round the day he returned from National Service; the inch-long scar above his left eyebrow where he fell off his bike when he was ten. She narrows her eyes with the effort of remembering, and a dark pain zips across her forehead.

A skinny little nurse with bony elbows and bad skin bangs down plates of food onto the tables. It can't be very hot, Maggie thinks, noticing how the nurse holds the metal plates in her bare hands. Then her memory leaps again; she can see Leonard holding a plate, the side of his hand covered with little red scars. He was always burning his hands on the hotel oven, a huge thing with double doors and eight gas rings. She remembers the heat in the windowless kitchen, steam, smoke from the steaks on the open grill, shouting, pans clashing, and rows and rows of white plates. She looks down at her own hands and sees similar scars.

The food in front of her is slopped on the plate willy-nilly, one thing on top of another; everything seems to be the same colour, and the whole meal is pale and insipid. It takes her a moment to identify what's on her plate: there's mashed potato on top of plain white spaghetti and next to it, a clodge of slimy white cabbage that's been boiled to within an inch of its life. 'I can't eat this,' she mutters. 'Potatoes and spaghetti shouldn't be served together. They're both starches. It's like having mashed potato and chips.'

Norma grins. 'Mashed potato and chips,' she sings. 'Ha ha! Mashed potato and chips! Cha cha cha.'

'Food not good enough for you, Madam?' the nurse sneers, her greasy blonde hair sticking out at all angles from under her white cap.

'There's nothing wrong with it; it's just that there's no meat or fish. And really, spaghetti should be served with a beef and tomato sauce, not potatoes. It's called spaghetti bolognese; it's Italian.' She's not sure how she knows this.

'Oh, *Italian*, is it?' the nurse says. 'And there was me, thinking our humble English food would be good enough! Well, forgive me, your ladyship. Pardoneh-moi.'

'That's French,' Pauline mutters, and Maggie feels her mouth twitch into a smile.

The nurse turns to Pauline. 'Something to say, Mrs Wilkes?'

'No. I didn't say anything.'

The nurse's eyes grow colder and they don't leave Pauline's face. 'Oh, come now. I think you did.'

Pauline shakes her head. 'I didn't, Nurse. Honest.'

'No? Talking to yourself then, perhaps?'

Pauline looks up sharply. 'No. I don't talk to myself.'

'Well, I most definitely heard something. I think you'd better stay on the ward this afternoon, where I can keep an eye on you. We don't want to send you off on a home visit until we can be sure you're ready, do we?'

'Oh no, please. I didn't mean anything; it was just a joke.'

Maggie is taken aback by the sudden wild panic in Pauline's eyes. Pauline, who seemed so calm and normal.

'I haven't seen my little girl for weeks ... please ...'

Pauline gets to her feet, knocking over a beaker of water, which spills onto her plate. Her voice is rising out of control. 'You've got to let me go home—'

'I haven't "got" to do anything, my lady.' The nurse's voice is like splintered ice. 'Now look at the mess you've made with your dinner. No, I really don't think it would be a good idea for you to go home this week. Not while you're so excitable.'

Maggie tries to mop up the spilt water with a couple of tissues but then Pauline begins to yell. 'Please, Nurse; please. I've got to go home; I want to see my baby. I can't stand it . . . please let me go . . . please . . .'

The nurse tries to lead her away but then Pauline rounds on her and kicks her hard on the shin. The nurse shrieks and others come running and one of them is blowing a whistle and then everyone is dashing around and shouting or crying or knocking things over. Norma puts down her spoon and looks around, eyes sparkling with excitement. 'What's going on,' she says in her sing-song voice. 'What's coming off.'

Maggie is frozen for a moment, sitting on a chair in the midst of this pandemonium. My God, she thinks, this is really happening: I am in a mental hospital.

CHAPTER FIVE

The visit with his parents has made Jonathan feel slow and heavy; Fiona is up in the spare room when he gets in, and he has to drag himself upstairs. She's wearing black leggings and a long, baggy green jumper that he hasn't seen before, and her hair is pulled back in a pony tail, making her look much younger. 'My sister came round earlier,' she says. 'Look, how about this for curtains? She bought it for Noah and Molly's room but never used it.' She holds up a length of fabric, tiny yellow chicks on a white background. He reaches out to touch it; it feels clean and new. There's a baby chair and a changing mat in the corner, and a huge pile of baby clothes on the bed. Lucy's obviously been having a clear-out. Fiona grabs a cushion and shoves it under her jumper. 'What do you think?' she grins, turning side-ways so he can get the full effect. 'Will you still love me when I look like a barrage balloon?'

He smiles. 'I expect so.' He can smell the fresh lemony scent of her shower gel as she passes him to toss the cushion back on the bed. He stands still for a moment, breathing it in, gathering up the imprint she's left on the air. She's in a good mood; he can tell by the way she's moving, like a dancer, full of energy and life. She was like this the day they found out. She'd bounded out of the bathroom waving the Predictor and grinning, and they'd stood together on the landing, foreheads touching, gazing at the pink line as though it were the baby itself. After two years of taking temperatures and filling in charts, he'd begun to wonder if it was ever going to happen, though he'd never voiced that fear to Fiona, nor she to him. They'd wanted to stay positive, but those things hung unsaid between them: the 'what if' discussions; fertility treatment; maybe even adoption. And then there was the pink line, and everything was going to be all right. At the early scan, he'd mistaken the baby's bottom for its head, and he couldn't tell the hands from the feet, but actually seeing it, the realness of it, he'd felt a surge of – not love, exactly, not yet, more like awe at the evidence that they'd done this amazing thing, created this real live baby, all by themselves.

'So,' she says, 'how did it go?' At that point, the doorbell rings. 'That'll be dinner,' she looks at him with mock guilt. 'I know it was my turn to cook but I couldn't think of anything. I promise I'll learn to cook one day. *Promise!*'

He smiles. 'Yeah, right!' It's only after they've unpacked the little brown paper carrier bags and spooned rice and saag and chicken balti onto heated plates that she asks again.

'I didn't get round to it in the end,' he says, pouring grape juice for her and opening some wine for himself.

She stops, her fork halfway to her mouth. 'Why the hell not?'

'The mood wasn't right. You know what they're like. It started off all right but—'

'The *mood* wasn't right? What does that mean? What *mood* do you need to tell your parents they're going to be grandparents, for God's sake?' She gets up, jolting the table and sending a balti-coated spoon clattering to the floor.

'It just didn't feel right. The atmosphere sort of . . . soured.' Gerald's face ripples into his mind. His father is old and sick; he tries to imagine him mellowed and smiling at the news. But it's like trying to imagine a colour that doesn't exist. *You? A father? May the Lord above preserve us.* He tries to push the image away.

'You don't want this baby, do you?' Fiona says, her back to him as she stands at the sink running water into a glass. 'Admit it.'

Her words punch him in the gut; he can hardly believe what he's hearing and for a moment, he can't speak. 'No, Fi,' he says when he finds his voice. 'That simply isn't true.' Gently, he touches her shoulder, but she shrugs him off and whirls round to face him. 'What then?' Her eyes flash. 'I can't start telling people until both sets of parents know. Why are you finding it so difficult?' Before he can reply, she stalks out of the kitchen, slamming the door behind her. He's about to follow her, then thinks better of it. He mops up the wine that spilt when she knocked into the table and then slumps onto a chair, drains his own glass, refills it, and takes another gulp. He's always wanted kids with Fiona; he knew almost from the moment he first saw her. It was at a party at the then newly-wed Malcolm and Cassie's on a warm, sunny evening in late summer, and when Jonathan arrived, everyone was in the garden, drinking chilled white wine. A slight breeze murmured through the grass, and there she was, standing in front of a bush that was heavy with full-blown roses, head thrown back and laughing at something Cass was saying. Her skin, tanned from a recent holiday, was the shade of toasted almonds and the sun had bleached her hair to pale amber. Her dress, which fluttered slightly in the breeze, was virtually the same shade as her hair and skin, so the whole effect was of a golden glow, illuminated by the sun. He can't remember what he'd said when Malcolm introduced them, but he'd had to stop himself from gibbering like an idiot as he shook her hand, because he knew right then, even though it was crazy: here was his soulmate; here was the mother of his children. It was so different to how he'd felt with Sian. He and Sian were together for five years, but it became a habit, easy and comfortable for both of them. Sian's body clock had begun ticking and they started to think about babies. That was when he realised. It wasn't babies per se, just the certain knowledge that he and Sian weren't right together, that any baby they made would be half of him and half of her, but never quite whole.

He tears off a piece of naan and dunks it in the balti sauce, but he barely notices the taste as he chews. He picks a bit more at the cooling food, finishes his wine and immediately pours himself a refill. The wine is soothing and he drinks it quickly, then empties the last of the bottle into his glass, surprised that he's finished it already. He drains it in one, enjoying the slight recklessness of it and wishing he still smoked. He looks at the remains of the takeaway and decides to leave clearing it up until the morning. Right now, he has to talk to Fiona. He has to *connect* with her again, and then everything else will come right. He wobbles slightly as he stands up – that wine was quite strong – and makes his way upstairs carefully; he doesn't want to stumble or bump into anything in case she thinks he's drunk, and he needs to tell her how much he loves her, how much he wants this baby. Better still, actions speak louder than words. Yes, that's what he'll do; he'll show her and tell her at the same time. Best idea he's had all day. He'll whisper to her, tell her over and over again while making love to her as tenderly as possible. She'll pretend to be asleep but she'll press herself back against him, gently encouraging him without turning round. It's a game they used to play: one feigns sleep while the other kisses and touches and strokes. The idea is to see how long you can go without responding. She likes him to lie spoon-like behind her, kissing her neck, cupping her breasts, running his hands over her thighs and belly; sometimes he can even enter her, thrusting gently once or twice before she'll turn over, grinning, pulling him on top of her and clamping her legs around him to draw him in deeper. When it's his turn he'll try not to move as she wriggles down the bed, but he knows that the moment he feels her warm breath on his belly or a strand of her hair trail across his thigh, he'll be lost.

When he opens the bedroom door, it takes a moment for his eyes to adjust to the dark, but he doesn't need light to tell him she isn't there. The room is cold and empty, the bed neatly made. The desire that has been building evaporates as he goes along the landing to the spare room. They never sleep apart, never. The door is closed and he opens it as quietly as possible then creeps across the carpet, picking his way through the bags of baby stuff she was looking through so happily just a couple of hours ago. She's lying on her back, her tiny form barely making a shape in the bed. He can't see her face because the covers are pulled right up, so he hooks his finger under the edge of the duvet and lifts it slightly. Her arm is curved up above her head, and she's got on the old pyjamas she wears when she has her period or if she's not feeling well. In the pinkish light from the landing, he can see her puffy skin, mascara smudged under her eyes, damp hair clinging to the side of her face. This is his fault. His parents are going on some church trip tomorrow, but he'll tell them about the baby when they get back. He wonders briefly whether to write to Gerald, expectant father to established father, try to break down this barrier. He'll think about it tomorrow. As he tries to silently navigate a path through the black bags, he stumbles, then veers sideways, cannoning off the wall and stubbing his toe on the wardrobe. 'Shit!' he says in a stage whisper. Fiona stirs but doesn't wake. He swears again under his breath as he limps back along the landing, toe throbbing, elbow stinging where he bashed the wall. He climbs into bed and lies there, straining to hear the sound of her footsteps coming back along the hall and aching for the closeness they used to share.

They'd met in late August and had married eight weeks later; both being teachers, they'd taken their honeymoon over the October half-term holiday. Fiona had moved into Jonathan's a while before the wedding, but it was that week in Cornwall when they'd really got to know each other. It had rained the entire time but they hadn't cared. They'd rented a little cottage on the edge of the moors and had spent the whole of the first day in bed, listening to the rain battering the leaded windows, drinking pink champagne and eating warm bagels with scrambled eggs and saying the words 'wife' and 'husband' as often as they could. They talked about their lives before they met. She once wanted to be a policewoman, she told him; he confessed to a brief childhood ambition to be a cat burglar. Her worst ever job was in a cake factory, taking clumps of raisins that were stuck together, separating them and putting them back on the conveyor belt; his was in a chip shop, digging the eyes out of potatoes before loading them into the peeling machine. They talked about his love of football and her preference for snooker; his liking of dogs, hers of cats. They discovered that they'd both had their tonsils out when they were six, that they could both play a guitar but that neither of them could sing. There was so much to talk about. It was as if they'd been together in a previous life but had been separated for thirty-odd years. That night, they'd ventured out to a pub across the moor, arriving wet and windswept and hoping for atmosphere and the ghosts of long-dead smugglers; instead they were greeted by a sign saying *kid's meal's half price*, and the smell of chips and stale beer. But they were still so intoxicated by the romance of their wedding and the thrill of their first day as husband and wife that the disappointment barely touched them. Later, when they got back from the pub, they'd lit the open fire and sat drinking brandy and gazing into the flames in silence, all talked-out and just basking in contentment, and then he'd become aware of a charge in the air, like a prickle of electricity. At the same moment, they'd put their glasses aside and turned to each other. He still wasn't sure who pulled whom down onto the rug, but they'd torn at each other's garments and had made love so suddenly and urgently that they'd still been half-clothed when they collapsed together, breathless and exhilarated. After a couple of moments, she'd begun to giggle, then he'd joined in and they found they just couldn't stop, and they'd laughed and laughed, still holding each other, until they had to wipe away the tears.

How have they moved from that to this, he thinks now, snapping at each other, shutting each other out? It is the last thought he has before sinking into a fitful sleep.

He dreams he's making his way along a sandy beach in a dim, thickening light. On his left is a sheer wall of barnacle-encrusted stone; to his right, the ocean. The beach ahead just comes to an end, tapering off to a point with the wall on one side, sea on the other. Ferocious, pewter-grey rollers close in on him. He turns to go back, but black seawater is powering towards him, filling in and obliterating his footprints. Fiona is looking down from the top of the wall, but it is too late; he is engulfed, the water closing over his head again and again as he struggles for air. He can hear her voice . . .

Jonathan . . . Jonathan!

He gasps, torn out of the dream as Fiona shakes him awake. He's instantly aware of several things at once: the fluorescent green digits on the alarm clock say 3.52; Fiona is standing next to him, holding the phone; she doesn't look angry any more.

'Wha . . . ?'

'Jonno,' she says gently. 'It's your mum.'

CHAPTER SIX

It's breakfast time. Hetty, who is Maggie's favourite nurse because she smells of Helena Rubenstein's Apple Blossom and reminds Maggie of her mother, is standing in the middle of the ward with a clipboard. She's done this before, but Maggie can't remember why.

'Okay, ladies,' Hetty says. 'Listen for your name, and remember, no breakfast if you're down for treatment.'

Thankfully, Maggie's name is not on the list, although Pauline's is. Pauline argued last time, said she didn't need it, but they said she was 'agitated' and they called her again the next day, and the next, and the next. When she stopped arguing, it went down to once a week.

'Treatment's at nine,' Hetty is saying, 'so make sure you've all been to the lav. I'll be back in two shakes and we can all go down together.'

She makes it sound as though it's something nice they'll all be doing, like an outing. Maggie stays curled up shrimp-like under the covers so that no one will see she's been crying. Pauline warned her. According to Pauline, you definitely get put down for treatment if they catch you crying.

Maggie has good days and bad days. This is a bad day. Sometimes, she feels as if she's full of poison, as if there's a huge fat boil inside her, ready to burst. Today, it's more of a hollow ache, a deep black sore yawning open somewhere between her heart and her stomach. She stays curled up with her hands around her knees until the feeling fades a little and she can bear to get up. She forces herself to eat her breakfast of watery porridge and a slice of cold toast and marge, and she tries as hard as she can to smile at Sister, and at Hetty and the other nurses.

After breakfast, she helps count the knives back into their box. If she's volunteering for jobs, they'll think she's doing well. When the knives are all accounted for and safely locked away until lunch, she heads back to the ward, silently praying that the others will have already gone down to the treatment room. But as soon as she goes through the double doors, she sees that they're still there, half a dozen women shuffling around, taking a long time to organise themselves. They're holding back, Maggie realises, desperate to put off the moment of bone-shaking agony.

'Come on, Dolly.' Hetty goes over to one of the beds where the humped shape under the blanket is visibly trembling. 'You're for treatment today, sweetheart,' she says gently. 'Keep your nightgown and dressing gown on, and take your teeth out. We need to be going down now.'

'Maggie,' Hetty calls, spotting her as she herds her charges, pale with terror, towards electrocution. 'Be a dear and pop along to the linen room for me, would you? I'm late getting these ladies downstairs.'

'Okay,' Maggie replies, trying to look keen and helpful.

'It's down the corridor, past the bathrooms, turn left and it's just opposite the craft room. There's a bundle of pillowslips I need bringing through. They'll be labelled "C" ward so you can't go wrong.'

Maggie walks back along the corridor, but the whole wing is so much bigger than she realised. She passes the long, narrow bathroom where there are five baths in a row and no screen or curtain in between, but the only other corridor goes to the right, so she turns into it and passes a row of locked doors that she thinks are to the single rooms, then there's another small kitchen and dining room, and one more unlabelled door. She goes back the way she came and walks further along; more bathrooms. She turns off by the next one and she can see the day room, thank goodness. But when she looks in as she passes, it's not the *right* day room. There's a recreation room and another bare door, which is locked. She sees more unlabelled doors, so she tries to push them open but they're all locked, and she just can't find the linen room, or even the craft room, and she turns round to try and go back but everything suddenly looks too big and vivid and her breathing comes too fast; the black hole in her stomach is widening and aching and trying to fold her in two. She leans against the wall for support, but then sinks to the floor and curls up in a ball until one of the nurses comes along with the tea wagon, hauls her to her feet and leads her back to the ward, where she crawls back into bed and tries to keep the tears in.

*

Today, Maggie's name is on the list. Hetty leads her and the other women along the corridor and down three flights of concrete stairs to the treatment room. 'Don't look so worried,' Hetty says. 'You'll forget all about it afterwards. You don't remember nothing about having it before, do you?'

'Well, no, but . . .' Maggie doesn't remember it specifically, but little snatches of memory keep flaring up, and they're enough to make her legs tremble.

As she follows Hetty along the corridor, two nurses come out of what Maggie later learns is the recovery room, each holding the arm of what looks like a slow-moving old woman. As they pass, Maggie sees that the woman is young, with a lot of ragged, straw-coloured hair. Her pretty dressing gown, which is midnight blue with a scattering of pink rosebuds around the neck and hem, is undone and the belt is trailing on the floor behind. On each of her temples is a livid red mark the size of a half-crown and there are more marks at the corners of her mouth. A line of saliva trickles down her chin. She looks in Maggie's direction, but her eyes are dead.

'Here we are then, ladies,' Hetty points to a long bench outside the closed doors of the treatment room. Just as Maggie sits, there is a loud shriek and a snort from behind the double doors, which then swing open as the previous patient is wheeled out, still convulsing, and taken into the recovery room. A minute or two later, the empty bed is wheeled back into the treatment room. Maggie sits rigid. There is a moment of stillness, a dense, frozen silence. Then the doors swing open again and a red-faced nurse with broad hips and a huge, shelf-like bust comes back out into the corridor. 'Can we have Margaret next please?' She looks along the row of women. 'Margaret?'

For a moment, Maggie allows herself to not respond. Instead, she marvels at the nurse's tiny shoes, and wonders how such dainty feet can possibly support that huge frame.

'Margaret Harrison.' The nurse is looking at her now. 'Come *along*, dear.'

There is a high bed in the middle of the room, and a black box with dials and knobs; there are wires, and straps and buckles. The doctor, an Indian man whom she hasn't seen before, smiles at her as she tries to get comfy, but he doesn't speak. 'Any false teeth or braces?' the nurse says, putting her finger in Maggie's mouth to look at her teeth as though she were a horse. 'Any watches or hair-pins?' Maggie shakes her head. The big nurse leans over and rubs a greasy substance into her temples. The woman smells of chip fat and cigarettes. She pushes a black rubber gag into Maggie's mouth and then stands behind her, holding her head with both hands.

Maggie wants to ask them to stop, to wait a second and let her prepare herself, but the rubber gag chokes her words. She tries to lift her hand to attract their attention, but someone is holding it down. The doctor puts two metal plates to her temples and she wills him to look at her, screams at him with her eyes so he can see that she needs to talk to him. Then her brain explodes. There's a thunderbolt of pain; lightning strikes her eyes; her bones melt and are crushed in an instant; her legs jerk and fizz and her arms flail and she can hear a gurgling in the back of her throat. She tries to free herself but it's as though she is in the grip of a giant vice. Then she feels herself falling, sinking fast until she is way down deep under the black water.

CHAPTER SEVEN

Frost sparkles on the steps of the crematorium. After the subdued lighting in the chapel, the brilliance of the sunlight glinting off the funeral cars is almost painful. Relatives and neighbours stand around in huddles, some stomping their feet and blowing into their hands, others smoking impatiently, keen to get back for the warming sherry they've been promised. Jonathan watches his mother stoop to read the cards on the floral tributes. She seems smaller than ever, her black dress and jacket accentuating her grass-like thinness and making her look so insubstantial he fears a sudden gust of wind might lift her over the rooftops like Dorothy in *The Wizard of Oz*. She's more composed now, graciously accepting condolences as she moves among the mourners. This morning, as they waited for the cars, he'd tried to comfort her, and was surprised by how inept he felt. It had made him think; how long was it since they'd had any physical contact – other than the perfunctory kiss on the cheek? Fiona's parents hugged him every time they met, and it always seemed so natural, but this morning when his own mother had leaned against him, it had felt strange and strained.

He looks at his watch. The funeral is making him twitchy now; he feels as though Gerald is watching him from beyond the grave, waiting for him to do something wrong or say something inappropriate.

'Jonathan.' His mother is coming towards him. 'Darling, would you and Fiona mind going back to the house to get the place warmed up a bit? And perhaps get the kettles filled and make sure everything's ready?' She looks flustered as she hands him her keys. 'Thank you, dear. You don't mind, do you?'

'Of course not,' he says, trying not to look too relieved at the excuse to get away.

*

As they walk up the drive to his parents' house, he starts to feel an unfamiliar lightness. For the first time, he can walk through that door without bracing himself against the weight of his father's disapproval.

Fiona hangs up her coat. 'How are you feeling?'

He considers this. His father is dead; that's it. Too late now to make amends; too late for everything. 'It's bizarre,' he says, 'but I can't say I feel anything really, except a mild sense of relief that I don't have to try and impress him any more.'

'That's hardly surprising, is it? After the way things have been?'

'But he was my own flesh and blood. I wish . . .' He sighs. 'Oh, I don't know. Even if I can't experience grief, I should at least feel some sense of loss, shouldn't I?'

'Don't be so hard on yourself. Lots of people don't get on with their parents; it's nothing to be ashamed of.'

'I suppose so,' he feels a momentary chill, and quite suddenly, he has an overwhelming need to be held. He pulls Fiona towards him; her hair smells of winter and yet her body is so warm against his. He's about to kiss her but she moves away.

'Let's get that fire on,' she says. 'It's bloody freezing in here.'

She looks great, he thinks, as she bends over the temperamental gas fire. Her skin is glowing, and there's a definite swell to her belly, even though no one else would probably notice. She looks ripe; bursting with life.

'Come on fire, light!' she says. 'Good fire!'

'You're mad.' He slides his hand across her buttocks. 'But you've got a gorgeous bum.'

'Jonathan!' she laughs and smacks his hand away.

He lifts her hair and kisses the soft white skin at the back of her neck.

'We shouldn't be snogging at a funeral,' she murmurs, kissing him anyway.

'I know.' He runs his hand up the back of her thigh, the smooth nylon hot against his cold skin. 'How long do you think they'll be?' He whispers against her ear.

'Oh, I don't know. Fifteen, twenty minutes?'

'Do you think we've got time?'

She pulls away and looks at him. 'You're not serious? Jonno, this is your dad's funeral! We're in his house.'

'I know, but I really, really want you.'

She makes a low noise. 'We can't,' she whispers, but her eyes are glittering.

'Let's go outside, then we won't be in "his house".'

'Outside? But it's freezing,' she laughs. 'Are you insane?'

He takes her hand and leads her to the back door. It does seem insane, but he can't fight it. It's not just desire, or even lust; it's an intense need to be close to her, to be as one, feeling the skin and the warmth and the wet and the beating of their two hearts close, close, together.

'Jonno, you really have lost it.' But she follows him, grabbing their coats on the way.

Ten minutes later, faces flushed, they hang up their damp coats and stumble into the living room just as the first car pulls up outside. The chemical-smelling gas fire is glowing like orange honeycomb and they warm themselves briefly in front of it before leaping into action. By the time the guests spill into the room, chatting now and clearly relieved to be over the more sombre parts of the proceedings, Jonathan has filled the sherry glasses and Fiona is pouring tea into china cups. The odd bubble of laughter rises up from the clusters of guests as they relax into the civilised pleasures of the funeral tea.

As he hands round the sandwiches, the combined smells of egg mayonnaise, sherry, strong tea and spicy aftershave begin to make him feel queasy, so he goes into the kitchen for some water. He stands at the sink looking out onto the well-tended garden, the only thing his father had really cared about. They'll never know now whether the baby would have made any difference; this is how it is. A picture flashes up in his mind: a late summer evening; he is very small, perhaps three or four; his father, in casual trousers, short-sleeved shirt and the ever-present tie, is bending over the rose bush, cutting a bloom almost tenderly. 'Careful.' He puts it into Jonathan's outstretched hand. 'Don't crush it.'

The image pops like a bubble and disappears.

After a few minutes, he goes back into the sitting room. Fiona nudges past him with a knowing smile; shame pokes him in the stomach, then begins to bed in more deeply, causing a surge of self-disgust.

'Fi, I'm sorry,' he says. 'I don't know what came over me.' This is true; even though he regrets what he's just done, he's still slightly stunned by the intensity of what he'd felt.

'Jonno, we haven't done anything terrible.' She puts her arms around him. 'I read somewhere that wanting to have sex is a common reaction to someone dying. It's a normal response to grief, to death. Something about needing to feel more alive when we're faced with the ultimate evidence of our mortality.'

That makes a certain sense, but it doesn't really help, because deep down, he wonders if it was more some sort of twisted two-fingered salute to Gerald.

'Look, it's your mum that matters now,' Fiona says. 'And she's coping; she has us both at her side and she's grateful. You're being a good son, so stop beating yourself up.'

A good son. As a child, he'd tried to be a good son, he really had. But that was before it dawned on him that his dad didn't actually like him. 'Do you realise,' he says, 'I'm now exactly the same age my father was when I was born?'

'And?'

'Doesn't it bother you? The idea that I might be totally out of touch?'

'Out of touch? In what way?'

'Like my dad was; you know, making me wear ankle-swingers; getting my mum to cut my hair because he wouldn't pay for a barber – I've told you this – then when I got beaten up for looking like something out of the fifties he told me not to be a crybaby.'

'That's nothing to do with age; it's just insensitive parenting. And I still think your mum should have stuck up for you.'

He mimics his mother: *'If they pick on you because your trousers are shorter than theirs, they're not the sort of boys you want to be friends with.'* They both smile, glancing along the hall to make sure she's not within earshot. 'The point is, if I don't get it right, if I misjudge it when the poor little sod wants to wear fluorescent purple pantaloons or whatever they'll be wearing by that time . . . well, I just don't want our child to go through that.'

'Right, listen. For one thing, you may be older than me but we agreed it's not too old, and for another, being older doesn't automatically make it impossible to relate to your kids.' She drops her voice again. 'There's no one in my antenatal group under thirty-five, and at least three of them are over forty. And most of the dads are older than the mums. You can't keep comparing yourself to your father. He's always been old, you said so yourself.'

He sighs, pulls her towards him and kisses the top of her head. 'All I'm saying is, don't let me become like him, will you?'

She tightens her arms around him. 'Jonno, you're not like him; you're about as different as it's possible for a father and son to be.'

*

After everyone's gone, they clear away and wash the tea things. The day has taken it out of Fiona and she's look-ing tired again, so Jonathan drives her home and then goes back to check on his mother. By the time he arrives, she's changed into her nightclothes; the long pink nightie and dressing gown make her seem vulnerable somehow.

'I think it all went off rather well, don't you?' She sits down surprisingly heavily for such a small woman. He notices the raised blue veins snaking over her feet. She nods towards the whisky bottle on the table by her chair and raises her own glass. 'I thought it would be acceptable, under the circumstances. Pour yourself one and sit down, dear. It's been a long day for all of us.'

He's driving, so he piles ice into his glass and pours in a tiny amount of the peaty-smelling scotch. Gerald's Old Holborn tobacco tin and silver lighter still lie on the bookshelf; his pipe, the mouthpiece dented with teeth marks, rests alongside. There's something both poignant and innocent about these things, placed there by his father yet never to be touched by him again. He looks back at his mother.

'I know,' she says. 'I've sent most of his clothes to the charity shop but I couldn't quite bring myself to . . . well, not yet. I'll get around to it, I expect.'

Jonathan is about to speak when she astonishes him by taking a packet of cigarettes and a lighter from her handbag. 'Bad habit, I know,' she mutters. 'But there's not much point in giving up now.'

'Giving up? But you haven't smoked for years!'

'I have, actually. But I told your father I'd stopped. Once he took up a pipe, he didn't like me smoking cigarettes, so I pretended I'd given up. Better to keep the peace.'

Jonathan sighs. 'But why did you always have to keep the peace, Mum? I don't just mean about the smoking. Why were you always so afraid of upsetting him?'

'Don't be tiresome, Jonathan,' she snaps. But then she sighs, and when she speaks again her voice is softer. 'I know your father could be rather ill-tempered sometimes but—'

'Rather ill-tempered? He threw his dinner at you because you'd overcooked the cabbage, for Christ's sake.'

'Don't blaspheme Jonathan, please.'

'He put my new train set in the dustbin because I'd left it on the floor—'

'That was to teach you to put your toys away.'

'Mum, he *knew* the dustmen were coming that morning.' There's a pause, then he sees the memory adjust itself. What he doesn't add is, *and so did you.*

She's always defended Gerald. He remembers coming home from school one day, aged eight or maybe nine, to find his guinea pigs gone. He'd gone straight through into the garden only to find an empty space where the hutch should have been. Bewildered, Jonathan had run into the kitchen where his mother was cutting up kidneys on a wooden board. He'd stopped, eyes level with the blood-smeared knife in her hands. 'Well?' she'd said. 'What do you want?' He tried to speak but he couldn't tear his eyes away from the kidneys, which bled in an almost human way, like a cut finger.

'Jonathan, I've a pie to make; I can't stand here all day waiting for you to—'

'Salt and Pepper,' he said. 'Where are they?'

'Ah.' She put the knife down, then picked up a cloth and wiped the worktop before turning back to him. 'Your father took them to the RSPCA this morning.'

'But . . . why?' Jonathan thought he could feel his heart beating in his ears.

'Because you haven't looked after them, have you?'

Her voice was sharp. 'You promised to clean them out every Saturday, and when your father went out there this morning, well, he said it was disgusting, frankly. I'm sorry, Jonathan, but your father's right. If you can't be trusted to look after them, they should go and live with someone who can.'

He'd fought the tears for long enough to argue that he'd been going to clean them out today, and it was only two days late, but she told him not to answer back.

The room is quiet apart from the hissing of the gas fire and the clink of ice cubes. His mother stubs out her cigarette and tops up her drink. 'We did a lot of things badly, Jonathan. We should have . . .' She falters and a tear runs down her papery cheek.

'Mum, I didn't mean to upset you.' He leans forward to put a hand on her arm. 'I don't blame you for the things he did, but I wish . . .' He stops; he shouldn't be getting into this, not now, but it's the first time she's even hinted at regret. Something a colleague said recently pops into his mind. They'd been talking about good and bad parenting, and the older man had said: *That's what's great about grandchildren – they're your chance to put right the balls-ups you made with your own kids*. Maybe that was true. He watches his mum dabbing her eyes with an embroidered handkerchief; perhaps the baby will change everything.

'I loved Gerald very much at first, you know,' she says. 'He was the most charming man I'd ever met, so gallant – a real gentleman.' She reaches for another cigarette. 'He treated me like a princess when we were courting. He had such presence.' He knows what'll come next – he could say it along with her. She needs something else to think about, something to take her mind off the past.

'My parents thought the world of him. Mother said his voice was so commanding he could have ordered the sun to come out and it would have.' She half-chuckles. 'Mind you, even after we married, I often felt like I should still call him Mr Robson.'

'Yes,' he nods, 'I remember you telling me.' A grandchild will give her something to look forward to, he thinks; a new purpose.

'He let me carry on working after we married. He was ever so good about it. I remember once . . .'

He stops taking it in. He's suddenly very keen to tell her; it'll make all the difference, and what's more, they'll have a common interest, a bond.

She's looking at him. 'I should have—'

'Mum, I've got something to tell you.'

She looks bewildered for a moment and he realises she was speaking.

'Sorry to cut in but I – we – meant to tell you, but what with Father being ill . . .' Guilt nips him sharply for using that excuse. 'I didn't say anything before but . . .'

She seems to recover herself. 'Oh darling, do get on with it.' She lights another cigarette and winds it towards her mouth with some difficulty.

'Yes, right. Sorry. Well, the thing is, Fiona and I, I mean . . . well, we're going to have a baby. You'll be a grandma!'

He waits. He doesn't know what to expect, but it isn't silence. Her face is blank. The only movement is her cigarette smoke, drifting upwards, greying the room.

'I said, you're going to be a grandmother.'

The gas fire continues to hiss and pop. The old mantel clock ticks so loudly that it's more of a clunk. 'Mum?' He tries to read her expression but she's looking through him.

'It's a bit of a shock,' she says.

He is so unprepared for this that anything else he might have said falls away. He searches for the right words but he can't come up with a single thing; it feels as if his mind is just a great void. 'A shock?' he manages eventually. But she doesn't respond. Several moments pass and the silence becomes increasingly brittle. His mouth and lips feel dry and he feels cold inside. 'Maybe I should be going,' he says after a while, 'and let you get to bed.'

She doesn't reply, so he stands and says goodnight. She's staring straight ahead, eyes blank, mouth turned down. He pauses at the door. 'Mum, are you all right?'

'What?' She turns towards him as though she's forgotten he's there. 'Oh, yes. Yes, thank you.' Her voice has changed and she seems distracted as she gets to her feet. 'I think I shall get off to bed now. I won't see you out, if you don't mind.'

Back at home, Fiona is standing at the fridge eating leftover pizza. Next door's cat is winding itself around her ankles, weaving in and out. 'Now the nausea's worn off, I can't stop eating.' She smiles. 'Well? How was she?'

'I told her.'

'Told her what?'

'About the baby.'

Fiona's smile dims. 'You told her? Just now?'

He nods. 'She, er . . .' He considers lying, saying his mum had been delighted and couldn't wait to be a grandma. But there's no point. He crosses the room and puts his arms around Fiona. 'There's no easy way to say it; she didn't seem very pleased.'

He feels her stiffen then she pulls away. 'It's hardly bloody surprising, is it? What on earth made you tell her today?'

'It may not have been the best –'

'Of course it wasn't! She's just buried her husband, for Christ's sake.'

'I know, but I thought—'

'Sometimes, Jonathan, you can be such a fucking idiot.' She pulls out a chair and collapses into it. 'What were you *thinking* of?'

'You, actually.' He throws his keys on the table and goes to the fridge, tripping over the cat, which hisses at him. 'You've been on about it for weeks.' He takes out a bottle and empties the last of the Chardonnay into a glass. 'When I finally—'

'When you finally decide to tell her, you choose to do it a few hours after your father's funeral. Un-fucking-believable!' Shaking her head, she gets up, takes a glass from the draining rack and tips up the wine bottle, but only a few drops drip out. 'Fuck,' she says, and bangs the bottle back down. 'Come on, then.' She looks at him, and the flame goes out of her voice. 'You'd better tell me what happened.'

'She said it was a shock.'

'A shock?'

'I know. Surprise would have understandable, I suppose, but . . .'

Fiona turns away from him. 'I really thought she'd be pleased.' There's a catch in her voice. She reels off a few sheets of kitchen roll and dabs at her eyes.

'Me too. Maybe when it's sunk in. Anyway, it's what we think that matters.' But he's shaken, too. He's used the term 'gutted' so carelessly after minor disappointments that it's become meaningless, but it describes perfectly how he feels now: like a fish on a slab with its guts, its very centre, cut out.

CHAPTER EIGHT

Maggie's sessions with Dr Carver are on Mondays, Wednesdays and Fridays; she remembers this now. And she remembers most of the nurses' names, and almost all the patients', at least, those from her ward. Her memory is beginning to grow, but the roots still aren't very strong.

'Don't push yourself too hard,' the doctor says. 'Relax, talk to the other ladies, and let nature take its course.' He taps his temple twice.

'I know.' Maggie speaks the words along with him: 'You can't force the old grey matter into action . . .'

'. . . before it's ready. Quite right.' He smiles as he shows her out. 'Now, mind you get yourself along to the social this evening,' he adds. 'Do you a power of good.'

*

There will be 'party food' according to Dr Carver; bridge rolls, cheese and pineapple, cocktail sausages – but not on sticks, apparently, because some patients can't be trusted. So the evening meal is light; liver sausage or luncheon meat with Heinz vegetable salad and brown bread and butter, or beans on toast. Maggie isn't hungry, so she just has a piece of toast and then heads back to the ward where she lights a cigarette and sits on her bed, legs stretched out in front of her, watching the smoke swirl up and up in the evening sunlight. What will this 'social' be like, she wonders? She's used to Pauline, Norma, and the other women on her own ward, but as for meeting new people, patients from the other wards . . . her stomach shifts at the thought. Although Pauline seems to think it'll be fun. 'I always enjoy them once I get there,' Pauline told her this morning, 'but I have to force myself to go.'

'Dolly!' Maggie calls out as the old lady passes. 'You going to this thing tonight?'

'The shindig? No, love, I ain't got time. I've got to get me stuff packed. I'm going home soon, see.'

'Oh, I see.' Maggie nods. 'That's good, then.' At first, she'd believed everyone who said they were going home soon, but now she knows it's mostly wishful thinking. After a couple of weeks of daily treatments, though, Dolly does seem to be going though a good patch. She walks upright, smiles at everyone and can even be heard singing to herself as she works in the laundry. At the moment, Maggie's working in the laundry too, but she's asked Sister if she can work in the kitchen. How long will she be here, she wonders? And what is her *real* life? A loud clapping breaks into her thoughts. 'Here we are, ladies.' Sister holds up a small cardboard box. 'You've got fifteen minutes to make yourselves beautiful.' She puts the box on the table and folds her arms. The women hurry down the ward. Maggie stubs out her cigarette and follows them. They crowd around, rummaging in the box and pulling out various items before scurrying over to where one of the orderlies is setting up a row of mirrors. When she can get near enough, Maggie looks into the box: there are stubs of lipstick, well-used pots of eyeshadow and rouge, pitted black cakes of mascara and mirrored compacts of pressed, pinky-beige powder. The scent reminds her of her mother, and a wave of childlike longing sweeps over her. She fights the urge to cry and concentrates on selecting some make-up. As she joins the other women at the mirrors, she is surprised to realise that she remembers her own face; it looks familiar, almost the same as she left it, apart from the puddles of darkness under her eyes. The cake of mascara is cracked and dry, so she spits a little saliva onto it and uses what's left of the brush to mix it to a usable consistency. She glances to her left and sees a line of women, all applying make-up at the same time. There is another rumbling in her memory, and she pauses with the brush in her hand. There was a long, narrow dressing room, and all the girls sat in a line, putting on thick, greasy make-up. She travelled by train to get there; she had a suitcase . . .

When she's ready, she goes along to the other end of

the ward to find Pauline, who's lying on her bed, clutch-ing a photograph and staring at the ceiling.

'Are you coming to this social thing?'

Pauline shakes her head and looks at the picture she's holding.

'Oh, come on,' Maggie says. 'You said you always enjoy it when you get there.'

'Can't face it tonight,' Pauline says. 'You go. You can tell me about it later.'

'I don't want to go on my own. Please come, Pauline.'

Pauline doesn't answer.

'Go on, just for half an hour.'

Pauline sighs, then she sits up, pushes the hair off her face. 'Oh all right; might as well, I suppose.' She swings her legs over the edge of the bed. 'Give me a minute, will you.'

Pauline's face is pale and gaunt. Her eyes are dull, the lids swollen and reddened; there are bruise-like crescents underneath and a deep red mark on each of her temples. She shows Maggie the photograph. 'Look. That's my baby, Angela. It's her first birthday today, but they won't let me go home because it's "not the right day for home visits". I'll see her on Tuesday, but it's not the same.' She takes a comb from her handbag and starts viciously backcombing her hair. 'A year old, and she barely knows who I am.'

Maggie looks at the picture. The child has fair hair and a tiny curl resting on her forehead. Her little starfish hand is clutching a fluffy toy of some sort – a dog, perhaps – and she's smiling at whoever is behind the camera. The smile is slightly lopsided, just like Pauline's. The genial-looking man holding her is gazing at her with pride. There is a tug at Maggie's memory and she remembers there's something she's supposed to do, in thirteen . . . or was it on the thirteenth? But she doesn't even know what month it is, let alone the date. Something else is coming back, but before she can grasp it, the nurse's voice cuts across her thoughts. 'Come along, ladies. Do get a move on!'

*

The day room is packed with people. There are patients and staff, some in uniform, some in civvies. The first thing Maggie notices is the pungent smell of body odour, and the men – the very presence of them. Apart from the doctors, the only men she usually sees are the orderlies who bring the dinner trolley from the main kitchen, and the pig-man – the rotund little Irishman who collects the buckets of pigswill from the ward kitchens on Mondays. She fans herself with her hand. The room is so crowded that she's lost sight of Pauline already. Even though the windows are open a few inches at the top and bottom, the heat is almost unbearable, and she can feel a film of perspiration forming on her upper lip. The ceiling fans rotate above her head, but they barely disturb the hot, heavy air. She tries to think about what it is she has to do; something to do with the picture Pauline showed her . . . but with the smell and the heat and the people jostling her, it's impossible to concentrate, so she stores the thoughts away for later.

She drifts around the room until she spots Norma sitting on the wide sill, looking out across the grounds. The bees are making the most of the last rays of evening sunshine as they hum lazily around the lavender that grows just beneath the window.

'Hello, Norma,' Maggie smiles. But the face that turns towards her is desolate; the eyes that yesterday twinkled with mischief are now flat and dead.

'Too far down the pole,' Norma says, her voice so faint it only just scratches the air. 'Too far down today.' And she turns back to the window. The sun slips behind the trees and in an instant the garden is in shadow, robbed of the pinks, reds and yellows that provide such a welcome contrast to the dismal hospital interior. Maggie hovers for a few moments. Apart from Norma, the only other women she's talked to are the other nervous breakdowns. *How long have you been in? Have you had ECT? When are you going home?* They ask each other the same questions, repeat their stories to anyone who'll listen, and compare notes about their sessions with Dr Carver. Maggie can cope with that; and she can cope with the sunny, childlike Norma who flits around the room like a butterfly. But this Norma is different, her cold misery impenetrable. Maggie lays a hand on her shoulder, but there is no response. A fat, glossy bee has slipped in under the window and is now buzzing around Norma's head and butting dementedly at the glass. Norma doesn't even seem to notice.

CHAPTER NINE

The phone rings just as he's getting out of the shower.

'Jonathan, it's your mother. I'm so glad you're there – I thought you might have gone to work. I – I couldn't sleep last night. I've been thinking about what you said. I'm pleased for you both, really I am, and I'm sorry for my behaviour. It was just that I wasn't—'

'No, *I'm* sorry. It was really bad timing.' A mental image of Fiona nodding pointedly pops into his brain.

'Listen, darling, could you come over? I'd like to explain properly.'

He hesitates. So far, yesterday is the only day he's taken off. He could take more time, but it would feel dishonest, given that what he's feeling isn't really grief. And anyway, when he's teaching, his thoughts don't keep returning to that last fraught visit with his father. Try as he might, he can't remember the last words they'd spoken to each other.

'Sorry, Mum, I told them I'd be back today, but I'll pop in on my way home, all right?'

*

Somehow, he muddles through the day, but he knows he's not on form; maybe he should have taken a few more days off. Darkness is falling rapidly as he drives through Blackheath Village; he looks at the fairy lights strung across the narrow roads and the Christmas trees twinkling in shop windows. Next Christmas, he'll be a father; his mother will be a – he thinks about the words – *grand mother*. She'd never been a particularly motherly mother, but that didn't mean she couldn't be *grandmotherly*, did it?

The sitting room is warm and smoky when he arrives. He glances at the half-full ashtray.

'I know,' his mother says. 'I shan't be able to do this when the baby comes.'

He smiles, disproportionately pleased to hear her say *when the baby comes*.

'You must have thought my response yesterday extremely rude.' She takes another cigarette from the pack and he notices her hand shaking.

'No, it was my fault. I don't know what I was thinking of.'

'I'm sorry, darling, could you light this for me?'

He takes the lighter and holds the flame steady for her, half-expecting a craving to take hold of him again, but it doesn't.

'It's not that I'm not pleased, it's just that it was, well, as I said, something of a shock. Oh, don't look at me like that; I know we've never discussed that sort of thing but you've been married, what, eight years? I suppose I thought you'd decided not to have children. One doesn't like to ask.' She takes a long draw on her cigarette. 'Jonathan, I'm thrilled you're going to have a baby, I really am. And I'll do my best to be what a ... what a real grandma should be.'

'Well, thank you,' he says, but she still seems agitated.

'There are some things I need to talk to you about; things I should have told you before, probably. Your news . . .' She smiles at him. 'Your *wonderful* news – put me in mind of something that happened long before you came along.' She pauses. 'I had a baby, you see, a little boy who died soon after he was born. We called him Gerald, after your father and his father. He only lived for two hours; such a tiny little scrap. Your father was heartbroken.'

'Mum,' he says gently. 'I didn't know—'

'Oh, there's a lot you don't know.' She takes a gulp from a cup of what looks like cold tea. 'They wouldn't let me hold him; they didn't in those days. Just took him away and told me to try again while there was still time.' She keeps her head lowered as she fumbles in her bag for a handkerchief and blows her nose, then she takes a deep, shaky breath. 'It changed Gerald a great deal, you know.'

Jonathan tries to think of something to say but nothing comes, so he just listens.

'You had to get on with life in those days. It took me a while, though. I barely got out of my chair at first, so your father had to look after me as well as the house. He was very attentive; even read to me to try and take me out of myself. But he wasn't as strong as people thought. Once I started to get back to normal, he went downhill; couldn't sleep, couldn't read; he even stopped listening to the wireless. Sometimes he'd sit in that chair for hours, just staring at the wall.'

Jonathan tries to picture them, grief-stricken, bewildered, trying to come to terms with the loss of their baby. Why hasn't she told him this before?

'I wanted another baby so much. I thought it might make things better, but . . .'

He leans forward. 'But what?' he asks softly.

'You see, your father didn't . . . I mean he wouldn't . . .'

'He didn't want another child?' Things are beginning to make sense now.

'It wasn't that, exactly. It was . . . oh dear, this is terribly difficult.' She stubs out her cigarette and reaches for another.

Part of him wants to press her, to ask her exactly how his father had reacted when he knew she was pregnant again. Had he been angry? Had he continued to be angry after the birth? Another part of him doesn't want to know. His mother's hand is shaking even more now. She seems to have second thoughts about the cigarette and tries unsuccessfully to get it back in the pack.

'Mum, look, don't talk about it any more now, not if you don't want to.'

She reaches for the handkerchief again. 'No, no, I must.'

He waits. But she's pressing the handkerchief to her lips, trying unsuccessfully to compose herself. How much longer can he sit here watching an old lady's distress? 'Mum, don't.' He rests his hand on her arm. 'It'll keep.'

*

That evening, he lies in the bath while the water cools around him. He thinks about his parents, going about their daily tasks despite their grief for the child who hadn't even lived a day; his mother cooking, shopping, struggling to contain her sadness. How the hell do you cope with the death of a child? It's something he can't even contemplate. He slides down, dropping his shoulders under the water to soak away the tension. Downstairs, Fiona has put on a CD – Elgar, because it's good for the baby apparently – and he's neither particularly listening to nor ignoring the music when he suddenly becomes intensely aware of it, moved by the deep, rich tone of some notes, the achingly melancholic quality of others. As he listens, the sound seems to soar up through the floorboards, spilling into the water around him and making his flesh feel raw. It is as though a layer of skin has been peeled off, exposing all the most tender places.

*

When he gets into bed, Fiona is sleeping soundly, her cheek resting neatly on the palm of her right hand and her lips parting with a little click as she breathes out. She'd seemed preoccupied tonight, and she'd wept when he told her about his mum losing her first child; perhaps he should have kept that to himself. He thinks about that long-ago baby, his brother. Would they have looked alike? He doesn't look like his father but people say he has his mother's eyes. He wants to ask his mum how she'd felt about being pregnant again, how she'd been after having him. Perhaps she'd had post-natal depression. He pictures his father looking down at him, seeing him both as a poor substitute for his dead brother and as the reason for his mother's suffering. He hadn't stood a chance of gaining a place in Gerald's affections, he sees that now. And the strange thing is, he can see the logic. After all, if anything happened to Fiona, would he be able to forgive the baby? He thinks about the Gerald his mother described, the heartbroken husband caring for his grief-stricken wife. She said Gerald had cried.

He turns over and closes his eyes tighter, but the more he tries to empty his mind, the more impossible it becomes. He turns onto his back and watches the beam of a headlight sweep across the ceiling. Fiona mutters something in her sleep and turns over. It's no good; he's wide awake now. Gently, he slides out of bed and pads downstairs.

He pours a small brandy then unlocks the back door and stands there for a moment, looking out into the garden. The smell of fresh pine cuts through the smoky December air. The Christmas tree is propped against the side of the house, waiting to be dragged in, decorated, then thrown out again a week or two later. The thought triggers a wave of childlike sadness which surprises him. His memories of early childhood are hazy, but perhaps it's just as well. Briefly, he pictures Gerald holding a newborn baby, and again he finds himself wondering whether, given the chance, his father would have mellowed in grandparenthood.

Despite the cold, he takes his glass, walks along the path to the bench at the end and sits down. The garden looks silvery in the moonlight, and there's hardly any sound. He pulls his dressing gown more tightly around him. A movement to his left startles him, but it's just a young fox, snaffling up the bread and scraps of meat Fiona put out for it. For a moment the creature looks up and their eyes meet. *See?* it seems to say. *You're not the only thing she cares about.* Then it disappears through a hole in the fence and he is alone again.

Already, Fiona loves their unborn child; she talks to it all the time with tenderness in her voice, even looking down at her stomach as she speaks. He tries to imagine his little son or daughter, curled up inside her, listening to the gentle rise and fall of her voice against the rhythmic beat of her heart, but he can only summon up an idea or impression; he can't seem to think of his child as a real person, not yet.

Soon, the combination of the cold and the brandy

numbs his mind enough for him to attempt sleep again. He climbs back into bed carefully, so as not to touch Fiona with his icy limbs, and as he sinks gratefully into slumber, his thoughts mangle into dreams.

He is playing in the garden of his parents' house when it begins to snow. He goes into the house through the French doors; the room is full of people, and there are two tiny white coffins on stands in the centre. His parents stare blankly through him. He turns back to the garden where he spots something moving. At first he thinks it's a couple of cats or fox cubs and he tries to open the door, but it is locked. He pushes his face up against the glass and sees that it's two babies, big enough to sit up, laughing and playing in the snow. He bangs on the glass and one of them looks up and reaches out to him. But the snow is so thick and heavy that the babies are already partly buried, so he needs to act fast. He turns back to the adults and tries to speak but no sound comes out, so he runs to each in turn and stands in front of them, tugging at their clothes and pointing to the disappearing babies. Still nobody sees him.

CHAPTER TEN

The day room is really filling up now. More patients are herded in, overdressed and over-made-up, and Maggie recognises hardly any of them. It occurs to her that she has no idea how big this hospital is. 'Ah, Margaret!' The familiar voice of Dr Carver cuts through the general hubbub. 'Glad you made it, well done.' His big bear-face grins at her. 'Having a nice time?'

She is about to say that she's not sure how she feels just now, when he nods encouragingly. 'Good, good. Try and make sure you mix with the other patients; don't want to be a wallflower, do we?'

Maggie smiles back. She doesn't want him finding someone for her to talk to. 'I'm just going to get myself a drink,' she says. 'Then I'll have a wander around.'

'That's the spirit,' Dr Carver smiles, patting her on the shoulder. 'Jolly good.'

She takes a paper cup of Pepsi-Cola from the long table

just inside the door. She is still slightly shaken by her encounter with Norma – Norma whom she'd thought was ever-smiling; Norma who seemed so happy in her girlish world of curtseys and dancing and funny little tunes. Maggie sighs. There are so many unfamiliar faces; so many who are obviously a bit funny in the head. If only she could see someone she could talk to. There's always Peggy, she supposes. Peggy is sitting on her suitcase in the corner, make-up all smudged and smeared as though applied by a chimpanzee. But if she goes over to Peggy, she'll have to sit there and look interested while Peggy opens her suitcase and counts the thousands of bus tickets she keeps in it.

After a while, she begins to get used to the heat and the smell. She looks around. In some parts of the room there are little pockets of normality, people at tables playing cards or ludo, or standing in groups, talking and smoking like normal guests at a normal party – normal except for the paper cups and lack of anything interesting to drink. A little cartoon deer with a blue bow capers across her memory; *I'd love a Babycham* . . .

At last she spots Pauline talking to a thin, dark-haired man who looks a bit like George Harrison. She starts at the thought; how on earth can she remember the name of some man from some stupid pop group when she remembers so little of what's happened to her in the last seven or eight months? Pauline, who looks more cheerful, is now beckoning her over. That picture of Pauline's husband and daughter comes into her mind again, making her wonder whether . . . but no. She looks at her hand: no wedding ring; no mark where a wedding ring might have been.

'Fancy a game of Monopoly?' Pauline says.

The man looks at her and smiles. He doesn't look too mad, so she pulls up a chair and joins them.

'Sam,' the man says, shaking her hand. His skin is warm and dry, and he has a gentle Scots accent, soft and dark, like damp earth. Maggie finds herself listening closely to the melodic rise and fall of his voice. As he sets up the game, the cuff of his shirt rides up, revealing a knobbly scar on the inside of his wrist. Maggie tries not to look. The three of them begin to play, talking generally about who's gone home recently and who's due to go. Soon, inevitably, they talk about their own breakdowns and treatment.

'I can still hardly believe I've had ECT.' Maggie rolls the dice and moves six spaces. 'Regent Street, I'll buy that.' She counts out the money. 'I vaguely remember going into the treatment room and them rubbing that stuff on my head, but I don't remember the actual shock.'

Pauline sighs. 'Sometimes, you don't remember it at the time but then you start to have nightmares about it. Not as bad as the real thing, but you can still end up hanging onto your head and screaming. Then they give you another lot.'

'Which makes ye scream again,' says Sam.

Maggie can't imagine Sam screaming, or even raising his voice.

'It's supposed to obliterate whatever horrible thing put ye in here,' he says. 'But it's no' that selective, is it?' His hair is so long that it almost touches his collar at the back, and it moves as he shakes the dice.

'I still don't know what put me in here,' Maggie says. 'Odd, isn't it? I can remember how to play Monopoly; I can remember all the words to "Love Me Do"; I can even remember the name of the cat I had when I was ten.' She pauses to take her turn, moving the miniature rocking horse three places along the board. 'But apart from blurry little glimpses, I can't remember anything important.'

Sam is looking at her, as though he's really listening. 'That must be hard,' he says. 'I used to think I'd rather no' remember anything, but some of them in here, they cannae even recognise their own families.'

'You can remember, then?'

He nods, lights a cigarette. 'I'm no' saying ma memory's intact – I cannae remember where I put ma socks or when I'm supposed to go to occupational therapy.' He takes a long draw of his cigarette. 'But I remember every detail of the day . . .' His voice catches and he closes his eyes.

Pauline gently touches his arm. He shakes his head as if to dislodge something, while the fingers of his right hand twist his wedding ring round and round.

'. . . of the day I lost ma wife and ma wee lad. Every detail.'

'I'm so sorry.' Maggie is aware that it's something she must have said a dozen times in the last couple of weeks.

But she is more sincere this time; she really wants to show her sympathy to this quietly spoken man.

'Thanks,' he picks up the shaker as though he's going to throw the dice again, but then he pauses.

'The sea took them; swept them off the pier. I jumped in, but I couldnae find them. Next thing I know, the life-boat is there, and they're pulling me out.' He shakes his head as though that is the worst part of the memory. 'I should have gone straight in after them, but I threw her a rope instead.'

'But that's *right*,' Maggie says. 'That's what you're supposed to do.'

'Aye, but the rope was rotten; it snapped.'

Maggie lays her hand on the back of Sam's. She's not sure whether it's acceptable to touch a man you've just met, but there are different rules in here. Sam's wrist is bony and the skin is warm and dry; she can feel the little hairs under her fingers. Surprised by the intensity of the sensation, she withdraws her hand, but he turns his over and catches her fingers briefly in his own.

The music is getting louder. They manage to sing along to 'She Loves You' while continuing their game. No one except Peggy and a few of the nurses join in with 'Summer Holiday' because the idea of going on holiday seems so far removed from their daily existence that even thinking about it is too painful. For Maggie, the song is also a reminder of home – she misses the sea and is about to say so when she remembers what Sam has just told her about his wife and child.

After 'Glad All Over' and 'Devil in Disguise', there's a pause in the music. Maggie glances over to where the record player is set up. A group of nurses are looking through a pile of 45s, then one of them selects a record. 'How about this?' she grins.

'Couldn't be more perfect,' says Julie, the skinny, spotty nurse who's always so horrible to Pauline. 'Put it on,' she orders, then she leans back against the wall, folds her arms and smirks as the air fills with a voice Maggie recognises: Patsy Cline singing 'Crazy'. The nurses try to stifle their laughter.

Sam shakes his head. 'Ignore them. Let them have their silly wee games.'

'Wait, I've got one!' One of the male nurses pulls the record off abruptly and puts another on the spindle. Patsy's voice rings out again, this time with 'I Fall to Pieces'. The nurses are still laughing, but Sister is marching across the room, her tree-trunk legs moving like pistons. Maggie would not want to be on the wrong side of Sister. A few patients, apparently oblivious, sing along to the song, encouraged by the nurses; others have made their way to the middle of the room and are trying to dance. There is another tremor in Maggie's memory, something deep. She remembers this song, people dancing and smoking cigarettes. For a moment, she has a vision of her real self: she is at a party, standing in the middle of the room, dressed up, smiling. The man is on his knees, singing along, singing to her.

The black hole is opening up inside her again, that

aching, hollow emptiness; then Pauline and Sam start to fade, the day room disappears and Maggie starts to shiver. She is outside, in the cold, in the dark; there is a buzzing in her ears and then the blackness rushes in. Her legs give way beneath her.

When she opens her eyes, she sees her legs stretched out in front of her and her feet in their flat black pumps, tilting sideways and making a 'V' shape. She is glad she's wearing slacks rather than a dress.

'Will ye stand back and give the lass some air!'

She can feel an arm supporting her head, and she tries to twist away, but then she realises where she is, and who is holding her.

'You'll be fine,' Sam says. 'Och, hush now; no need to cry.'

*

Back on the ward, she pulls the covers over her head and pretends to be asleep. She hears the others come back from the day room, the drugs trolley being wheeled through the ward and the nurses reading out each patient's name and the details of their medication. She tries to blot out the sound of their voices because she wants to concentrate on what she's remembered. She thinks about the George Harrison man, Sam, but then pushes him to the back of her mind – she can think about him tomorrow. The night nurses are talking about someone needing medicine for a chest infection. *Infection.* The word catches on a ragged edge of memory. She needs to think about that, too, but she is more tired than she'd realised, and soon the thoughts and words and pictures begin to jumble and tangle as she sinks into sleep.

*

Just after midnight, she sits up in bed with a gasp, eyes so wide they feel like they'll never shut. Now she remembers; now she knows why she's here.

CHAPTER ELEVEN

A glimmer of winter sunlight forces its way through the clouds, briefly turning the wet playground silver before disappearing back into the greyness of the afternoon. Jonathan braces himself as he walks towards the prefab classroom. He's teaching a challenging Year 10 group next period, and again it flits through his mind that he could have taken more time off. He's not sure whether it's his father's unexpected death that's shaken him up or his mum talking about the baby that died: his brother. He still doesn't understand why she hasn't told him before.

The classroom smells of nylon carpet, damp plasterboard and unwashed adolescent. A faint trace of dope hangs in the air, but with no evidence of anyone actually smoking, it's probably safe to ignore it. He rubs his hands together. It's like a bloody icebox in here.

'Come on, you lot, settle down. We've got a lot to get through. Amber, stop chatting and turn to the front please.'

Amber turns around, her face screwed up in a sulk. The others keep talking. 'Can everyone pay attention please.' He claps his hands loudly. 'Come on now, that's enough.' Gradually, the noise dies down.

'Right,' he says, 'let's get back to *The Woman in Black*—'

'Why ain't we going theatre, Sir?' Amber folds her arms across her chest. She looks furious. 'The Fawcett says we ain't allowed.'

His heart sinks. '*Mrs* Fawcett. Now, what do you mean you're not allowed?' They all start speaking at once. 'Hang on, hang on. One at a time. Amber, what's all this about?'

'Fawcett, right, she comes into Business Studies yesterday, and she's like, you lot can't go "Woman in Black" now, and we're like, why not, Miss? And it's because some dude from the business and industries thing was supposed be giving us a talk on Wednesday, but now he's coming Thursday instead and she's like, "You can't afford to miss this excellent opportunity, blah blah".'

Jonathan sighs. 'How many of you does this affect?' Nine hands go up; almost half the group. He sighs again. This lot would get more out of one trip to the theatre than half a dozen visits from some fat-bellied, shiny-suited businessman.

'You said we was allowed, Sir. How come she says we ain't?'

'I don't know, Daniel,' he says. 'This is the first I've heard of it.' He drums his fingers on the desk. 'Look, I can't promise anything, but I'll speak to Mrs Fawcett to see if it's possible to rearrange things.' But as he speaks he remembers what Malcolm said about this new deputy head: *Fawcett? About as flexible as a bloody crowbar.*

The door opens and Ryan Jenkins saunters in. Great. Ryan bloody Jenkins, back already. The boy starts high-fiving his mates as he makes his way to a seat.

'Come on, Ryan,' Jonathan says. 'Hurry up and settle.'

A week ago, he'd had to physically stop Ryan from pummelling the head of a Year 8 kid during morning break. Ryan was bright, but incredibly disruptive. Most of the teachers turned a blind eye rather than deal with him, but that made him think he was untouchable, and Jonathan certainly wasn't going to walk past while Ryan beat the younger boy to a pulp. He'd hauled him up to the Head's office and Ryan had been promptly suspended. Now here he was again.

'Ryan, sit down now, please.' He keeps his voice level, but he can sense trouble already. Ryan leans across the desks to talk to Chloé Nichols, who is still scowling at Jonathan, probably because he told her off in the previous period – a geography lesson he'd had to cover at the last minute. Chloé turns her attention to Ryan and gazes at him with rapt attention, then she and the other girls laugh at something he tells them.

'Okay, everyone.' Jonathan still tries to keep it light, lets the boy have his moment. 'I know Ryan's far more entertaining than I am, but we've got to get on now. So, if you don't mind, Ryan.' He gestures to a seat and, miraculously, Ryan sits. 'Okay, let's make a start. Who can tell me—'

'Look!' Ryan points at Jonathan's knees and he looks down automatically. 'You've pissed yourself, Sir.'

There's an eruption of laughter and he curses himself for the reflex action.

'Made you look, Sir!' Ryan rocks his chair back on two legs, grinning, emboldened by the obvious admiration of the girls. The whole group is talking again now.

'Okay, everyone, very funny. Now let's have some quiet, please. Come on, Ryan, stop behaving like a two-year-old and concentrate on what we're supposed to be doing.'

Ryan yawns and stretches expansively. Jonathan ignores it, but Ryan yawns again, loudly this time. 'Ryan, do you want me to write on your report card?'

Ryan shrugs. 'You can't, Sir. Ain't done nothing, have I?'

'He was only saying, Sir.' Daniel; usually a good kid, but easily led.

'Yeah,' Craig Willis chips in. 'That you'd, like, pissed yourself, Sir.' He turns, grinning, towards Ryan. 'Innit?' Laughter spatters around the room.

'It's not piss.' A girl's voice from the corner. 'It's jizz!' Another burst of giggling. Lauren? He can't be sure. Eight or nine girls clustered together, all looking at the boys for approval. He hesitates; fatal indecision. They're revving up now, gathering power.

'Mr Robson, did Chloé's tits make you dribble?'

Don't react, he tells himself; just don't react. They're all paying attention now, watching to see what he'll do. He used to be able to distinguish the good kids from the troublemakers, but they seem have merged now into a single unit, a pack. He hears his father's voice: *'Savages, most of them'*. No. They're just kids; difficult kids.

'Perhaps him like boys, innit? I bet him want to get in Kieran's arse.'

'No, he ain't no batty boy,' Craig calls across the room. 'Me seen his wife.'

'Bet she's a dog,' Lauren chimes in. Chantelle jumps to her feet and starts barking. The class erupts in more laughter; they're all at it now.

'Quiet!' he yells, banging his hand down on the desk. 'Or each and every one of you will stay behind at the end of the day.'

A brief hush falls over the room, and for a blissful moment he thinks he's got away with it. Then Ryan turns to the others. 'Yeah, shut it, you lot. Mrs Robbo's well fit.'

Craig grins. 'Innit? I'd give her one.'

'That is *it*! Craig, *out*! Lauren, Chantelle, this is your last verbal warning. And unless the rest of you want a detention at three forty, I suggest you put a sock in it – *now*! Ryan, bring me your report card.' His throat aches from shouting; he's cocked it up – badly.

Lauren starts to cry. Chantelle puts her arm around Lauren and looks at Jonathan as though he's just strangled a kitten and stamped on its head. Ryan sits down and leans back, looking at the ceiling with exaggerated boredom.

'Ryan. Report card. Now!'

Ryan makes a big deal of searching through his

rucksack, taking out every item and examining it closely before showing it to the class.

'Get on with it!'

'I *am,*' Ryan says, facing Jonathan and rolling his eyes theatrically before turning back to his mates. The noise is dulling now as the rest of the group, sensing fresh sport, watch to see who'll back down first.

'Found it, Sir.' Ryan holds the card up and waggles it back and forth. He turns to grin at the class, and then he begins to walk towards Jonathan, slowly, ostentatiously – and backwards. As he gets to the front, he spins on his heels and follows it up by moonwalking towards the door.

'Ryan Jenkins,' Jonathan says steadily. 'Do not even think about leaving my classroom without permission.'

'I weren't, Sir,' he says, in mock outrage.

Jonathan takes a breath. Maybe he can still save this. He tries a conciliatory tone. 'Come on, then. Let's have that report card please.'

Ryan offers the card. But just as Jonathan is about to take it, the little shit jerks it up out of his reach. Briefly, Jonathan considers sending him over to Malcolm or to one of the assistant heads. But what sort of teacher is he if he can't deal with this himself? He makes a grab for the card, but the boy whisks it behind his back, swapping hands before holding it up again. Jonathan moves fast but his fingers fail to grasp it before Ryan yanks it away again. He can hear the other kids laughing; he knows he's not thinking straight now, he's just reacting. The card flashes up in front of him, then vanishes; it appears to his right, then is gone, to his left, then disappears; now you see it, now you don't; his face is too close, the smell of bubble gum is too near . . .

He is aware of the silence before he registers the gasp that precedes it. Ryan is standing still now, an unmistakable air of smugness beginning to settle around his features. The kids are whispering. There's a dent in the plasterboard wall, and tiny drops of blood are blooming from the grazes that are beginning to smart on Jonathan's knuckles. His fist had seemed to move independently, smashing into the wall just inches from where Ryan was standing – how he'd not punched the little sod on the nose he'd never know.

'Sit!' he tells Ryan, then he walks out of the classroom, closing the door behind him as quietly as he is able.

*

There are piles of blue exercise books all over the floor of Malcolm's office. He leans back in his chair and sips coffee from his *World's Best Dad* mug while Jonathan goes through what happened.

'I don't think I've ever felt so close to thumping a kid before,' Jonathan says. 'I *let* him wind me up. Oh, and did you hear that Fawcett woman's cancelled the theatre trip? So they were pretty unsettled before we even started. Then Ryan comes in and, well, that was it. Why's he back so soon, anyway? I thought he'd be excluded for at least another week.'

'I know,' Malcolm sighs. 'Not much of a deterrent, is it? Look, don't worry too much. I'll have to put in a report, and you'll get a ticking off from on high, but everyone knows what an arrogant little tosspot Ryan Jenkins is. He'd probably benefit from a bloody good hiding.' He pauses. 'How was the funeral?'

'It was fine. Well, as fine as a funeral can be, anyway.' He doesn't add that he'd managed to upset his mum *and* Fiona straight afterwards.

'Everything else all right? Fi okay?'

Jonathan hesitates for a millisecond, then nods. Malcolm's a good friend, but talking to him about their marriage doesn't feel right. 'She's fine. We're both a bit tired, that's all.'

Malcolm nods. 'Cass was tired in the first few months. Fiona's about the same age as Cass was when we had Poppy, isn't she?'

'She's thirty-nine.'

'Yeah, Cass was forty. The tiredness goes off a bit after the first few months and they have a burst of energy. Then once it's born, you'll both be exhausted. And you can say goodbye to a good night's sleep for at least two years.'

'It's been a while since I've had one of those anyway, to be honest.'

'No wonder you look like shit. I prescribe a large Scotch before bed.' Malcolm stands up and takes his jacket from the back of the chair. 'Seriously though, I'm sure this'll all blow over, and I know you've just had the funeral and everything, but you need to watch yourself. I wouldn't be a mate if I didn't mention it. I reckon our Mrs Fawcett wants to put a few heads on spikes to justify her existence.'

Jonathan nods. 'I'll bear it in mind.' He stands up.

'No, you stay there. I'll go and have a word with those charming young ladies and gentlemen while you chill out here for,' he looks at his watch, 'a whole fifteen minutes before period seven.' He slaps Jonathan on the back as he opens the door and disappears, whistling, into the corridor.

CHAPTER TWELVE

January 1962

Although it is well past twelfth night, there are still faded paper chains hanging from the ceiling and straggly bits of tinsel draped over the hunting prints on the wall. The place smells of burnt sausages and tomcat but the rooms are cheap, and as she'll only be earning five pounds ten a week, that's the main thing.

The room is part of a converted attic, and the ceiling slopes either side of a tiny dormer window through which Maggie can see the rain-varnished rooftops of Sheffield. The flinty eyed landlady stands behind her, puffing and wheezing from the climb. There is a half-crown of rouge on each dusty cheek; her mouth is a red scar. 'Thirty bob a week,' she says after she's caught her breath. 'In advance.'

Maggie looks at the green linoleum, pockmarked with cigarette burns; the litter of spent matches beneath the gas fire; the faded orange candlewick bedspread and the vase of dusty red plastic tulips on the bedside cabinet.

'I don't allow food in't rooms, no loud music, and no lads. Lavvy's two floors down and bathroom's in't basement. Take it or leave it.'

'Oh, I'll take it please.' Maggie is conscious of how high and tinkling her voice sounds compared to that of her landlady who, she later discovers, smokes forty Players a day. Maggie wishes her accent wasn't so obviously southern, although Mr Howard – Clive – seemed to like it. 'Pretty voice, that,' he'd said at her audition. 'Might find you a speaking part if you make out well.'

'Is tha working?' The landlady does not smile, nor does she remove her hands from her hips as she eyes the ten-shilling notes in Maggie's outstretched hand. She'll not let rooms to lasses without jobs, not under any circumstances.

'Yes,' Maggie says quickly. 'I'm starting at the Playhouse on Monday – Assistant Stage Manager.'

The landlady relaxes. 'Ta, love.' She counts the money with practised rapidity before putting it in her apron pocket. 'I'm Dot. You'll meet Alf, me husband, and the other boarders at teatime – that's half past five sharp. What'll we call thee?'

'Maggie,' she says. 'Maggie Harrison.'

Dot nods. 'There's a washbasin in't lavvy but if you want a bath, it's a shilling and I'll need a day's notice. No baths on Sundays – that's mine and Alf's bath night – and Mr Totley downstairs has his on a Friday.' She then runs through the rules of the house: keep the wireless turned down, no music after nine o'clock and no visitors after eight. Maggie can rinse a few things through in the bathroom if she puts a shilling in the meter, but there's a launderette – Dot pronounces it 'laundriette' – on the corner. There's a telephone box on the main road by the bus stop. The house telephone is Dot's private number and only to be used by the boarders in special circumstances and if they put thruppence in the box. The gas fire is operated by a coin meter, which takes one- and two-shilling pieces, of which Dot has a supply should Maggie need to change a ten-bob note. Maggie is beginning to wonder quite what the 'all' in 'all included' in the advert meant.

'Get thi sen unpacked, then, love, and I'll see thee at teatime – in't big kitchen, second door on't right as tha comes down ' stairs.'

The bed almost caves in as she sits on it, and there is a musty smell about the bedding. It's no palace, but it's hers.

After Maggie has settled in, she telephones her brother from the call box. 'I'm here, safe and sound.'

'Good.'

'I've got the room I rang up about. You should see the landlady! Sixty if she's a day and plastered in make-up – like those mannequins in C&A's window.'

'Really?'

'Oh, Leonard. Stop sulking.'

'I'm not.'

'You are. You're talking in that sulky voice.'

'It's too quiet here without you.'

'You'll get used to it. Anyway, it's not like I'm never

coming back, is it? You can come and see me once I've settled in. And we can write.'

'I was going to write today anyway. I didn't get a chance to tell you what happened at work last night – you'll wet yourself!' He sounds happier now, but she feels a pang. She'll miss her old job; at least, she'll miss the dramas and scandals that are part of life in a hotel kitchen. But if she doesn't get away now, she'll end up doing the same job, in the same place, for the next thirty years. Both her parents had cooked for a living, working in hot, windowless kitchens all their lives, and now Leonard was doing it too.

The pips go and she puts in another tuppence.

'I'm going to have to go in a minute,' she says. 'The landlady's strict about mealtimes. We're having toad-in-the hole tonight. It smells awful.'

'You can't eat muck like that; you'll die!'

'Quite possibly. What's on at work this week?'

'Veal escalopes in Marsala sauce, beef Wellington and lobster risotto. See what you're missing? Listen, I was looking through the *Stage* this afternoon and they're auditioning for ASMs in Brighton.'

Maggie sighs. 'I want to try somewhere different, smell something other than the sea every time I go out.'

'I thought you liked the sea?'

'I do but . . . oh, Lenny, you know this is what I've always wanted to do.'

'What about London? We know loads of people there already.'

'Exactly! And even if I could get into a theatre in London, which I doubt, I'd be bumping into them all the time. I want to go where I can move around without people saying hello every five minutes and telling me I'm looking more and more like my mum.'

Since their mother died, Maggie has felt like she was growing up under a microscope: would little Margaret have her mother's looks? Would she be as good a cook? As good a seamstress? As thoughtful and kind-hearted as her dear mother? It was as though her only purpose in life was to step into her mother's shoes and tread her mother's path.

'What's wrong with looking like—'

'Nothing. I just want to look like *me* sometimes.'

CHAPTER THIRTEEN

'Hadn't you better make a move?' Fiona glances up from the *Guardian*. 'The milkman'll be here in a minute for his daily shag.'

'Do we still have a milkman?'

'Ah,' she says. 'Good point.'

She has an antenatal appointment this morning, so she's still in her dressing gown, wearing her old glasses so she can read the paper before putting in her contact lenses. The dark, heavy frames make her look stern and intellectual, but they always slip down her nose and there's something exquisitely touching about the way she keeps pushing them back up with her finger. He watches as, barely taking her eyes from the paper, she spreads thick honey on her toast. Her dressing gown is loose at the neck and as she bites into the toast, the fabric falls forward to reveal the enticing curve of her breast.

'I'm not looking forward to today,' he says.

She puts the paper down and takes her glasses off. 'No, I'm sure you're not. There's bound to be some sort of disciplinary, but let's hope Malcolm's right and it'll just be a ticking off. It's not as though you actually hit the kid, is it?'

'True,' he leans over to kiss her. 'Wish I was coming with you.'

'No need. It's just weight and blood pressure today. See you tonight. Good luck!'

*

Traffic is heavy, slowed by that nasty, misty drizzle that never quite becomes rain. As he turns carefully into the school's steep approach road, kids swarm over the tarmac. Some of them peer in at him as they pass. There's a loud thud on the roof and a scuffle behind the car. 'Sorry, Sir,' a Year 7 boy shouts as he grabs his rucksack and slides it down from the car roof. Jonathan pulls into a parking bay and switches off the engine. Then a face appears at the window. Leah Richards, Year 8, grinning, forcing a fat pink bubble from her mouth, bulging forward, bigger and bigger, then splat, it hits the glass and she runs off, shrieking. At least it's only gum. Malcolm's had nail varnish poured on his windscreen and obscenities scrawled on the bonnet in marker pen. Everyone's had their tyres let down at some point, and the new computer studies teacher came out of a staff meeting one night to find a load of Coke cans superglued to the seat of his motorbike. Jonathan sighs. Teaching's supposed to get easier over the years, but sometimes it's like walking up the down escalator.

As he locks the car, he becomes aware of someone nearby. Ken Pinkerton, one of the assistant heads, is standing right beside him. 'Morning, Ken,' he says. The man reeks of body odour. Stinky Pinky, the kids call him.

'Will you come with me, please, to Mrs Fawcett's office.'

'What, now? But registration's in five minutes. Can't I pop up after period two?'

Ken adopts an even graver expression and repeats the instruction word for word.

'Come on, Ken,' he says. 'Who's going to register my form? They'll go feral if I'm not there by eight forty.'

'Cover for your registration period has been arranged.' Ken gestures for Jonathan to follow him.

'Oh, right,' Jonathan says. For some reason, this makes it all feel more serious, and as he follows Ken up the stairs it feels as if he's being escorted to the gallows.

'Come in, Mr Robson. Take a seat.' Mrs Fawcett waits with her hands clasped under her pointy chin while he sits down. 'Early this morning, I received a complaint . . .'

He opens his mouth to speak but she raises a traffic-stopping hand. 'Your head of department has put me in the picture as far as he is able. But I need to hear your version.' She takes off her glasses. 'At this stage, of course, it's informal. But you may want to talk to your union rep.' She leans back. 'So, what happened?'

'Well, the group was a bit agitated right at the start.' He

tries to look her in the eye, but it's like making eye contact with a dog that's considering ripping your throat out. He steels himself. 'They were upset; they'd just heard that their theatre trip's been cancelled.'

'Oh?' She manages to get two syllables out of the word.

'They were looking forward to it. And to be honest, I felt at a bit of a disadvantage, considering I knew nothing about it.' He waits for her to apologise, and then he'll ask if there's any way round the problem.

'I think you'll find I put a memo in your pigeon hole, Mr Robson.'

He feels the proverbial wind being sucked from his sails. 'I must have missed it,' he mutters. He almost mentions having been off on Tuesday to attend his father's funeral, but he knows it's irrelevant. He never checks his pigeon hole; no one does. Why can't she use email like everyone else? 'Anyway,' he says, 'when Ryan came in, it started to get out of hand.' He goes over everything as accurately as he can, conscious that his hands are sweating. When he's finished, the room is silent apart from a fluttering above him where a moth has become trapped in the lightshade, its wings batting frantically against the sides.

'Ryan says you hit him.'

He feels a thud in the pit of his belly. 'No, no way. Definitely not.' He shakes his head.

On go the bifocals again and she peers at the paper in front of her. 'He told his mother that you struck him on the side of the head.' She looks at him over the top of her glasses, reminding him briefly of his father.

This can't be happening. 'I don't know what to say. I did feel stressed; I did thump the wall and he *was* standing nearby, but I certainly didn't hit him.'

She allows another silence to grow. 'So you're telling me that at no point did your hand make contact with his head?'

'Absolutely not.'

'Very well.' She straightens the papers in front of her. 'The incident still constitutes a disciplinary offence, but it's considerably less serious than a physical assault.' Again she takes off her glasses. 'Jonathan.' Her tone softens, and he gratefully registers her use of his first name. 'You wouldn't be the first teacher to be falsely accused and you won't be the last. We'll take statements from the students and hopefully we'll clear the whole thing up quickly.' She rises and gestures towards the door. He stands, obediently. 'However, I'm suspending you while I carry out a full investigation. I'll telephone as soon as it's been completed. In the meantime, you're going to have to trust me.' She opens the door.

Physical assault; *physical assault*. Does the boy really hate him that much?

Ken is still out in the main office. 'Okay, Mr Pinkerton.' She nods at Ken, then turns to Jonathan. 'I'm afraid you'll have to be escorted from the premises.'

His legs are weak as he walks to the car and he can feel his heart rate speeding up. He fumbles with the key, but can't get it in the door.

'Oh well,' Pinkerton can barely contain his smirk. 'See you *anon*!'

Bastard. He looks like he's just won teacher of the fucking year. Jonathan starts the car, crashing the gears as he puts it into reverse, then he accelerates out of the parking area and swings onto the approach road, his brain reeling. He wants to get home, away from Ken's mocking eyes, so he can think about this properly. He turns sharply into the main road, whacking the back of a very new-looking silver Volvo parked on the corner. He slows down and looks in the rear-view mirror. There's no one around, no one running after him waving their arms. He puts his foot down again and doesn't stop until he gets home.

*

There's a pleasing rhythm to chopping, and Jonathan starts to feel calmer as he flicks the shallots into the pan with the butter, lemon zest and rice. Then he turns up the heat and sloshes in white wine, which makes a loud hiss and sends up a cloud of fragrant steam. When the rice is just right, he'll add lemon juice, rocket and parmesan, a good grind of black pepper and a drizzle of extra virgin olive oil. Risotto requires patience; you have to add the hot stock little by little so that the rice expands slowly, becoming plump and creamy but still retaining a little 'bite'. But he messes it up; he adds the stock too quickly and he cooks it for too long.

'Sorry,' he says as he puts the plates on the table. 'Not a culinary triumph.'

'Better than I could make, though.' Fiona looks at him. 'It'll blow over in a couple of days, Jonno.'

He leans over and kisses her forehead. 'Thank you for being calm and sensible. What would I do without you?'

She forks up a mound of risotto. 'Less cooking and more ironing, probably.'

After dinner, they watch a programme about bears in Canada. 'Oh wow, look at that,' Fiona says. On the screen, the bears have positioned themselves at the top of a waterfall where salmon are travelling upstream to spawn. As the fish make their incredible leap, the bears simply open their mouths. Some of the salmon make it back to their birthplace to lay their eggs, but many don't. Jonathan wonders how they felt when they realised they'd leapt right into the mouth of a hungry bear. Probably not that different to how he's feeling now. Christ. How can he have been so stupid? Why hadn't he just sent Ryan to Malcolm instead of trying to face the boy down?

*

Malcolm rings on the Wednesday to see if he's going to rehearsals. Their am-dram group is doing 'Snow White' this year, and he and Malcolm at six feet and six-one respectively are playing dwarves – Smiley and Blushful. They can't use Happy and Bashful because, much to Malcolm's disgust, Disney holds copyright on all the original names (except Sneezy, apparently). Cassie makes an equally ironic Snow White with her vast hips, her butterscotch skin – courtesy of her Guyanese father – and her short-cropped hair, currently a fiery orange, but she might dye it a festive red and green for the Boxing Day performance, she says. 'Give the thing some colour. Everything you guys do is so damn black and white.'

Jonathan had totally forgotten. 'Tell them I've got the trots or something,' he says. 'I won't be able to concentrate. All week, I've been pouncing on the phone, thinking it'll be Linda Fawcett, but nothing. So I rang her today; I thought they must have finished interviewing the kids by now, but do you know what she said? She said things are taking longer because of the planning for the Christmas activities. My job's on the line and she's worried about the fucking Christmas activities. Can you believe that? Perhaps I should go in and see her.'

'I wouldn't if I were you. Our Mrs Fawcett doesn't like being hurried. You don't want to risk pissing her off and slowing things down even more.'

Jonathan nods. 'True. The waiting is driving me nuts, though.'

'I'm sure it is. But at least you can use the time to catch up with your marking.'

'That's what I've been doing, but it still feels like I'm sitting on my arse while Fi has to drag herself out of bed to get to work in the morning.'

Malcolm sighs. 'I know. I wouldn't like it either, but listen, if you start hiding yourself away, people might think there's a reason.'

'No smoke without fire, you mean?'

'Remember that bloke who taught geography when old Wilkins was Head? What was his name? You know, Welsh chap. Lovely bloke.'

The guy had been young, mild-mannered. It was his first teaching post. He'd taught art as well. Or was it music? Anyway, he'd been accused of 'inappropriate behaviour' by some Year 9 girls. Apparently the girls' stories hadn't tallied and the police felt the whole thing was a nonsense. But the teacher hadn't ever returned to school, which had prompted vindictive mutterings from a particular corner of the staffroom.

'Oh, all right,' he says. 'You win.'

*

He's glad he went to rehearsals in the end. Fiona came to watch, and then they all went back to Malcolm and Cassie's where Jonathan and Malcolm knocked up a pretty reasonable Spanish omelette which they had with ciabatta and red wine while they debriefed. Throughout the whole evening, he realises as he gets into bed, his thoughts haven't once strayed towards school. Fiona is already asleep even though she was only ten minutes ahead of him. She looks exhausted; her reception class is pretty demanding and she's really feeling the strain now.

He wakes refreshed for a change, having dreamt of summer, of sitting on the beach, looking out to sea. The dream makes him think about days at the seaside as a boy, watching the waves and marvelling at the thought that even after he'd gone home, even when he was at school, or asleep in bed at night, the tides would continue their inevitable, rhythmic movement. The day is cold, but sunny outside. Malcolm says he should make the most of this enforced time off. If Fiona wasn't at school they could have driven down to Hastings for the day, had a wander around the Old Town, got fish and chips from The Mermaid like they used to and eaten them huddled together in the bus shelter overlooking the fishing beach. He loves Hastings, even at this time of year. It's not as trendy as Brighton but there's something about the place. He first went there on a school trip when he was ten. He and Alan Harper would stand gawping at the tall wooden huts where Victorian fishermen used to hang their nets to dry, then they'd wander around the fish market where you could buy fish caught just a few hours earlier. Glittering piles of mackerel and herring, red-spotted plaice, crabs the size of saucers and other fish he couldn't identify without his *Observer's Book of Sea and Seashore*. With the typical blood-lust of the schoolboy, they'd watch, fascinated, as the men took fish from the pile, deftly slit them open and scraped out the innards, then tossed the bloody, stringy bits of flesh into plastic buckets. Seagulls, flapping their huge wings and shrieking and screaming at their rivals, swooped down to steal from the buckets, then soared off with mackerel guts streaming from hooked beaks.

Perhaps he should go fishing. A couple of hours of tranquillity will do him good, and at least it'll mean he's not sitting here waiting for Linda Fawcett to call. The doorbell rings. He ignores it; probably someone selling dishcloths. But it rings again, longer, more insistent this time, so he gets out of bed, puts on a pair of boxers and a t-shirt and goes downstairs. The police uniforms show through the glass. It must be about that car he hit – he'd completely forgotten about it, and an apology is already forming on his lips as he opens the door.

'Jonathan Hugo Robson?' the male officer says, then defers to his partner, a great heffalump of a woman with an unexpectedly jolly-hockeysticks voice that makes Jonathan think of gymkhanas. He can't take in what she's saying at first, but the gist of it is that he has to go to the police station this evening to make a statement regarding an 'alleged assault'. Six o'clock, she tells him; report to the desk.

CHAPTER FOURTEEN

In the weeks since Maggie arrived in Sheffield, she has become so good at her job they're calling her 'Queen of the Props'. She can find – or make – anything that's needed, whatever the play. Nothing has yet defeated her. Her particular talent is furniture and in a couple of hours, with a bit of padding and some old brocade curtains, she can transform a battered settee into a Victorian chaise-longue or a cheap fireside seat into a winged armchair. She loves this feeling of being part of a large family that extends to the theatre up the road, a family that throws frequent parties to which everyone from both theatres is invited. Tonight she's going to one with Jack, who's almost as new to the company as she is. She puts on the new underwear she bought from Swan and Edgar just before she left – bra, pants and suspender belt, all lacy and matching; proper, grown-up underwear. When she was little, she didn't understand matching underwear. She smiles, remembering how her ten-year-old self would watch her mother dress for an evening out. 'It's not as though anyone's going to see it,' she'd say, hands on hips, shaking her head at her mother's silliness. She fastens her stockings and pulls the half-slip up around her waist, then she props the hand mirror on the washstand and empties out the contents of her make-up bag. She brushes on several layers of sooty mascara, making it extra thick on the outer lashes because she's read somewhere that it makes your eyes look bigger. She notices her mouth is open and she smiles. Last week she was in the dressing room under the stage, watching some of the girls getting ready to go on; they were all sitting in a line, all opening their mouths as they brushed on the mascara. She adds a good slick of Max Factor Strawberry Meringue, backcombs her hair at the crown and then sprays it with lacquer.

It's cold tonight, even for February, so she chooses a sweater dress, mustard-yellow with a nipped-in waist and a wide belt. She checks her appearance one last time; good – she looks just how she wants to look: like an independent young woman on her way to a date.

'Watch thi sen, mind,' Alf says as she passes the kitchen on her way out. 'I know all about them actors – them what aren't pooftas is ha'penny snatchers.'

*

The wind is wrecking Maggie's hair. Should have worn a headscarf, she thinks as she waits for the bus. The smell of liquorice is strong tonight; she thought she was imagining it until Dot mentioned something about one of the other boarders working at the Bassett's factory where they make the Liquorice Allsorts. It's a comforting smell, especially on a cold night.

'A right lazy wind, is this, duck,' the bus conductor says as he takes her fare. 'Too lazy to blow round you, so it goes right through you!' Maggie smiles. She takes out the powder compact Leonard gave her for her twenty-first and runs her thumb over the shiny lid. It is a beautiful thing, emerald green with a circlet of twinkling, diamond-like stones. She can smell the powder as she flips it open, a sort of dusty caramel, dry and perfumey; it reminds her fleetingly of her mother. She turns her face this way and that. Does she look theatrical enough? She snaps the compact shut and puts it back in her handbag. She hopes they won't all be too sophisticated and actor-ish at this party; after all she is just the Assistant Stage Manager, the lowest of the low.

The wind is really getting up now. There are bits of newspaper blowing all over the street; a plastic bag floats high above the trees, which are bending right over, looking as though they might snap. She gets off the bus and walks to the telephone box where she's supposed to be meeting Jack. He's not there. Doubt begins to creep under her skin. Maybe he only asked her as a joke. Maybe the others put him up to it. *Ask the new girl, the stuck-up one from down south. We'll all wait to see if she turns up, go on, Jack, it'll be a laugh.* How could she have been so foolish? Jack is very tall and good-looking; why would he want to go out with her when he could have his pick?

A woman shrieks as her umbrella blows into the road. Maggie watches it, inside out with all its spiky bits revealed, bowling along like a young girl doing cart-wheels and showing her knickers.

Then she sees him walking towards her, hands in his pockets, collar turned up. His hair, usually slicked back and perfect, is blowing all over his face.

'Come on,' he says when he spots her. 'It's only down the road. Let's get out of this bloody wind.' He slips his arm under hers and steers her along. She is slightly put out that he doesn't look at her, because she's made a lot of effort and she looks good, even though she says so herself.

Like the other women they pass, she keeps one hand on her hair as they walk. Jack doesn't speak but his hand on her elbow is reassuring. They turn down a side street where there are no front gardens, only a doorstep between the house and the pavement. Jack peers at the house numbers.

'Here we are,' he says, turning into a passageway that runs between the houses.

Maggie hesitates. The alley is as dark as a dog's guts, as her mother would have said, and she can't see the way out at the other end.

'Why are we going down here?'

Jack looks at her, irritation creasing his face. 'Because we're here; this is where the party is.' Then his expression changes. 'Oh, I forgot. You don't do this down south, do you?'

Maggie looks blank.

'Use the back door, I mean.'

She still doesn't understand. So far, she hasn't really been anywhere apart from her lodging house, the launderette and a couple of pubs. This is the first time she has been to someone else's home.

'If you used the front door, you'd be stepping straight off the street onto their front-room carpet. My digs are the same – my landlady's got her settee pushed across the front door. Come on,' he says, taking her hand. 'I'll make sure you don't trip.'

At the end of the passageway – the gennel, he calls it – light spills out from the kitchen window and she can just make out a small yard. A bicycle stands against the creaking fence and there are a couple of things on the washing line, flapping madly as though they're about to fly off.

There is laughter from inside, and music. The back door is unlocked and they step into the little kitchen, which leads into a room packed with people chatting, laughing and smoking. The music's in the front room: Del Shannon singing 'Runaway'.

A woman with long red hair and huge eyelashes emerges from the fug of cigarette smoke in the back room. Her outfit – purple slacks and a baggy orange sweater with enormous black buttons – makes Maggie feel both overdressed and boring.

'Vanda, darling!' Jack grins. 'Long time no see.'

Maggie is still getting used to the theatrical tendency for everybody to call everybody else *darling*. She wonders whether she'll soon have the guts to do it herself; she imagines ringing her brother: Leonard *darling*, she'll say, it's *me* . . .

'I didn't know you were coming,' the woman says to Jack, her tone bordering on hostile. 'I certainly don't remember inviting you.'

'The message I got was "the more the merrier".' He puts his hand on the small of Maggie's back and pushes her gently forward. 'I don't believe you've met Maggie.'

Vanda seems to shake herself, as though remembering her manners. 'No, no I haven't. Hello, darling.' She smiles broadly now. She is older than Maggie first thought: late thirties; forty, even.

'Maggie's our new ASM. Maggie, this is Vanda. Vanda does something rather marvellous with a bathing suit and a boa constrictor.'

'A *snake*?' Maggie's eyes widen.

'Don't talk nonsense, Jack. Boris is harmless.' She turns to Maggie, relieved, it seems, to be talking to someone other than Jack. 'Absolutely adorable and absolutely harmless. He's a docile old thing and he's terribly fond of me.' She gestures towards a framed picture on the wall. The photograph shows an extremely glamorous Vanda in a sparkly costume and high heels, smiling at a large snake that is coiled around her leg and waist, its head level with hers.

Maggie shudders. 'It looks, er, impressive.'

'Thank you, darling,' Vanda says, then leans towards her. 'Actually, the name's Elsie, but the stage name sort of stuck. Help yourself to drinks and I'll see you later.

Remind me to introduce you to Boris.' She flashes a look at Jack and disappears through the crowd.

'What was all that about?' Maggie asks.

Jack shrugs. 'She's a bit potty. Come on, let's get a drink. Got any ciggies? I forgot to buy any.'

She takes a new pack of Embassy Tipped out of her bag and hands it to Jack, who takes out two, passes her one and tosses the other into his mouth, catching it by the tip perfectly between his teeth and winking at her as he does so. He pockets the rest of the pack.

He really is incredibly handsome, she thinks as he takes the lids off two beers and hands her one. She would rather have something else, a gin and orange, perhaps, but she takes the beer and stands next to him as he leans against the wall, nodding to the music and smoking without removing the cigarette from his mouth.

'So,' she says, or rather shouts – someone has turned the music up. 'Where are you from originally?'

He laughs. 'It's not where you're from – it's where you're going.'

She smiles and sips her beer before trying again. 'Which company were you with before?' But he has his back to her. She looks around the room. Why is she finding it so hard to relax? It's not as though she's not used to parties, although the parties in Hastings and even those in London when she was at stage school weren't as packed as this, or as loud. She can hear 'Let's Twist Again' from the front room, but Chubby Checker is being drowned out by the voices singing along.

A few people have spilt out of the room and are twisting in the hall. She'd love to dance, but Jack is engrossed in talking to Clive about the play. She's just wondering whether to try and join their conversation when Vanda appears panting and breathless.

'Aggie, darling! Found a friend of yours in the front room! Come and say hello.'

'It's Maggie,' Maggie says.

'What?' Vanda puts her hand to her ear.

Don't say what, say pardon. Maggie can hear her mother's voice, clear and sharp. 'Oh, never mind.' Maggie allows herself to be led into the front room, which has been almost completely emptied of furniture to facilitate the dancing. On a table in the corner is a record player surrounded by record cases, carrier bags, a cardboard box and stacks of loose 45s. A skinny boy with a bootlace tie and Buddy Holly glasses seems to be in charge of the music.

'Hello, Little Mags!' The familiar voice makes her turn and she is delighted to see Una, Clive's assistant, sticking her leg out and twisting impressively down to the floor.

Maggie laughs, shouts 'Amazing!' and is about to join in when the record comes to an end. There is a brief pause as the arm swings back and another disc drops onto the turntable. The breathless dancers wait expectantly, then as Patsy Cline's voice fills the room, they groan, shake their heads and move away to let couples take the floor.

Una shrugs. 'Can't dance to this. Come and talk to me in the kitchen.'

Maggie follows her, leaving the couples moving around the room to 'I Fall to Pieces'.

'What do you think of Jack?' Una says, unscrewing a bottle of gin.

'Don't know really. This is our first date – ooh, could I have one of those? I don't really like beer.'

Una sloshes generous measures into two glasses, tops them up with tonic and hands one to Maggie.

'Lovely, thanks.' Maggie takes a sip. It flashes through her mind that Una might have designs on Jack herself. Or maybe she's an ex-girlfriend. 'Has he been with the company long?'

Una shakes her head. 'Joined just before you. Vanda knew him before, though. They were both in rep in Leeds.'

At that moment, Vanda stumbles into the kitchen. 'Oops!' she grins, and puts a hand out to steady herself. 'Did I hear my name being taken in vain?'

Maybe it's Vanda who's the ex, Maggie thinks. Jack looks the sort who'd like older women, and Vanda is very attractive.

At that moment, Jack pokes his head around the door. 'What's this then,' he winks at Maggie. 'A mothers' meeting?'

'Jack!' Vanda spins round, wobbling again. 'You're neglecting little Aggie, here.'

'Maggie,' Maggie says. Yes, this Vanda must still have a thing for Jack; she's deliberately calling her by the wrong name to make her feel awkward.

'Maggie? Oh darling, I'm so sorry. Why ever didn't you say? I've been calling you Aggie all night!'

CHAPTER FIFTEEN

The phone feels cold and heavy in Jonathan's hand as he waits for Fiona to answer. He didn't call earlier because he thought it would be a formality and he'd be home by now.

'Hello?' There's note of irritation in her voice.

'Hello, it's me.'

'Good – I was beginning to wonder where you'd got to. Where are you? When will you be home?'

'Soon, I think. Look, don't worry, but I'm at the police station.'

'What? Oh God, what's happened?'

*

It's almost nine by the time they've finished with him. After the statement, they took his fingerprints and a DNA sample. 'Standard procedure on arrest,' the PC said as he

125

swabbed the inside of Jonathan's cheek. 'There,' he'd smiled, 'all done.' Jonathan felt like a kid at the dentist. He starts the car and pulls away from the police station, driving ultra-carefully. *Assault occasioning actual bodily harm. Assault. Bodily harm.* He stops at Costcutter to pick up a couple of beers, enjoying the brief distraction of walking around the shop. As he waits at the till, his eyes stray to the shelves behind the counter, stacked with fat, shiny packs of cigarettes. He should have cracked it by now, but every so often a craving seems to crawl up from somewhere dark and settle into a yearning ache at the back of his throat. No, he tells himself. No, no, no.

As soon as he gets back into the car, the whole evening crowds in for an action replay. The large woman constable, Sandy Clark, had been friendly at first – her brother-in-law was a teacher in Lambeth, she said, and she didn't know how he put up with it. 'I wouldn't do your job for fifty grand a year, a top-of-the-range BMW and a month in Barbados,' she said with an exaggerated shudder. 'Would you just confirm that this is a new and sealed tape.'

Jonathan nodded.

'Aloud, please.'

'Yes, it's a new tape.'

'Now, in your own words . . .'

So he told her how the lesson had started badly, how Ryan was just back from being excluded after Jonathan had caught him beating up a younger boy, how he'd been playing up and showing off to his mates, and how finally,

Jonathan had lost his temper and thumped the wall. Just when things seemed to be going not too badly, another PC came into the room and handed a note to PC Clark, who then stood up. 'Interview suspended at . . .' She checked her watch '. . . 20.13.' She switched off the tape machine and left the room.

It's like being in *The Bill*, Jonathan thought as he sat there while they talked in low voices outside the door. Only he couldn't just turn it off.

'Interview resumed at 20.16,' she said after pressing 'record' again and sitting down. 'So, Mr Robson.' She looked less friendly now. 'You've never been in trouble with the police, you say?' She tapped her pen annoyingly on the desk. His fingers itched to confiscate it and threaten her with a detention. 'You'd call yourself a law-abiding citizen?'

'Absolutely. I've never been in trouble. Not so much as a speeding ticket . . .' It hit him before he finished speaking. An unmistakable smirk crept across PC Clark's plump face.

'And so if, for example, you were to have – hypothetically – been involved in a road traffic accident where, for argument's sake, your moving vehicle made contact with a stationary – let's say parked – vehicle, you would either leave your details for the owner of said vehicle as you are no doubt aware you are required to do, or you would report the incident to the local constabulary at the earliest opportunity?'

'Oh God, no, it was—'

'So you *wouldn't* report the incident?'

The male officer by the door stifled a laugh. They were enjoying this. He shook his head and tried again. 'Okay, I know,' he said. 'I hit a car; I didn't stop. Whether you believe me or not, I did intend to report it. It's no excuse but it was the same day they told me about the complaint from Ryan; I'd just been suspended on a false allegation. Look, I'll pay for the damage, obviously. And I'll apologise personally to the owner.'

'Failing to report an accident is an offence,' PC Clark said, adopting a stern expression. 'The vehicle's owner was not best pleased to return from a business trip and find the offside rear wing of her brand-new car significantly dented. Neighbour heard it, apparently; took your number. Thanks to the wonders of modern technology, a DVLA trace threw up your name and by a happy coincidence, you're already here!' Both she and the male officer were grinning now.

'I'm not going to argue,' he said. 'Would it help if I paid for a hired car while it's being repaired?'

PC Clark chewed her lip as she looked at him. Was there a microthread of sympathy?

'There may yet be charges. However . . .' She seemed to be weighing him up. 'You're in enough trouble already, aren't you? I'll put your offer to the vehicle's owner; she might be prepared to let it drop.'

*

Fiona opens the door as he's walking up the path. 'Thank God,' she says. 'You've been ages.'

'Sorry.' He follows her into the kitchen. 'I should have called again.'

'So, what's it all about?'

'Well, it seems it wasn't enough to get me suspended. Ryan's now saying I hit him. He says I deliberately hit him on the side of the head so it wouldn't show; told his mum he couldn't hear properly afterwards.'

'Oh, my God. Didn't they talk to the other kids?'

'Yes, but most of them say they didn't see what happened – which is rubbish, because they were all watching – and Chloé Nichols reckons she actually saw me hit him.'

'*What?* But why?'

For an awful moment, he wonders if she doubts him. 'I don't know. She and Ryan are an item, so maybe that's it. As for the others, God knows.' He sighs.

'Shit, Jonno, this is scary.'

'I know, but don't be too worried. I'm sure it won't come to much – I overheard them saying they thought Ryan's version was probably a load of tosh.'

'Then why arrest you?' She takes a plate out of the oven and puts it in front of him. 'It's only out of a jar, I'm afraid. And it's gone a bit manky now.'

'Thanks.' Some of the pasta bows are so dry they look crispy in places, but there are a few soft ones in the middle, protected by the congealed pesto. 'That's what's so annoying – if the other copper had been handling it, I don't think they would have. I heard him say he thought it was a waste of time, then she – PC Clark – said she wasn't taking any chances and why not just "let the CPS sort it out".'

'So how was it left?'

'If nothing changes, in other words, if Ryan doesn't own up, it'll go to court. They said the court'll write with a hearing date.'

'I can't believe this is happening,' Fiona says.

'Me neither. But if I have to go to court, then I'll just tell the truth.' It doesn't sound as reassuring as he'd hoped. 'Anyway, let's hope it doesn't come to that.'

Fiona starts chewing at her thumbnail. Neither of them speak. The only sound is of a distant police siren fading away into nothing.

The night passes like a film in front of him, sharp definition, bold colours, distinct sounds. Consciousness refuses to let him go; he's trapped. Frame by frame, his father, *idiot boy, upsetting everyone*, his mother, *we did a lot of things badly, Jonathan*; smoking a cigarette, but she doesn't smoke; *it's a bit of a shock*. Ryan, mocking, *do you often piss yourself, Sir?* Fiona, *such a fucking idiot; what were you thinking of?* Linda Fawcett, *a physical assault; Ryan says you hit him; you hit him; Ryan says . . .*

CHAPTER SIXTEEN

'Are you a virgin?' Jack whispers. Maggie has drunk rather a lot of gin and has somehow found herself in a darkened bedroom, lying on a pile of coats that are still damp from the rain. She can hear the hollow whistling of the wind trapped inside the chimney and the occasional chink as a puff of soot and other debris falls down into the bedroom fireplace. 'It doesn't matter if you're not, you know.' His breath is warm and thick on her neck, his voice tight and strained. 'I don't mind. I don't think girls should have to behave differently. I bet you're a right little raver when you get going, aren't you?' He is pushing against her and she can feel his thing, hard and swollen, pressing against her thigh.

Maggie *is* a virgin; she nearly did it once but neither she nor the boy really knew what they were doing, so they gave up.

Jack is beginning to sweat. His fingers are brushing the inside of her thigh, playing with her stocking top.

'Jack, slow down. It's our first date.'

'So what,' he murmurs, kissing her again. He's a good kisser, she'll say that for him. His hand is moving again, more insistently this time, up to her panty girdle. He groans as he touches her. She is breathing heavily herself now and instinctively flattens her stomach so his hand can slip inside her pants. His fingers make her gasp and she wonders what it would be like to go all the way. She is wondering whether to ask if he has a French letter when the door bursts open.

'Oops! Sorry, pal.' She recognises Jimmy the set-painter and his girlfriend, who giggles.

She and Jack sit up, dishevelled. Her heart is pounding and she can hear the music downstairs, more subdued now. The door closes again.

'Now, where were we?' Jack says, pulling her back down.

The wind is getting stronger; she can hear what sounds like a metal dustbin lid being blown down the road.

'No, Jack.' She sits up, smoothes her hair. 'Sorry, but not yet. Let's wait until we've been going steady for a while.'

'Oh, come on, Little Mags.' He pushes her back on the bed; his hand shoots up her dress and tugs at her pants. 'I'll be careful.'

She can feel his tongue in her ear, warm and solid and slimy. She doesn't want to do it after all, she decides. It just doesn't feel right. 'No, Jack, really, I don't want to.'

'Yes, you do,' he breathes. His breath is hot and damp on her face. It smells disgusting, a mix of beer, tobacco and Twiglets. 'Come on,' he says again. 'You want it, don't you? Tell me you want it.'

'No!' she shouts and pushes him away. She leaps up and straightens her clothes. He looks furious.

'You know what you are, don't you?' He fumbles for the cigarettes, throws one at her and squints against the smoke as he lights his own. 'A prick-teaser.' But then he grins. 'Can't blame me for trying, can you?'

*

Downstairs, things are quieter. The party has thinned and people are sitting on the floor in the front room, the tips of their cigarettes glowing in the dark, singing along to 'I Fall to Pieces', which must be playing for the third time. The street door rattles in the wind, lifting the carpet slightly with each gust.

'Jack,' Maggie says. 'I should be getting back to my digs.'

'Yeah, it's late; we'll go in a minute. Dance with me first.'

She hesitates.

'Oh, come on,' he says. 'You don't want me to *fall to pieces* like poor old Patsy, do you?' Then he makes a big show of falling to his knees, spreading his arms and singing along.

Maggie is glad it's dark so no one can see how much she's blushing. 'Stop it, Jack,' she says, but she can't help smiling.

His voice gets louder as the record nears the end then he mimes heartbreak and collapse. Everyone laughs and claps, and she can't help feeling just a little proud when he takes a bow. Then he grins at her. 'Get your coat then; I'll see you home.'

*

Outside, the wind is far stronger than it was earlier. Maggie allows Jack to take her arm as they make their way along the street towards the bus stop. She leans in to him as a particularly powerful gust assaults them and a sheet of newspaper flaps around her legs, trapping her until she manages to kick it away. A cardboard box blows past and there is a crash further down the road as a slate flies off a roof.

Maggie opens her mouth to speak but the wind grabs her words and tears them away. Another slate hits the ground behind them.

'Fuck!' Jack yells, pulling her close to the wall. She hasn't heard him swear before. Bits of houses are flying off and tumbling along the road. Dogs are barking and she can hear glass smashing in the distance.

Having lived close to the sea all her life, Maggie is used to strong winds and severe weather. She has seen a huge section of the pier torn away by a sea storm and tossed about on the waves like a matchstick; she has seen the coastguard called out, watched the lifeboat being launched and seen the fishermen's wives and mothers huddled together on the east cliff steps, waiting for news. But she has never seen anything like this. Is it possible to have a hurricane in England? Something is rolling down the church roof, too big for a slate or a tile. There is a massive, thudding crash as it hits the ground. The Holy Mother, dashed to pieces.

'Come on,' Jack shouts, pulling her towards a passageway.

She holds back. The passageway is completely dark and there are no lights on in the houses, but she can see curtains blowing out into the street through a smashed window, waving frantically for attention. Another piece of debris falls from above, catching her on the side of the head. She yells, and allows Jack to pull her into the darkness.

'We'll wait here until it drops,' he says. 'It's got to let up soon, surely.'

He puts his arm around her shoulders and strokes the hair out of her eyes. He kisses her, a gentle, tender kiss, and she responds.

CHAPTER SEVENTEEN

Jonathan carefully disengages the carrier bags from the deep red grooves they've made on the insides of his fingers and sets them down on a bench outside Mothercare where he's supposed to be meeting Fiona. He glances up. Those angels, he thinks, are wearing too much make-up. For a moment, he pictures them, not suspended from the glass roof of Lewisham shopping centre on tinsel-covered wires, but sitting in a prefab classroom, chewing gum and looking bored as he tries to interest them in *Hamlet*.

The play area is packed with prams and pushchairs. Parents, mostly mums but there are a few dads too, mill around, rubbing hurt knees, peeling satsumas or giving bottles to their babies while watching their toddlers negotiate the slide. Did his own father ever play with him like that, he wonders? He can't remember going to parks when he was very little, although he does remember the odd walk in the woods, and a trip to Windsor Safari Park when it first opened. They'd ended up going home after a couple of hours because a chimpanzee pulled off one of the windscreen wipers and Gerald was so full of rage that no one could enjoy the rest of the day anyway.

This time next year, he might be right here, giving his baby a bottle, holding him or her on the baby slide while Fiona pops into Mothercare. Looking after Malcolm's or Lucy's kids is easy, but it's not the same as your own baby. You can care for someone else's child, love them, even, but you're only responsible for their physical well-being, and even then only while you're *in loco parentis*. You're not responsible for their happiness, for whether they feel safe and secure, for whether they grow into confident, socialised, fulfilled adults.

'Robbo!'

A boy's voice, rasping, thick with testosterone. Jonathan turns around, but he can't see anyone.

'Robbo!' A different voice, louder. 'Punched any more kids lately?'

He leaps up this time, spins around to look. He can hear sniggering but he still can't see anyone. It's always the same if they see you out of school: *I saw you in the holidays, Sir. You was down Lewisham on Saturday, Sir; you said hello.* They can't quite get over the fact that you exist outside of the classroom. He spots Fiona walking towards him. She obviously heard the comment, as did some of the play-area parents. 'Just kids from school, trying to wind me up,' he says, loud enough for the parents to hear. He takes her bag. 'Come on. Let's go home.'

'Bloody hell, is there anyone who *hasn't* heard?'

'What do you mean?'

Her eyes flicker and she looks away.

'Fi?'

She sighs. 'I didn't tell you before, but Laura – you know, teaches Year 2 next door to me – well, she knew you'd been suspended. Not about the police, though.'

'Well, that's something. How did she know?'

'Some of her kids have brothers or sisters at your school. Some of mine probably do, come to that. I just hadn't thought about it.'

'But it's only Laura who knows?' he asks as they reach the car. He unlocks the boot and lifts the bags in.

''Fraid not. I was getting a lot of pitying looks, and Judy Wickson said she thought it was "common knowledge".'

He slams the boot shut. 'Common knowledge,' he sighs. 'Great.'

On the way home, he turns the radio on in the hope that the afternoon play might distract them both, but he's not really listening. Neither of those voices in the shopping precinct sounded like Ryan. But perhaps they've all heard by now, every child from Year 7 upwards; every teacher from the newest NQT to the Head herself; every parent. Christ. And according to his union rep, there's nothing, *nothing* he can do but wait.

They drive past the bottom of the school's approach road. There are quite a few kids around, even though they're not supposed to be out at lunchtime without a pass. 'I bet half of this lot don't have passes,' he says. 'But it's not my problem, is it? Not while I'm suspended.'

'Good grief,' Fiona says. 'How can their parents let them go out like that? Oh God, I'm turning into my mother. But honestly, are they allowed to wear skirts that short to school?' The girls she's pointing at are chatting and giggling as they head up towards the school, bare thighs moving scissor-like beneath their tiny skirts as they totter on ludicrously high heels.

'No. Supposed to be no more than four inches above the knee, but even if it's the right length, they roll it over and over at the top until you can practically see their bum cheeks, then when you send them to their head of year, they unroll it on the way there and say you're picking on them.'

Fiona smiles. 'I used to do that. You have to. You don't want to be different.'

'I suppose so,' he says. 'What I don't get is why they can't be allowed to wear trousers like they want to.'

Fiona shakes her head. 'Crazy, isn't it, in this day and age.'

They drive past a couple of Year 10 girls from that geography group he'd covered the day after the funeral, just before it kicked off with Ryan. It was first period after lunch, when they were still hyperactive from an hour and ten minutes of smoking themselves silly and consuming vast quantities of E-numbers and chips. They sat there, fully made-up, staring at him with the top buttons of their blouses undone and thrusting their little chests at him. They were all trying to look older, but most of them were still growing; their heads were still too big for their bodies, for Christ's sake. Chloé Nichols sat near the front as though she'd practised in front of the mirror: how to sit so Sir gets the best view of my breasts. Her hand frequently went up to her collar to pull her blouse open a little more and she kept turning slightly so he couldn't look in her direction without seeing clearly the swell of her left breast rising out of a lacy green bra. She tossed her streaked blonde hair and, playing with the silver hoops in her ears, smiled up at him. Then her lips parted and he could see the raspberry pink of her tongue as she churned the chewing gum over and over.

'Are you looking at my tits, Sir?' she said, fixing him with her smoky eyes.

The truth was, *Yes, Chloé, how could I not look at your tits? You think you're being very clever and grown-up by thrusting your tempting, creamy little breasts towards me, but the fact is, I'm a married teacher with a pregnant wife and you're still a child.* What he actually said was, 'Leave the room, please, Chloé. Come back when you've got rid of the earrings. That goes for the bracelets too.'

'Don't you like a woman to make an effort with her appearance, Sir?' She glanced at her mates for approval. He wasn't going to fall for that again – the last time he'd questioned a girl for referring to herself as a woman, he'd been treated to a loud and graphic account of her latest sexual encounter. He repeated the instruction. Chloé's smile disappeared. She got up sulkily, mumbled something and slouched towards the door.

'And make sure you're wearing the correct uniform when you come into school tomorrow, please.'

He hadn't realised at that point that he was teaching Chloé next period; and that was the day she'd sworn blind she'd seen him punch Ryan Jenkins. Why hadn't it dawned on him before? Hell hath no fury.

CHAPTER EIGHTEEN

Maggie's feet go slap slap on the pavement as she charges downhill in the darkness, so fast she fears she will be unable to stop. The street is so littered with debris she has to keep leaping over things. The gale is at her back and seems to be aiding her flight, so she lets herself go with it; all she knows is that she must keep moving. A lump of wood falls right in front of her and it's too late to avoid. The palms of her hands sting as they hit the cold pavement; she scrambles to her feet but then falls again, and her head hits the ground with a smack. That is the last thing she remembers.

*

She is lying on the cold, damp ground. She raises her head, and tries to make sense of why she's out in this vicious wind in the middle of the night in a place she doesn't recognise. There was a party; she was with Jack. She's trying to hang on to details, half-glimpses, but her mind is pushing them away. She hauls herself to her feet and tries to run, but the debris swirls all around her, blocking her way, making her stumble. She glances behind her but there's no sign of Jack. She tries to get her bearings but she doesn't know this area, and anyway, everything looks different in the dark. Something hits her leg and she leaps out of the way as a slab of wood – it looks like an entire garden gate – skids down the road. She must get back to her digs. If only she could just magic-ally be there, in her little room with the torn lino and the creaky bed and the doorknob that falls off every time she turns it. She starts to run again, though with more purpose. If she can get to a main road, she'll be able to find her way. She begins to head downhill and then – and this is what makes her think she must be dreaming – she sees a little house blowing down the street. She blinks: the ground is littered with slates, broken glass, chimney pots, odd bricks and whole piles of rubble. Things are flying around in the wind and there is a small building – she sees now that it's not actually a house – moving by itself, with people hanging on to one side, yelling at each other over the scream of the gale. It is as though she has suddenly landed in *The Wizard of Oz*. As she runs, one of the men calls out to ask if she's all right, but she ignores him, because it can't be real.

*

Dot and Alf have been up all night, and they and the three other boarders are in their dressing gowns in the kitchen. Half the back roof is missing, Dot tells her, animated by the drama, and the chimney stack is nowt but a pile of bricks in't yard. She pours hot water into a bowl and adds TCP, turning the water milky. Any other night, she says, as she bathes the cuts on Maggie's head and the grazes on her hands and knees, she'd have wondered why a young girl wasn't home at a decent hour, but she can see Maggie was caught in the storm. All those slates flying around, it's a wonder she isn't cut more badly than she is; in fact it's a wonder she got home at all. Dot's friend Mrs Hallam – her as lives over in Burngreave – rang up just before ' telephones went down. Mrs Hallam would be stone-cold dead now if it weren't for her Kenny making her wear his crash helmet when she went to use outhouse in't yard. What a carry-on. Dot changes the blood-pinked water and sloshes in more TCP. It stings and stinks, but Maggie really doesn't care. Alf's greenhouse is smashed to smithereens, Dot says, blown right up in the air and over into next door's garden. Maggie says nothing. She hasn't spoken since she came in, but with the drama of the hole in the roof and the outrage of Alf's flying greenhouse, nobody has noticed. Dot empties the bowl again, turns back to Maggie and pauses, head on one side.

'Make ' lass a cup of tea, Alf,' she says. 'She's in shock.'

Maybe she is in shock; all she knows is that she wants

to stop hurting. She didn't feel any of this while she was running, but now her hands and knees smart from the grazes; her head hurts at the back and at the side; and the other thing that's bothering her is the soreness, a raw, burning soreness between her legs.

'Come on, duck,' Dot helps her to her feet. 'Good job your room's at ' front where it's not so bad. I'll help thee get tucked up. Bring ' tea up, Alf,' she calls over her shoulder as she guides Maggie up the stairs.

When they reach her room, Maggie sits on her bed, so glad to be there she starts to weep.

'Don't take on, love,' Dot says. 'Come on, now. Where's tha night things?' She helps Maggie out of her dress and then she freezes. Maggie looks down and sees what Dot sees: bruises, bigger than a half-crown; the torn slip; the patches of blood; the ripped stocking.

Maggie begins to shake, her teeth rattling, clashing together. Why can't she remember what happened?

There is a knock at the door and Alf's voice calls, 'Is tha decent?'

Dot opens the door. 'What d'you call this?' she snaps. 'Weak as old maid's water, that is.' But then her voice wobbles. 'Make it a bit stronger, will you?' She half-closes the door, then opens it again and calls after him, 'And Alf – put a few sugars in.'

CHAPTER NINETEEN

Jonathan drops Fiona off at Lucy's and promises to have at least some of the present-wrapping done by the time she gets back. The phone's ringing as he lets himself in. It's his solicitor with the promised update, but she doesn't really have any news. 'The CPS throws these cases out all the time,' she says. She sounds confident, cheerful almost. 'Weak evidence submitted by risk-averse coppers terrified of making a decision. It's just buck-passing.'

'Can't we do anything to speed things up?'

'No, just a question of waiting, I'm afraid. I'll be in touch again after Christmas – try and enjoy the break.'

He flicks through the CDs for something noisy to listen to while he wraps the presents. Led Zeppelin, maybe, or Deep Purple; something to stop him thinking about Ryan Jenkins and Chloé Nichols. He goes for the Led Zep, slots it into the machine and turns up the volume so that the chunky guitar and insistent drumbeat fills the room. He's just placed a brightly coloured wooden xylophone in the centre of a sheet of wrapping paper when there's a loud knock at the window.

He turns the music down and opens the door.

'Sorry,' the man says. 'I did ring the bell, but . . .' His smile is broad, but with a certain truth about it that rules out double glazing. He's as tall as Jonathan, late fifties maybe, and he wears a dark waxed jacket that's all press studs, flaps and pockets. Too scruffy for a Jehovah's Witness. 'Mr Robson?' he asks. He has thick, dark eyebrows and a slightly wonky eye.

'Yes?'

'Don Hutchinson.' He holds out an ID card. 'I know it's nearly Christmas, but I wanted to catch you before the country shuts down for a fortnight. I just need a few minutes of your time.'

Jonathan looks at the card, hesitates, then stands back. 'Okay, come through.'

Hutchinson smells faintly of peppermint, Jonathan notices, and he walks with a slight limp.

'So,' Jonathan says. 'What exactly can I do for you?'

'I'm with the Unsolved Crimes Review Unit,' the man explains, his eyes darting around, taking everything in. 'South Yorkshire Police. We're re-investigating some old cases and you may be able to—'

'No,' Jonathan shakes his head. That's all he bloody needs. 'I've never been in trouble with the police before this assault nonsense.'

'That's as maybe,' Hutchinson says. He's a big man.

Solid, like those cartoon characters with muscles so hard that the crooks hurt their fists when they punch them. 'I'll get to the point.' He smiles. 'The police database has thrown up a partial match between your DNA profile and that of the perpetrator of a number of unsolved crimes.'

Jonathan immediately feels a guilty expression gathering on his features, like being a kid in assembly when the Headmaster vows to find the culprit of some misdemeanour. 'I swear I haven't—'

Hutchinson puts his hand up. 'Not accusing you of anything, Mr Robson. It's a *near* match; we know you're not the perpetrator. You're too young, for a start – some of these crimes date back to the sixties and seventies.'

'You're joking!'

'Extraordinary, isn't it? Analysis techniques are so advanced now that the forensics lads can build an accurate DNA profile decades after the crime – as long as the evidence was collected and stored properly at the time, of course. The thing is,' and here Hutchinson looks him in the eye, which is unnerving, because while one eye meets Jonathan's head-on, the other stares over his left shoulder as though watching for something else to happen, 'there's a possibility that the perpetrator of these particular crimes is related to you.'

Jonathan forces himself to take in what the man is saying.

'So I just need to ask you a few questions about your family.' Hutchinson rummages in the pockets of his jacket and pulls out half a roll of Polo mints, which he puts on the table, and continues to rummage.

'What sort of crimes—'

'Ah, here we are.' He produces a notebook and pen. 'Should only take a few minutes.' He picks up the Polos, peels back the green outer paper and then the silver layer to reveal the sweets, stacked together like little white tyres. 'Mint?'

'No thanks.'

Hutchinson pops a Polo into his mouth and crunches it loudly as he flips open the notebook and writes something at the top.

'So what's this "perpetrator" supposed to have done?'

'I'm afraid I can't . . .' Hutchinson begins, then he pauses. 'I couldn't trouble you for a glass of water, could I?'

Jonathan feels a prickle of irritation, although he supposes asking for water isn't exactly unreasonable. He fills a tumbler from the tap. His hand is hot and slippery on the glass.

Hutchinson nods. 'Thanks.' He tips his head back and empties the glass in one. Before Jonathan can push him for more details, he nods towards the newspaper that's on the table. 'Did you see the Liverpool game? First half was dire; like watching paint dry.'

'No, I didn't.' He tries to keep his voice level. Football: the universal language of blokes, Fiona calls it. But why is the man stalling?

'I support Sheffield Wednesday, me; we're playing like a field full of donkeys at the moment.'

'Sheffield? That's where I was born.'

'Really?' Hutchinson's voice is alert now. His stable eye meets Jonathan's, while the other remains on look-out duty. 'So your family's from the north. When did you move down south?'

'No, they're from Sussex, actually. They didn't live in Sheffield – I was born three weeks early, apparently, while they were up there staying with friends.'

'Did they ever live in the north?'

'Not as far as I know. Look, what *is* this crime you're—'

'Hmm.' Hutchinson writes something down, then pops another mint into his mouth and begins to crunch. He looks puzzled.

Jonathan goes to the sink for some water for himself, takes a long swallow and tips the rest away. 'Right, now I really need to know what this is about.'

'Okay.' Hutchinson takes off his jacket, revealing a red sweater with a once-white shirt collar showing at the neck. 'My team looks at "cold cases", old crimes where there's evidence on file but no one was ever charged. The forensics lads use that evidence to create a DNA profile of the offender. Then if the suspect's DNA profile matches the one on the database, bingo!'

'But what *suspect*?'

'We don't have a suspect at the moment, but when your sample was fed into the national database – standard procedure – it threw up a partial match to an existing profile, in this case a male, offending in the sixties, seventies and early eighties.

'But—'

'No two people have the same DNA,' Hutchinson continues, 'except identical twins – so the fact that your DNA showed such a close partial match means there's a good chance the man we're after is related to you. We all share fifty per cent of our DNA with each parent, and so given the period we're talking about—'

'You're not saying it's my father?'

'No, not necessarily. There are a lot of other things we need to take into consideration – whether the suspect was in the right area at the right time, for one thing. But what I *am* saying is that I need to know more; and I will need to talk to your father.' Hutchinson's manner is matter of fact, unapologetic. Jonathan walks back to the table without speaking. He wipes his damp palms on his jeans and sits down. Images of Gerald loom in front of him. Gerald's silent rage, throbbing through the house; Jonathan and his mother, tiptoeing around so as not to trigger a wave of anger that might rear up and engulf them all. Gerald was always angry; anger defined him. But a serious criminal? No, that couldn't be.

Hutchinson looks up from his notebook and takes two more Polos. 'Sorry,' he says, crunching the mints and offering the pack to Jonathan again. 'I'm giving up smoking and these seem to help. The wife says chewing gum's the thing, but I can't stand the stuff.' He wrinkles his nose.

Jonathan doesn't reply; he'd rather not get into a discussion about nicotine cravings.

'So.' Hutchinson looks at him. 'What can you tell me about your dad?'

'He died. The funeral was two weeks ago.'

Hutchinson's wonky eye flickers. 'I'm sorry.'

Sorry. That's what people say when someone dies; it's what you're supposed to feel. 'Thanks, but there's no need. We weren't very close.'

'I see.' Hutchinson asks more about Gerald, whether he'd had trips away from home – training courses, conferences, anything like that.

'He was away a few times when I was a kid,' Jonathan says, 'but not many. I always wished he'd go away more often – things were always easier when he wasn't around.'

'Why? Was he a difficult man? Drinker? Violent?'

'Not a drinker, no. Why do you ask if he was violent? Was it—'

'Just trying to get a picture, that's all. So was he? Capable of violence, I mean?'

Jonathan can feel the pressure building up behind his eyes. Was Gerald capable of violence? When he thinks of the frail old man his father had become, it seemed impossible. But the younger Gerald? He clears his throat. 'He did hit my mum once. He pushed her over and she banged her head on the fireplace.' He tries to swallow but his mouth is too dry. 'That was unusual, though. Mostly he was just extremely bad-tempered.'

The whole atmosphere in the house would change when things were not to Gerald's liking – his newspaper rumpled, the television too loud, a meal served at the wrong temperature. Once, when Jonathan was about eight, he'd brushed past his father's chair and knocked over the ashtray that was balanced on the arm. Gerald stared at the pile of grey and black ash, the mahogany pipe and the upturned ashtray lying on the rug, then he got to his feet, jaw rigid, fists clenched. Jonathan had frozen, bracing himself for the thwack of the stick that his father kept next to his armchair. But instead, after a torturous pause, Gerald had stalked pointedly from the room, eyes dark with fury, silence gusting all around him.

'Just tell me, what did he do?'

Hutchinson looks at him; this time the rogue eye seems to be facing almost the same way as its twin, and the effect is even more unnerving. 'So you think it's definitely your father, then?'

'No, I just want . . . oh, for Christ's sake, I don't know.' Jonathan stands up again. 'What am I supposed to think?'

Hutchinson sighs, reaches for the pack of Polos but then changes his mind. 'Let's establish the facts first. So, we know he went away a few times when you were a child; now, can you think back to when you were – what, teens? Early twenties? How often was he away from home then?'

'Sorry. I've no idea. I tended to avoid him as much as I could by then.'

The room is quiet while Hutchinson writes it down.

'Look, even if it *was* my father – whatever it is – isn't it a bit late to come looking for him now?'

'It may seem that way,' Hutchinson says, closing his

notebook. 'Especially since there's been no further movement on the case in thirty years. But it's not so much about
catching our man, not after all this time. It's about peace
of mind. I'm not fond of the expression *closure*, but it's
apt. If we can establish who's responsible, even if that
individual is now deceased, we can close the file, knowing he's not still out there thinking he got away with it.'
He stands up. 'I appreciate your help.'

They shake hands. 'So, are you going to tell me?'

Hutchinson smiled. 'Sorry?'

'What they were, these unsolved crimes. Don't I have a
right to know?'

'I'm afraid not. Not until I can be sure, anyway. Which
reminds me, where can I find your mum?'

CHAPTER TWENTY

The morning after the storm, Maggie eases herself pain-
fully out of bed. The back of her head hurts, and so do the
bruises on her arms and thighs. There's one on her breast,
too; she unties the bow on her nightdress so she can see it
better. It's reddish-purple, like a birthmark, but with a
semi-circle of smaller, darker areas in the middle. She
catches her breath; it looks like . . . but it can't be. She runs
her fingers over the small marks; they're slightly raised
and are beginning to scab over. She feels her eyes fill with
tears as she realises what they are: bite marks. For a
moment, it is as though her heart is thudding in her ears;
she can hear her own breathing too, shallow and fast. She
wants to run but she knows that would be crazy because
she's here, safe, in her room. After forcing herself to take
deep breaths, she feels a little better. She takes a sip of
water from the glass on the bedside table, and she tries –
again – to remember what happened after Jack kissed her.

She is thinking so hard it almost hurts. She searches every corner of memory, but that one part is still empty.

She puts her dressing gown on. It's almost nine and she should be getting ready to go to the theatre, but the idea of going in as though nothing has happened . . . And what is she going to say to Jack?

'Maggie, love,' Dot calls up the stairs. 'Young lass from ' Playhouse were just here. What wi't phones being down she's having to go round in person, like. Anyway, ' next few performances are cancelled, so't lass says, so tha's to stop at home unless you hear owt different.'

'Thanks, Dot,' she calls back down. Thank goodness for that; she couldn't have gone in today, she just couldn't.

'And I've run a bath for you, love, under't circumstances. When you've got yer sen sorted out, do you want to come down and keep me company for a bit? I were going to make a brew soon.'

The idea of a warm bath followed by a cup of tea in Dot's kitchen suddenly seems like the nicest thing in the whole world. 'Yes, please,' she replies, trying not to cry. 'Thank you.'

*

It seems the whole of Sheffield is reeling from the freak gale, which swept in across the Pennines, funnelling through the city and smashing it to pieces. Dot has been out in the street since dawn, sweeping up the aftermath with the other women and gathering as much information as she can. 'It's like a scene from ' blitz out there,' she says as she puts the teapot on the kitchen table. 'It said on't wireless more than half ' houses in Sheffield's been damaged. Them prefabs at Heeley came down like a pack of cards, our Mr Totley says – his ma lives ower that way. There's folk homeless and injured – some even killed, so they're saying.'

Maggie shivers. While taking her bath, she'd discovered that as well as being sore, she's bleeding a little, but at least she's alive.

Dot looks at her. 'About last night, lass. We've no telephone just now, but I were wondering if you wanted to ring your mam up? Once it's back on, like?'

'No,' Maggie shakes her head. 'No thanks.'

'Tha's had a nasty shock, duck. I'm sure your mam would want to know. I could ring her up for you . . .' She is twitching with anticipation.

'No. I mean, I don't have a mum. She died when I was sixteen.' If her mother were still alive, what would Maggie tell her? *I seem to have lost my virginity but I don't remember how it happened?*

'Oh, I'm sorry to hear that, love. Who's tha got at home, then? Your dad?' Maggie has seen Dot scrutinising the boarders' letters, putting on her spectacles to read the postmark. *One for you from East Sussex, duck. And I see Mr Totley's got another one from Manchester.*

Maggie shakes her head. 'There's only my brother.'

'Well, you could tell him you was hurt in the storm. He might want to come up. I could let him have the back room for a couple of nights. I'd have to ask a few bob for his breakfasts and so on, but—'

'No, Dot. Thanks for offering, but there's no need.'

Dot pauses. 'Maybe,' she says gently, 'I know it's none of my business, but . . .' She stirs her tea, taps the teaspoon on the side of the cup several times, then looks at Maggie. '. . . has tha thought about telling ' police, love?'

Maggie doesn't answer. The idea of telling the police had crossed her mind. Jack raped her, she's certain of that now. She's covered in cuts and bruises and she's bleeding down below, but how can she report it if she can't remember what happened? The police would laugh. She shakes her head, 'No.' Her voice is barely more than a whisper.

Dot nods, then tilts her head. 'Tha looks washed out, love. Why don't you stop here and take it easy for a bit? You don't want to be up there by yer sen, not after a bump on't head. Heads is funny things. Come on, lass.' She nods towards the fireside chair. 'Sit by 't fire and make yer sen comfy; I'll make another brew as soon as ever I've finished outside.'

Maggie does feel a bit wobbly. Apart from the bruises and the soreness, there's a plum-sized lump on her head, and a gash above her ear where a slate caught her as it fell; maybe she should take it easy for a day or two. 'All right, Dot. Thanks.'

When Dot isn't outside leaning on her broom and gossiping with the neighbours, or making Spam and pickle sandwiches for Alf and his brother while they rig up a makeshift cover for the roof, she makes endless cups of milky tea and sits with Maggie, chain-smoking her way through an entire pack of Players. Maggie is surprised at how much she wants to just carry on sitting here in Dot's comfy chair, soaking up the warmth from the gas fire and trying to work out what to say to Jack when she sees him.

Dot hasn't asked directly, but she's clearly desperate for Maggie to talk, and Maggie feels she owes her some-thing, some little titbit. 'You'll never guess what I thought I saw last night,' she says when they're on their third cup of tea. 'It must have been the bump on the head, I suppose, but I thought I saw a little house being blown along in the wind.'

Dot looks aghast for a moment, then shakes her head and smiles. 'Oh, that,' she says. 'That weren't a house. Lads at ' foundry were talking about it, according to my friend Mrs Bowden – her Frank were on't early shift. It were a sheet-metal garage, apparently, skating down the road with half the street chasing after it. I should like to have seen that me sen.' She chuckles and lights another cigarette. 'They're saying on't wireless it were a hurri-cane. Only hit Sheffield and a bit of Chesterfield, by all accounts.' She shakes her head again. 'Never seen owt like it, honest to God, I haven't. Garages floating down ' road – I bet tha thought tha was going mental.'

CHAPTER TWENTY-ONE

After supper on Christmas Eve, they pack their presents for Fiona's family into the laundry bag she keeps for the purpose. Now Jonathan has got used to the idea that they're going to her parents, he's quite looking forward to it. But the visit from that policeman is nagging at him. His mother is at her sister's in Edinburgh for Christmas, but Hutchinson wants to talk to her as soon as she returns. 'What do you think?' he asks Fiona. 'Should I call her at my aunt's or wait until she's back?'

'I think you should leave it,' Fiona says. 'Why worry her now?'

'Hutchinson wants to see her alone; he said there might be things she'd "find difficult to talk about" in front of me.'

'Sounds fair enough. You don't have to be there at the same time as him, do you? Here, hold this for me.'

He holds the edges of the bag while Fiona zips it up. 'I

suppose not. But he doesn't even want me to tell her he's coming. I can't let him just turn up, can I? I mean, he's as good as said he thinks my father was a violent criminal. What's that going to do to her?'

Fiona stops what she's doing and sweeps a strand of hair away from her face. She looks tired. It seems ages since he's seen her smile. 'I thought you said there's only a chance it could have something to do with your dad?'

'A strong chance, Hutchinson said. And I suppose it *is* plausible, don't you think?'

'I don't know.' She looks down, finishes zipping up the bag. 'If you phone her now, it'll spoil her Christmas and she'll want to come rushing back. You had to talk her into going as it was.'

'True.' He lifts the bulging bag down onto the floor.

'Let this Hutchinson guy talk to her when she gets back from Edinburgh, then you can go and see her when it's had time to sink in.' She pulls out a chair and sits down. 'He won't just go round there and blurt it out, surely? She's an old lady.'

'That's what I said. He said he wouldn't be "insensitive" but that basically, he's got a job to do.' He sighs as he sits down opposite her. 'And the DNA aspect means I'll have to tell her about being arrested – she'll want to know how the whole thing came about.'

Fiona shakes her head and sighs. 'Do you really think – I mean, *really* – that it's your dad they're looking for?'

'At first I thought it couldn't be, but from what Hutchinson said about the DNA ... the odds are pretty high.' As he thinks about what that might actually mean, he feels like a hole is opening up in his chest.

Fiona sighs again. 'It's just one bloody thing after another, isn't it?'

He walks over and puts his hand on her shoulder, but she gets to her feet. 'I'm going up,' she says.

'It's only half past nine, I thought—'

'It'll be a long day tomorrow.' She moves towards the door as though she's dragging a heavy weight behind her. 'And I'm tired. See you when you come up.'

A wave of disappointment breaks over him. They usually exchange their gifts on Christmas Eve; it's always been their time together before diving into the cheery celebrations of her family or the frigid, restrained hospitality of his. He sits down again heavily. He always enjoys Christmas with Fiona's parents; the friendly chaos of Jean's warm, messy kitchen; Nick's gleeful 'let's have a little nightcap', which usually meant a whopping great whisky or two. But this is their last child-free Christmas, and he'd hoped they'd spend it here, just the two of them. She'd seemed keen, too, until the other night. He'd started telling her what he was planning to cook on Christmas Day – rare beef with fresh horserad-ish, crispy potatoes and red wine gravy, followed by mini Christmas puddings made with fresh figs and served with clotted cream – when he noticed she wasn't smiling. 'What's wrong?' he'd said.

'It sounds lovely, Jonno, but . . .' She sighed. 'Do you mind if we go to Mum and Dad's after all?'

'But I thought . . .'

'It's just that, what with everything that's going on, I think we both need the distraction.'

He'd been about to disagree, but then she said, 'And I know this sounds silly and childish, but right now I feel like, I don't know . . . like I want my mum.'

But he assumed they'd still have their own little celebration tonight, as usual. And now it's Christmas Eve and she's gone to bed, and the empty kitchen feels cold and miserable. Faint laughter from next door's television wafts through the walls; the fridge shudders then resumes its humming. He should go to bed as well, but he knows he won't sleep, so instead he wanders into the living room. It smells of Christmas – the green, fresh-pine scent of the tree overlaid with a citrus tang of oranges. He switches on the telly and lies down on the sofa to watch some celebrity chef shoving half-pound slabs of butter inside a turkey and telling viewers that Christmas was no time to be worrying about heart attacks; then the camera switches to a homely kitchen and a voluptuous woman in a low-cut holly-green sweater who, in between piping whipped cream onto mince pies, appears to be fellating her own thumb. He grabs the remote and hits the off button. As he lies there, listening to the house quieten around him, his eyes begin to close. He's too drowsy to control his thoughts, but not drowsy enough to slip into unconsciousness, and in this state, his agitated mind begins to turn his father into various incarnations of murderers from the Yorkshire Ripper to Dr Crippen.

It takes a supreme effort to rouse himself from this no-man's-land, but he manages to force his eyes open, then he stands and switches the lamp on in the hope that the light will chase out the shadowy images lurking in his brain. In the kitchen, he pours a glass of milk, takes a sip then spits it in the sink; it's on the turn. The foul, sour taste jolts him back to reality. 'Sod it,' he mutters aloud. He rummages in the bags by the door until he finds the port they're supposed to be taking with them tomorrow; he pours a generous measure and goes back into the living room. Their presents for each other are still beneath the tree, which is hung with golden baubles and draped with ropes of twinkling fairy lights. But no matter how long he stares at it, he can't quite absorb its cosy cheer.

CHAPTER TWENTY-TWO

It is Sunday so there's no performance today, and Maggie is sitting at the props table with a Peak Frean's Teatime Selection tin full of broken eggshells in front of her. In the coming week's play, the leading lady bakes a cake and is seen cracking two eggs into a bowl. With matinees three times a week, that's a lot of eggs, so the entire company brings in their eggshells and it's Maggie's job to stick the halves together so they look like new. She's mastered it now: she takes half an eggshell, wedges it just inside the other half, dips her brush in some fresh egg white and paints over the join, then sets it to dry. She is at her calmest when working. They tell her she's the best ASM they've ever had and her willingness seems to impress them, so she tries to ignore the way her stomach churns when she sees a particularly gluey strand of albumen in one of the shells. Concentrating on work helps her to stop thinking about Jack. When the theatre reopened after the storm, Clive sent someone round to his digs, but his land-lady said he'd left. Paid his rent up to the end of the month and moved out. 'Huh,' Vanda said when she heard. 'That's just what he did in Leeds, buggered off out of the blue without so much as a by-your-leave.'

At first, Maggie was relieved that she didn't have to face him, but now she's angry. How dare he do that to her and then just disappear, leaving her bruised and battered and bloodied? For a while, a tiny part of her had wondered whether she could possibly have got it wrong, whether there was some other explanation for her ripped clothes and torn body. Part of that night is still a blank, but every now and then, when she's least expecting it, her memory dredges up some image or sound to throw at her, making her start and tremble until it fades away again. She feels her throat constrict and tears threaten, but she will not cry; she will *not*.

Jimmy is up the ladder, whistling as he paints the flats for the new play. Right now, there are just a few new strokes beginning to obliterate the reds and golds of last week's Victorian drawing room. You can't see yet what the new set will be, but when Jimmy has finished, it'll be so realistic you will feel you could walk into it.

She picks up the next half-shell and is about to hold it against another when she spots a streak of blood in the sticky remains. Her stomach heaves. She drops the eggshell, scrambles to her feet and runs to the nearest lavatory where she brings up most of her breakfast. As she makes her way back, everything becomes suddenly oversized and vivid. And then there is a most curious occurrence: the next thing she is aware of is sitting on the wooden floor, leaning up against the leg of the props table with the battered biscuit tin in her lap. But now eight of the shells are stuck together, and she's sure she has only done three. She shakes her head; perhaps she's been daydreaming. But her mind is blank. No matter how hard she thinks, she cannot bring to the surface any memory of the last – how long? She looks around like a new-hatched bird, and that's when she notices the flat Jimmy was working on. It is transformed. It now shows a cluttered farmhouse kitchen with a great oak dresser at one end and a blackened kitchen range at the other. Pots and pans hang from the walls and there's a huge kettle on the range; he's even painted flowers on the plates that adorn the dresser. Jimmy is an artist, a genius. She looks around, but he's gone, and when she walks over to the board and gingerly reaches out a finger, the paint is unmistakably dry.

*

Over the next few days, Maggie feels increasingly unwell. She keeps getting a peculiar, detached feeling and yester-day she fainted. That must have been what happened the other day. And hadn't Vanda warned her about Jimmy's practical jokes? Apparently, he's always sewing up the bottoms of the cast's trousers while they're onstage, or filling their gloves with dried peas. He must have stuck the extra five shells together while she was unconscious, just to give her the heebie jeebies.

Not long after the eggshell episode, as she is washing her smalls in the basement bathroom of her digs, it happens again. It's Dot's laundry day and the old copper is bubbling away in the corner, the room damp and full of steam. Dot prods around in the soapy water with her wooden tongs then hauls out great steaming tangles of bedlinen and drops them into the bath with a splat. She grunts every now and again with the effort. One minute, Maggie is standing over the stone sink, wringing out her nylons, the next, or so it seems, she is lying in bed fully clothed, her face wet with tears. Dot is knocking on the door and calling her name.

She stumbles across the room and opens the door; the hot, clean smell of Robin's starch floods the room.

'Whatever's the matter, duck?' Dot's face is flushed from ironing and she's wheezing from the effort of the stairs.

'I don't know,' she says slowly. She's not sure what time it is, or what she is supposed to be doing.

'You must have had one of your turns,' Dot says. 'You looked a bit queer so I thought I'd pop up and check, and as soon as I came up them stairs I could hear you breaking your heart. Rooaring like a babby, tha was. You want to get yer sen to't doctor's, if you ask me; get summat for tha nerves.'

CHAPTER TWENTY-THREE

On Christmas morning, they barely speak. Fiona insists he's probably still over the limit, so they take her car. He's in no position to argue. She drives with her jaw clenched, knuckles whitening on the steering wheel and eyes fixed straight ahead.

'I really am sorry,' he says again.

She shrugs. 'Yes, well.'

They exchanged presents before they left, but she isn't wearing the bracelet he bought her. And when he gave her the early edition of *The Velveteen Rabbit*, a childhood favourite she's wanted a copy of for years, she barely smiled. Her gift to him was a boxed set of fourteen Hitchcock films on DVD. 'Fantastic!' he'd smiled as he unwrapped them. The first weekend they'd ever spent together there'd been a Hitchcock Season on television and they'd spent the entire two days in bed watching the movies, eating snack foods and having sex. 'That's a wonderful present, and I know I don't deserve it.' He'd looked at her, hoping for a glimmer of shared memory, but by then she was putting her coat on and pointedly looking at her watch.

The drive to her parents' house takes just over an hour. The silence in the car creates a vast, deep crater and each time he tries to talk, his words just fall into it and disappear.

*

The festive atmosphere at Nick and Jean's means they have to make an effort, and they manage to get through lunch and a game of junior Cluedo with Noah and Molly fairly cheerfully. After lunch, they all settle to watch *It's a Wonderful Life*, and Jonathan is relieved to be able to stop smiling. He steals the odd glance at Fiona, but she refuses to meet his gaze, so he gives up and tries to concentrate on the film. James Stewart's character, convinced it would be better if he'd never been born, is about to throw himself off a bridge when Clarence, his guardian angel, intervenes. Jonathan suspects that right at this moment, even if he had his own jovial, avuncular guardian angel, it would probably tell him to just go ahead and jump.

Fiona had got up before him this morning, so she'd found the half-empty bottle as soon as she went downstairs. She'd come storming back up just as he was getting out of bed.'You selfish bastard!' she'd yelled. He could see tears glinting in her eyes but at that point, he honestly hadn't known what she was talking about.

'Have you any idea how much this cost?' She waved

what was left of the port at him.

'Er, no, not—'

'Almost fifty pounds,' she said. 'You've had about thirty quid's worth.'

'*How* much? Why the—'

'It was for my dad; for his birthday.'

He looked at her. He'd completely forgotten it was Nick's birthday just after Christmas. 'Oh God, I'm so, so sorry. I honestly didn't realise it was a special bottle; I thought we were just taking it like we take a bottle of wine.'

'But I *told* you I'd chosen it as a treat for my dad.'

And now he remembers: she *did* tell him, but he's been so preoccupied with the arrest and with Hutchinson and the DNA thing that it went right out of his head. *What possessed you?* she'd demanded. The obvious answer was *too much vintage port*, but that wouldn't go down well.

After *It's a Wonderful Life*, they play a torturous game of charades, followed by a falsely cheery walk with Lucy, Matt and the kids while Jean prepares a supper of cold turkey, pickles and mashed potatoes. Over supper, Fiona knocks back a second glass of red and then bursts into tears because it's bad for the baby. Then she goes to bed, leaving Jonathan to fumble for an explanation.

*

They set off home after lunch on Boxing Day, with Jonathan driving this time. 'Well, that was nice, wasn't it?' he says as they turn onto the dual carriageway.

'Yes.'

'The kids clearly had a great time.'

'They seemed to, yes.'

'And I thought Lucy and Matt were on good form.'

'Mmm.'

He glances at her, but she's looking straight ahead. He starts to say something else, but her silence fills the car like expanding foam, so he shuts up.

They pull up outside the house, and as he draws level with his own car ready to reverse into the space behind, he sees a deep gouge in the paintwork, running the whole length of the offside. It looks like someone's dragged a screwdriver or a key along it. He gets out and bends to examine the damage, running his finger along the rough metal.

'Oh, my God. Who'd do something like this?' Fiona says.

He hesitates. He's not sure why, but a little voice is screaming at him that Ryan Jenkins has something to do with this.

Fiona is frowning. 'You think it's that kid, don't you?'

'Could be.'

'But he doesn't know where we—'

Then he remembers. 'He was boasting in class a while ago about how easy it is to find addresses on the internet if you know the name and the area, and that wasn't long after we saw him in Greenwich Market that time.'

Fiona looks doubtful, and just for a moment he wonders if he's being paranoid. But then he sees her glance nervously up and down the road before going into the house.

CHAPTER TWENTY-FOUR

The waiting room is dark and dingy-looking, with blistered, flaking paint covering the rough-rendered walls. The doctor's receptionist is also his wife and, according to Dot who knows these things, the house is their home as well as his surgery. Dr Sarka, she says, is 'coloured, but very nice' while his wife, a statuesque middle-aged German called Herta, is 'a bit of a Tartar'.

Herta presides over the waiting patients from a hulking oak desk in the corner. Periodically, she throws a dart-like glance over the top of her tortoiseshell spectacles to silence a coughing child. A heavily pregnant woman, also with a hacking cough, asks for a glass of water. With a click of her tongue, Herta grudgingly obliges.

Herta has what Maggie thinks is a knowing expression. Maggie has seen the family planning posters on the walls; she knows what the terrifying Herta probably assumes, seeing her sitting here with no obvious cough or bandage. Since she arrived in Sheffield she has learned that, in some people's eyes, girls who work in the theatre and live in digs are little more than prostitutes.

There is a loud buzz from the metal box on the wall and a red light flashes.

'*Miss* Harrison,' Herta announces, 'you will see the doctor now.'

Dr Sarka is a foot shorter than his wife and as broad as he is tall. The little hair he has left is combed, black and gleaming to disguise the baldness, and he is wearing the same spectacles as his wife. Maggie wonders whether this is deliberate, to make them at least match each other, even if they don't match anybody else in this town.

Maggie lists her symptoms – fainting, blurred vision, nausea, a feeling of disorientation, and she tells him about the slate hitting her during the storm. He makes a note, asks if she ever suffered 'these fits' before that night. He picks up a miniature torch and stands over her, leaning his face down towards hers so she can see the hairs protruding from his cavernous nostrils. She flinches. He is not going to hurt her, he says; he just wants to see how her eyes react to the light.

She apologises. His tone is kindly, reassuring. But he is so near she can smell his breath, pear drops, overlaid with a faintly oniony tang. There is a hint of spice about him, and of male underarm odour, almost masked by the heady richness of his aftershave. She looks left and right as instructed, tries to relax.

She is holding her breath and her hands are clenched tightly together.

'Something else is troubling you?' he asks, putting the lid back on the torch, which looks just like a fountain pen. He takes his spectacles off and turns to face her, using the desk as leverage; his feet, she notices, do not quite reach the floor.

'No.' She shakes her head. 'No, nothing else.'

He puts his spectacles on again and turns back to his desk. 'Bowels okay?'

She nods.

'When you pass water, any pain? Any burning sensation?'

She hesitates, shakes her head.

'When did you last menstruate?'

She lowers her eyes. This is the thing she's been trying not to think about. She's read that missing one month is normal. It happens during times of upheaval, like moving away from home. That must be the explanation. But even as she thinks this, she knows it's not so; everything is not going to be all right. They call it *the curse*, but it is surely the absence of her period that will damn her.

*

A week later, Dr Sarka confirms the thing that she has most dreaded, the thing that cannot possibly be true. She feels different somehow, not herself. The doctor suspects her funny turns may be connected: strange things happen to women when they're expecting, he says, especially when the pregnancy is unplanned. He asks if she and the baby's father are intending to marry, and she shakes her head. He raises his eyebrows as he looks at her.

Maggie looks at her hands. *Tell him what happened,* she urges herself. *He's a doctor; just tell him.* But how can she tell him when even she doesn't know?

The doctor looks at her again, not unkindly. 'Maybe if you tell him about the child?'

Without looking up, she shakes her head again. 'I – I don't know where he is.' She can feel her face colouring. What must the doctor think of her?

The doctor sighs. He writes the addresses and telephone numbers of three nursing homes on a notepad, tears off the paper and hands it to her.

There was a waitress Maggie knew at the hotel in Hastings who went to one of those places. It turned out to be more like a workhouse. She stuffs the note into her handbag, thanks him and scurries out through the waiting room, past Herta and her accusatory stare into the sleety March morning.

The doctor watches the door close, sighs again, and presses the buzzer for his next patient.

*

When Maggie wakes on Sunday morning, the appalling truth of her condition has crept across her brain and is hanging there like poison ivy. Usually, she enjoys

Sundays; she doesn't have to go in until lunchtime because it's the day they strike the set, pack away the old props and lay out the new ones. Jimmy will be painting the flats and everyone will be moaning about having to read a new script while trying not to muddle the play they've been performing all week with the one they're rehearsing.

She puts her housecoat on and paces a little, smoking cigarettes as she tries to think what to do. Gin; there's something you can do with gin and a hot bath. And mustard. She's not even sure whether you're supposed to drink the gin or bathe in it. And there are pills, she's heard. Quinine? If she's going to do the gin thing, she needs to do it soon. Who can she ask? For the first time since she's been in Sheffield, she's aware of how far from home she is. Back in Hastings, there are people she could talk to, but she's been here for three months now, and apart from a couple of hurried postcards when she first arrived, she hasn't been in touch with any of her old friends. She can't just suddenly get in contact now and ask them if they know how to get rid of a pregnancy.

Later, when she's packing away the rubber snake from the last play, it comes to her: Vanda! She gets the address from Una, and manages to slip away from the theatre that afternoon, ostensibly to search for props for next week's play. As she walks up the hill towards Vanda's, she almost veers into the road to avoid the passageways between the houses. Her heart beats too fast and her breathing is shallow. Halfway up the hill, she hears someone cry out as if in terror. She stops and flings her head around but the street is empty; then she realises, because its echo is still caught in her throat, the cry came from her own lips.

She tries to walk on but there's a whooshing sound in her ears and she's struggling to take a breath. Something is crushing her, a hot, suffocating mass, sucking the air from her lungs. The next thing she knows, she is lying on the pavement and someone is throwing water at her face. She gasps as she opens her eyes.

'Come on, lass. That's ' ticket. Let's get thee to tha feet.' A solid, whiskery man who smells of pipe tobacco helps her up. A stout woman in a wrap-around apron dips her fingers into a glass and flicks more water into her face.

'Give over, Florrie; ' lass is coming round.'

The woman mumbles an apology and offers the glass to Maggie's lips. A small crowd has gathered and someone suggests calling a doctor.

'Thank you,' Maggie says, taking a gulp. 'I'm fine now, really.'

'You passed out cold,' the woman says. 'I was cleaning me windows and I saw tha grab on't lamp post, then tha dropped like a stone, didn't she, Stan?'

'Aye. Gave tha head a right crack, lass. How's tha feeling now?'

The concerned faces make Maggie feel a fraud. She declines the offer of tea and a sit down and is assuring them she's fine when she sees Vanda hurrying towards her.

'Maggie, darling! What happened? I was nosing out of my window and I saw you sprawled out on the ground. I thought, I'm sure that's young Maggie from the Playhouse down there taking centre stage.'

There is an audible click of the tongue from the whiskery man. 'Lass fainted, Elsie,' he says. 'In't it obvious?'

Maggie had forgotten about the name, and wonders whether Vanda has a completely different personality to go with 'Elsie'. She thanks the neighbours again and allows Vanda to lead her up the road. As they walk down the passageway, Maggie realises she is holding her breath and gripping Vanda's arm a little too tightly.

The yard is like a bomb site, with piles of rubble and broken fencing heaped all around. 'The back wall and both fences came down in the storm,' Vanda explains. 'Could have been worse, I suppose. Next door's chimney collapsed into their front room.'

Vanda fills the kettle while Maggie looks around, surprised at how different the house seems now the furniture is back. The room is an odd mix of old and new, dark and light. A glass-fronted oak cabinet stands next to a G Plan sideboard; the settee looks modern, with thin wooden legs and tweedy black and white covers, but the fireside chairs remind her of her grandma's. Theatrical photographs cram the mantelpiece – Vanda and Boris, the chorus, a magician, and various other performers, all with great flourishing signatures. There's one of a man who looks like James Mason. Maggie used to have a crush on James Mason, but that was a thousand years ago.

'So.' Vanda takes two cups and saucers from the kitchen cabinet, bright yellow with white polka dots – vivid, like Vanda herself. 'What are you doing in this neck of the woods?'

'I was coming to see you, actually.' Maggie's stomach is doing somersaults as she sits at the little Formica table watching Vanda spoon tea into the pot. 'I need some advice, really. You see, I . . .' She can't make the words come.

'Advice about what?' Vanda shouts over the whistling kettle. 'I haven't found the secret of fame and fortune, if that's what you're after.'

'No, it's . . .' She hesitates again.

'Maggie darling, do spit it out. I'm dying of curiosity.'

Maggie takes a deep breath. 'I'm pregnant.' It sounds harsh and vulgar, but *expecting* or *going to have a baby* don't seem right at all. 'I've seen a doctor so I know it's definite.' Just get to the point, she thinks; just ask her. 'And I was wondering whether you knew, well, I don't have much money, and I know there are pills you can get to bring on your monthlies but I don't know what they're called.' She is babbling now, the words spilling out like water from a leaky gutter. 'And I was wondering if you knew how to, you know, there's that thing you can do with gin, isn't there? But I don't know how much you need or whether you have to use mustard as well . . .' She stops. While she has been talking, she has ripped the tissue she was holding to pieces. She looks down with some surprise at the little bits of white, dotted like snow over the lino. She kneels to gather them up, failing to notice that Vanda has fallen silent in the kitchen and has stopped fussing around with sugar bowls and spoons.

'And what makes you think I would be able to help you?' Vanda is standing very still with her back to Maggie, her arms spread and her hands resting on the wooden draining board. Her voice has a steely edge; her back is rigid and seems to crackle with tension. Maggie gets to her feet.

'I just thought—'

'Did you think I was a prossie or something? Some sort of loose woman, just because I show a bit of leg on stage and I don't have a husband?' Vanda turns to face her, and she's shocked at the black lights flaring in Vanda's eyes.

'No, no. I didn't think that.' She says it clumsily. She *has* made assumptions; not what Vanda thinks, but maybe not that far off. And based on what? The make-up? The flamboyant clothes? The fact that Vanda is older? She can feel her face flush.

'You listen to me,' Vanda almost spits. 'It's not my problem that you've gone and got yourself into trouble, and I have no intention whatsoever of helping you to get out of it.' She turns away again, pours the tea so it slops into the saucers and says, icily, 'Sugar?' She stands with the sugar bowl in her hand, apparently impatient for an answer.

'It's not quite like that.' Maggie looks down. 'I'm sorry I've upset you. I didn't know who else . . .' But she is making things worse. 'I'd better go.' Mumbling apologies, she opens the back door and says goodbye.

She walks quickly through the passageway, feeling her breath quicken. Despite the chilliness of the morning, she is aware of a fine sweat breaking out on her forehead.

*

That night, Maggie does not sleep, not at all. She lies in her little bed, eyes wide open in the darkness, thinking. If Vanda won't help her, she decides, she'll have to do it alone. She spends the morning sitting on her bed, smoking, waiting for the off-licence to open. At ten to eleven, she puts on her coat and headscarf, grabs her handbag and hurries down the four flights of stairs to the hallway, pausing to check that Dot has definitely gone out. She heaves open the door to the basement. The damp, mushroomy smell triggers a wave of nausea, but when it has passed, she goes down to light the copper so that by the time she gets back with the gin, the water should be hot enough. There's a sense of urgency now, a need to get this *thing* out of her. She has begun to picture it, its face grotesque, pitted and gnarled like something that's been in the sea for days.

*

Drink a lot – no tiny tot! Where did she read that? She takes another gulp. She can hardly see to turn off the water, partly because the steam is so dense, and partly because she is so drunk. Drunk as a skunk, as Leonard would say.

At first, she'd poured it into a glass and lit a cigarette to go with it, but now she's swigging it straight from the bottle and telling herself it's medicine. She holds it up to see how much she's drunk, but there are two of everything. She tries what she's seen Leonard do when he's really sozzled; she puts her free hand over one eye, and it works! The two bottles move back into one and she can see she's had just over half. Surely that should be enough? She puts the bottle on the floor and lurches forward, almost falling into the bath. This gives her the giggles. She fumbles with the tin of Colman's mustard powder, and the lid comes off so suddenly she drops the whole lot into the water where it billows out like deadly yellow bath salts. She positions the wooden chair next to the bath so she can reach the bottle, takes another gulp and starts to undress. But as she pulls her sweater over her head, she loses her balance and stumbles, knocking the chair and the bottle onto the floor. She curses, grabs a towel and bends down to try and mop up the gin, but the room begins to spin and she hears a roaring in her ears before she is overtaken by nausea. She tries to stand but the room won't keep still, so she crawls through the puddle of gin on the lino to the sink in the corner.

The retching comes from so deep within her she wonders if she will vomit the baby right up into the stone sink. She's never been so sick. It seems to go on forever and she's so consumed that she doesn't hear Dot shouting down the stairs.

Dot has made a mistake; she forgot her WRVS meeting

was cancelled this week so she came home, planning to get on with her needlework and then put her feet up and listen to the wireless.

'Who's in there?' Dot shouts, banging on the door which immediately swings open because Maggie hasn't bothered to lock it.

Maggie is hanging over the sink, thinking she's about to die, when she feels a cold blast of air and notices the movement of the steam.

Dot is looking at her as though she cannot believe her eyes. Maggie retches again, then the roaring in her ears makes everything go red and she passes out cold on the floor.

She comes round to find Dot wiping her face with a flannel. It takes her a moment to work out where she is, then she remembers why she's in the bathroom. She sits up, then tries to stand, but Dot tells her to stay still. The steam has cleared now and she can tell by the gurgling noises that Dot has emptied the bath.

'Right,' Dot says, straightening up. 'How much did tha drink?'

'About half,' Maggie replies. She feels remarkably sober, considering.

'With a bit of luck, you'll have brought it all up.' She doesn't look at Maggie and she is talking through her teeth. 'This is a respectable house, this is. I'm going upstairs now but I'll be keeping an eye on thee. If owt starts to happen, I'll call an ambulance.'

'No, please . . . I'm sorry. I didn't know what else—'

'A respectable house,' Dot says again, opening the door. Maggie can hear her muttering as she climbs the stairs: *After all I've done . . . no gratitude . . . that sort of girl.*

Maggie starts to gather her things. She is too tired, too drained even to weep. Then her legs tremble and she feels dizzy again. She mustn't faint; she puts her hand on the steam-wet wall to steady herself, but then a powerful cramp grips her stomach and spreads around her middle. *My God*, she thinks. *This must be it; it's actually working.*

CHAPTER TWENTY-FIVE

The six of them, all with white beards and pointy hats, are squashed together in what is little more than a broom cupboard at the rear of the auditorium. The idea is that if Sneezy appears in front of the stage just before curtain up, the audience will be so busy watching his antics that they won't notice the rest of the dwarves creeping out behind them in the darkness, ready to hi-ho their way down the aisles and onto the stage.

Jonathan peers through the crack in the door. It's airless in the tiny space, humid with exhaled breath. He tries to shift position but given the proximity of the other dwarves he can barely move. Sweat starts to prickle under his arms, and he runs his finger under his collar to lift it away from the clammy skin on the back of his neck. What doesn't help is that he is absolutely certain he saw Ryan Jenkins just now, hanging around outside with a couple of other boys.

'I'm sure it was him, you know,' he whispers to Malcolm.

'Unlikely. Not really their manor, is it? And – oh, here we go.'

Sneezy has started his major sneezing routine so the rest of them begin sliding out of the cupboard. At the cue, Dozy lifts his shovel onto his shoulder and sings a long, loud *hi-ho*. The others follow suit with their shovels, then begin singing the hi-ho song as they march down the darkened aisle towards the brightly lit stage. Jonathan is last in line, and as he sees all the heads turning around to watch them, everybody smiling, the rapt faces of the little kids, he begins to think that maybe life isn't so bad after all.

And then smack, he's on the floor. He scrambles to his feet. His wrist hurts and he's grazed the side of his face.

'You all right, mate?' A pony-tailed man with a gold stud in his nose and a toddler on his lap hands him the shovel. 'You must have tripped.'

Jonathan looks behind him. There's no crease in the carpet, no handbag left carelessly in the aisle. The audience laughs.

'Smi-ley!' The other dwarves are standing at the front, hands on hips; Malcolm is giving him a look, doing his best to make it all part of the show.

Jonathan scans the laughing faces, but the lighting makes it difficult to see more than the few that are nearest to him. For a moment, he thinks he recognises a Year 10 boy a little way along the row, but he's mistaken. Even the nose-stud man is grinning now.

'Hurry up, Smiley,' Malcolm shouts, still in character. 'Snow White'll be here soon and if she finds you hanging around down there, it'll be early to bed and no telly for you!'

They're all laughing at him now, enjoying his humiliation. He can feel the sweat beading on his upper lip; his heart is beating hard, like he's just run up a flight of stairs. He looks around the auditorium; Fiona's out there somewhere, witnessing this, seeing him made a fool of. He looks again at row upon row of laughing faces, but doesn't recognise any of them. Maybe he *is* overreacting. He tries to gather himself, knows he should put on his biggest smile, sing a loud *hi-ho* and march merrily down the aisle with the others. But what if Ryan Jenkins is out there, poised to start heckling or throwing things at the stage? Jonathan's anger is pulsing in his temples; he's not sure he trusts himself any more. He begins walking slowly towards the front, trying to balance reason against suspicion. He can feel them all watching. They're only kids, he tells himself; it was a coincidence. It's just an audience full of kids, laughing at the panto like they're supposed to. Now is his chance to pull it back; just march the march and sing the bloody song. Just do it. He continues down the aisle. All he has to do is walk up those wooden steps and onto the stage, then smile and bow and carry on with the show. But his legs seem to be acting on their own. As he walks, he has the strangest sensation that he has stepped outside of his own body. The expression *beside myself* comes into his mind as he watches himself walking towards the stage, then on past Malcolm and the others, and out through the door at the side. A moment later, he is almost surprised to find himself, light-headed and slightly shaky, standing behind the stage in the darkened space that doubles as a dressing room. He sits down among the bags and coats and boxes of props and considers what he's just done; he's actually walked out of a performance. What he wouldn't give now for a cigarette. And then he hears the voices onstage, a wave of laughter, then another, louder, no doubt at his expense. Well, fuck them. Fuck the lot of them.

*

'It's just for a few days,' Fiona says, putting her suitcase by the door. 'I'm not leaving you. I'm just, I don't know . . . tired.'

'If you're tired, rest. Why do you need to go to your mum's, for God's sake? I can look after you here,' Jonathan says. He's been trying to sound rational and calm, but he can feel panic beginning to rise. This can't be happening, not to him; not to them.

'I don't just mean that sort of tired.' She sighs irritably. 'I mean I'm tired of . . . of all this; of everything that's happening. I need a break.'

'A break from me?'

'Look, I can't even think straight now. Just let me do this, okay?' She is standing next to her case, with her car keys in her hand. She won't look at him; he feels sick.

'Is it because of the other night?'

She sighs again. 'It's not just that. Though it was pretty bloody embarrassing to have to sit there watching while you walked out like a stroppy child.'

He opens his mouth to defend himself, but what's the point. She's right.

'Everyone was looking at me, Jonathan. And I was right in the middle of the row so I couldn't even get out of the place quickly – they all had to stand up to let me pass.' She shakes her head. 'And now it's in the bloody local paper.'

This week's *Mercury* is still open on the kitchen table. The headline reads: *Smiley turns Grumpy*. Which really doesn't help. 'It's only a tiny article.'

'Plenty of people'll see it. And anyway, that's not the point. I know it's a difficult time, but tipping half a bottle of vintage port down your neck on Christmas Eve isn't a very mature way of handling stress, is it?' She's looking at him now, her face tight with anger.

Well, you buggered off to bed at half past nine, he wants to say, but even in his head it sounds selfish. He looks at the floor. 'I know; you're right.'

'And you're not even trying to cope. You're drinking too much, you're still not sleeping—'

'That's hardly my fault, is it?'

'No, but refusing to see the doctor is. You've not been sleeping for months now, and all you need to do is—'

'Please don't shout.'

'I'm not shouting,' she yells, banging her keys on the

hall table. 'I just want you to take some responsibility.' She grabs her coat from the rack. 'Seeing a doctor doesn't make you less of a man, you know.'

'All right, all right. I'll see the bloody doctor if it'll make you happy.'

'It's not to make me happy, it's . . .' She runs a hand through her hair. 'Look,' she says more gently. 'This isn't helping. We'll talk in a while. Just let me have some time on my own, okay? Please.'

She reaches up and kisses him briefly but without warmth, and when he tries to hold her, she moves away. She opens the front door. 'I need some breathing space. I'll call in a few days. I promise.' And she is gone.

Breathing space, he thinks as the house tingles with the silence of a just-closed door. When someone says they need space . . .

*

Jonathan grimaces at his reflection as he pulls the razor through five days' growth of coarse black stubble. His eyes are bloodshot and his skin has a yellowish tinge. These sleeping tablets make him feel like death, but they certainly work. Thank God his mother insisted on taking a taxi back from Euston. She'd taken the sleeper service from Edinburgh, so her train got in at 6.40; he'd never have been able to drag himself out of bed in time, never mind have his wits about him enough to drive through central London. He stands under the shower for several minutes, allowing the hot water to bring him back to life. He uses Fiona's shower gel, closing his eyes so that he can imagine the familiar lemony scent is coming from her newly washed skin instead of his own. She's been gone a week.

It starts to rain as he leaves the house. Next door's cat is on the windowsill, sitting upright with its tail curled around its body in a perfect 'C'. Jonathan pauses, holding the front door open behind him. 'Well?' he says to the tortoiseshell. 'You coming in or not?' The cat's eyes narrow in a slow blink, its ears twitch, and the tip of its tail flicks very slightly. 'Come on, Puss,' he coaxes, reaching out to tickle it under the chin. But the cat, who usually spends more time with him and Fiona than with its owners, arches its body and hisses, then settles back down and eyes Jonathan as if he is the most unpleasant creature it has ever had the misfortune to encounter. 'Sod you, then,' he says, pulling the door shut behind him.

*

The windscreen wipers are on fast as he pulls up outside his mother's, but even through the grey veil of rain, he recognises Hutchinson's waxed jacket and the slight limp as he walks away from the house towards the main road. He sighs and switches the engine off.

She looks surprised to see him. 'That man said you'd probably come today, but I didn't expect you just yet.' Her voice is thin and shaky. She motions him to follow her into the kitchen. The luggage from her trip is still in the hall. 'You look dreadful,' she says as she fills the kettle. He notices her hand is trembling. 'Why didn't you tell me about what happened? With your school? With the police?'

'I didn't . . . I don't know. I suppose I was worried about what you'd think. That you might think I'd hit the boy . . .'

There is a silence. 'Is that what you truly believe?' She looks him in the eye. 'That I'd think you capable of striking a child?'

He drops his gaze. 'I didn't think, I suppose. Not properly.'

'False allegations against teachers: it's happening all the time these days, according to the newspapers. Where are you up to with the whole thing?'

'They can't lift my suspension while I'm waiting for the court case, even though my solicitor's fairly sure it'll be thrown out. Seems teachers are different to the rest of the population – we're guilty until proven innocent. Anyway, what did Hutchinson have to say?'

'Well.' She turns away and reaches for the cups and saucers. 'He told me about all this DNA whatnot and that they're looking for somebody who committed . . . and that . . .' There's a clatter as she drops both cups, one of which breaks.

'Mum, sit down.' He speaks softly as he guides her to a chair. His chest feels tight and he is almost afraid to breathe. What has she just discovered?

She takes a breath. '. . . and he said that that person was almost certainly closely related to you.'

'Was it him? Could it be? Just tell me, Mum, please.'

'Jonathan, I should have told you this before. I tried to, but . . .' She tries to take a cigarette from the pack on the table, but her hands are shaking too much. He's never seen her in this state before. This is it, he thinks. Nausea ripples faintly through him.

'Mr Hutchinson wanted to know all about your father. But I couldn't tell him anything, because, you see, darling . . .' She looks up at him, her eyes small and frightened. 'Gerald wasn't your father.'

CHAPTER TWENTY-SIX

Maggie paces the floor. All that pain and it still didn't work. She is wondering what to do next when Dot raps on her door. Dot is grim-faced. She's discussed it with Alf, she says, and they're sorry but they can't have that sort of thing going on under their roof.

'But nothing happened,' Maggie protests.

'That's not ' point. How do I know you won't try it again? Or summat worse? End o't week, love. If you please.'

After Dot has gone downstairs, Maggie walks over to the window and lights a cigarette. Her head is packed with voices and pictures and everything is in a tangle. She looks out over the rooftops, many still covered with tarpaulins after the storm. It's been raining all morning and over to the east the sky is inky-dark, heavy with the promise of another downpour. It seems to have rained every day for weeks. She stubs out her cigarette, puts her coat on and grabs her umbrella. She'd better go and have a look in the newsagent's window, see if there are any cheap rooms available. As she pushes the door handle back on – it comes off in her hand every time – she hears voices in the hall: Dot's low, gravelly rasp and a higher sound, a female voice she recognises.

'I got your address from Una,' Vanda says as she reaches the top of the stairs. She's not smiling but nor is she looking as fierce as when Maggie last saw her. 'I came to apologise. I shouldn't have gone off at you like that.'

Maggie looks at the floor. 'I'm sorry, too. I truly didn't mean to offend you.'

'I'm sure you didn't. I *was* angry but I suppose I can be a bit sensitive. Anyway, I just wanted to say . . .' She glances over her shoulder, down the stairs. 'Look, don't do the gin thing, it rarely works; just gives you a dicky tummy and a nasty hangover.'

Maggie nods. 'I know; I tried it. Now my landlady's throwing me out.'

'Oh dear. I should have told you before.' She sighs. 'I tried it myself once. Didn't work. I ended up going to a woman. I thought she knew what she was doing, but . . .'

'That didn't work either?'

'Oh, it worked all right – made sure I wouldn't be lumbered with a kid. Ever.'

It takes a moment for her meaning to sink in. 'I'm very sorry,' Maggie says. Vanda walks over to the window and looks out. 'The boy, I mean the father. Is there no chance he'd —'

'No, it's not ... it wasn't ... it ...' Maggie's voice is barely more than a whisper, and then she stops because she really doesn't want to cry.

Vanda turns to look at her. 'Oh God. It was Jack, wasn't it? Did he ... did he force you?'

Maggie nods, and now she can't stop the tears. Then Vanda's arms are around her, and she allows herself to sob while Vanda rocks her like a baby. Vanda's sweater feels warm and soft against her cheek, and she can smell Wright's Coal Tar soap.

'I'm sorry,' Maggie says after a few moments. She straightens up and rummages in her pocket for a tissue. 'I'm not even sure how it happened. I can only remember bits. I must have led him on, I suppose. I didn't mean to. I'm not very experienced, you see. I shouldn't have kissed him back.'

'Don't be so bloody daft,' Vanda says. 'I don't hold with this nonsense that men can't control themselves. They just say that to make us feel guilty.' Vanda lights two cigarettes and hands one to Maggie. 'Did he hurt you?'

'Yes,' Maggie nods. And she tells Vanda about the torn clothes and the cuts and the bruises and the bite mark.

Vanda is listening intently, then she shakes her head. 'I'm so sorry. I should have ...' She covers her face with her hands. 'Christ.'

Maggie looks at her.

'There was always something about him that worried me.' She takes a long drag of her cigarette. 'When I was in rep with him in Leeds, he took this girl out, Pat. She was lovely, a bright, cheerful little thing; but after she went out with Jack that one night everything changed. She was off poorly for a couple of weeks, which is virtually unheard of in rep, as you know, and when she came back – by which time he'd disappeared, incidentally – it was like she was a different person.'

'How do you mean?'

'She hardly spoke. Looked awful, turned up late, missed performances. They kicked her out in the end, and she didn't even seem to care. This was a girl who'd been in the chorus since she was fourteen and wanted to be a star.' Vanda stubs out her cigarette. 'That night at the party, I should have warned you.'

Maggie shakes her head, remembering how she'd suspected Vanda of being Jack's ex. 'I probably wouldn't have listened. Anyway, there's no point in . . . the important thing now is to do something about . . . this.' She gestures towards her belly, still not quite believing something is actually growing in there.

'You could probably get it done legally,' Vanda says. 'Under the circumstances.'

'They wouldn't believe me. For a start, most of it's still a complete blank, and even if it wasn't, I thought Jack was my new boyfriend, and you can't be raped by your own boyfriend.'

Vanda sighs. 'I see what you mean.' There is a pause. 'I do know someone,' she says. 'Someone I wish I'd known twelve years ago. He's a doctor so he'd do it right, everything sterilised. I can ask him, but I'm not promising. And you'll have to promise not to tell anyone I gave you his name.'

Maggie nods. There doesn't seem to be any other option.

*

Maggie has a part in the current play – a maid, with one line, 'very good, Madam' – but she can't enjoy the matinee because somehow she's going to have to convince Clive she's too ill for the evening performance. As it turns out, Clive can't get her out of the theatre quickly enough – he doesn't want flu sweeping through the entire company like it did in '58, he explains.

The man who opens the door is tall and thin with a lot of grey hair and a carefully trimmed beard. 'Can I help you?' he asks. He's wearing a blue and white flowery apron over dark trousers and a sagging grey cardigan. He doesn't look like a doctor.

'I'm not sure I have the right address.'

'Who are you wanting to see?' He looks her in the eye. 'Maybe if you told me *your* name?'

'Miss Harrison,' she says. 'Margaret Harrison.'

'Ah yes. Miss Harrison. I'm expecting you, aren't I? I'm Dr Montague. Come along in.'

He's older than she'd imagined, quite elderly, in fact, and his movements are slow. He takes the apron off as he leads her along a narrow hallway, down some steps and along another corridor into a dark room at the back of the house. How odd it is to be seeing a doctor in the evening. He switches on the light. The room smells damp. It's barely big enough to accommodate the oversized oak desk and the examination table, which pokes out from behind a dark-blue curtain. The wallpaper is bright red, spattered with big white flowers and tiny black birds, and on the chimney-breast there are three ceramic ducks in mid-flight, just like the ones in Dot's front parlour.

'Sit down, please.' He waves her to the only chair. There's a hissing sound as he turns on the gas fire. He fumbles with the matches for so long that she fears the place will blow up, but then there's a loud pop and the fire begins to glow and warm the room.

He leans against the desk and folds his arms. 'How far along are you?' He doesn't write anything down.

'About eight weeks.'

'I assume the young man is not prepared to marry you?'

She looks at her hands, shakes her head. Should she tell him the truth? Would he believe her?

'Very well,' he sighs. 'The operation is simple but not entirely without risk.'

He explains what he's going to do and what she can expect afterwards but Maggie isn't listening. She doesn't want details, she just wants it over.

'You'll need to empty your bladder,' he says at last, 'then we'll get started.'

As she walks up the stairs to the toilet, she notices a moth, belly-up on the dusty windowsill, its legs shrivelled and its wings powdery with death. Poor thing; what a place to die. The walls are lined with pictures of the royal family, mostly formal – Princess Elizabeth as a young bride; her and Philip with Prince Charles and Princess Anne; being crowned queen at her coronation. But one picture, clearly torn out of a magazine and then framed, shows the queen dressed casually, no hat or gloves, holding baby Andrew in her arms and smiling at the camera. Maggie slowly reaches out and touches his chubby leg.

While she's in the lavatory, she can hear raised voices. Briefly, she considers running down the stairs and out of the house. She could say she was afraid of the shouting. But then she hears the theme from *Z Cars* and she wishes she was back in Hastings with Leonard, a bottle of Tizer and a plate of toast on the floor between them, watching their brand new Rediffusion television set and gossiping about their colleagues at the hotel. Instead, she's using the toilet in a strange house, in a strange town, prior to letting a strange man kill the thing that has attached itself to her womb.

She's reassured to see that he's now wearing a white coat. The examination couch is made up like a bed but with a heavy, dark-green cotton sheet tucked over the top of a brown rubber one. He's standing on a pair of wooden steps, fixing something to the ceiling. His hands are spotted with age, the knuckles swollen and shiny with arthritis.

'Twenty-five guineas, is that right?' She reaches into

her handbag for her post-office book with the crisp new notes tucked inside.

'Ah yes.' He steps down, and she sees the stirrups dangling from a bar on the ceiling. 'Leave it on the desk, then slip your underthings off and pop up onto the couch.'

She turns away from him and starts to unclip her stockings.

'Keep your nylons on. And your slip. I only need you to remove your, erm . . .'

She removes her briefs and puts them in her handbag, then she steps onto the footstool and climbs up onto the couch. She feels clammy, and she's shivering.

'Try to relax,' he says, taking things out of the desk drawer and laying them on a metal tray.

Her legs are shaking so much she can see them moving. Her teeth start to chatter and she can hear her own breaths. She tries to hold on, tries to relax. Not long, and it'll all be over. She watches the white-coated figure fussing around, lining things up. Why can't he just get on with it? But when he turns towards her, the darkness closes in and she hears someone scream.

*

Vanda hands Maggie a cup of sweet tea. 'Here, drink this,' she says. She opens a packet of cigarettes and hands one to Maggie. 'You really, truly don't remember?'

Maggie shakes her head. 'I remember climbing onto

the couch, but after that it's all hazy. I know I screamed, and I vaguely remember him slapping me.'

'You were hysterical.'

'I know – I just can't remember why.' She's still shaky, and the teacup rattles in the saucer when she puts it down.

'Well, you can't go back to Ted, that's for sure. He was in a right old tizzy when he rang me up. Said he was amazed he hadn't had the police round, what with the racket you were making.'

Maggie sighs. 'I don't know what he must have thought of me.'

'Ted's a good man, not a crook like most of them,' Vanda says, rummaging in her bag. She takes out an envelope and hands it to Maggie.

'What's this?'

'It's your twenty-five guineas – he wouldn't take a penny.'

And sure enough, the envelope contains all the notes and even the two half-crowns. Part of her doesn't want to look at the money or think about it; it was intended as blood money, after all. Briefly, she's tempted to tell Vanda to give it back to the doctor, but she knows that would be stupid. 'Tell him . . . tell him thanks. And I'm sorry for . . . tell him I hope I haven't caused him any trouble.'

Vanda nods. 'I will. So,' she lights her cigarette, then Maggie's. 'What now?'

'I don't know.' Maggie sighs. 'I suppose I'll have to . . .' Her stomach shifts at the enormity of it all. 'I suppose I'll have to have it, then have it adopted. Dr Sarka gave me some addresses – nursing homes, he said. But whatever happens, I can't go through with an abortion.'

'It would have been all right, you know, with Ted.'

Maggie nods. 'I know. But I just can't.' She draws deeply on her cigarette. 'Do you think Clive'll sack me?'

'Not until it shows, so you'll be all right for a while. Those homes aren't much fun from what I've heard.'

'I know.' Maggie sighs. 'I knew a girl who was in one. The nuns made her clean the parquet floor with a toothbrush. Still, it'll only be for a couple of months, I suppose.'

'Listen, I've been thinking. You need somewhere to live, right? I've got a spare room – I used to have a lodger but since he went I haven't bothered to look for anyone else – and I could do with some help with the rent. If I were to let you have it really cheap, perhaps you could do some bits and pieces for me when you can't work any more – you know, cooking, cleaning, mending my costumes; that sort thing.'

Maggie is doubtful.

'Go on,' Vanda says. 'It'll help us both out and we'll be company for one another. I get fed up only having Boris to talk to of an evening.'

Boris; she'd forgotten about Boris. 'Where do you keep it?'

'Come and meet him.' Vanda grabs her hand and leads her upstairs into the little back bedroom, where a tank, more of an enclosure, really, stretches across the entire wall and almost to the ceiling. Inside is a large, coiled snake, asleep under one of the lamps. Its body, which is as thick as Maggie's wrist, is chestnut brown with a rich pattern of greyish, diamond-shaped patches and deeper brown saddle shapes. The chestnut brown becomes brighter towards the tail, turning almost brick red. It is, Maggie has to admit, a handsome creature.

'He's a Columbian Red Tail. Very good-natured. He's nearly twenty, so he's getting on a bit. I've had him for sixteen years – bought him off an exotic dancer called Lola in Eastbourne just after the war.'

'What were you doing in Eastbourne?' Maggie doesn't take her eyes from the snake. If it moves, she wants a head start out of the room.

'That's where I'm from. Well, near there anyway. My mum's still there.'

'I'm from Hastings.'

'Never! We're neighbours! Do you miss the sea? I do.'

'A bit. And I miss my brother.'

'I envy you, having a brother. There's only ever been me and Mum.'

'At least your mum's still alive.'

'Yes, well. So anyway, what d'you say? Eighteen bob a week and you help out here. Then you'll only have to go in for a couple of weeks. Maybe you could even come back afterwards – you'll get a job easily enough once it's all over.'

Maggie is still doubtful about sharing a house with Boris, but she needs to move out of Dot's by Saturday, so she agrees.

CHAPTER TWENTY-SEVEN

After pouring him a brandy 'for the shock', his mother places a shoebox on the table in front of him. 'It contains all the papers and so forth. And also, I always thought you might like to, well, I assumed . . .' She rests her hand on the lid. 'I kept the clothes you were wearing when you came to us.'

He drinks the brandy in two gulps, hoping its medicating qualities will kick in quickly. The lid of the shoebox bears remnants of the discoloured, brittle sticky tape that once secured it, and in the centre, written in his mother's flawless copperplate, is his name in faded violet ink. He lifts the lid. Inside is a pile of clothing and a large, fat envelope. He shakes out the contents. There are official-looking letters, county court documents and medical records referring to blood tests and vaccinations, but he can't keep his hands still enough to read them properly. He rests his head in his palms for a moment, but he's aware of his mother hovering anxiously behind him. He needs to keep it together. He takes a breath and clears his throat before returning to the things on the table in front of him. On top of the pile is a little woollen cardigan, navy blue, quite thick, with five yellow wooden buttons shaped like ducklings. He runs his thumb over one of the buttons, then lifts the cardigan out of the box. Underneath is a pair of heavy cotton dungarees, blue with white stripes, and a thin white jersey. His mother is looking at him.

'Jonathan?'

He's never seen her look so worried. He wants to say something but he can't.

'It's all there, darling. All the paperwork, your clothes, and the few things they sent with you.'

He picks up the wad of papers again. *We are pleased to inform you that your application has been accepted. In due course, we hope to place a baby in your care* ... He shuffles the letters. *Baby will be ready for collection at twelve noon.* Ready for collection, like a pair of patched-up old boots. *Baby will be dressed and have food for a journey. We ask our adopters for a voluntary financial contribution. The cost to the society of each adoption is currently estimated at £10.* So he'd been bought for a tenner. The words shimmer in front of him; these documents are all dated 1964, but he was born in 1962. He picks up the dungarees, folds back the tag and reads: *To fit age 12-18 months.* He looks again, but there's no mistake. Gerald and Daphne Robson took him into their care on 27 February 1964, not as a newborn, but when he was almost sixteen months old.

During the thirteen-week probationary period, he reads, *the mother may change her mind.* Why *thirteen* weeks, he wonders? Fiona would say it was unlucky. He flicks through the sheaf of papers again, pulls out one headed *Matter of the Adoption Act.* It's the formal adoption order, showing that the application was heard in Hastings County Court, although he doesn't notice that immediately, only that it's dated 28 May 1964. The adoption had gone through unimpeded.

Thirteen weeks; so she could have changed her mind. At any point during those thirteen weeks, she could have just picked up the phone and said she wanted him back. He thinks about Poppy, Malcolm and Cassie's seventeen-month-old who, when they'd visited just before Christmas, had delighted everyone by toddling around the room picking up micro-scraps of wrapping paper and saying 'hare-wah' as she handed each one to Cassie. The dates, the facts, are beginning to organise themselves in his mind. His biological mother hadn't been a weeping teenager, forced to hand over her newborn by an unforgiving family or a stern-faced nun; she had given away a child who could walk and talk, who had probably waved goodbye.

He stands and takes his coat from the back of the chair. 'I need some air,' he says. 'I can't . . . I mean, I need some time to . . . to take all this in.'

*

This morning's rain has turned to sleet, so it's wet and freezing; the worst of both worlds. But he's got to get out; the air in his mother's kitchen is thick and heavy with revelation and he fears what he's just been told will crush him if he doesn't give it room to expand and take shape. He walks quickly along Lee Terrace and turns into Blackheath Village. The sleet is icy on his scalp, wetter than rain. He can feel the wetness trickling down the back of his neck inside his collar. As people around him scurry into doorways, he breaks into a run. At first he doesn't seem out of place because so many people are sprinting to the shelter of a shop's awning or a bus stop, but Jonathan is picking up speed. Shoppers move out of his way. He is breathing hard now, and getting hot; he unbuttons his coat and it billows out behind him. He can feel his feet slamming against the pavement and water splashing up over his ankles as he runs through puddles. He begins to move his arms for momentum, but the coat is restricting him so he shrugs it off, bundles it over his arm and, after trying to carry it for a while, gives up and throws it over a wall. Sweat breaks out on his back, neck and forehead. The icy drops are almost welcome now, soothing his overheated body as he pounds on through the wet streets and up through the village towards the heath. His jeans are soaked through, and the flapping wetness slaps raw against his legs as he runs and runs, stopping only when the ground becomes soft underfoot and his feet begin to squelch on the boggy grass.

Still panting, he stops to rest under the shelter of an

ancient oak tree. He stands there for a while, leaning against its rain-blacked bark, looking out across the greyness and listening to the white noise of heavy rain. He's trying – really trying – to properly absorb what he's just been told, but his mother's words are still tumbling around in his head. His instinct is to call Fiona, but he hesitates. He feels like an imposter, as though he'd somehow got her – if indeed he still has her – under false pretences. He knows it's ridiculous – he is the deceived, not the deceiver. But seeing those clothes, those papers; tangible evidence that's real and solid, whereas he seems to be fading: not quite a teacher, not quite a father, not quite a son.

Her mobile's switched off, and there's no reply from Nick and Jean's landline. He tries Malcolm, but his phone is off as well. Things have been pretty cool between him and Malcolm since the panto, but at least they're still speaking.

His breathing has slowed now, and he tries to gather his thoughts as he watches the sleet jumping and spitting off the pond. As a boy, he'd often spent long, sunny days squatting at the edge of this pond, net poised, trying to see past his reflection to the tiny fish that darted back and forth beneath. Whose was the face that would look back at him now? This time yesterday, despite everything that was going on, he'd known who he was. He kicks a mud-caked twig into the water. After the initial shock of his mother's bombshell, he'd actually been relieved that it couldn't be Gerald the police were looking for; but that only lasted for about thirty seconds, and then it dawned on him that his DNA was still linked with – with whoever it was.

The temperature is falling by the minute; his nose, ears and even the surface of his eyes feel cold. Iron-grey clouds tinged with yellow crouch above him as he stands looking out across the black water. The sleet suddenly eases, and now barely pierces the surface, but the sky seems to be gathering itself, filling up with snow ready to smother him. He should make a move. But still he stands there. He reaches into his pocket for his wallet, takes out his driving licence and looks at it. The photo was taken five years ago; he's smiling. *Robson*, it says next to the photo. *Jonathan Hugo*. Ha. Still holding the photocard, he lifts his arm, curls his wrist around, and flicks. The licence goes spinning out across the pond, then slices through the surface in a flash and disappears down into the sludge.

He is walking slowly back towards his mother's, soaked through but barely noticing the discomfort, when his phone rings. 'Fi, thank God—'

'What is it, Jonathan?' Her voice is colourless. 'You promised you wouldn't call—'

'I know. Look, I'm sorry, but I need to tell you . . .' He stops. She'd wanted a break from all this, and now he's going to burden her again. He takes a breath, then speaks more steadily. 'I don't see how I can *not* tell you about this.'

He hears her sigh. 'Go on then,' she says.

'Well, it turns out I'm . . .' But he finds he can't say it

straight out. 'I've just come from my mum's. She told me more about what happened after that first baby died. It seems she did get pregnant again, four more times, in fact. But she lost them all; miscarriages. All boys, apparently.'

'But . . .'

'Hang on. There's more. She said part of her wanted to keep on trying, but by that time she was becoming convinced that she and my . . . that she and Gerald were somehow "biologically mismatched" and that they'd never produce a live child. So she started thinking about adoption.'

Fiona doesn't say anything but he can tell that she's listening closely now.

'He was against the idea at first. But she was in such a state. She begged him to consider it, and eventually he agreed.' He waits. 'Fi?'

There's a pause before she says, 'I'm still here.'

'Say something.'

'I . . . I don't know what to say.' She speaks slowly. 'So let me get this straight. You're saying that Daphne and Gerald . . .'

'Yes. They're not my real parents.'

CHAPTER TWENTY-EIGHT

Maggie is only five months gone when Clive tells her she must leave. He's very nice about it, but her condition is now so obvious that he really can't keep her on any longer, so she takes up her role as Vanda's housekeeper-cum-wardrobe mistress. Monday to Wednesday, Vanda works shifts at the pub on the corner, and from Thursday to Sunday, she plays the clubs and theatres in Sheffield, Leeds and Manchester. Sometimes, Maggie goes along to watch. On stage, Vanda sparkles like the sequins on her costumes. Even Boris livens up under the powerful stage lighting, slinking around Vanda's shoulders, waist and legs, then drawing his head back as though about to strike, eyes fixed, tongue flicking menacingly. Vanda buys dead things from a greasy little man who comes to the door once a month and looks shifty as he hands them over, packed tightly together in a plastic bag. She dangles them in front of Boris, who widens his jaw and swallows them whole. To her own amazement, Maggie has overcome her fear of Boris. She's even become rather fond of him, and spends many an evening with the dozing snake draped around her shoulders and resting his head on the warm boulder of her belly.

The baby – she is forced to think of it as a baby now – must be huge, because she is like a fat, round pod about to burst. According to Dr Sarka, the child's size means there's not much room for manoeuvre within Maggie's womb. On the mercifully few occasions when there is movement, Maggie flinches, but bears it; after all, considering she is going to give the child away without even looking at it, she feels it's entitled to give her the odd kick.

*

Two weeks before her due date, Maggie feels a band of pain tighten around her middle as she heaves herself out of bed. It isn't much, but it's enough to trap her breath in her lungs. After it subsides, she makes her way slowly downstairs.

'Morning, Fatso,' Vanda smiles, pulling out a chair for her.

Maggie butters a slice of bread, spoons pale amber honey onto it and is just biting into it when another pain flings its steely arms around her and grips until she is forced to let out a low moan.

Vanda's eyes widen. 'What is it? It's not starting already, is it?'

When Maggie is able to speak again, she lets out her breath. 'It's probably just practice contractions.'

But then her waters break, and Vanda's back-room floor is awash. Maggie wedges a tea towel between her legs while Vanda calls the ambulance, her voice rising in panic and settling again in response to the operator's words.

Maggie tries to relax. She'd asked the midwife how much it would hurt. 'Worse than having a tooth filled, not as bad as having a leg cut off,' the midwife said without looking at her. 'Maybe tha should have thought about that before tha jumped into bed.'

The pain is monstrous. It rises up and swamps her, then retreats, leaving a tidemark of fear. Just as Vanda says she's going to call 999 again to find out what the bloody hell in the name of Jesus H. Christ is going on with this sodding ambulance, two ambulance men walk past the kitchen window.

The men fill the room; they are big, smiley and capable-looking. The older one rubs his hands together and says not long now, an early Christmas present and where's the proud dad then?

'There isn't one,' Maggie says quietly. 'And the baby's being adopted, so I won't be bringing it home.'

His smile only falters for a second. 'Right you are, duck,' he says. 'We'd better have a look at you, see how you're going on.'

'It's not due for another two weeks.'

'Well, you're definitely on't way, love. Better get you into hospital to be on't safe side.'

Maggie nods; the sooner she goes in, the sooner this will be over. And when they take the baby away, everything will be back to normal.

*

Maggie labours for two days. When she was first admitted a lifetime ago, she thought she would be strong enough to get through this. Pain tears through every cell and nerve ending, but it comes from outside of her, opening its cavernous jaws and clamping down, carrying her off to another place. She has her eyes closed against the harsh light of the delivery room, but she can hear them talking.

'This one should have been straightforward,' the doctor mutters, sliding his stethoscope over Maggie's enormous belly. 'Heartbeat's there, but it's feeble.'

He hands the stethoscope to his colleague, who listens intently, then nods. 'Bit echoey; I don't think we can wait.'

From up on the ceiling, Maggie looks down at the woman and the people around her. There's something familiar about that great bloated body, but that is all.

'Wait!' the midwife shouts. 'It's crowning!'

Maggie lands back in her body; someone is trying to suffocate her and she fights the mask, which smells of hot rubber. Then she hears bumble bees, senses them buzzing in her nose and begins to feel a little calmer. *That's it*, a voice says, *good girl, deep breaths, ready for the next one.* Next what, Maggie thinks. Then the pain rips through her again. *Bear down now,* a voice says. *You can do it!*

She feels a mighty urge to expel the thing that is taking up two-thirds of her body, and that's when she remembers: she's having a baby. The deep-red curtains of pain pull back briefly. All these people, she thinks. Then the curtains close again, and she is sinking.

Come on, lass. You don't want us to have to cut it out, do you? They're shouting now: *Come on! One more push should do it.* Maggie makes a supreme effort, hears a noise coming from so low down inside her that it seems like another country, and then the pain changes, rushes up to the surface and burns as though she's passing a ball of fire.

The head is born and everybody seems pleased. *One more,* they say, *one more little push.* She feels it slither out of her and opens her eyes just in time to see them whisking it away. She remembers she's not supposed to look, but she catches a glimpse and it's not what she expected at all. Not pink and plump, but blue-grey and scrawny, like a bird thrown from the nest. There is no cry.

'Is it all right?' she asks the student midwife, who looks terrified and doesn't answer. The doctors huddle over the baby, poking around in its mouth, holding it upside down. She knows it's nothing to do with her, not now, but do they have to be so rough?

After all the noise and shouting, the delivery room is eerily silent. Apart from the little student who looks tearful, everyone is clustered around the baby, but Maggie can't see what they're doing. She asks again if it's all right, but they ignore her. She bites her lip. *Please don't let it be dead, I didn't mean to hate it, please don't let it be dead.*

Then, to her surprise, another pain grips her, forcing her back against the pillow and causing her to cry out.

The senior midwife, a stout, thunderous-looking woman, looks round from where she is helping attend to the baby. 'That'll be the afterbirth,' she tells the student. 'You can deliver it. Give her more gas and air and if it doesn't come away after three or four contractions, just knead her stomach.'

Maggie grabs the mask this time, hangs onto it like a life raft. She'd assumed the afterbirth was something that would just slip out, not this huge thing that she was going to have to 'deliver'. The next contraction reaches up, grips her and pulls her down into the depths. Bubbles of pain pop in front of her eyes. She barely rushes back up to the surface before it drags her down to its lair again, and this time she lets herself go with it, and finds that in doing so, she becomes oddly lucid. This, then, is her punishment for wanting to kill the baby, for thinking it a monster. The student midwife starts to pummel her stomach and Maggie lashes out, pushing her away.

'Don't make a fuss now. It's just to help bring the after-birth along,' the girl says, attempting the same patronising tone as the older midwife.

The next pain looms, and before Maggie closes her eyes – she needs to lock herself in – she sees the older midwife whisper to the student, and then she sees the young girl's tears. As her pain peaks, she opens her mouth and lets out a long, anguished cry. She has no reason to be brave.

But as her own cry subsides she hears another, high, furious and insistent, surrounded by whoops and cheers and well-dones and thank the lords and other things, in among which Maggie detects the 'she's and 'her's. So she has given birth to a little girl.

Again Maggie cranes her neck and tries to sit up, and they don't try to stop her. In their joy at having got the child breathing, they seem to have forgotten the instructions not to let the mother see it.

'She's perfect!' The student brushes a mascara-stained tear from her cheek. And Maggie sees the little squirmy thing, pink now, its cries settling to an outraged grizzle.

The older midwife comes over to the bed just as another pain begins to rise. 'Come along now,' she says, her tone impatient. 'This is taking too long.'

Maggie is about to yell that she can't bloody help it when the pain mutes her. The midwife starts to knead her stomach, then stops, turns to the student and adopts a teacher-like tone. 'What must we always check before delivering the afterbirth, Nurse?'

'But you said—'

'I repeat, what must we check before—'

'Oh, just shut up and get it out of me, *please*,' Maggie yells, then grabs the rubber mask and clamps it over her face.

'Quiet now, Mother,' the midwife says, and Maggie wants to scream *I'm not your bloody mother* but she needs all her energy to stay afloat in this ocean of pain.

'A twin!' the student says. 'We should always check for a twin.'

'That's right, now if you . . .'

Maggie feels the pain change, like it did before. It burns but not as brightly, and suddenly they are all around her again, both doctors, the midwife and the student, all shouting, all excited. And then she feels the same slithery feeling only all in one go this time, and they are lifting it up, another bruise-coloured thing, smeared with blood and greasy white, a thatch of golden hair. It cries immediately and fills up with life, its little face hot and red and screwed up in fury.

'Twins!' The young student is grinning, ecstatic. 'One of each!'

CHAPTER TWENTY-NINE

Jonathan sits in his mother's kitchen, trying not to shiver in his wet clothes. He looks at his birth certificate again. *Name and surname of father* is blank. *Name, surname and maiden surname of mother: Margaret Letitia Harrison.* Only a maiden surname. He pulls out the adoption order. *In respect of Jonathan Hugo Harrison*, it says, *an infant.* He wonders why they didn't change his first names, but he's glad; these are the names his birth mother gave him. It feels like some sort of connection with who he might really be. Beneath the clothes and papers there's a little lace-up boot made of soft red leather, a tiny knitted teddy bear, and a small bundle of something in a piece of black velvet, which he unwraps to reveal seven pebbles, all with holes in.

'It was just those few things,' his mother says as she brings the teapot to the table. 'The agency said they were to stay with you. You loved that teddy bear; and the little boot – the other one must have been lost before you came to us, but you hung on to that one for dear life. You never showed much interest in the stones, though; I suppose you'd picked them up on the beach near where you lived.'

'The beach? I thought I was born in Sheffield. Or wasn't that true either?'

His mother flinches.

'Sorry,' he says. 'I didn't mean to sound so—'

'You were. The short version of your birth certificate is accurate – your birth was registered in Sheffield. But when you came to us, it was definitely from East Sussex. We lived just outside Hastings then, but we moved; we didn't want to be too near your . . . your natural mother.'

'Hastings? So that's where you adopted me from?'

She nods as she lights a cigarette. Jonathan digs his thumbnails into his fingertips to stop himself reaching for one. He's been doing fairly well up until today, but now he wants to rip the filter off a full-strength Marlboro and smoke it down to the very last fibre.

'They wrote to say we'd been accepted, and a few days later, the lady from the agency telephoned. She said she was sure they'd find a match quite soon – they used to try to match the baby's hair and eye colour with that of the adoptive parents—'

'So there wouldn't be any awkward questions, no doubt.'

'Jonathan.' She looks at him steadily. 'Things were different then. There were so many babies coming up for adoption; so very many. Was it really wrong to try and minimise the physical differences between them and their new parents? Goodness, there were enough other differences people had to cope with.' She stands and switches on the light; the room has grown dark even though it's still only the middle of the afternoon.

He glances out of the window; a few flakes of snow are beginning to fall. It's the coldest January for twelve years, apparently. He thinks of the thick cardigan with the duckling buttons and wonders whether it was this cold in the winter of 1964, whether it was snowing on the day he'd become a Robson instead of a Harrison. He turns back to his mother.

'But why was I so . . . I mean, why was I the age I was?'

'I'm coming to that.' The edge of impatience to her voice is reassuring; her vulnerability is harder to cope with than the tetchiness he's used to.

'Mrs Wells from the agency – ever such a nice lady – said they'd probably have a match in a few weeks. They knew they had more babies coming in.' She glances up at him. 'I know; it does sound a bit like a shop, doesn't it? But they had their own mother and baby homes, you see. Anyway, Mrs Wells said it could be sooner if we were prepared to consider an older baby. They told me about you, and I said yes immediately. She told me to think about it, talk it over with Gerald. But I knew I wanted you. With the miscarriages, I'd already lost five babies, and you'd lost your mother . . .'

He starts and looks up, but she shakes her head. 'No, no, I'm sorry, I don't mean she'd passed on. She'd gone away somewhere apparently; left you with a brother.'

But he mishears her. 'I had a brother?'

'No, *her* brother. She didn't have any other children. She was quite young, I think.'

Momentarily, he pictures a brother, fourteen or fifteen; the two of them, stranded like orphans, depending on each other. He shakes away the fantasy sibling. 'So, what, she just got fed up with me and set off round the world?'

His mother shakes her head. 'I'm sorry, darling. I don't know the details.'

'And what about . . .' he feels his stomach contract, '. . . what about the man who . . . I mean, my biological father?'

She sighs. 'We never knew anything about him. I don't think they knew who he was.'

So, these people who created him: his father did something so bad that they're still looking for him forty years on, and his mother . . . had she known who his father was? Maybe she had; maybe she just kept his name off the birth certificate in order to protect him. What sort of woman did that make her? These were his parents.

'I wonder what he did?'

'What's that, dear?'

'My . . . the biological father; the one the police are still after. I'd like to know what I'm descended from.'

His mother clicks her tongue. 'I shouldn't think about that if I were you.'

'Mum, you can't always avoid difficult—'

'Darling, listen.' She reaches across the table and lays her hand on his. He almost pulls away, purely out of surprise. Her skin is cool and dry, the weight of her tiny hand negligible. 'Whatever it was, there's nothing that can be done about it now. That policeman, Mr Hutchinson, he said they never close these cases, but I don't know what good ever comes of raking up the past, I really don't.' She sighs and shakes her head. 'It's best to move on.' She looks at him. 'Isn't it?'

'I don't know. I don't even know what I'd be moving on *from*.'

As he prepares to leave, he sees her slide a small white envelope under the lid of the box. She looks more than tired, he thinks; she's haggard with exhaustion. He feels a powerful impulse to reassure her, but of what? Her status as his mother? His as her son? He should kiss her; embrace her, at least. But he hesitates and the moment is lost.

He drives a little way up the road before pulling over and taking out the envelope he saw her add to the box.

My dear Jonathan,

As I said this morning, I shall always regret not telling you sooner. You have a right to know who you are, and I hope you will be able to forgive me. Your father thought it was for the best; his manner of thinking was that if you knew the truth, you would never become a Robson, and as you know, the family name was very important to him. I went along with it at first – I suppose I thought we would tell you when you were older, but your father became agitated if I mentioned it. I've been thinking about it a lot since he passed away, and I believe he realised he'd made a dreadful mistake, but, as you know, he hated to admit he was wrong.

I am, I'm afraid, a little like your father in that I sometimes find it difficult to say kind things. I have been very foolish. It is rather late, I know, but please understand now that my love for you is as deep as that of any mother for her son.

He reads it twice before noticing that she hasn't signed it. He pictures her sitting at the dining-room table, agonising over whether to use the word 'Mum'. Still holding the note, he tips his head back against the seat and closes his eyes, both to shut out the image and to hold back the tears that are starting to form. Gerald often used to refer to her as 'Daphne' rather than 'your mother'; maybe he's even done the same himself. He hopes not; he really hopes not.

He swallows back the tears and sets off again, and as he does so his stomach growls; the last thing he ate was the greasy remains of a chicken chow mein at eight this morning. It's still only just gone three; how can so much have happened in so few hours?

CHAPTER THIRTY

When Maggie wakes, it is dusk, and the nurses are switching on the soft orange lights above the beds. She looks along the ward and sees that some of the women have babies by their sides. That's when she remembers. She summons every thread of strength she has left. 'Nurse!' she calls. 'Nurse! I've changed my mind; I'm going to keep them.'

'Don't be so silly,' the nurse says. 'You're just exhausted. You've been very poorly, but you'll feel better in the morning.'

Maggie starts to shout, demands to see her babies.

'Now, now, now.' The ward sister bustles in and smoothes the bedcovers. 'Whatever is this commotion, Mrs Harrison? You'll upset the other ladies.'

'It's Miss Harrison,' Maggie says weakly.

'I know, dear. It's a courtesy title. Now, what's all this nonsense? Are you going to settle down or am I going to have to call Matron?'

'I've changed my mind, Sister. I was going to have the baby adopted, but now it's twins and it's not their fault and they might have died and I'm their mother and I need to look after them and—'

'Hang on, there!' The sister holds up a palm. 'Slow down, now. You're bound to feel a little emotional for a few days – giving birth upsets the nerves, especially with young ladies in your particular situation. But you'll get over it. Why don't you get a good night's sleep—'

'No! I don't want to sleep. I want to see Matron. They're my babies and you've got no right to keep them from me, and if you—'

'That's enough, Mrs Harrison! Matron will be along directly, so save it for her.' Sister plumps the pillows and, Maggie is almost certain, smiles.

*

Three days later, Maggie looks up to see Dr Sarka walking down the ward. He's wearing a dark grey overcoat and a matching hat, which makes him seem taller. He removes the hat as soon as he spots her, and when he stands next to the bed, she can smell the faint spiciness of his skin and feel the cold on his clothes.

He asks how she is, and nods gravely when she says she's sore but not too bad, considering. Then he looks her in the eye and says that Matron has told him, and does Maggie really think she's being sensible. How will she cope with two babies and no husband, he asks, and what's more, no income?

Crossing her fingers, she tells him her brother will look after her. 'I know they all think I'm mad. Matron says I'll be denying them a happy life with proper parents. But I can be a proper parent, I know I can. It's not their fault they were born, and I can't just throw them away like last week's cheese.'

Dr Sarka sighs. 'Life can be difficult for unwed mothers,' he tells her, 'and for illegitimate children. You mustn't be afraid to change your mind again, you know.' He picks up his hat, bows slightly, and says he'll see her soon.

She nods, and thanks him. But she knows she won't change her mind.

Soon after Dr Sarka leaves, Vanda pops in on her way to work. She's wearing an old army greatcoat and brown Crimplene slacks, but Maggie can see that underneath, she's wearing her stage costume, a turquoise sequinned one-piece that she usually wears with glittery silver tights. Vanda kisses her and hands her a bag of oranges and a bar of chocolate.

'Lovely, thanks. Where's Boris?'

'In his bag on the back seat of the taxi. Hope he doesn't wake up!'

They both smile.

'Van,' Maggie says, 'I . . . I've decided to keep them.'

Vanda's mouth drops open. It's the first time Maggie has seen her literally speechless.

'But you can't', she says eventually. 'What will you live on? *Where* will you live?'

Maggie reassures her that she'll move out as soon as

she leaves hospital. She'll probably go back to Hastings to stay with Leonard, she explains, at least for the time being. Then she falls silent. She wishes she felt as confident as she sounds. She's written to tell Leonard she's keeping the babies, but the letter only went yesterday and she's not sure how he'll react.

'I've asked Leonard to employ me as his housekeeper, at least until the twins are old enough for nursery. He's been paying a daily ever since I left, and he never wanted me to move away in the first place, so it should be all right.'

Vanda nods slowly. 'I can't say I won't miss you.'

'Me too.' A wave of sadness washes over her. She'd arrived in Sheffield so full of plans and dreams. This was going to be her home; a new place, a new self. 'Thanks for letting me stay, and for everything else – you know, before.'

Vanda waves the words away, seems about to speak but then hesitates.

'What is it?' Maggie asks.

'Well, I was thinking, what if the babies, I mean what if they start to look like . . .'

Maggie shakes her head. 'They're nothing to do with him. Nothing!' After a pause, she glances up and down the ward. All the nurses are busy with the new mother who came in during the night, pale, bruised-looking and exhausted, just as Maggie had been a few days ago. 'Would you like to see them?' she whispers.

Vanda nods. 'Are we allowed?'

'Not really. I'm only supposed to go to the nursery when it's feeding time.'

'Sounds like a zoo,' Vanda says.

'Smells like one as well,' Maggie laughs. It's so long since she's done so that she is acutely aware of the unfamiliar sensation in her facial muscles.

The twins lie facing each other in the cot, curled into one another like the petals of a tulip. They have to sleep together, according to the nursery nurse, or they 'get right mardy, rooaring and carrying on like it's end o't world.'

'What a pair of little poppets.' Vanda's face softens as she gazes at the sleeping babies.

Maggie reaches into the cot, suddenly craving the warmth of a newborn infant in her arms. When she'd held her babies for the first time – once the staff had finally accepted that she was determined to keep them – she'd been enchanted by the weight of each tiny head resting against her shoulder, intoxicated by the warm, talcum-powdery smell of her son's skin, the salty damp- ness of her daughter's hair. Her son; her daughter; how could she have considered giving them away?

'Mother! What are you doing out of bed?'

Maggie snatches her hand back. 'Sorry, Matron, I—'

'Nurse will fetch you when Baby needs feeding. Now run along.'

Hot tears gather in Maggie's eyes. How can Matron have already forgotten there are two babies, not one? And isn't *run along* the most ridiculous thing you can say to a new mother? As she makes her way slowly back along the ward, placing one foot carefully in front of the other, she wonders if she'll ever be able to walk normally again.

CHAPTER THIRTY-ONE

The familiar green and cream sign of the Blackheath Tea Hut comes into view. There are three lorries parked on the grass alongside the hut, plus a couple of vans, a taxi, a horsebox and a police car. Some of the drivers stand around warming their hands on polystyrene cups, others sit in their vehicles. This place is always busy, day and night, whatever the weather. Jonathan pulls over and gets out of the car. By the look of the purple clouds skulking above the treetops, it's going to snow properly soon. There's been nothing but rain and sleet for days, but the air is different now, it's drying out, sharpening. He buys tea and a bacon roll and sits back in the car. He should go home. He pictures himself sitting in the living room, watching telly with a tray on his lap, and he can hardly bear the thought. The house is just a symbol of his failure: he's in it all day instead of being out there earning a living, and Fiona *isn't* in it. He chews and swallows mechanically, barely tasting the food. This time yesterday, he was Jonathan Robson, son of Daphne and Gerald. A few weeks ago, although life hadn't been perfect, he'd been a full-time teacher of English, with a wife who loved him and wanted to be with him.

His phone rings and he grabs it, certain it'll be her.

'Mr Robson? Don Hutchinson here. Sorry to trouble you again, but I was wondering if you'd spoken to your mum yet?'

Jonathan sighs. 'I've just come from there.'

'So you'll be aware, then . . . ?'

He lets the silence spool out.

'I mean, you've had a chat, you and your mum?'

Oh, what the hell; it's not Hutchinson's fault. 'Yes, she told me. I'm adopted. So it's not my father – the man I thought was my father. So what now?' There's a pause, and then he hears the sound of crunching. Hutchinson and his bloody Polos.

'That's why I'm calling. I'm sorry to hassle you, but I need to ask whether you're planning to trace your real parents—'

'They're not my real parents.'

'Sorry – bad choice of words; your biological parents.'

Jonathan sighs again. 'I've no idea at the moment. I don't know my biological father's name, so there's no chance of tracing him without finding my mother first – that's if she even knows who he is.'

'I'm aware that it's a tough time for you, but I'm afraid I still have a job to do. Given the familial link with your

DNA, it's essential that I talk to your mother – your birth mother, I mean. You have a legal right to see your adoption file, so . . .'

'Look, to be honest, I'm still trying to get my head round the whole thing.'

There's another pause before Hutchinson speaks again, his voice softer, a hint of sympathy. 'Just keep me posted, eh? I'll be in touch.'

Jonathan finishes his tea, throws the empty cup onto the passenger seat and pulls out onto the A2, but instead of driving across the heath towards home, he soon finds himself driving up the long road that leads to the school. The kids must have been out for a while, because they're already piling into the sweet shop and crowding around the bus stops. He carries on up the hill, but then has to swerve so sharply to avoid a speeding red and white Mini that he almost hits a parked car – it's so close he actually braces himself for the impact. That's the last thing he needs. He was lucky last time – the woman who owned the Volvo was more than reasonable about the whole thing, but he can just imagine PC Clark's smug grin if it happened a second time.

At the top, he pulls over and turns off the engine. God knows how fast that Mini must have been going – and right near a school, too. Boy racers; probably not much older than some of the kids in school. He finds himself watching the kids as they pass, searching the faces for Ryan's arrogant stare. Most of them have already gone, so it's just the stragglers now. What is he doing here anyway? He's just about to start the engine again when he spots Chloé Nichols, sauntering down the middle of the road with her mates, bag slung over her shoulder, not a care in the world by the looks of her; planning her weekend, most likely. If she hadn't backed up Ryan's story, the whole thing would be over by now. He almost certainly wouldn't have been arrested; and if he hadn't been arrested, they'd never have taken his DNA, and if they hadn't . . . Christ, had she any idea what she'd started? And all because she had the hots for Ryan bloody Jenkins. What if he went over and spoke to her? *You're a bright kid, Chloé, why lie for Ryan?* Chloé shrieks with laughter at something her friend is saying, then she tosses her hair and hitches her bag up on her shoulder. Does she have *any* idea? He gets out of the car and lets the door fall shut without locking it, then he begins to walk across the tarmac towards Chloé and her friends. There are a few teachers walking down the hill, some of whom he knows. Well, so what? It's a free country.

Chloé looks up as he approaches; her eyes meet his.

He doesn't look away, but he can't quite read Chloé's expression. The next second there's a red blur to his left, a screech of brakes, and then Chloé is flying through the air like the Christmas angels in the shopping centre. She seems to sit briefly on the wing of the Mini before rolling over the bonnet and landing in the road with a thud. Time holds its breath as Jonathan takes a step forward; in a split-second he takes in several things: the red Mini is full of passengers; Chloé's leg is twisted under her; there's blood on her cheek and her blonde hair is streaked with mud. He moves nearer and then becomes aware of another blur to his left. A second high-speed car is plough-ing straight towards them. Chloé's friends scream. He bounds forward, grabs her by the ankle of her boot and pulls, yanks her hard so that her head bobs on the ground as her hair trails through a puddle. It flashes into his mind that you're not supposed to move someone who's been hit by a car; what if there's a spinal injury? What if she's in a wheelchair for the rest of her life and it's his fault? Even as he thinks these thoughts, he's aware of the strange trick that time is playing on him. How can he be thinking all these things in this micro-millisecond? He's read about this phenomenon somewhere; it's to do with the brain speeding up the thought processes when under stress; there's a name for it. The wheel of the second car comes so close to Chloé's head that he half-expects to see tyre tracks on her hair. Unlike the first car, this one doesn't brake or even slow, but accelerates away, leaving only the reverberating echo of its jumbo-sized exhaust.

*

By the time Chloé is taken off to hospital and the police have taken statements, it's completely dark and begin-ning to snow again. Jonathan sits in his car. They all saw him pull Chloé out of the path of the second car. He's a minor hero. Joyriders, the police said, the same two cars that had been reported earlier in the day, racing each other on Shooters Hill. One of them had mounted the pavement and run over an elderly Labrador. 'Heartless bastards never even stopped,' the copper said, shaking his head. Jonathan didn't point out that they hadn't stopped after hitting Chloé either.

He takes out his phone to call Fiona, but she probably wouldn't answer so he puts it away again, starts the engine and heads home, though the thought of walking into the empty house makes him feel almost achingly bleak. As he drives across Blackheath, huge white discs of snow begin to fall, lightly at first, then heavier, and soon it seems like a billion flakes are falling around the car. On the far side of the heath he can see All Saints' Church, impressively lit from below so its tall spire glows golden against the darkened sky; a white crust is beginning to settle Christmas-card-like on its many sloping roofs. Further on, orange light spills out of the pub onto the snow-dusted wooden tables on the forecourt. He imagines pushing open the doors and hearing the hubbub of conversation, the clink of glasses and the familiar smell of beer and old wood. The idea is attractive. But at some point, he'd have to come out of the warmth and back into the real world. There would be more snow on the ground by then, more of the landscape obscured; but everything would be the same underneath.

After finding no one in at Malcolm and Cassie's, he considers going over to Lucy and Matt's, but it doesn't seem appropriate somehow. So he drives aimlessly for over an hour, not really noticing his route, just allowing himself to be soothed by the falling snow, the passing headlamps of the other cars, the rhythm of the wind-screen wipers. Eventually, he finds himself in Brockley, where he'd lived with Sian. Apart from a few new shops and cafés, the area is unchanged. He slows as he approaches the old wine bar, then hits the indicator, pulls over and gets out of the car. Maybe someone he knows from the old days would be there, someone to talk to. He peers into the dimly lit interior, but instead of the cheery crowd he'd anticipated, there are just a few early evening drinkers standing at the bar, still in suits, laptops and briefcases resting on the high stools next to them. The tables are empty apart from a tired-looking man of about thirty who sits alone, staring out of the window. A copy of *The Times* lies unopened in front of him and he's about two-thirds of the way through a bottle of red. No one in the place seems to be talking; no one is smiling. Jonathan gets back into the car and pulls away.

A couple of years after they'd spilt up, he'd bumped into Sian in Greenwich. What had she told him about the flat they'd rented overlooking Hilly Fields? She'd definitely stayed on there after he left. Had she bought the place? Yes, he's sure she'd mentioned a mortgage, a boyfriend who wanted to settle. She's probably moved away by now. He turns into the crescent and drives halfway up. There it is; and there's a light on in the living room.

CHAPTER THIRTY-TWO

Maggie names the twins Elizabeth and Jonathan. When she feels their tiny fingers curl around her own, when she smells their vanilla-scented skin and wonders at their navy-blue eyes and miniature shell-pink toenails, she marvels at such perfection; such exquisite innocence.

After watching some of the proper mothers, Maggie decides to try feeding the twins herself. Elizabeth's reluctance causes some concern, and she needs to be 'topped up' with powdered milk, but with a little help from Sister, a routine is established. Despite the initial hostility caused by her lack of wedding ring, Maggie forms a tentative friendship with the woman in the next bed. Pearl is older than the other mothers, with a round, doughy face which is not flattered by the severe cut of her greying hair; her arms are pudgy and her sturdy legs are spidered with purple thread veins. This is her fifth child – the first girl – so she knows what she's doing. She shows Maggie three different ways to fold a nappy, and also how to swaddle the twins, *so's they feel all snug and safe like as when they was inside you*. When her husband, a thin, balding man clearly older than Pearl, comes in on the dot of seven every evening, Pearl smiles girlishly and her face becomes young and glowing and as pretty as her namesake. Maggie watches them, holding hands the whole time, their faces so close they're almost touching. Their tenderness almost makes her weep.

When Pearl goes home, she comes over to say goodbye and to wish Maggie luck. She's holding a large bag. 'I got Bert to bring in a few of ' boys' old things,' she says. 'There's rompers and nightdresses and leggings and the like. Mostly blue, I'm afraid, but they might save thi a bob or two, just until thi gets on tha feet.'

Maggie takes the bag of clothes and looks inside. There's much more than Pearl mentioned; she can see vests, matinee jackets, bonnets, bootees, all in the most delicate blue or the snowiest white. 'Oh, Pearl,' she says. 'These are beautiful. But don't you want some of the white things for little Anne?'

Pearl laughs and shakes her head. 'Not on tha nelly. After four lads on't trot, I've made me mind up; our Anne's wearing nowt but pink frocks and frilly bonnets until she's twenty-one at least.'

A few days before Maggie and the twins are discharged, Vanda brings in two little matching outfits that she has knitted herself – leggings, matinee jackets, hats and bootees, both in the softest, palest lemon wool.

'They're beautiful.' Maggie looks in wonder at the tiny bootees. 'I didn't know you could knit.'

'I used to knit all the time as a kid, scarves and shawls mostly, then baby clothes as I got older – I loved doing matinee jackets. Always thought I'd have lots of children, see? Listen, I've been thinking. Why don't you stay on with me for a while? I'd have to put the rent up a bit if it was going to be long-term, but I could babysit during the day so you could get a few hours' work, and – well, we could just see how we go.'

*

Vanda collects Maggie and the twins from the hospital in a taxi. She's made a few preparations, she says. There is a large, old-fashioned pram waiting in the back room, donated by the lady next door who's had it in her attic for nigh on twenty years, 'but ' lass is welcome to it,' she'd told Vanda. 'It's hard enough with one babby, never mind two.' Upstairs in Maggie's room, two deep drawers have been turned into makeshift cribs. Vanda has made little mattresses by stitching together layers of an old eiderdown and there are proper white cot sheets, knitted blankets and quilted white coverlets, one trimmed with pink ribbon, one with blue. The pillowcases are embroidered with blue-birds and sprays of flowers, and tucked under each coverlet is a tiny teddy bear, knitted in honey-coloured wool. Maggie's throat tightens. She feels strangely raw now she's out of hospital, as though some of her outer layers are missing. She trails her hand along the edge of one of the drawers. 'They're like little nests,' she says, feeling her voice break.

That night, the babies are unsettled. As soon as one goes to sleep, the other starts crying. The house is cold, especially compared to the sheltered warmth of the hospital ward, and Maggie shivers as she paces the floor, first with Jonathan, then Elizabeth. For the first time, a sliver of doubt creeps in; she hopes to God she's done the right thing.

CHAPTER THIRTY-THREE

Sian has gained weight. He remembers her as having a rather boyish figure – straight up and down and flat-chested. She's short, like Fiona, but she was always incredibly strong and athletic – she'd have beaten him in an arm-wrestle any day. Now she looks softer and more rounded. 'You look well,' he says as she pours red wine into chunky blue goblets. The flat looks different. *Of course it's different after nearly twelve years, idiot!* There's a proper Victorian fireplace with a real fire flickering in the grate; an oversized rectangular mirror hangs above the fireplace.

She grins. 'Hmm – is that a euphemism for fat?' She's wearing a long purple skirt with a baggy red jumper and a purple headband to keep her curly dark hair off her face; she always did love purple.

He shakes his head. 'No, not at all. It suits you—'

'Don't worry, Jon,' she laughs, and he catches a glimpse

of a gold tooth. That's new. 'You won't offend me. It was giving up that job at Martino's that did it. All the time I worked in a kitchen, I hardly ate a thing. The minute I left, it was like I'd suddenly remembered you can eat food as well as cook it.'

He smiles. They'd met at Martino's. Sian had been a chef for a couple of years, but it was Jonathan's first night in a kitchen, and it had been terrifying. No one bothered to introduce him, he was just shown into the basement and told to make himself useful. The windowless room was sweltering, steamy and chaotic. The massive stainless-steel sink was already heaped with giant-sized mixing bowls, pots and colanders. A battered radio in the corner played inane pop music, although he hadn't even noticed it at first because of all the shouting and crashing of pans. The owner came thundering down the stairs. 'Where the fuck are table four's starters?' he barked at Sian, who was standing in the centre of the room by the industrial cooker, a blue striped apron tied over her chef's whites, tea towel slung over her shoulder. 'And table six is leaving if their mains aren't there in three minutes flat.'

'Give me a break, Martino,' she shouted back without looking up. She was shaking a pan with one hand and turning fish on the griddle with the other. 'I'm going as fast as I can.'

Minutes later, Martino came down the stairs again, this time carrying two plates, which he banged down on the stainless-steel worktop. 'Table nine wanted theirs well done and there's still blood running out of this.' Again

Sian answered without missing a beat. 'Tell the peasants to go to a steak house if they want a well-done fillet. This is a restaurant, not a fucking crematorium.'

Jonathan had walked over to her then and there. 'Do you – would you fancy coming for a drink with me?'

She turned to look at him. Her eyes were startlingly mismatched, one a conker brown, the other hazel. She flicked her gaze down his body then up again. 'You're a bit previous, aren't you? What's your name?'

'Jonathan. Jonathan Robson.' He squirmed at the eagerness in his voice.

She'd weighed him up for a moment. 'Go on then, Jonathan Robson; I'll have a drink with you.'

He feels himself colour as he remembers what had happened after that drink, and he has to shake his head to rid himself of the pornographic images that are now romping across his memory.

'I put on even more weight when I got married,' Sian was saying. 'Everyone said it was "contentment", but it was more down to misery.'

'I'm sorry it didn't work out.'

She shrugs. 'Some you win; some you lose. So.' She tucks her legs underneath her as she curls onto the sofa beside him. 'Come on then; tell me all about it.'

He'd forgotten how hypnotic those eyes were; when she turned them on you, you were compelled to bare your soul. First he tells her about Chloé, how he'd dragged her clear of the car, and how he'd been worried about her spine until the paramedics reassured him.

'Bloody hell.' Sian uncurls herself and sits up straight, her face a study in concern. 'You're probably still in shock; do you want a brandy?'

He smiles; the famous medicinal brandy again. 'No.' He shakes his head. 'No thanks.' He nods towards the wine. 'This seems to be doing the trick.' Then he tells her about the baby, and how worried he is about being a crap father.

'But I thought you didn't want kids?' she says, and for a moment, a silence opens up between them as each remembers the last unhappy days of their time together. 'Anyway, sorry.' She turns away to refill her glass. 'You were saying.'

Then he tells her the rest: how he'd lost his rag with Ryan, the arrest, the DNA and Hutchinson, and finally his mother's revelation this morning – *this morning? Surely not only this morning?* 'So basically, the only clues I have as to the genes I'm passing on is the fact that my father's still wanted by the police and my mother's name was Margaret Harrison – and she dumped me when I was a toddler.'

'Wow.' Sian lets out a slow, whistling breath. 'That's quite a story.'

He takes a long swallow of the spicy wine, then twirls his glass around as he looks into its depths. 'This afternoon,' he says after a minute, 'when I saw Chloé Nichols coming out of school, I felt – for a moment, anyway – I felt physically violent, like I wanted to hit her.' He carries on twirling his glass, and then he looks up. 'What if . . . I mean, what if I can't control it? What if it's an inherited trait or something?'

'I think you're reading too much into it. Everyone feels like that occasionally. And not only that, but you're under a lot of pressure and you've had some almighty shocks.' She takes a sip of her drink. 'What are you going to do? I mean about your birth parents?'

Threads from an unknown past are tangling together into a knot deep in his guts; he wants to reach down inside himself, tear it out and throw it into the fire. But it's started to take hold and grow, like an oily black cancer. He empties his glass and allows Sian to refill it. 'I don't know.' He sighs again. 'I really don't know.'

When he was little, he'd been convinced there was a monster in his wardrobe. 'Oh, for the love of Mike,' his father had said, stalking across the room so the windows rattled. 'There are no such things as monsters.' Jonathan, curled tightly under the covers, heard the squeak and bang as his father wrenched open the wardrobe doors and flung them wide. 'See?' Gerald's voice boomed. 'Nothing but clothes. Now stop being such a sissy and go to sleep.'

But Jonathan never did know for sure, because he'd averted his eyes at the last minute in case the dark, shapeless thing he saw there was too terrible to behold.

'Hey, let's dial out for a pizza,' Sian says, getting to her feet. 'No one can deal with that sort of trauma on an empty stomach.' She stops and turns to him. 'Or will Fiona have something ready for you?'

'Actually, Fiona's . . . she's staying with her mum for a few days.' He tries to laugh. 'You know, so the grandma-to-be can fuss around her a bit.' He avoids her gaze so she won't see the truth. What was that he'd read about lying and body language? You look to the left if you're recalling something, and to the right if you're making it up. Sian pauses only briefly before picking up the phone. 'That's all right then,' she says. 'Veggie or full-on carnivore?'

After they've eaten, he puts his head back against the sofa and closes his eyes. He can hear the fire spitting and crackling in the hearth, and he can smell Sian's perfume, a familiar, woody scent – sandalwood. She always used to put sandalwood oil in her bath; so that hasn't changed. But Sian has; she's softer, less prickly than he remembers. She moves closer and leans back. Her hair touches his cheek and then he feels the warm weight of her head on his shoulder. He takes a breath. 'I should make a move.'

'In this weather?' she says. 'Don't talk bollocks.'

Now that's more like the old Sian. He opens his eyes. She's sitting forward now, looking at him, the glow of firelight on her cheek and a golden flame dancing in each of her eyes. She lays her hand on his thigh. 'It's been so nice,' she murmurs. 'Why not stay? I mean,' she moves closer, 'with me?'

More images tumble through his brain. He wonders if she still sleeps naked, even in the winter; if she still checks under the bed for spiders every night; if she still occasionally cries in her sleep.

'Sian, I'm sorry. I shouldn't have come.' He starts to get to his feet. 'It was thoughtless of me, coming here, dumping all this on you. I – I'm not saying I wouldn't like to stay, it's just that . . .' He knocks his glass over. 'Shit, sorry. I'm an idiot. I hope you don't think—'

'Don't worry. It was empty.'

'No, I meant—'

'Oh, put a sock in it, for fuck's sake,' she says, standing up. Her voice is clipped and hard now. She goes out of the room.

Why had he come here? He looks around. This was once his home, but he has no connection with it any more; nor with Sian.

When she returns, her voice has softened. 'Here.' She throws a bundled-up duvet onto the sofa. 'You've had a bottle of wine; you shouldn't drive. That thing pulls out into a bed.'

'No, look, I'm sorry. I'll get a cab—'

'You'll do no such thing. Get some kip and I promise I won't creep in and take advantage of you.'

He smiles. 'Thanks, Sian.'

*

Ten past three and he hasn't slept a wink. The fire's gone out now and the room is freezing. How can he face Sian in the morning? Yet again, he's managed to think only about himself; turning up on her doorstep, accepting wine and food and virtually crying on her shoulder in the flickering firelight; what did he expect? He gets up, pulls on his jeans and sweatshirt and then scrabbles around the room for a pen and paper.

Feel very sober and very stupid. Sorry for turning up out of the blue and behaving like a twat. Thanks for letting me talk. Jon

He puts the note on the coffee table, then folds up the sofa bed and duvet. Before he leaves, he goes back and adds a kiss after *Jon*, and as he clicks the front door shut behind him, he wonders whether he should have done that.

With the moonlight and the vast expanse of snow on the fields opposite the flat, it is almost like daylight outside. A line from a poem pops into his head: *The moon on the breast of the new-fallen snow gave the lustre of midday to objects below.* As he walks to the car, his footsteps squeak in the powdery snow. When he stops, there is no sound or movement, just him, incongruous, clumsily dark and uneven against a smooth white background. Not part of it, but alien; an interloper.

CHAPTER THIRTY-FOUR

Maggie hadn't planned to go back to Hastings, not so soon anyway. But there's no alternative. Leonard drives up in early February to collect them. The drive takes twice as long as usual because of the snow. It's even worse in the south, he says. They've had drifts fifteen feet deep, and the sea froze last week. It's a record, according to the BBC.

The twins, now twelve weeks old, are sleeping at either end of their extra-large carrycot, which is wedged on the back seat of Leonard's packed-to-bursting Morris Traveller. Vanda leans in and kisses them, slipping a five-pound note under the coverlet when she thinks Maggie isn't looking. Maggie tries not to cry as she hugs Vanda goodbye. This wasn't the plan; this wasn't what was supposed to happen.

Everything had been all right before Christmas – that was when the snow started. It had seemed magical at first, and late on Christmas night, Maggie had stood at the back door, blowing her cigarette smoke out into the freezing night and watching the lacy flakes float down, fast and silent like a moving Christmas card. The world seemed to quieten by the second, a soft white hush settling over the little back yard and on the rooftops beyond. Someday, she would take her children out into their own back garden and show them how to build a snowman.

On Boxing Day, Una, Jimmy and a few of the others had turned up. Maggie hadn't expected to see any of them again, yet here they were, treating her like an old friend. No one called her 'Little Mags' now. With the tree lights twinkling and Christmas records playing on the radiogram, they'd sipped whisky, eaten Maggie's mince pies and played endless games that no one but Jimmy seemed to have heard of. Una volunteered to give Elizabeth her top-up bottle, but swiftly handed her back when she regurgitated most of it. 'Darling! I'm *so* sorry,' Una said, holding Elizabeth at arm's length. 'I appear to have spilt your baby.'

Later, after they'd all gone, Maggie and Vanda watched the Dick Van Dyke show on television. Maggie took out her sewing box to finish repairing Vanda's costume. She and Vanda made a good team, she thought. Money was tight now, but once the twins were older, she'd be able to bring more in.

When the show finished, Vanda stood up, stretched, and turned the set off. Maggie watched the white dot shrink and disappear while Vanda wandered over to the window and lifted the net curtain. 'It's getting heavy; I'd better go and get ready – it's going to be a bugger getting across town in this.'

Maggie folded the sequinned costume and packed it along with the green shoes and the heavy bag of make-up. Then she tidied up a bit, made a turkey sandwich for Vanda to take with her and put more coal on the fire. She'd just begun to wonder why Vanda was taking so long when she heard her footsteps on the stairs, slow, one step at a time, not the way Vanda usually clattered up and down stairs at all.

'Hurry up,' Maggie said. 'You'll be—'

'He's dead. Boris is dead.'

*

Vanda cried for two days.

'It's only a bloody snake,' Leonard said when Maggie rang him on New Year's Eve. 'I mean, I could understand her being upset about losing a faithful old dog, but—'

'Boris was a faithful old snake. It was probably old age, but she thinks he froze to death because she forgot to check the bulbs on Christmas Day. And don't forget he's been her livelihood for seventeen years. In fact, without Boris . . .'

'So what's she going to do for money now? What are *you* going to do?'

*

As they drive slowly out of the still-frozen city, she is struck by how unfamiliar the town looks. The snow changes the shape of the buildings and trees, makes everything bigger and startling white against the inky sky. On her way into Sheffield just over a year ago, she'd noticed the dark stone buildings, blackened by smoke from the steelworks, and the giant furnaces, casting an orange glow on the skyline. At twenty-one, ambitious and eager to make her mark, that view had symbolised industry, the busy-ness of getting on with life rather than waiting for it to start.

Now it's as though that Maggie was another person. She turns and looks over into the back seat; the twins look different somehow. There's something vivid about their faces; something more demanding, more real.

They've only travelled about thirty miles when it starts again. At first, there are big, heavy flakes that fall straight to the ground, but then the wind gets up and soon they're driving through a blizzard, snow flying at them horizontally then swirling in front of the car so they can't see more than a few feet ahead. After three hours, they're still only just past Chesterfield. They pull into a roadside café so that Maggie can feed the babies. Leonard goes inside to get their bottles warmed while Maggie attempts to give them their breastfeed. Elizabeth won't latch on, so Maggie ignores her pathetic little mewling noises while she feeds Jonathan instead. Mercifully, he takes his feed, burps, and goes back to sleep. She tries Elizabeth again, but although she roots frantically for the nipple, as soon as she finds it, she spits it out in disgust. 'Come on, darling,' Maggie coos. 'Have some of Mummy's milk.' But Elizabeth's bottom lip juts forward and she starts to howl.

Maggie is on the verge of tears when Leonard comes back to the car. He averts his eyes as he climbs into the front seat.

'Thank God for that,' she takes one of the bottles. 'Here you are, sweetheart. Is this what you wanted?' But Elizabeth twists and pulls away, her crying reaching an even higher pitch.

'Oh, for Pete's sake,' Leonard says after a few moments. 'Give her here and go and warm yourself up a bit.'

Elizabeth stops crying almost as soon as Leonard takes her. 'See,' he smiles, as Elizabeth settles immediately to her bottle. 'You just need the magic touch.'

She hates me, Maggie thinks as she makes her way carefully across the café's frozen forecourt. She doesn't want me as her mother.

The warmth of the café is cheering, even though the place is empty. Maggie lights a cigarette and drinks her tea, ignoring the lipstick mark and sugar crystals around the edge of the cup. With each sip, and each puff of her cigarette, she is further revived.

Vanda hadn't had the heart to train a new snake. She'd worked a few extra shifts at the pub, but it wasn't enough. Maybe if it hadn't been for this endless snow . . .

One night soon after Christmas, Vanda had set off for

work as usual, dressed in a fur coat and hat, leather gloves, a knitted scarf and gumboots with two pairs of thick socks over her stockings. Less than half an hour later, she was back. Maggie had been huddled in front of the gas stove trying to warm her chapped hands when the back door opened and Vanda leapt in, a flurry of snow blowing in after her. 'The beer's frozen,' she said. 'First time in living memory, apparently. They're closing until the weather lets up.' She stomped her feet to get the snow off her boots. 'So there'll be no wages for a while.'

Maggie filled the kettle for tea. 'I've still got a bit in the post office,' she offered.

'That's if we can *get* to the bloody post office.' Vanda peeled off her gloves and blew into her hands. 'It's probably closed. Everything else is.'

Even when the pub reopened, the takings were down and the landlord cut Vanda's shifts to four a week, then two. So she started at the sweet factory. Maggie smiles at this memory. Poor Vanda. At the end of her first day, she'd stumbled home through the snow, reeling and giggling as though drunk. 'God, I feel peculiar,' she said as she fell into the house. Then her skin turned pale and she passed out on the back-room floor.

'Vanda!' Maggie knelt next to her and shook her. 'Vanda, are you all right?'

Vanda stirred, burped, and then scrabbled to her feet, only just making it to the back door to be violently sick. When Maggie asked if it might have been something she ate, she admitted to having consumed a lot of uncooked sweets at work. 'My supervisor said I could eat as many as I liked – perks of the job. I was preparing them for the oven, see, and they were so soft and gooey, I just kept popping them into my mouth.' She paused and her skin seemed to fade again. 'God, I must have eaten about thirty or forty of the things.' She groaned. 'I need to go to bed. My head's going to come off.'

Although she still felt rough the next day, she went to the factory, but was only out of the house for two hours before she was back, looking a delicate shade of green. Maggie fetched her a glass of water and a blanket so she could lie on the settee.

'You'll never guess,' Vanda said in a feeble voice. 'You know I told you how I ate all those raw sweets? They were Victory Vs; seems they contain ether – and chloroform. All right when they're cooked, but . . .'

'No wonder you were ill. Isn't that what they use to knock people out?'

Vanda nodded, closing her eyes.

'You didn't eat more today, surely?'

'No, it's the fumes. They make the mixture in these huge vats and even the smell makes me ill.' She let out a weak groan. 'Can you bring me a bucket?'

Vanda didn't return to the factory. Three weeks later, she took a job at the Picture House as an usherette, permanent, but badly paid, and so when she came into Maggie's room a week or so later and said, 'I need to talk to you,' Maggie knew what was coming.

'I'm behind with the rent already and it could take

months to find a better-paid job. I'm . . .' She sighed. 'I'm going to have to take a room instead. I'm sorry, Maggie.' She looked at the floor. 'You'll be able to go back to Hastings, won't you?'

*

They make three more stops along the way, twice so Maggie can feed the twins and once so Leonard can buy another pair of socks because his feet are so cold he can no longer feel them. The twins, huddled together under the patchwork coverlet Vanda knitted, are warm as toast and by some miracle, or perhaps lulled by the movement of the car, they are quiet. Jonathan sleeps peacefully, the odd windy smile pulling up the corners of his mouth, but Elizabeth's eyes are wide open. 'Hello, darling,' Maggie whispers. Elizabeth blinks, but does not return Maggie's smile. She's watching me, Maggie thinks; weighing me up.

Maggie tries to doze but she can feel her daughter's eyes on her as she drowses. She's becoming increasingly certain that Elizabeth is cleverer, wiser than her, and that her purpose for being here is to replace Maggie, to become properly what Maggie has failed to be.

CHAPTER THIRTY-FIVE

'Fi, can we just talk, please?'

She's standing at the sink, her back rigid as though the muscles themselves are angry. They'd had a shouting match last night, and she'd gone to the spare room, slamming the door so violently that next door banged on the wall. It was only after she'd gone to bed that he'd spotted the little pile of new cookery books on the kitchen worktop. He hadn't noticed them before. He'd looked at each colourful, glossy jacket: *The New Baby and Toddler Cookbook, Organic Baby Food from Scratch,* and the one that really made him want to hug her: *Cookery for Beginners.*

Right now, though, she doesn't look very huggable. She hurls the potato she's just peeled into the sink, picks up another and begins gouging its eyes out. 'What is there to talk about? I go away for a few days and as soon as—'

'Eleven.'

'What?'

'Eleven days; you were away for eleven days. That's more than "a few".'

'Whatever. The point is that the minute my back's turned, you're off sniffing round your ex-girlfriend.'

'Don't be disgusting.'

'Me? *Me*, disgusting? That's rich, coming from you.'

'Christ, can't you stop that for a minute and come and sit down?'

'No.' She scalps another potato and throws it into the bowl.

'Fiona, listen to me.' He bangs his fist on the table. 'I didn't sleep with her, all right? Ask her. Just fucking ring her up and ask her.'

She spins round to face him. 'Oh, so you've taken her number, then?'

Their eyes lock for a moment. 'No, actually; no, I haven't.'

There's a heavy silence as they each try to think what to say next.

'Fiona,' he says more quietly. 'I swear to God, there's nothing going on and I didn't sleep with her. I shouldn't have gone round there, I know that. It was stupid and thoughtless. I didn't even intend to end up in Brockley. But after everything that happened yesterday, I couldn't think straight. I just drove around because I couldn't face coming home to an empty house.'

'I was here.'

'I didn't know that, did I?'

More silence.

'I called you.'

The flame has gone from her voice. He takes a step towards her and she doesn't back away. 'I'm truly, truly sorry. Please let's not argue any more; at least for a while.' He risks a smile; she almost smiles back.

*

Over the next few days, Hutchinson leaves several messages, but Jonathan ignores them. He's more concerned with not messing up his marriage any more than he has already. Fiona seems quite agitated, though. 'I'd understand if you made a firm decision not to go any further,' she says, 'but I don't get this . . . dithering. Surely it's best to just find out whatever there is to know?'

He doesn't say anything. He doesn't want to get into another row, not when she's only been back a week and they're just beginning to get close again.

'Anyway.' She hands him a slip of paper. 'He called again when you were out. These are his work, home and mobile numbers – says he's left four messages.'

He folds the note, shoves it into his back pocket and picks up the local paper.

'Well? Aren't you going to call him?'

'I don't know. Not yet.' He starts reading the match reports.

'Jonno.' She comes over and sits on the arm of his chair. 'Perhaps if we just talked about it . . .'

He puts the paper down. 'Look, I know Hutchinson needs to do all he can to find . . . the man he's looking for. But I can't make the decision to trace my mother based on the fact that she's the only link to whoever it was. I need to think about it a bit more. Can't you understand that?'

She tilts her chin in that same way he's seen her mother and sister do. 'No, Jonathan,' she says. 'Quite frankly, I can't. The uncertainty's eating you up, and it's making you a right bastard to live with.' She walks out of the room, returning minutes later with her coat on. 'I'm popping over to Lucy's. See you later.'

*

Jonathan walks to the Rose and Crown, hands in his pockets, breath crystallising as it hits the cold night air. It hasn't snowed for a week but the front gardens are still streaked with traces of grey ice and there are sludgy mini-drifts under the hedges. It'll snow again soon; he can taste it, sharp, flinty on the sides of his tongue. He knows Fiona's right, but he has to try and make her understand that he can't take decisions at the moment, not until he can think straight again. So much has happened lately that he feels like his brain has been in a food mixer. When he'd phoned the school to see if there was any news on Chloé, Linda Fawcett had treated him with such suspicion and unpleasantness that he'd hung up on her, which wasn't clever. Malcolm told him later that Chloé was out of hospital – a few cracked ribs and a broken leg that had to be pinned, but already badgering her mum to let her go back to school, which was a surprise; Chloé was bright, but not particularly conscientious. Maybe dicing with death had given her a whole new outlook.

The pub is at the end of a row of trendy white-painted terraced cottages where tasteful lighting spills out through wooden blinds. He can hear someone tuning a guitar as he passes one house, and behind the darkened windows of another, the plaintive ringing of a telephone.

The woodsmoke hits the back of his throat and he is cheered to see a fire crackling in the huge fireplace. Malcolm is already at the bar. 'Black Sheep?' he mouths. Jonathan nods. He puts his phone on 'silent' in case Hutchinson calls again, and looks around the room. It's quiet for a Friday; a couple of old boys at the bar as usual, an overweight couple squashed side by side on the bench seat, silently drinking their halves of lager, and two young women with large glasses of white wine and the remains of a meal in front of them. As Jonathan sits down, the women stand, pick up their bags and glasses and go out through the glass doors into the smoking area, a covered patio with several tables and tall gas heaters that double as lamps. The women settle themselves at a table and Jonathan watches the dark one take a luxurious drag on her cigarette and exhale through her nose.

That does it. He heads out into the vestibule and begins feeding pound coins into the cigarette machine.

'Hiya, Sir.' The voice makes him jump. Petra Simmons, Year 13; smart kid. He forgot she works here at weekends – she is saving hard for university.

'Hello, Petra.' He asks her how she is, tells her not to work too hard then makes his way back to Malcolm, who dutifully follows him out to the smoking area. He tears the cellophane from the vending pack. 'What a bloody rip-off.' He counts the cigarettes. 'I don't even like Silk Cut.'

'Me neither,' Malcolm says, helping himself to one. 'Still, desperate men and all that. Speaking of which, did you see the game on Tuesday?'

They spend the inevitable ten minutes talking about football before Malcolm says, 'Anyway, you sounded fed up on the phone.'

Jonathan sighs, takes a long pull at his pint and then tells Malcolm about Hutchinson's interest in his birth mother. 'Fiona's on about it too. But I'm just not sure I want to know.'

'Why the bloody hell not?'

'For a start, what sort of woman walks out on a toddler? I was only a few weeks younger than Poppy, for Christ's sake. And this DNA business means that my biological father was . . .' He pauses, swills his beer around the glass. 'Well, God knows what.'

'Bank robber?' Malcolm suggests. 'Diamond smuggler? Or perhaps he was some great forger or something. Hey, you might have inherited some hidden talent that you could exploit and make shitloads of money.'

'It's not funny.' Jonathan grabs his pint clumsily,

THE THINGS WE NEVER SAID

spilling it. 'What if . . .' He watches a tiny fly struggling to free itself from the puddle of spilt beer. 'What if he was a child killer or something? Supposing I've inherited – oh, I don't know.' He glances at Malcolm. 'Whatever he did, it must be pretty bloody serious for the police to still be interested after all this time.'

'Yes, but they open up these "cold cases" all the time now, don't they? And if—'

'And what if my birth mother knew? What if they were like the Moors Murderers or something?'

Malcolm looks at him, then at the table. 'All right, mate. I see what you mean.' He drains his pint. 'Drink up.' Before Jonathan can find his wallet, Malcolm is heading back inside towards the bar.

'So, what are you going to do?' Malcolm sets the second pint down.

'To be honest, it feels like if I don't do anything about it, it can't become real. But if I start looking into it—'

'You're stuck with whatever you find out.'

'Precisely.'

They each lift their glasses and drink, then Jonathan takes out two more cigarettes. Malcolm shakes his head.

'Oh, come on. One more and then we'll go in.'

'You're a bad influence, Robson.' Malcolm takes the cigarette, lights up then shakes out the flame. 'Why's this cold-case bloke pestering you about it, anyway? Surely he can just go and find out whatever he likes?'

'Apparently not – well, not easily, anyway. Data Protection Act and all that. He reckons he can probably get round it if he has to, but he's hoping I'll save him the trouble. Thing is . . .' He stops as Petra comes out into the smoking area and begins cleaning the empty tables around them, then moves to their table to change the ashtray. Malcolm asks her how her revision's going and they chat about her forthcoming exams. After a few minutes, Malcolm rounds off the conversation by repeating Jonathan's warning to Petra not to work too hard. 'I won't, Sir,' she smiles. 'Enjoy your evening.'

'Why's she so nice?' Jonathan says as soon as she's out of earshot.

Malcolm nods. 'Model student. Just goes to show, though.'

'What?'

'You met the parents? Dad's always at the dog track – a waste of space that grass could grow in and . . .'

'I know. Pond life.'

'Well, that's the point; just because your parents are arseholes it doesn't mean you'll automatically follow in their footsteps.'

'Even so, if it's in the genes, well, don't you think it's something that – oh, I don't know; maybe you're right.' Jonathan stands. 'Come on, it's getting cold; let's go back inside.' He feels for his wallet. 'Fancy a short?' They've been friends for over ten years; both know this is code for *I may not say it but I value your opinion and friendship.*

'Why not?' Malcolm grins, swallows the remains of his pint in two gulps and declares, 'When you're out, you're out.'

At last orders, Jonathan stands up, jolting the table. 'Another, my friend!' he says with some theatricality.

'Go on then.' Malcolm drains his glass. 'Bloody hell, I can see two of you.'

Jonathan hasn't been this pissed for years. He orders the drinks and is pleased with himself for remembering to ask for water as well. 'Decided to be sensible,' he says, handing Malcolm a pint of water. It comes out as 'sessibel'.

'Which one of you said that?'

Jonathan grins. Malcolm's eyes are glassy-bright and the lower half of his face has collapsed. Jonathan hopes he doesn't look as drunk as Malcolm; they're too old for this. Petra and the barmaid, an older woman, are now putting chairs and stools up on tables. 'D'you think they're trying to tell us something?' he says loudly, the words ridiculously slurred. He's about to make some quip about the company being so charming that it's hard to leave, when he catches a glance from Petra. It stings his face and makes him look away. It's nothing like the *haven't you got homes to go to* look being fired at them by her colleague, it's more, what, concern? No. Disappointment.

Soon they're outside in the frosty darkness. They fall silent as they concentrate on negotiating the icy pavements, each less steady on his feet than he'd like to admit. The fuzzy warmth in Jonathan's head is seeping out into the cold air. He sighs audibly and steps off the kerb without even glancing along the road. He feels Malcolm grab his arm and yank him backwards at the same time as he registers the big dark shape to his right. There is a screech of brakes and the angry sound of a car horn. His heart thuds as he remembers Chloé Nichols flying through the air. He jumps back onto the pavement as the taxi driver leans out of his window. 'Fucking idiot!' the man yells. 'Look where you're fucking going!'

Jonathan opens his mouth to shout back but the taxi pulls away, the driver shaking his head in an exaggerated way. He puts his hand out to steady himself before attempting to cross the road again. A police car passes them at high speed, blue lights flashing but no siren.

'Devious,' Malcolm says. 'Trying to catch them in the act.'

'Yeah, bloody coppers.' Jonathan thinks of how they mocked him at the police station; how he'd heard that policewoman say the allegation was probably rubbish before she arrested him. And he thinks of Don Hutchinson and his unsolved crimes. 'Bastards,' he mutters, quickening his step. The booze sloshes around in his stomach and he's dying for a wee.

'Whadya say?' Malcolm's words are dissolving.

'The police. They bloody loved it when I failed to report hitting that Volvo.'

Malcolm slips on a patch of ice, grabs Jonathan's sleeve. 'Yeah. Gits,' he says with overstated loyalty.

If they'd done their job properly all those years ago, Jonathan is thinking, his natural father would be in prison, wouldn't he? And if they'd caught him in the first place, they wouldn't be interested now. And if Mr-Cold-Case

Hutchinson had simply retired and taken up golf or fishing like any normal bloke . . .

'There's one,' Malcolm says.

'One what?'

'A police-git.' Malcolm points, swaying slightly.

On the other side of the road is the police station. A uniformed policeman is punching in numbers to the door-entry system.

'Police Constable Git,' Malcolm says, flinging his arm out as he wobbles again.

Jonathan catches his arm, whether to steady Malcolm or himself he can't tell. God, he's pissed. The street is spinning. 'S'all the bloody police's fault, you know,' he says as the pair of them lurch across the road.

And that is the last thing he remembers.

CHAPTER THIRTY-SIX

More than twelve hours after leaving Sheffield, they finally drive along the coast road.

'Where are we?' Maggie says sleepily.

'Home. Don't you recognise it?' Leonard turns into a side road and they immediately go into a skid. Maggie clutches the carrycot in terror but Leonard quickly manages to right the car. The sky is dark now, but the snow makes everything lighter. They pull up behind a hulking white shape that she assumes is another car. Glancing down the road, she counts five snowmen standing in front gardens, their hats, scarves and carrot noses already half-covered by the most recent fall. The wind coming off the sea has blown snow up against the houses and sculpted great curves and arcs out of the whiteness, making unexpected shadows and giving the place an eerie look, like a Salvador Dali landscape. The drifts are so deep that some of the front doors are completely obscured.

'You wait here,' Leonard says. 'I need to clear a pathway to the door or you'll go base over apex.'

She smiles. That was one of their dad's expressions. It takes a few minutes to clear the path, and there's a foot-long icicle hanging threateningly from the windowsill above. Leonard bashes it several times before it finally snaps, and at last they make their way carefully up the steps.

Home. Perhaps she's been away long enough to make herself appreciate it. The first thing she'll do is light the fire and make some cocoa. Cocoa-by-the-fire; it was a ritual their mother had established when she'd first started teaching them to cook. She'd call them in as she prepared the evening meal. 'Now, you two watch closely,' she'd say as she rubbed cubes of butter and lard into the flour with her fingertips, lifting the mixture high and letting it trickle back into the bowl. 'More air makes it lighter. And a pinch of bi-carb will make it nice and short.'

Maggie's pastry was never as good as her mother's, but Leonard's was sublime: pale and biscuity, crisp to the bite but crumbly and light on the tongue. 'It's his cold hands,' their mother explained. 'Good pastry needs a cool touch.' Maggie's own talent was for stews and casseroles. She knew how to trim a neck of lamb and brown it slowly to reduce the fattiness, then season it and stew it gently with sliced onions in a pan of delicate golden stock until it was tender. After an hour or so, she'd add potatoes, pearl barley and sweet baby carrots, then leave the whole thing to cook until all the flavours had infused and a rich savoury aroma filled the house. On winter nights, they'd sit around the kitchen table eating steaming plates of lamb stew and mopping up the fragrant gravy with hunks of home-made bread. Afterwards, the three of them would have cocoa by the fire, hands curled around their mugs as the hot coals scorched their cheeks and shins while the draught from the ill-fitting window chilled the backs of their necks.

The lock is frozen and Leonard struggles with the key. Then the door swings open. Maggie wrinkles her nose; the house smells of mice. She recognises the smell, because the hotel kitchen was frequently overrun and she'd had to set the traps.

Leonard flicks on the light. Maggie puts the carrycot in the hall and walks into the kitchen, her shoes making a sticky-tape noise on the tacky lino. Everything is grimy. There are newspapers stacked on every chair, there's a build-up of brown grease on the stove, and mouse droppings surround the half-loaf of bread that Leonard has left on the table. Used saucepans are piled on the draining board and next to it, the twin tub is almost hidden by the pile of grubby chef's whites.

'Lenny,' she says. 'What on earth? This place is a pigsty!'

He looks sheepish. 'I know. I've been doing split shifts. And the daily left in November . . .' He looks around as though he's seeing the room for the first time. 'It is a bit of a state, isn't it?' Then his face brightens. 'I forgot – I've got a surprise for you.'

He leads her along the hall to her old room, tells her to close her eyes. When she opens them, she smiles. 'Oh Lenny, it's perfect.'

'I made it,' he says, running his hand along the sidebar of the wooden cot. 'Not bad for a beginner, is it?'

'It's beautiful, Len. Thank you.' She smiles as he shows her the blue teddy bear he's painted at one end and the pink rabbit with the bright yellow bow at the other.

The tall, draughty windows in Maggie's bedroom rattle in the wind, and ivy has started to grow into the room through a gap in the frame. She keeps finding things she left here before she went to Sheffield – hairspray, perfume, eyeliner – but it's as though they belong to someone else. She picks up a record: 'All I Have to Do is Dream'. Yes, she thinks, and boil a dozen nappies, and wash a mountain of woolly jackets and cot sheets. She shoves the record back in its sleeve just as the twins start to grizzle. Jonathan's easier to feed, so she sees to him first. Breastfeeding certainly saves money, she thinks, but she wonders how long she'll be able to stand it. Both twins clamp onto her nipple as though they're terrified she'll get away. As they take in the milk, she fancies she can see them filling up, becoming plumper and more rosy-cheeked while she herself becomes thinner, paler, weaker. She feels as though she may look in the mirror one day and find that she's no longer there. Is that the sole purpose of mothers, she wonders: a source of nourishment that simply fades away when no longer needed? After all, hadn't her own mother died as soon as her children became independent?

When she tries to nurse a wailing Elizabeth, the child just pulls and twists at the nipple, stretching it out until Maggie winces in pain. Eventually, Elizabeth settles and drops off to sleep, milk spilling out of her mouth as though she's overflowing.

Maggie lights a cigarette and sighs as she looks out of the window. March. It's snowed every day for weeks; how much longer can it last? It was bright and crisp this morning, but now it's clouding over again and the sky is heavy and bulging. It's all there, waiting.

CHAPTER THIRTY-SEVEN

Jonathan is only out for a few seconds. He can't remember Malcolm trying to bring him round, nor can he recall being hauled into the police station. In fact, the next thing he remembers is sitting on a long bench, slumped against the wall next to a lad with a nosebleed and a shrivelled-looking man in a donkey jacket. Every few seconds, the man, who stinks of cider and vomit, mutters and waves an uncertain fist at anyone who's passing.

A few feet away, Malcolm is leaning against the desk, partially supported by a skinny policeman who looks about sixteen. An older officer with a boozer's nose is taking details. Jonathan opens his mouth to speak, but nothing happens, so he leans his head back against the wall and lets Malcolm do the talking.

'Postcode?'

'Sierra echo three,' Malcolm slurs, 'two fosstrot Zulu.'

'Smartarse,' the copper says without looking up. 'Right,

follow PC Linton here and get your heads down for a couple of hours. Then we'll see.'

'C'mon then, lads,' the young copper says, pulling Jonathan to his feet.

'Lads? We're nearly old enough to be your fathers.'

'Time you acted like it then, isn't it? Come on.'

They follow him down some stairs where he unlocks the door to a small cell. 'Not both of you. This isn't bloody scout camp.'

Someone is throwing up in the next cell. 'For fuck's sake,' the copper mutters. 'You,' he says, nodding at Jonathan and indicating a concrete bench covered with a thin blue mattress. 'Lie down before you fall down.' He turns to Malcolm. 'You, follow me.' He jangles his keys and calls back into the cell, 'Sleep tight, and don't bother ringing for room service.' The door slams and Jonathan hears the key turn.

He lies down on the mattress and groans. How on earth has he ended up in this state? In the corner there's a stainless-steel lavatory – just the pan, no seat, and as far as he can tell, no paper. He hopes he won't be needing it, but he's desperate for . . . actually, his bladder doesn't feel so uncomfortable now. He can probably wait. Something tugs at the sleeve of his memory, then everything begins to spin and he surrenders willingly to oblivion.

*

It seems like only minutes later when someone shakes him awake. He sits up too quickly and pain hammers into his skull.

'Come on, rise and shine.' It's the same PC that put him in here earlier, only now he smells of sweat and cheeseburgers. 'It's all kicked off in New Cross and we need the space.'

Jonathan looks around. 'What, you mean I can go?'

'You can, Sir. No tea in bed though, I'm afraid. It's the maid's day off. Your mate's waiting upstairs. Sobered up quite quick after he puked. Report to the desk, then you can both sling your hooks.'

Jonathan shuffles up the stairs, heart pounding with the effort. He feels sick, dizzy, and desperately thirsty. How could he have been so stupid? According to the clock on the wall, it's almost half past three. Fiona will be worried sick; he needs to call her. Reception is crowded with loudmouthed youths, shouting and swearing at the officers trying to manhandle them into the processing area. The unmistakable smell of marijuana hangs in the air.

'Lucky we've been so busy,' the custody sergeant says, as Jonathan signs for his things. 'If it weren't for the paperwork I'd have done you for Drunk and Incapable.' He raises his eyebrows. 'Not to mention Indecent Exposure.'

'What do you mean?' A fragment of memory skitters through his mind.

'Good job PC Collins came along when he did.'

The policeman's beard shifts as a grin spreads across his big face. He shakes his head slowly, in an exaggerated way. 'Dear oh dear oh dear. Much longer with it all hanging out in this weather and you'd have been singing soprano.'

The jigsaw of the final moments before he passed out begins to reassemble itself in Jonathan's head. He groans.

The sergeant nods in the direction of a room off the reception area. 'Your mate's through there,' he says, whistling 'Baby, It's Cold Outside', as Jonathan walks towards the door.

Malcolm's face is not so much pale as translucent. 'That was Cass,' he says, putting his phone away. 'Her mother's going over to babysit and then she's coming to pick us up. She tried to get hold of Fiona, apparently, but she's not answering.'

'That's us both in the shit then.'

'Yep. I told Cass we'd get a cab but she doesn't trust us. She said I should thank the lord she didn't get the kids up out of bed and trail them down here to show me up for the worthless streak of snake-shit that I am. Quote, unquote. Then she hung up on me.'

'Oh fuck, fuck, fuck.'

'Yeah, well.' Malcolm is quiet for a minute. 'This business with . . . you know, all this bollocks that you might have inherited some killer streak or something—'

'I know you think it's bollocks, but for God's sake, it was bad enough thinking I might take after my—'

'Just belt up for two bloody minutes, will you?' Malcolm

snaps, lunging towards him so violently that, for a moment, Jonathan thinks he's going to hit him, but instead he grabs his shoulders. 'Listen, for fuck's sake. There's something I've never told you before. Something I don't like to even think about.' He leans forward, head bowed, arms resting on his knees; he laces and unlaces his fingers.

The anguish etched on Malcolm's face shocks Jonathan into silence, but then the door swings open and a spiky-haired teenager in a leather jacket and ripped jeans swaggers over to the vending machine and punches in his selection. Malcolm's hands drop to his sides and he turns away again. An older man follows the younger, his eyes flicking nervously around the room. He leans and says something to the boy who shrugs him off, grabs a can from the mouth of the machine and stalks towards the door. The man looks around with an apologetic expression as the youth snarls at him from the doorway. 'Dad! I need to get my head down, innit?' As the man hurries after his son, Jonathan glimpses an inch of pyjama-bottom poking out beneath his trousers. He is wearing carpet slippers.

The heavy door swings shut behind them, causing a brief draught before the stillness returns. Malcolm turns to Jonathan again; he looks crushed. 'Listen,' he sighs. 'My father . . .' His voice catches. 'My father started touching me up when I was ten.'

Jonathan thinks he's misheard.

'I had five younger brothers and sisters; my mum locked herself in the spare room most nights – we'd all heard her telling him she couldn't cope with any more kids. One night, they had this huge row. She screamed at him that he wouldn't be such a good Catholic if it was him who had the babies. He yelled something back, then he ripped the bathroom cabinet off the wall and chucked it through the window.'

'Bloody hell.' Jonathan speaks in a whisper.

'We were picking slivers of glass off the front path for days after. Anyway, that's when he started on me. I won't go into what he did, but shall we say it progressed. He'd come into our room while my mum was on nights. I'd lie there watching the door and waiting for the handle to turn, trying not to cry in case I woke my brothers up.' He takes a breath. 'Then, after two years, it stopped.'

Jonathan lays his hand briefly on Malcolm's arm. A wave of nausea threatens to engulf him but he fights it down.

'I was so glad I didn't have to watch for that fucking doorknob that it never occurred to me to wonder *why* it had stopped. I only found out a few years ago; he'd moved on to my sister, Karen. She was ten – that was the magic number. *You're into double figures now*, he used to say, as though it was some sort of grown-up privilege. According to Karen, he got at our brother Andy as well. Andy's never told me himself. I just thank God the old bastard dropped dead before he could touch the little ones.'

'Malc, I don't know what to say. Here I am, going on about my problems when all the time . . .' A series of images flashes through his mind: Malcolm as best man at his and Fiona's wedding, Malcolm's wedding to Cass, Malcolm with his sons from his first marriage, flying kites on Blackheath. And the everyday stuff, Malcolm bringing beer when they built the shed, Malcolm backing him up at school, Malcolm cajoling him back to am-dram when he was about to drop it. In every mental snapshot, Malcolm is smiling, encouraging, not a trace of self-pity. 'I had no idea.' He moves to place a comforting hand on Malcolm's shoulder, but their arms knock awkwardly together. 'Sorry, I was . . .'

'I know.'

'What about your mum?'

'We never told her. What he did was down to him; no one else.' Malcolm turns towards him, a stricken light in his eyes. 'All this *like father, like son* stuff is nonsense. I've got kids, remember?'

'Oh God, no, I didn't mean . . .'

Malcolm picks up his cup and drains it. 'So any more genetic inevitability claptrap, and I might just have to knock your block off.'

'Point taken.'

'I don't want to talk about it again, all right?'

'Okay, but—'

'Never. I mean it.' Malcom stands. 'Right.' He jingles the coins in his pocket. 'Let's grab another coffee to fortify ourselves before Cass gets here.'

Just then, the door opens and an officer they've not seen before informs them that Cassie is waiting in reception. 'You naughty boys *are* in trouble, aren't you?'

CHAPTER THIRTY-EIGHT

After a few weeks, it becomes clear that they can't all survive on what Leonard earns, so Maggie finds a job she can do at home – making rubber pants for babies. She gets Leonard to set up their mother's old Singer sewing machine in the living room, and she starts work. A box containing pieces of transparent rubber, cut out and ready to sew, is delivered each week along with two bags of white rubber bands – small ones for the legs and bigger ones for the tops. Maggie stitches up the sides, then sews the bands in and hey presto, rubber pants! She works throughout the summer, clattering away at the sewing machine, her foot rhythmically working the treadle. When she pauses to light a cigarette, it's as though the machine is holding its breath, waiting for her to start again. Occasionally she looks out at the sun, high in the sky. Maybe she could take a short break, take the twins down to the beach perhaps. But no; she has a quota to fill.

As she machines away, much faster now she's been doing it for a while, she thinks back to the day she'd got talking to Janine, who'd put her in touch with the people for whom she makes the rubber pants. It was back in May, the first day that it had been warm enough to go to the beach. The sun had still been weak, but doing its best to melt the grime-streaked snowman remains that still lingered in some of the front gardens even then. Maggie had looked down at the twins as she wheeled them along the promenade, Jonathan gnawing on a teething ring, Elizabeth leaning against him and just looking around, blinking at the world. Flashes of sunlight glanced off the water; the air smelled salty and carried the tang of freshly caught fish. She got them down the slope to the beach, and managed to drag the pushchair across the pebbles to a spot nearer the sea. They were trying to wriggle out of their straps, so she unbuckled them, lifted them out and set them down on the stones, where they gazed in wonder at seagulls as big as themselves, and waves gently fizzing onto the shore. She gave them each an Ovaltine rusk and they gnawed away happily while she flicked through a copy of *Woman's Realm*.

Within minutes, the twins had an admirer – a little girl called Diane, whose heavily pregnant mother was sitting nearby.

'I'm Janine,' the woman smiled. 'You *are* lucky having twins – all the agony out of the way in one go!' Janine wore pearls and a pale-green frock and apart from being in the family way, she looked just like Jackie Kennedy. She took out a pack of Park Drive and offered one to Maggie, and the two of them spent the afternoon chatting and smoking in the warm sunshine. Diane, besotted, entertained the twins with her new 'Tressy' doll – a rather creepy thing in Maggie's opinion, with hair that 'grew' when you pushed a button in its back. It was as they were packing up to go that Maggie mentioned being short of money. 'Have you got a sewing machine?' Janine asked. And she told Maggie about the rubber pants. 'It's not much money,' she'd said as she wrote down the telephone number on the back of Maggie's cigarette packet. 'But I've done it since Diane was born, and if it weren't for junior here,' she gestured to her swollen belly, 'I'd still be doing it.'

Maggie could kick herself for not asking Janine for her number; she barely sees anyone except Leonard these days, and she could really do with a friend.

*

By the time the chill of autumn settles once more around Maggie's shoulders, she is heartily sick of rubber pants. It's difficult to sew when her fingers are so cold, but she needs the money. She hates this weather. The air smells damp and smoky, and a dense fog is trying to push its way in from outside. This isn't exactly a 'pea-souper', but fog unsettles Maggie almost as much as it did her mother. It was, after all, what killed her father. He'd been covering for another chef in London during the smog of 1952 when he went down with bronchitis. The hotel sent him back home to Hastings, but he never recovered.

The twins sit side by side in their high chairs. Jonathan eats impatiently as usual, his mouth opening up like a little bird for each spoonful. He chomps twice, swallows, opens again then bangs the plastic tray in protest at the delay while Maggie tries to spoon mashed banana and custard into a reluctant Elizabeth, who clamps her mouth shut and twists away, her face wrinkling in misery. Jonathan reaches for his sister and his fingers brush against her forehead. She stops her fretting and rests her head against her brother's hand. 'Mimbet,' Jonathan says, his eleven-month-old attempt at 'Elizabeth'. His fingers flex and scrunch in her hair as though testing its silkiness. Briefly, Elizabeth is calm.

How different they are: Jonathan with his scrubby little tufts of golden hair, robust and solid and always laughing; Elizabeth with her satiny white-blonde curls, tiny, fragile, skin almost translucent.

'Come on, darling,' Maggie coaxes. 'Just one mouthful.' But Elizabeth refuses and resumes her whimpering. 'Come *on*.' Maggie pushes the plastic spoon against her child's firmly closed lips. Elizabeth is testing her; Elizabeth knows she is not a proper mother, merely an accidental one who is failing. 'Please, darling. Be a good girl for Mummy.' But Elizabeth shakes her head. 'Oh, for crying out loud!' Maggie scrapes her chair back and tries to wipe spilt food off her already-stained slacks. 'Can't you eat the damn stuff just one time without a fuss?'

Elizabeth starts to cry. 'You're doing this deliberately,' Maggie snaps. Jonathan's eyes widen and his lower lip trembles. He too starts to yell. 'Now look what you've done!' She lifts Jonathan out of the highchair, moves aside the overflowing laundry basket with her foot and sets him down on the rug, then puts Elizabeth down next to him. Jonathan, easily distracted, starts happily tearing off strips of the *Daily Sketch* and trying to eat them. Maggie disengages the paper from his tightly curled fingers and gives him some wooden bricks instead. Elizabeth makes no attempt to play, despite Maggie's open handbag being within her reach. Her skin is pale, the pallor emphasised by the redness of her eyes, which seem tiny and piggish in her moon-face. When Jonathan tries to interest her in a green brick, she continues to sit immobile. He tries a red brick, but to no avail. Maggie touches her daughter's forehead and is shocked by the intensity of the heat. How could she not have noticed? Thank God Leonard insisted on having a telephone put in. But when she asks if the doctor can call round, the receptionist can barely keep the outrage from her voice: 'Doctor has *far* too big a round to be coming out to snuffly babies,' she says. 'Bring her along to evening surgery. Five o'clock.' And she hangs up.

Maggie crushes a baby aspirin and mixes it into a jar of egg custard, Elizabeth's favourite. But she won't open her mouth. She even refuses rosehip syrup. Maggie telephones Vanda, who is sympathetic but can't offer practical advice: *Darling, the only thing I've ever looked after is a boa constrictor, and even he died!*

Maggie lights another cigarette. If only her mother were alive; she'd know what to do. She drums her fingers on the arm of the settee; Jonathan is playing contentedly with his bricks while Elizabeth sits listlessly on her lap, coughing occasionally. The hands on the mantel clock seem paralysed. She picks up her book, but after two pages she realises she hasn't taken any of it in. How is she going to get through until the surgery opens?

After half an hour or so, Elizabeth brightens, and she doesn't feel quite so hot.

'Look, sweetie,' Maggie says, reaching for *Tabitha and her Kittens*, one of the books Vanda sent down for the twins' birthday in November. 'Where's the pussycat? Show Mummy the cat.'

Elizabeth touches the page. 'Tat!' She turns to Maggie, her little mouth widening into a smile and revealing four snow-white teeth.

'Clever girl!' Maggie kisses the top of her head.

Elizabeth puts her thumb in her mouth, curls her index finger around her nose, then leans back onto Maggie's chest and closes her eyes, as though her work is done. She must be teething again, Maggie thinks. Or it's another bloody cold.

Maggie reaches for her cigarettes. Damn, it's her last one. She looks out of the window. The fog seems to have lifted now. Perhaps the air will clear Elizabeth's nose. She dresses the twins in padded leggings, coats, hats and mittens, and straps them into the pushchair. Jonathan wriggles and frets. He too is looking slightly red-eyed and pale. Please don't let them both have colds.

The air is damp, and the pavements look wet even though it hasn't rained. The seagulls seem to be shrieking particularly loudly. She wishes they'd just shut up, stupid, useless birds. As soon as she manoeuvres the huge push-chair into the tobacconist's, a smiling Mrs Dean comes out from behind the glass-topped counter. She has known Maggie since she was a little girl and must now be well into her seventies, though still slender and attractive, pearls in her ears and at her throat, her hair an improb-able shade of auburn and her face carefully made up. 'Hello, my poppets!' she cries, ducking her head down to the pushchair to kiss the twins. But then she freezes and the smile evaporates. 'Goodness.' She looks at Maggie. 'Ought you to have them out?'

Maggie looks at her, then at the babies. 'Elizabeth's got a cold,' she says. 'I'm taking her to Dr Cranfield later, but he'll probably only give her a linctus.' Then she looks more closely and begins to see what Mrs Dean sees. Red patches on Elizabeth's face; a rash. Jonathan looks blotchy as well, screwing up his eyes against the light and pulling at his ear. She puts her hand to his head and feels the heat before she touches him.

'Measles!' Mrs Dean announces. 'They shouldn't be out while they're infectious, dear. I'd take them straight back home to a darkened room and get Dr Cranfield out.'

Maggie is flustered. 'Measles? I thought they were too young for measles.' But now she looks at them again she can see that it's not just any old rash. 'They said I should go to evening surgery . . .'

'Poppycock! Those children should be tucked up in the warm and if . . .' She stops. 'Never mind.' She nods towards the wooden chair in the corner of the shop. 'Sit yourself down for a minute, pet. I'll sort this out.'

Maggie watches her disappear into the back room, hears the whir and click-ker-ching as the telephone dial spins round. Mrs Dean shouts into the receiver, demands the doctor come out immediately. She doesn't give a tinker's cuss whether Dr Cranfield is about to have his tea; she's had three children and seven grandchildren and she knows a measly child when she sees one. There is a clunk as she slams the receiver back into its cradle.

CHAPTER THIRTY-NINE

Before now, Jonathan has only ever seen Cassie smiling and laughing; this is like a different person. Her face is dark and her mouth has gone thin and hard; when she looks at him, her eyes seem powered by an electric current, as though she might zap him with one laser glance. He and Malcolm sit meekly side by side in the back, the frost that sparkles on the deserted streets failing to rival the iciness inside the car. Talking is clearly not permitted. He glances at Malcolm, whose skin is now the colour of an old bandage. It must have cost him a great deal to talk about what he'd been through, Jonathan realises. As he gets out of the car, he catches Malcolm's hand and holds it for a moment.

As he walks up the path, he braces himself. It's gone four now, and yet the lights are still on downstairs. She'll be furious, and she has every right. He should have phoned; she'll probably accuse him of going to Sian's again or something. At least her car's here – when Malcolm said Cass couldn't get hold of her, it crossed his mind that she might have gone again. He's surprised she didn't call, but then he reaches into his jacket for his phone. Shit. It's still on 'silent' and there are four missed calls and a text. He scrolls down as he fumbles for his keys. But there's only one from Fiona – the others are from Lucy. He switches it back to 'outdoor', puts his key in the lock and pushes the door open.

He stares at the big red drops on the carpet and bloody handprints on the wall; he bounds up the stairs, feeling the sticky wetness as soon as he touches the banister rail. He pushes the bedroom door open and freezes. The smell hits him first, a rusty, coppery tang. The duvet is on the floor, one corner completely sodden with blood. The bed is covered too, and there are bloody handprints on the chest of drawers. He can't move; he can't think. Perhaps this is some sort of drink-induced hallucination. His phone rings. Lucy. He presses *answer* but he still can't speak.

'Jonathan? Where the fuck have you been, you selfish bastard?'

He's never heard Lucy swear before. 'What . . .' But his voice still won't work. He clears his throat and tries again. 'What's happened?'

'Fiona's been rushed to hospital,' Lucy says, in a tone that suggests it's his fault. 'She was bleeding, and yet again you—'

'Lucy, please. Just tell me what's happened.'

'Lewisham hospital; the labour ward.' Then her voice fractures. 'Just get here.'

'Lucy!' But she's gone.

He knows he shouldn't be driving but bollocks to it. He almost falls down the stairs in his hurry to get out of the house and into the car. Labour ward; why is she on the labour ward? She's only twenty-four weeks.

He stopped believing in God when he was about ten, but now he's desperate to believe there's something out there that can influence what's happening. *Please, please, please*, he prays as he drives. *Please don't let us lose this baby. Let Fiona be all right, I'll be a better person, I swear. I'll be a good husband and a good father and I'll try my hardest to be a good son; just let our baby be born safely and I swear I'll bring him up properly and I'll take him to church. Show me what to do; I'll do anything, I promise, anything if you'll keep them both safe.* He coughs to hold back a sob that threatens to slip between his lips.

*

The car park is full, even at this time of night, so he parks in a disabled bay and runs into the hospital. One of the midwives buzzes him into the ward and meets him just inside the doors. She's wearing what look like green pyjamas. 'Your wife's very poorly,' she says as she leads the way along the corridor. 'She's lost a lot of blood but we managed to find a match fairly quickly and we're giving her a transfusion now.' The woman's buttocks are so large that each seems to move independently of the other, but she walks quickly despite her size, and Jonathan has to hurry to keep up with her. It's only five in the morning and many of the rooms are still in darkness, but there's a feeling of activity, a sense that the ward is awake, alert.

As they pass one of the side rooms, he can hear a woman crying out in pain. For one awful moment he thinks . . . but the midwife marches straight past, thank God. A heavily pregnant woman in a pink and black dressing gown is pacing the corridor, supported by her dishevelled-looking partner. Behind the door of another room, a baby cries insistently.

'Nurse!' An older woman comes out of one of the rooms, her face creased with anxiety. 'Please, when are you going to see to my daughter? She's in such a lot of pain.' Behind her, an enormously pregnant teenage girl is leaning over the bed while another girl of about the same age rubs her back. The first girl is crying loudly.

'We'll be along to check on her in a little while,' the midwife snaps without breaking her stride. 'There are other patients besides your daughter, you know.'

Up ahead, there's a hubbub of activity. A lot more people in green surgical pyjamas are going in and out of one of the rooms. They move quickly and purposefully; the sense of urgency is palpable.

'She's in here,' the midwife says, pushing the door open and standing aside as someone else hurries out. 'You'll have to stay out of the way; they're still trying to get her stable.'

Lucy is standing just inside the door, her hair a mess. She's wearing glasses instead of her usual contacts, and she looks as if she's been crying. Instead of yelling at Jonathan, she almost collapses into his arms. 'Thank God you're here. I thought . . . I thought she might . . .'

Men and women in green surround the bed, moving in and out of the little cluster like bees around a hive. They're all frowning, intent on what they're doing; they speak in sharp, clipped sentences but he can't make out what they're saying because they're talking so quickly. One of them reaches up to adjust a bag of blood that's hanging from a stand next to the bed.

'She was fine when she left me earlier on,' Lucy is saying. 'Then she phoned at about half two and said she was bleeding and could I come over, but by the time I got there . . . oh God, it was . . . I've never seen so much blood.'

Then a gap appears in the group around the bed and he can see her. She looks smaller, somehow. At first he thinks she's unconscious, but then she opens her eyes. He steps forward and she looks at him, but her face doesn't register anything at all; it's as though she isn't actually there. He's never seen her so pale. Her face is ashen; her skin glistens with sweat and there's dried blood on her forehead and in her hair. She tries to speak but it's very faint.

'All right, Fiona,' one of the men says in an extra-loud voice, as though she's deaf or stupid. 'You're doing fine. Everything's under control now.'

Fiona murmurs something again, but no one takes any notice.

'Pulse is coming down, but it's still one-twenty,' someone says.

'Give her another two units,' the man who appears to be in charge shouts. 'Come on, let's speed it up a bit, shall we?'

One of the women fixes another bag of blood to the stand beside the bed. There are so many of them, all around her, all doing things to her.

Jonathan watches what's happening as though it's a film. He wants to intervene, to stop them prodding at her or at least to ask what they're doing and why, but he's in limbo; frozen.

'We're getting there,' someone says after a while. 'BP's picking up.'

'Thank Christ,' says the man in charge. 'Good girl, Fiona. You're doing just fine.' He says something to the woman next to him, then turns to Jonathan. 'Right, you the husband?'

Jonathan nods.

'We've given her six pints of blood; the trick with this is to get the blood into her faster than it's coming out – pretty basic, really. She seems to be stable now and her blood pressure's looking much more healthy, so it doesn't look like we need to do a caesarean—'

'Caesarean? But the baby's not due until—'

'Only option if the bleeding doesn't stop spontaneously – we're risking mum and baby otherwise. Placenta praevia can be a life-threatening condition, but I think we're out of the woods now.'

Jonathan looks at the doctor, who clearly expects some response.

'He doesn't know,' Lucy chips in. 'She hasn't told him.'

'*What?*' Jonathan turns to Lucy. 'You mean she knew there was something wrong—'

'Not like this. They didn't think it was serious.'

'But why didn't she—'

'Because she didn't feel she could tell you,' Lucy sighs. 'I know it's not your fault, Jonathan, but with everything else . . .'

The doctor is speaking again, and Jonathan tries to focus on what he's saying.

'We still need to see how the baby's doing. We'll get a CTG on her now she's stable – sorry, that's a cardiotocograph – it measures the foetal heartbeat so we can tell if the baby's in distress. Then we'll need to get her scanned so we can see what's been happening in there.'

The midwife who'd let Jonathan in fits a strap around Fiona's belly and pulls another screen into place. Fiona mutters something. 'It's all right, sweetheart.' The midwife lays her big paw of a hand on Fiona's forehead and strokes her hair. 'No more bleeding now; you're going to be just fine.' Her voice is considerably less strident than when she spoke to him outside. 'Hey now, look who's here to see you. And you with no lipstick on!'

Jonathan moves nearer to the bed, but Fiona looks right through him. 'The baby,' she whispers.

There are tubes going into the back of both her hands, and there are wires and loops everywhere, but he manages to curl his fingers around hers as he leans over and kisses her. Her lips are dry and cracked but her skin is clammy to the touch.

'Okay, Fiona,' the midwife says. 'You see that line on the screen there? That's your baby's heartbeat, still nice and strong. And listen . . .' She adjusts something on the machine. 'There we are – listen to that! Good, normal, healthy heartbeat.'

'Thank God,' Jonathan whispers, gently squeezing Fiona's fingers. Her gaze flickers towards him and she smiles weakly.

Lucy bursts into tears, kisses Fiona and Jonathan, and says she's going outside to phone home. Everyone else in the room is smiling too, and there's a sense of 'job done', of tidying up. The room begins to empty until the only people left apart from himself and Fiona are the man in charge, who's writing something on a clipboard, the big midwife and a tall, red-haired man who Jonathan has only just realised is also a midwife. He looks ridiculously young and is so slender he could play Laurel to his colleague's Hardy.

'Well done, Fiona,' the doctor says. 'Things are looking good, so you try and get some rest now, okay? I'll pop back and see you later.' He nods at Jonathan. 'She'll look a lot better in a few hours, but she'll be staying with us for a while. Sister'll fill you in.' He smiles at Jonathan for the first time, and Jonathan is struck by an absurd desire to embrace the man. Instead, he tries to thank him, but his teeth start to chatter and he can't get the words out.

He turns back to Fiona. She's still hooked up to a drip and the male midwife is attaching another bag, this time of clear fluid, which looks far less terrifying than the blood. 'Just some saline,' the midwife says, as though that explains everything.

Fiona is watching the jagged line on the monitor. Jonathan strokes her hair back and kisses her damp forehead. 'I'm sorry,' he whispers. 'I'm so, so sorry I wasn't there.'

She turns her head away, and he realises he probably still stinks of whisky.

CHAPTER FORTY

Throughout several long days and nights, Maggie nurses the twins exactly as the doctor told her. She sponges their fevered foreheads, dabs calamine lotion onto their itchy skin and bathes their swollen, crusted eyelids. Leonard helps out on his day off, bringing her cups of tea and cheese on toast, and Mrs Dean pops in with Lucozade and cigarettes. When Maggie finally sinks into bed, she lies rigid as the babies thrash around in their cot, their dry, rasping coughs ripping though her.

On the fifth day, Jonathan's fever breaks. He stands up in the cot, holding out his arms. Thank heavens. She lifts him out, and he snuggles into her neck, sucking contentedly on his little finger. At lunchtime he manages some scrambled egg and by teatime he's almost back to normal. But Elizabeth is no better.

'The rash is fading,' Dr Cranfield says when he calls in on his evening rounds. 'But I'm surprised she's still feverish.' He takes off his bottle-end spectacles and cleans them with the hem of his jacket. 'Hmm.' He purses his lips and taps his stethoscope in the palm of his hand. 'Keep sponging her down and I'll call in again tomorrow.' He puts the stethoscope back in his bag and clicks it shut. 'This little chap's on the mend, anyway,' he adds, as a grinning Jonathan clutches his trouser-leg and pulls himself to a standing position.

The following morning, Elizabeth's temperature is a hundred and three. Jonathan, disgruntled by the lack of his mother's attention, whinges and pulls at her sleeve every few minutes. Maggie crawls through the day, and by the time she puts the babies down for their nap, she is almost crying with tiredness. Jonathan fidgets when she tucks him in at the other end of the cot – he doesn't understand why his sister isn't up and playing. Elizabeth's forehead is still burning, but for the moment, she's quiet, so Maggie allows herself a short rest. Just ten minutes, she thinks as she curls up on the settee. She picks her housecoat up from the floor, throws it over herself like a blanket and sinks immediately into sleep.

*

The shrill ring of the doorbell rips her from sleep and she looks incredulously at the clock; she has slept for almost two hours. She calls to a protesting Jonathan as she goes to open the door. 'Mummy's coming, darling. Just a minute.'

She's still disoriented as she opens the door to Dr Cranfield. 'Sorry,' she mumbles, pulling her hair into place. 'Fell asleep.'

The doctor smiles. 'I'm sure you needed it.' She steps back to allow him in and then follows him along the hall. 'How's the patient today?'

'Much the same. Not as grizzly as she was, but—' She stops. Something about the doctor's posture as he stands over the cot . . .

He drops his bag and leans over to Elizabeth, then he turns to Maggie. 'Are you on the telephone?'

'Yes, yes, we are. What—?'

'I want you to telephone for an ambulance. Put me on the line when you get through.'

After twenty minutes of pacing the floor and looking anxiously out of the window, Dr Cranfield drives them to the hospital in his own car. Jonathan wails with indignation at being dropped off with Mrs Dean, but there's no time to stay and settle him. Elizabeth is limp and heavy in Maggie's lap. The rash that had seemed to be fading is now more blotchy and livid than it was even at the start, and although Elizabeth's eyes are open, they are vacant and stare through Maggie as though she isn't there.

The doctor swings the car into the ambulance parking area, leaps out and runs round to the passenger side. Elizabeth's eyes are now rolling back in her head. He takes her from Maggie's arms and runs into the hospital, kicking open the double wooden doors as he enters. He doesn't break his stride as he hurries past the reception desk and into the treatment area, barking something at the nurse as he passes. Maggie tries to follow but the nurse takes her arm and guides her to a seat in the waiting room, where rows of weary-looking people with nothing obviously wrong are slumped in their chairs.

Maggie came here when she was little after breaking her wrist. They'd waited hours but her mother, a force to be reckoned with in her own home, was so in awe of doctors and nurses that she wouldn't even ask when they'd be seen. Well, Maggie is not her mother. She marches up to the desk and demands to be told what is happening.

The nurse tells her not to worry, her daughter is in good hands. 'Sit down and look at a magazine, dear, and let the doctors do their job. I'll bring you some tea.'

Panic starts to rise in her chest and her instinct is to scream at the nurse, tell her not to be so bloody ridiculous, but she recognises the genuine attempt to calm her. The nurse is smiling, asking if she takes sugar. 'One, please,' she says, and makes as if to go back to her seat. But as soon as the nurse turns away, she darts through the double doors, ignoring the signs that tell her not to. The treatment area is deserted but for an elderly lady holding a handkerchief to her mouth while a nervous-looking doctor stitches a gash on the side of her foot. For a moment, Maggie's thoughts are suspended as she tries to work out what to do, then she sees another set of double doors, another 'No Admittance' sign, and she charges towards it. Just as she is reaching out to push the door, it opens from the inside, and Dr Cranfield appears. He starts as he sees her, then his whole body slumps. 'Margaret,' he says. It is the first time he has used her name.

'What's happening? What's wrong with her?'

Dr Cranfield starts to talk, and Maggie tries to listen but she can't take in what he's saying. She identifies a few words, *complications* and *rare* and *sometimes, after measles*, then she realises he's waiting for her to speak, but her voice won't work so she just looks back at him.

'They don't usually allow it,' he says, 'but as I'm your family doctor . . . I thought, well, if you held her for a . . .' He takes his spectacles off, wipes his eyes, then puts them back on and looks at her. 'You mightn't want to, of course, but . . .'

Might not want to hold her baby? Of course she wants to hold her baby! She follows him back through the doors and there is Elizabeth, a little scrap of a person adrift in the high hospital bed. Maggie is vaguely aware of several pairs of eyes turning towards her as she approaches, but it is not until the young hospital doctor gently lays Elizabeth in her arms and starts to remove the tubes from her tiny body that she realises her child is already dead.

CHAPTER FORTY-ONE

After moving the car to an ordinary bay and putting six quid in the pay and display, Jonathan climbs into the back seat and sleeps. He wakes dry and nauseous with a crick in his neck. His hangover now hits him with a vengeance, thudding in his head when he moves and sticking the walls of his parched blood vessels together when he's still. He buys paracetamol in W. H. Smith, swallows two with water from the basin in the gents then goes to the hospital café for coffee and toast before heading back up to Fiona.

They're just wheeling the ultrasound machine into the room when he arrives. Fiona looks better, but still pale and blotchy, and there are dark circles under her eyes. The sonographer seems bored as she checks Fiona's name and enters something on the computer. She rubs the gel over the neat little bump they've been calling Fred for the past few weeks. 'We just need to check to see that everything's in order, and make sure the placenta hasn't started to come away from the wall of the uterus.'

Fiona's legs are shaking visibly. The sonographer looks at her for the first time, then squeezes her shoulder. 'Try not to worry,' she says. Fiona grabs Jonathan's hand and grips it so hard it hurts.

He says another silent prayer as the image starts to form on the screen. His eyes have barely adjusted to the fuzzy black and white picture when the sonographer says quickly, 'Baby's fine,' and smiles at them both.

'Are you sure?' Fiona whispers.

'Lively as a little jumping bean, look.'

Tears spring from Fiona's eyes now, but they're tears of relief.

'The placenta's lying about halfway across the cervix,' the sonographer explains. 'There's roughly a fifty per cent chance that it'll still move up and out of the way as the pregnancy progresses, but we'll need to scan you every two weeks now to monitor it. If it doesn't move, we're looking at a caesarean, I'm afraid.'

'I don't care how it's born as long as everything's all right,' Fiona says.

Jonathan is mesmerised. At the last scan, he'd been distracted, and although he'd pretended he could make out hands and feet, it had just looked like a blurry negative, whitish blobs in a blackish sea. This time, there's no doubt that he's looking at a tiny human baby. At one point, it seems to be kicking at the device the sonographer is running over the bump, and it is very clearly sucking its thumb. This, he tells himself, is my child. This is what is real; this is what it's all *for.*

'I can tell you the sex, if you'd like?'

They look at each other; both shake their heads. As they watch their baby doing somersaults as though playing in a swimming pool, it suddenly puts out a hand and seems to wave, then it turns very definitely and faces them.

'Hello, baby,' they say in unison.

*

Soon after the sonographer leaves, the doctor from last night comes into the room. There are two fresh shaving cuts on his neck, and his eyes look tired and bloodshot. He stifles a yawn as he pulls up a chair next to the bed. Fiona will have to stay in for at least a couple of weeks, he tells them, and then, all being well, she can go home, although she'll be on bed rest right up until the delivery. Still slightly stunned, they both nod and thank him, not really processing what he's said but incredibly, overwhelmingly grateful for what he's done.

Fiona needs to sleep, so Jonathan heads off to pack some things to bring in later. As he walks towards the car, he sees Lucy coming the other way.

'How is she?' Lucy says. She looks pale and there are bags under her eyes. 'Matt's taking the kids to school so I thought I'd pop back.'

'She's tired, and they're keeping her in for a while, but

she's okay. And we've just had the scan – the baby's fine, too.'

He sees Lucy's shoulders relax. 'Thank heavens for that. I know they said it was looking good, but I was still worried.' She looks at him. 'Did you get any sleep?'

He nods. 'Couple of hours.' He rubs the back of his aching neck. 'On the back seat of the car.'

Lucy grimaces.

'Luce, do you fancy a quick coffee?'

She nods, and they walk back through the car park to the hospital canteen.

'So,' he says, putting the two polystyrene cups on the table. 'When did she find out about this? And why the hell didn't she tell me?'

Lucy sighs. 'They told her after the last scan. But it didn't seem to be a big deal; they said the placenta would probably move, and that—'

'But it's my baby too. Why—'

'I know. She should have told you. But you have to see it from her point of view. You've had all this carry-on with your school, and then that policeman turning up . . .' She hesitates.

'Go on.'

'Fiona felt . . . well, the way she put it was that she didn't think there was room in the marriage for any more problems. She felt you'd sort of cornered the market.'

He shakes his head. Part of him is angry that she didn't tell him, but also angry with himself for making her feel she *couldn't* tell him.

'Don't be too hard on her; she's been pretty down recently. She said you thought she wasn't being very supportive, that she was too wrapped up in the baby.' Lucy rummages for her sweeteners in her enormous handbag – her 'mummy kit', Fiona calls it. He catches a glimpse of a toy bus and a Mr Men book among the usual handbag contents.

'I didn't think that.' But as he speaks, he realises he hasn't been thinking about Fiona at all. He's been totally preoccupied with his own worries.

'It's hard to understand what it's like to be pregnant,' Lucy says, 'even for the dad. For a woman, it's the most important thing in the world – for that period of time, anyway.'

Jonathan nods. 'I've been rather self-obsessed, haven't I? I don't think I did understand how she felt, not at first, anyway.' He takes a mouthful of coffee. 'Do you know what?' He smiles. 'I caught her stuffing a cushion up her jumper at one point, just so she could see what she'd look like when she got big.'

Lucy laughs. 'We used to do that when we were kids, playing Mummies and Little Girls. I'd have tantrums because Fiona always got to be the mummy; she used to wear our mum's high heels and clip-clop about saying, "I'm the eldest, so I have to get in practice."' They both laugh, then she's serious again. 'She's always wanted kids, Jonathan. And she's good at pretending she's not worried about being nearly forty.'

He nods, then looks at her. 'Thanks, Luce.'

On the way home he goes over it in his head. He hasn't been 'involved' with the pregnancy; all he's really done is to worry about what sort of father he'll make, and that isn't the same thing at all. What a total dick he's been. And now, as he drives, he keeps trying to recreate the moment their baby – their very own child – turned to face them. It's the most profound thing that has ever happened to him: exciting, yet calming at the same time. All his anger – at his parents, at Ryan and Chloé, at Don Hutchinson and his 'cold case' – is starting to dissipate. Right now, nothing – *nothing* – matters except Fiona and the baby. He can feel the connection at last. It's like a game of tag, like lighting a fresh new candle from the flame of one that's already burning down.

CHAPTER FORTY-TWO

Maggie's grief attaches to her body like a parasite, dragging at her throat so that she can hardly speak, hanging off her in great heavy folds and trailing on the floor behind her as she moves.

Leonard takes some time off work, and Auntie Alice, her mother's sister, comes to look after Jonathan. Auntie Alice has a fierce shampoo and set and three chins that wobble when she talks. She smells of ginger biscuits and faintly of body odour, probably because of her fondness for Tricel blouses and Bri-Nylon frocks. But she does her best.

Leonard puts Auntie Alice in the room above Maggie's. One night when Maggie goes to lie on her bed – she no longer sleeps, merely moves to a slightly less painful level of consciousness – she notices the cot has gone. Then she hears Jonathan crying upstairs, and Auntie Alice's soothing voice. She knows she'll have to start looking after him again soon, but right now she can't bear to hear him asking for 'Mimbet' over and over and over.

The grief-drenched days roll one into another. Maggie moves around in a trance-like state. The air in the house feels thick and stiff, difficult to breathe. She stares out of the window. A few flakes of snow swirl in the golden light from the streetlamp. Snow. Isn't it too early for snow? But she has no idea what day or month it is, so probably not. They say it won't be as bad this year, but how can they be sure? Her mind creeps back to last winter. She lights another cigarette to steady her nerves. It was the worst winter on record: the 'big freeze'. She should never have brought the twins back to Hastings in those horrendous blizzards; why hadn't she waited until the weather improved? Elizabeth had never been right, not since the day they left Vanda's. Tears spill over her hand as she takes a drag of her cigarette. She'd snapped at Elizabeth when she wouldn't feed on the journey back, and had bundled her over to Leonard while she'd gone off and sat in a café. Even once they were home, she shouted at Elizabeth. She'd always treated her two babies differently; she sees that now. How many times had she left the poor child wailing in her cot while she fed Jonathan, simply because he was easier? Had she cuddled Elizabeth as often? She wriggled and fidgeted so much that Maggie thought she didn't like to be cuddled, but maybe Maggie simply hadn't been holding her properly. Maggie now sees her own ineptitude with such startling clarity that it almost dazzles her, a great bright orb of blame, bouncing at her from all angles.

*

After four weeks, Auntie Alice returns to her home in Cornwall. She can't leave Uncle Dennis to fend for himself any longer and heaven only knows what sort of a mess the place'll be in when she gets back. Before she leaves, she makes a huge pan full of soup and puts a steaming bowl in front of Maggie. 'Come on, Margaret, love,' she says, her powdered chins wobbling. 'You don't eat enough to keep a sparrow alive.'

Maggie looks at the thick green soup. Pea and ham; she used to love this when she was little, especially when Auntie Alice let her cut dry bread into cubes for croutons. She picks up her spoon. Her throat feels stiff and paralysed. She forces her lips to open and although she can feel the warmth of the soup as it floods onto her tongue, she cannot taste it.

'Time's a great healer,' Auntie Alice says. 'And at least you've still got Jonathan.'

With all her might Maggie tries, but the soup just will not slip down her throat.

'And you're still young; you can have another baby some day.'

*

312

Jonathan watches her warily from his cot when she curls up on her bed, pulling her knees up to her chest in an attempt to soothe the hollow, empty pain inside her. He sighs a lot, she notices. He shouldn't sigh like that, but she is unable to do anything about it. At least he's stopped calling for Elizabeth now. For a while, Maggie thought she'd never be able to be in a room with him again. 'Mimbet,' he'd whimper, flexing his little fingers in his own hair as if it was a substitute for Elizabeth's. Then there was the day he found one of her shoes down the side of the settee. Maggie had bought the little bootees when Elizabeth started pulling herself into a standing position, just two weeks before she died. They were made from soft, pliable leather with two metal eyelets for the single lace, exactly like Jonathan's but cherry-red instead of navy. As soon as Maggie put them on her, she'd pull them off again and turn them over and over in her star-fish hands, concentrating fiercely as she examined them.

'Mimbet,' Jonathan said when he found the shoe. He held it out for Maggie to see. *'Mimbet, Mimbet.'*

'No!' Maggie shrieked. 'No Mimbet! Bad boy!' Then she'd fled from the room, flung herself on her bed and sobbed. When Leonard came home, he found Jonathan sitting miserably under the kitchen table, cold and soggy in nothing but a wet nappy and a dribble-soaked cotton vest, the red boot clutched tightly in his hand.

Since then, Jonathan has barely made a sound. Occasionally, he'll mouth a little tune, or point to the pushchair and say 'out'; but mostly, he just sucks his little finger, clutching Elizabeth's red boot as he watches Maggie silently, his eyes wide and round, so dark they look like black marbles.

*

Maggie takes to asking everyone she sees about measles; have they had it, have their children had it, how ill were they, how long did it last? She asks Dr Cranfield again and again why Elizabeth died. All children get measles at some point, don't they? She can vaguely remember having it herself: she and Leonard, spotty and miserable, tucked up together in their mother's bed, surrounded by colouring books as their mother fed them chicken broth and warm orange juice.

The doctor explains patiently: 'Yes, measles is very common, but there can be complications, which is what happened in Elizabeth's case. She developed a secondary infection that caused inflammation in her brain. It's very rare, but it happens sometimes.'

And you did nothing to stop it. That's what he wants to add, she can tell. But he doesn't say it, and so she returns to his surgery almost every day and asks him again why her baby died, and every day, he talks about this 'infection'.

'Margaret.' The doctor leans back in his chair, laces his fingers and taps his thumbs together. He's looking at her very oddly now. 'As I've already said, I want you to come and see me whenever you feel . . .'

Maggie nods, a quick, short nod to shut him up.

'. . . but I think, well . . . I'm not sure it's good for you to come here every day like this.' He leans forward again, looks at her notes. 'You're taking the tablets I gave you?'

Maggie nods, begins to get to her feet.

'Just a minute.' He stands and puts his hand out towards her shoulder. 'Sit down again, Margaret, please. I'm trying to think what would be best for you.'

She doesn't want to sit down again; she needs to get outside, needs to be walking. She moves towards the door. 'I have to pick Jonathan up,' she says curtly.

'Margaret,' he sighs. 'I'm not saying you shouldn't come. I'm concerned, that's all. I think you might need a little rest . . .'

But she doesn't hear any more because the door swings shut behind her.

CHAPTER FORTY-THREE

The man at Social Services says he'll send Jonathan a leaf-let, *Access to Birth Records*, and an application form. Jonathan should state on the form where he would like to receive his counselling, and he shouldn't be surprised if there was quite a wait.

'But I don't want counselling. I just want—'

'Counselling's compulsory.' The voice sounds bored, as though he's heard the same thing a hundred times before. 'The waiting list is for access to your adoption file.'

'But it's my legal right, isn't it?'

'Yes,' the man sighs, 'but it has to be *supervised* access. Some of the information can be distressing . . .'

'Look, I realise—'

'. . . and you need a social worker to go through it with you. Except there aren't enough social workers to go round.'

'So how long?'

'The waiting list is currently at ten to twelve months.'

Jonathan hangs up.

A quick internet search confirms that there are a number of agencies prepared to find people for a small – or sometimes not so small – fee. He calls one that advertises its rates as 'from £50' and speaks to an avuncular man who set up the business when he retired because of his fascination with family history. Tracing someone can take anything from a few minutes to several months or longer, he explains. The cost depends on the amount of work involved, which in turn depends on how common the name is. 'If birth mum turns out to be a Mary Smith, for example, we could be in for a long slog. The first step is to get hold of your original birth certificate—'

'I have it,' Jonathan says. 'Her name was Margaret Letitia Harrison.'

'Excellent! That would give me a very good start if you did want to go ahead – there's bound to be a few Margaret Harrisons, but there can't be many with Letitia in the middle.'

The man, Bob, goes through some of the possibilities – she might refuse contact, she might have gone abroad, she might even be dead. He advises Jonathan to think carefully about the implications before deciding to go ahead. Sometimes, he adds, as if he can read Jonathan's mind, sometimes clients discover things they'd rather not know.

'Bob,' Jonathan says, 'I just want to stop *not* knowing.'

*

After scanning the documents and emailing them to Bob, Jonathan lays out the contents of the shoebox on the bed: the little red boot, forlorn without its partner, the thin jersey, the dungarees and the hand-knitted cardigan. Fiona asked him to take in some wool and knitting needles because the woman in the next bed has offered to teach her to knit. Had his birth mother knitted this while she was pregnant, he wonders? They didn't have scans in those days, but maybe she'd pictured him floating around inside her, maybe she'd wondered whether he would be a boy or a girl; whether he'd be like her, or like his father. A dark cloud looms in his mind every time he thinks about his biological father. He looks at the red boot, the sole slightly worn along the outer side, perhaps because he'd been learning to walk. Why only one? And the pebbles; why had they been sent with him? He shuffles through the papers and pulls out the document from Hastings County Court, then his birth certificate which, having been unfolded and refolded many times in the past few weeks, is beginning to lose its crispness. He was born in Sheffield, and then his mother had taken him to Hastings. Had she returned to the north after the adoption, perhaps to be with his father? Could she still be in Hastings?

Fifteen minutes later, he's in the car heading for the A21. He doesn't know what he'll do when he gets there, but a walk along the seafront will clear his head. He selects a CD, pushes it into the slot and turns up the volume. Fiona hates The Smiths. She says they depress her, but they always cheer Jonathan up because no matter how miserable he's feeling, Morrissey always seems to feel worse.

He parks on the seafront, and the wind bites his face as soon as he opens the door. It's the sort of wind that flings wet sand and salt at your cheeks, burrows into your ears and rips across the surface of your eyes. But he turns up his collar, puts two pounds in the ticket machine and heads up into the Old Town. He wanders along George Street with its trendy vodka bar and arty little gift shops, then High Street, which is full of antiques and dusty second-hand books, and then back along All Saints' Street, with its narrow passageways, stone steps and sloping Tudor cottages. Through habit, he counts as he climbs the East Hill Steps, losing count after a hundred or so and panting by the time he reaches the top. The wind batters him and his ears hurt, but he loves the view from here. He looks down at the fishing boats, nets piled up around them, and at the wooden net huts, mostly fresh fish shops now, with the day's prices chalked in blue and pink on blackboards outside. Beyond the Stade, a restless gunmetal sea throws huge waves inland, each thudding heavily on the shore. Had his mother taken him onto that beach, let him play with the pebbles, pointed out ships on the horizon? It's starting to rain. The houses below are built at angles, little rows facing this way and that, all on different levels.

Seagulls stand on the blackening rooftops looking majestically out to sea, their feathers ruffled by the wind. He watches the gulls swooping and gliding above the net huts, incandescent white against a rapidly darkening sky. Women are putting up umbrellas and hurrying home out of the rain. Could Margaret Letitia Harrison be one of them? The rain's getting heavy now, so after one last look at the view, he heads back down the steps in search of fish and chips, checking his phone as he walks – he's paranoid about it now. Three missed calls from Malcolm; must have been while he had the music on in the car. He calls back but it goes to voicemail.

Sitting in a shelter on the promenade, he eats the steaming cod and salty chips with his fingers as he listens to the rain drumming on the roof and watches it bouncing off the tarmac. Bob had sounded confident. He'd start with the marriage records – apparently young girls who'd given up their babies often married within three to five years. If she was alive, Bob said, he'd find her. Jonathan is quite sure Hutchinson would be able to find her if he gave him his birth certificate and the court documents, but whatever there is to discover, Jonathan wants to know about it before the police.

Out of the corner of his eye, he sees a woman pushing a baby in a buggy. He screws up the empty wrapper and stands as the woman approaches. It's a very old lady, using the ancient pushchair for support. Strands of yellowed grey hair stick out from under her red baseball cap and a pair of cheap-looking earrings blow around the sides of her head like a pawnbroker's sign in a gale. She's wearing brown woollen tights and men's shoes.

'Don't you touch my baby,' she scowls at Jonathan.

The 'baby' is a life-sized plastic doll, dressed in blue leggings and a sunflower-yellow knitted coat with matching mittens. Its sparse nylon hair has been woven into tiny plaits, with coloured beads threaded onto the ends.

'It's all right,' Jonathan says, keeping his voice low, as though soothing a child. 'I'm not going to hurt your baby.'

She looks at him blankly. 'Fuck off and leave me alone,' she says and, oblivious to the downpour, continues her laborious progress along the promenade towards the pier.

As he watches her walk away, he thinks of his mother, and how unforgiving he's been of her often sharp tone and distant manner; and of Gerald, and how he's hated him at times. A memory flickers into his mind, of being in hospital at the age of six after having his tonsils out: there was Gerald, sitting beside the bed, feeding him ice cream and reading him a story. As a child, he'd often wished for different parents; he hopes to God his own child will never do the same. He watches the old lady shuffling along, the hem of her dress hanging below her filthy coat. He'd taken care how he spoke to this fragile person; it probably wouldn't have occurred to him before. From now on, he will keep his voice gentle, no matter what he discovers. As he throws the empty wrapper in the bin, a seagull lands in front of him, fixing him with its eye and screeching at him in outrage. He looks at the huge bird, then his mobile rings and the creature flies away. Malcolm.

'Have you heard from the Fawcett yet?'

'Have I heard . . . ?'

'Obviously not. Mate, I call bearing good news.'

Jonathan smiles. 'That makes a change. What's happened?'

'Ryan Jenkins has admitted it. His father brought him into school this morning – dragged him by his ear, from what I heard – and he stood in front of Linda Fawcett and admitted you never laid a finger on him.'

Jonathan can hear the sea, the shrieking gulls, the traffic noise behind him. 'What? He's actually—'

'Yep! Down to Chloé Nichols, apparently – she confirmed it to Ryan's dad. Who, by the way, turns out to be a decent bloke. Divorced from Mum, had Ryan for the weekend and accidentally read a text Ryan had got from Chloé asking him to own up to "getting Robbo done" – seems she has a conscience after all. Anyway, Dad duly confronts Ryan, and Ryan spills the beans.'

'Bloody hell.'

'Indeed, my friend, indeed. So, that's that. There's probably a message from Linda on your landline. She'll tell you more, obviously, but it's definite. It's all over the school.'

*

On the drive home, he doesn't put the radio on or listen to CDs, he just focuses on the rhythmic sweep of the windscreen wipers and the clattering of rain on the roof.

He should be ecstatic, but instead he feels flattened out, empty.

As Malcolm predicted, there's a message on the landline. Ryan's father has also contacted the police, Linda says, and Ryan and Chloé are both making statements. The school's own investigation will naturally be dropped and Ryan will be excluded for an unspecified period. Jonathan would be welcome back in school the following day or may want to take a further day or two to 'readjust'. Jonathan deletes the message. He wants to ask why Ryan won't be permanently excluded. But that can't happen, can it? Because Ryan has a 'right' to an education, whereas Jonathan is merely a teacher, which means he has no rights. Linda sounded like she expected him to thank her, but if anyone deserves thanks, it's Ryan's father. No matter how badly your child behaves, Jonathan supposes, he's still your child. As he replaces the receiver, the phone rings. It's his solicitor. The police are dropping the case, she tells him, and he might like to know that the CPS threw it out anyway, as she'd predicted.

CHAPTER FORTY-FOUR

Infection. The word sounds so nasty, so dirty. It haunts Maggie's thoughts. When she lies down at night, she sees the letters dancing around, jumbling up and re-forming in her mind. She shakes her head but then starts to hear the word. First it's in the doctor's voice, like a stage whisper, blowing into her ears. Then it's in the sound of the waves, washing over the shingle as she walks on the shore. She hears her mother, scolding her when she was little for picking at a scab: *Don't do that, you'll get an infection.* And then the higher, accented voice of George, the head chef at the Grand after she'd turned up for work once with a cough. *Crazy girl; you crazy come here with zis infection.* Another voice drowns out the others, a rich, booming sound: *I don't want you spreading the infection.* Clive, the director who'd thought she showed promise as an actress. He'd sent her home once because he thought she had ' flu. The voices merge so that all she can glean from the cacophony is that it is her fault her baby is dead, that she as good as killed Elizabeth by allowing her to pick up an infection.

Soon, Maggie cannot escape the word at all. Even when she tries to concentrate on other words, 'infection' is the only one she can see or hear. One day, she picks up a newspaper, but when she looks at it, she finds the word on every page, in every paragraph, in every line; when she turns on the wireless for *Listen with Mother*, instead of the usual nursery rhymes and stories about teddy bears, every song, every rhyme is saturated with infection. If she goes out into the street, the word is on billboards, on road signs, on the sides of buses. She starts to see it even in her dreams, where infection mutates from a proper word made up of black letters and white spaces into a spiky red, crab-like creature that beds down in her belly and then bursts open, disgorging hundreds of tiny replicas of itself. The little red things force their way out through her pores, scurrying from her body in search of new flesh. They approach the cot, swarming over her babies and marking their perfect skin with their long, prong-like fingers . . .

Maggie wakes with a scream dying in her throat.

Jonathan is awake and crying. She moves instinctively to the cot and is about to pick him up when she remembers; she is suddenly quite certain that if she touches Jonathan, those little creatures will get at him, infecting him all over with their red spots. She must not touch him with her bare hands, not under any circumstances.

She hesitates. Jonathan is wailing, fat, shiny tears spilling from his eyes as he holds out his arms. 'No,' she says, shaking her head. 'No, you don't understand.' And then she runs from the room, along the passage and into the kitchen. She pulls open the door of the built-in cupboard, praying that what she needs is there. She moves aside bottles and jars, pulls out a box full of dusters, a spare mop, a polythene bag containing bandages, lint and gauze. Jonathan's cries become more insistent and Maggie's search more frantic, then at last, she sees what she's looking for. First, she scrubs her hands and forearms with the carbolic soap. Then, she runs fresh water into a bowl, adds Dettol (double what it says on the bottle, just to be on the safe side) and stands with her hands completely immersed for two full minutes until she is sure she is clean.

*

After that, as she tells the health visitor, Miss Knowles, she is careful never to touch Jonathan unless she is disinfected. She washes her hands with Dettol, she pours it in her bath and even gargles with it.

Miss Knowles scribbles in her big blue notebook, her busy little head bobbing away as she writes. 'And why do you think you need to gargle with Dettol?'

Maggie doesn't answer immediately; isn't it obvious? Since Elizabeth died, Miss Knowles has been coming here too often, looking around and generally poking her beaky nose in. Maggie doesn't like her; doesn't like her expression, her stupid questions.

'Well?' The health visitor looks over the top of her heavy-framed glasses, a false smile loitering on her face.

'It's so I don't pass on any infection. It might be in my mouth, mightn't it? Then it might escape when I speak.'

Miss Knowles' smile is wearing off now. She tilts her head, looks at Maggie oddly and writes something down.

Maggie follows her eyes as they stray from the grubby lino and stained rug to the nappies drying over the chair backs and the saucer doubling as an ashtray on the arm of the settee. Maggie knows the room is in a bit of a mess, but she's more concerned with keeping herself clean for when she has to touch Jonathan. After all, she is the source.

'I can smell it,' Miss Knowles says.

'What?' Maggie jumps up from her chair and looks around. 'What can you smell?' She thought she could smell the infection herself this morning, but then she realised she didn't know exactly what it smelled like.

'Dettol. It's ever so strong. Doesn't it get on your nerves?'

Maggie sighs and shakes her head. 'Of course not.' Leonard's mentioned the Dettol smell; he doesn't like it, but he's hardly ever here these days, so why should she worry? If he's not at work he's with his new girlfriend, Sheila, at her bedsit in Bexhill. Maggie has asked Leonard not to bring Sheila to the house; Sheila didn't have measles when she was a child and so she could have it now, couldn't she? And she could pass it on to Jonathan. Dr Cranfield says not; he says Jonathan will be immune for life, but Maggie knows he's lying just to pacify her. And anyway, there's always the risk of some other infection. That was what killed Elizabeth; a *secondary infection*. The words are loud in her head, as though someone is shouting them.

'Well.' Miss Knowles stands up. 'I'll pop back and see you again quite soon.'

'Why?'

The woman smiles her fake smile. 'Why? What a funny question! I like to keep an eye on all my ladies, especially when they've been through . . .' She looks uncomfortable. 'Especially when they've . . . er . . .' She stuffs her notebook and papers into her bag, a cross between a doctor's bag and an ordinary handbag. 'Ladies, families who've . . .'

Maggie catches a glimpse of the other notes in the bag, names and addresses of other people this woman has visited; other families, other children who are ill, dozens and dozens of nasty, germ-riddled people. The words in her head get louder still, several voices shouting: *Infection; secondary infection.* They are so loud that she cannot hear what the woman is saying any more, she can only see her mouth moving, her lips, opening and closing, and suddenly she knows what the voices are trying to tell her: this woman is not a health visitor at all; she is dangerous, and she must be stopped. Maggie hesitates for a moment, but then she knows the voices are right because now she can see those little red infection creatures coming out of the woman's mouth. There are hundreds of them, pouring out in a torrent, scurrying all over the floor and up the curtains and across the ceiling. She looks around for something to swat them with; she must do something, because Jonathan is asleep in the room along the passageway, and the woman is walking towards the door, her whole body a heaving, crawling mass of infection.

CHAPTER FORTY-FIVE

Jonathan has been back at school for over a week, but each time he walks into the building, he feels more and more alien. It's not the kids – some of them seem genuinely pleased to see him, and his form gave him a 'welcome back' card, which they'd all signed and which touched him more than he cared to admit. Chloé Nichols had even written him a letter of thanks and apology. But despite these things, he is becoming increasingly plagued by the sense that things are just . . . wrong.

'How about what I was saying before? About going part-time?' Fiona says as they eat. She's home from hospital now, but she's only allowed out of bed to go to the loo so he's set up a small table next to the bed so they can eat together. 'We could each do three days. I'm sick of us both being knackered.'

'It's not just the hours, though. It's . . . I don't know; I don't *feel* like a teacher any more. I'm not sure I ever really have.'

Neither of them speaks for a moment. 'Hey,' he says, noticing her expression. 'Ignore me; I'm just feeling a bit hard done by. I've been suspended and arrested, we've both been through hell because of it and what happens to Ryan Jenkins? A ten-day exclusion! He'll be back on Monday.' He hasn't told Fiona, but today he came dangerously close to just walking out. Not only has he grown up with the wrong parents and the wrong name, he'd stumbled into the wrong career for the wrong reasons.

Fiona puts her hand on his arm. 'I know; it pisses me off too. But it's over now. And compared to . . .' she points to the bump '. . . how much does it really matter?'

He nods. 'Yes, you're right.' He leans towards her, picks up her hand and holds it to his lips. 'God, I was scared.'

'Me too.' She leans into him so their foreheads are touching. 'If I'd lost this baby . . .'

The idea of losing the baby is awful; horrible. But at one point, he thought he might lose Fiona, and that . . . well, that just didn't . . . he closes his eyes, kisses her hand. 'I'm sorry I've been so crap,' he says. 'Things are going to change from now on, I swear.' His voice catches and he doesn't trust himself to say any more.

'Hey.' She slips her other hand into his and squeezes it. 'It's been a tough time; we've had a lot to cope with. Let's take this as a new beginning. For a start,' she lightens her voice, 'we've still got to get through the next few months with me lounging around on my fat arse while you do all the work.'

He smiles. 'Your arse isn't fat.'

'It will be if you keep cooking stuff like this,' she says, nodding towards her plate. He'd poached the chicken breasts in white wine and stock so they stayed moist and tender, and served them with a creamy peppercorn and brandy sauce, new potatoes and green beans. 'Come on, it's getting cold.' She picks up her cutlery and starts eating again. 'Work-wise,' she says, 'what if you could do anything you wanted? And don't say a milkman or a train driver.'

'I don't know. Social work crossed my mind, but . . .' He thinks for a moment. 'Do you know what, if money wasn't an issue, I think I'd go back to cheffing. Not the fourteen-hour shift stuff I did before, but just being in a kitchen again, doing something people appreciate.'

She nods, running her thumb around the rim of the plate to scoop up the last of the sauce. 'Well, you haven't lost your touch.'

'It's badly paid, though. Not a problem if you're young and mortgage-free, I suppose.' He takes a mouthful of wine and smiles as he remembers his time in the kitchen: pans flying through the air when the head chef threw a wobbly; the heat; the shouting and swearing on some nights, the intense silent concentration on others. And then afterwards when the customers had gone, upstairs in the restaurant, exhausted but finally relaxing with cold beers and steak sandwiches while they shared out the tips and praised each other for a good night's work. 'I loved it – much to my father's dismay.' Gerald had been furious when Jonathan decided to train, even when he said it wasn't something he planned to do for life. It was wasting his degree, in Gerald's opinion. But Jonathan found a strange synergy in the way he thought about literature and the way he felt about food. When you studied literature, you looked at how the author put certain characters together, created dialogue between them, sketched out the fictional place they inhabited. And then you searched for the layers of meaning in the text, noticed how those layers were built up to produce just the right balance, the right texture for the story. As a chef, you had to blend the ingredients, putting together flavours that worked with each other, just the right amounts of each so that the overall dish had depth and complexity, was exciting on the palate and stayed in the memory long after the last mouthful had been savoured.

Fiona sucks the last of the sauce from her thumb. 'If we won the lottery, you could open your own restaurant.'

'We don't do the lottery.'

'Ah – a flaw in the plan! Seriously, though, what about doing dinner parties for the rich and lazy?'

'Wouldn't make enough money, not at first anyway. Oh, I don't know; maybe one day.' He stands up and begins to clear the plates. 'Let's not worry about it now.' He kisses her on the head.

'Okay,' she smiles. 'And we've got plenty to be cheerful about – the baby's fine, I'm fine, and you've still got a job, despite almost ending up doing time for being drunk and disorderly.'

He looks at her. It was bound to come out at some point anyway, so he decides to risk it. 'There's something else I haven't told you about that night.'

Her expression changes. 'Oh?'

He finishes clearing the table, picks up the tray and walks to the door. 'The reason I ended up in the cells . . .' He opens the door with one hand, ready for a quick getaway – there are books and other missiles within her reach '. . . was that I was so drunk I pissed on the police-station steps and my zip got stuck so I couldn't put my cock away and that's when I passed out.' He slips through the door and then peeps back round it. 'It was stupid and embarrassing and I'm really, really sorry.'

But she's laughing; hallelujah, she's really, really laughing.

*

He's painting the ceiling in the nursery when the call comes.

'Jonathan,' Bob says. 'Is this a good time to talk?'

'Yes, fine,' Jonathan says, assuming Bob just has another question.

'I've managed to locate her. Told you it could be quick! Do you want the details now or shall I call you in a day or two when it's had a chance to sink in?'

Jonathan's legs go suddenly weak and he can hear a buzzing sound. He holds the phone away from him so Bob won't hear how shallow his breathing has become. 'No,' he says eventually. 'No, it's fine. Just hang on a sec, would you?' He moves a paint-covered rag, the radio and his coffee cup off the old bentwood chair and sits down.

Outside, the sky has darkened and there's a smatter of rain on the window.

'Sorry, Bob. Go on.'

'Right you are. Birth mum was born in 1940. She's called Margaret Kielty now – married in 1968.'

Jonathan tries to speak, but only makes a dry, half-formed sound. He clears his throat. 'Where does she—'

'She lives in Hastings.'

Jonathan lets out a breath. That day a couple of weeks ago when he walked around the Old Town and up onto the east cliff, he might have walked past her; all those times he'd been there as a child, loving the place, feeling at home; she might have been *there*.

'Jonathan?'

Pictures flash through his mind: what she might look like, what sort of life she has. Kielty; Margaret Kielty. 'Bob, you say she got married; did she have any more children?'

'Nope. I checked right back to the date you were adopted.'

Bob speaks as though that's good news, but ever since his mum told him about the baby who'd died, Jonathan has been thinking about what it would be like to have a sibling. When he'd discovered he was adopted, he'd felt doubly cheated; he'd been given a brother, albeit one who'd died, and then had him snatched away again.

'I think it's best if I make the first approach,' Bob says. 'If you're in agreement, I'll write a careful letter – she may not have told her husband about you – to see if she's amenable to further contact. We can take it from there.'

CHAPTER FORTY-SIX

Hastings, February 2009

Maggie stands at the top of the steps, getting wetter and wetter. She should go back inside. Sam'll wonder what on earth she's doing. She puts the letter back in her pocket. She wants to tell Sam, but not yet. She needs to think about it a little more first. When she goes back down the steep steps, he's standing at the door. 'Och, hen. Look at you! You're wet through. Come on in, now; ye'll catch your death.' Sam's face is creased with concern. His hair is almost white now, but still thick and strong. There are loose threads hanging from the hem of his navy bathrobe. She'd better mend that before it comes down completely. It's a detail she'll remember; part of the picture of this day. When big things happen in Maggie's life, they don't sit around at the back of her mind, fading with the years like an old painting; they come back, stronger than before, shimmering into her memory and settling there, the colours and smells deepening, the shapes and sounds becoming more defined.

'I . . . I need to go for a walk,' she says.

He smiles. 'Aye, but do ye no think it's a wee bit wet to be walking out in your dressing gown?' She manages to laugh, but she really does need to go outside again soon because she recognises the warning signs. Everything she looks at seems huge and vivid, then her vision goes black around the edges and her breathing comes too fast. She dresses quickly in the first things that come to hand – the old skirt she wears for gardening, a sweater of Sam's, the raincoat she bought from the charity shop just last week. She transfers the letter from the pocket of her dressing gown to that of her raincoat, then heads off, up the steep steps and into the wet morning. She turns right onto the coast road and walks briskly past the fish market and the old net huts and along towards the pier.

Maggie was never a heavy woman, but there's even less of her now, and she has trouble keeping her footing in this wind. She can hear the waves thudding against the sea wall, and see the seawater spraying high into the air and crashing down onto the road with a heavy splat. Her hand is in her pocket, her fingers curled around the letter that she has both dreamt of and dreaded. The wind gusts hard at her again, taking her back through the years and across the miles to that night in February 1962.

The wind rages through the city, tearing down trees and branches, ripping slates from roofs and flinging them to the ground. There are bangs and crashes, glass breaking, a dog barking in the distance. Jack kisses her harder, and she can feel the back of her head pressing against the cold stone wall.

She tries to draw away, but his hand is on her breast, rubbing and squeezing. She yelps in pain and tries to twist out of his reach but he pulls her back. 'Oh, no you don't,' he says. 'Not this time.' He kisses her again, slamming her head against the wall. His tongue jabs into her mouth and she can feel his teeth against hers. He pushes his hand down the front of her dress, yanking at the neck. For an absurd moment, all she can think about is that he'll ruin the neckline. Then her breast is exposed and she feels a blast of cold air before his mouth clamps over her nipple, biting so hard she cries out.

'No,' she shouts, trying to push him away. But this time, she cannot move him. His knee is wedged between her legs and he is leaning his whole weight against her, pinning her against the wall.

'Jack,' she says, more quietly. But he is fumbling with his belt. She freezes. His hand flies up her dress, his nails scratch her thigh as he tugs at her pants. There is a hollow clattering as a dustbin rolls past, a crash as yet another tile hits the ground.

She can hear her mother's voice: 'Knee 'em in the balls, love. That's what you do if you're in trouble. Knee 'em where it hurts.'

With all the effort she can muster, she pushes against his shoulders and brings her knee up as sharply as she can.

'Oh, spitfire, are we?' He grabs her knee and twists her off-balance. She flings out her arms to steady herself and he grabs them, holds her wrists together and pulls up her dress with the other hand.

'Fucking little prick-teaser,' he snarls. 'You're all the fucking same.'

She is crying now. 'I'm sorry,' she says. 'Please don't . . .'

His nails scrape her groin as he wrenches her underwear aside, then there is a hot, sharp pain. The shock makes her gasp. She thinks about screaming but knows no one would hear, not with the noise of the wind and the houses falling apart around her.

'No, please.'

He jabs into her again, and again the back of her head hits the wall. She cries out. He slaps her on the side of the head and pain flushes behind her eyes. 'Shut up, you little bitch.'

Just as Maggie thinks she cannot bear this for another moment, something happens: she realises she can no longer feel what's going on. From where she is hovering a few feet above the ground, she watches herself being pummelled, shaken around like a rabbit in the jaws of a slavering dog. She can see a sticky dark patch of blood spoiling her lovely hair, trickling down her forehead and into her eye, and she can see the back of Jack's head. She considers this calmly, and comes to the conclusion that she must have died, which is a shame, because she was only twenty-one and she really did have plans. But it is over, and that is that.

*

The crash of a wave breaking over the sea wall brings her back to the present. She realises she's crossed the busy coast road without even noticing. She stops by a bench on the promenade, clenches and unclenches her fists, moves her toes, shakes her head and coughs to try out her voice. Good; she can feel everything, which means she's properly back.

Tucking her head down against the gale, she carries on towards the disused pier, where she ducks under the padlocked chains and makes her way past the little art galleries, cafés and bohemian gift shops – *Covent Garden by the sea*, they'd said the last time it re-opened. Now it was closed again, everything boarded up. It was always a false hope, this pier, and building a few pretty shops on top couldn't change what was underneath. The very fabric of the thing was rotting; the waves had torn off great sections of the metal supports and hurled them out to sea; barnacles clung to the salt-softened wood and the whole thing was in danger of imminent collapse. Through the gaps in the boards she can see dark, meaty waves, chopping and rocking beneath. It's inevitable, she thinks; if the sea is determined to destroy this great foreign body that has waded uninvited into its waters, then it will. What if it were to collapse now, with her on it? She's used to her life flashing before her, although these days it's only when something snags on her memory and rips back through the years, like now.

Down on the beach huge seagulls, strangely vulnerable with their feathers fluffed up by the wind, pick along the strandline for scraps. Behind them, up on the coast road, the tail end of the rush-hour traffic pushes slowly through the rain. Maggie holds on to the metal rail and looks down into the slaty sea, unsure whether the water on her face is rain or spray from the waves below. With the cold reddening the skin on the backs of her hands, she stands on tiptoe and leans right over, so she can see nothing but the waves bashing against the pier's rusty underskirts. Rivulets of icy water run down her neck and she can feel loose flakes of paint under her fingers. There is something inviting about deep water, she thinks; a certainty that beneath the thrashing surface there is a soothing silence, a velvet-blue calm, there for the taking.

Then she thinks of Sam, and of what he lost all those years ago. She forces herself upright again, unfolds the letter and watches it flap in the wind. If she lets go now it'll be whipped up into the air, then tossed down into the ocean where salt water will eat the print away. But even if she throws it out to sea, even if it is torn from her hand and carried off by a shrieking seagull, the words will still exist; the *fact* remains.

CHAPTER FORTY-SEVEN

Jonathan expected it to be weeks before he heard from Bob again, but he calls back within days. Margaret Kielty is willing to meet, he says. How about next Saturday?

On Friday night, he buys fish and chips but he can't eat; his stomach feels hollowed out and he keeps going hot and cold, as if he has a fever. The kitchen is silent apart from the humming of the fridge. Next door's cat, who's been curled up on top of the tumble drier, now stretches luxuriously and, sensing fishy leftovers, jumps down and begins winding itself around his legs, its loud, rasping purr filling the room. Jonathan scrapes the remains of his skate into a dish and sets it down on the floor, then watches as the animal eats greedily, still purring, its metal name-tag clinking against the plate. With its yellow-green eyes and fat, bottle-brush tail, it reminds Jonathan of the cat he'd had as a child, *Johnny*. He'd chosen the name himself, and he smiles now at his six-year-old narcissism. A flimsy memory slides into his mind, of Gerald coming into his bedroom to tell him that Johnny had been run over. When Jonathan had started to cry, Gerald sat down on his bed and put his arms around him. He remembers the warm, bony feel of his father's chest, the hard shirt buttons and the combined smells of starch and pipe tobacco. He's forgotten so much about Gerald. And about Daphne, come to that. In fact, his entire history has tilted; he needs to go back, not just over the last few weeks, but over his whole life, crossing bits out and putting bits in; revising. But he can only revise the life he's ended up with, not the one he started with; the one with which he is about to come face-to-face. A chill blows over him. What will she be like? What will she tell him about the man who provided the other 50 per cent of his DNA?

He lies in bed, watching the changing numbers on the digital clock, each luminous new hour mocking his attempts to sleep. She is 'willing' to meet him; does that suggest she'd be pleased to, or only that she's prepared to? He even looked it up: *inclined or favourably disposed; done or given without reluctance*. Through the gap in the curtains, he can watch the night sky, but there's not a star to be seen. Instead he focuses on a building in the distance, a high-rise block with a few windows still lit. He watches the lights go out, one by one.

*

It's five past ten when he arrives in Hastings, almost an hour early. The sun is struggling to peek through the clouds, but the day is chilly. He'll probably only be here for a few hours, but he dropped Fiona off at Lucy's on the way because he didn't want her getting out of bed to get drinks or snacks. Lucy made up the sofa for her in the living room and the two of them were going to spend the day watching DVDs. He finds a café and sits in the window with his coffee, watching the Saturday shoppers and trying to pretend it's a normal day. He's bought a *Guardian* but he doesn't open it.

At twenty to eleven, he walks down to the seafront. For a moment, he's tempted to run across the road and jump down the steps onto the beach so he can crunch along the shingle, pretending he's here for a day out. He carries on along the front, glancing at the map as if he doesn't know it off by heart. A few yards further and he turns the corner into her road, then counts along the house numbers. He calls Fiona. 'I'm here. I'm outside.'

'Good. Well, good luck, then.' She sounds so quiet, so far away. 'Call me as soon as . . . well, just call me, okay?'

'Will do. Speak to you later then. And Fi . . .'

'Yes?'

'I love you.' She's the only one, the only thing in his whole life that is *right*.

'I love you, too, Jonno.'

He turns towards the tall, white-painted house, part of a once-beautiful Regency terrace but now rather forlorn with its flaking paint and chipped windowsills. They all look weathered and tatty; he's heard that seaside houses need painting more often because of the salt. He can see the concrete steps down to the basement flat behind a row of black iron railings. He runs his hand along them like a child, then starts to walk down the steps. There's a plant pot outside the front door, a small tree of some sort. A gardening glove lies on the ground next to it. Heavy sage-green curtains are drawn to the sides of the large bay window, and he risks a quick look through the glass. An old-fashioned lamp with a fringed shade stands on a square dining table in the centre of the bay; beneath the lamp is a folded newspaper with a pair of steel-framed glasses resting on top. As he nears the door, a sensor light comes on, making him feel suddenly exposed. There's a movement to his left; he glances at the window and catches a glimpse of her hand as the curtain falls back into place.

CHAPTER FORTY-EIGHT

She's not how he'd pictured her, this woman who bore him. She looks younger, for a start, and taller – he's used to looking at the top of Fiona's head, so it's quite a shock to find that his birth mother is almost as tall as he is. Her face is softer than he imagined. What *had* he imagined? Her hair must be quite long because she's pinned it up in a bun, although bits have escaped and are hanging down all over the place. Fiona will want to know what she looks like, so he takes note of these details. For a woman in her sixties, he'll say, she's quite attractive but not very well groomed. Unlike Daphne, she wears neither make-up nor jewellery, apart from a plain wedding ring, and her clothes seem slightly old-fashioned and mismatched.

When he first arrived, almost two hours ago, she could barely meet his eye. He'd taken it for guilt, but now he's heard her story, it is he who has lowered his eyes. He feels slightly sick; it's all buffeting around in his head now, all clashing and clanging together, making sounds he can't bear to hear and pictures he can't bear to see. Part of him wants to run, to fling open the door of this stuffy flat, to bound up the steps into the sharp seaside air and then sprint down towards the sea, where the tide comes in and goes out and does what it's supposed to do, according to nature, on and on, for ever.

He takes a breath and looks at her. 'I'm so sorry,' he says.

She presses her hand to her forehead. 'Excuse me for a moment,' she says. 'I've such a headache . . . I must take something . . .' She gets to her feet and walks to the door. She carries herself well, he thinks, almost elegantly, but at odds with her clothes.

While she's gone, he casts his gaze around the room. It's shabby but comfortable, with patchwork cushions on the sofa and rag rugs on the floor. A radiator under the window blasts out heat. On the mantelpiece are several cacti and a dusty spider plant with its babies hanging over the side like little umbrellas. There's an empty pill bottle, a key with a paper tag and a name scrawled in pencil, and an old mantel clock with a couple of post-cards and a thank-you card tucked behind it. The shelving in one alcove is filled with books: hardbacks on garden-ing and cookery, and paperbacks including the Brontës, several Kahlil Gibrans and a fair collection of what Fiona calls Sunday afternoon books – Catherine Cookson, Maeve Binchy, Rosamunde Pilcher. He's about to look at what might be a photograph album when he hears her coming back.

*

Maggie pauses with her hand on the doorknob before she goes back in. Her head is pounding, and the paracetamol she's just taken feels like it's stuck in her throat. She can actually see her fingers trembling. She pushes the door open and there he is: Jonathan, her son. She's so glad they kept his name. She can hardly believe he's here in the same room, breathing the same air. But there is one more thing she needs to tell him, and then he will leave, she is certain. She settles in her chair and takes a sip of orange squash to moisten her lips before she continues: 'By the time it all came back to me in the hospital, I'd been remembering little snippets for quite a while,' she says, 'but none of it made sense until the night of the social.' She pauses, looks down at her hands. 'It didn't all come back at once – some of it never did, in fact. But when I sat up in bed that night, I'd remembered about Elizabeth, and I'd remembered attacking that poor health visitor. But that was it. It was only later that I . . .' How can she put this into words? She takes another sip of the sweet, artificial drink '. . . that I remembered what had happened . . . what I'd tried . . .' She can hear her own breaths coming too fast. Oh, why won't her head stop hurting? She's really struggling now, but she must tell him the truth; she owes him that much. 'It was a while before it came back to me what, God forgive me, what I almost did to you.'

She glances at him; he's waiting for her to carry on. He has kind eyes, but she can see the anxiety in them, even without her glasses on. She's grateful for this brief time with him, for the way he has sat here listening with barely an interruption. How proud his . . . his other mother must be of him. She hesitates, desperate to prolong this moment. Why hadn't she asked more when he first arrived? She wants to know all about him, all about his wife and his life and the future he hopes for. But she has no right. She draws a deep breath and prepares herself. When she tells him the rest, he will go and she will not blame him.

*

With the aid of the cut-glass fruit bowl, Maggie has managed to knock the infection woman to the floor, but those little creatures are swarming all over the place, scuttling, multiplying into a huge mass which surges along the hallway in a red tide towards Jonathan's room. She leaps over the groaning woman and reaches the bedroom in two bounds. Hoisting her crying child onto her hip, she heads for the front door. The shock and suddenness of it all seems to stun Jonathan into silence, and Maggie is aware of his startled expression as she begins to run through the cold streets. As they near the beach, he starts to whimper again. He is shivering; so is she. She hugs him tighter and tells him to shush, shush, Mummy's going to keep you safe. She strokes his damp hair, notices the salty smell from his scalp and the heat from his soft cheek as he lays it against her own. Despite the coolness of the day, his forehead is burning. Fear rips through her. He has a fever; she has failed to protect him. She starts to unzip his little sleepsuit, but then she has a better idea. Wrapping her arms around him again, she hurries down the stone steps onto the shingle. She is still wearing the thin leather pumps she keeps for indoors and she can feel the hard stones through the soles as she crunches down to the water's edge. She pauses only for a second, then takes a step forward. The lacy surf froths over her foot, sending a chill through her whole body. Another step and the cold water floods right up over her shoes, slicing at her ankles. A noise makes her look round; a figure is coming down the beach towards her, that woman, a red mass, boiling with infection. Maggie wades further out, the water chopping at her thighs. Then a dark wave swells in front of her and she feels the icy water rise up in a shock over her shoulders. Her whole body rocks sideways and the seabed disappears from beneath her, leaving her flailing in the water, one arm desperately clutching her child as the current tries to tug him away. Briefly, she sees the sky before the water closes over her face, sending an acid pain zinging up her nose. The shouts from the beach become distant and muffled; she twists round to try and gain her footing and her elbow touches the ocean floor as she stumbles, gripping Jonathan more tightly. But then she feels him start to slip and the next minute, he is gone. Half-choking on the briny water, she flings her arms around, frantically searching for his solid little body. But all she finds are fronds of seaweed that brush against her face and hands. She kicks and twists in panic, and her knees scrape against the shingle. Just as she thinks her lungs will burst, her head breaks the surface and she is coughing and gulping the dry air.

*

Sitting there in her living room over forty years later, Maggie is unable to subdue the strange half-gasp that bursts from her throat, as though she is fighting for air once more. Now she is starting to shiver. 'They took you to hospital, but apart from being cold and shocked, you weren't hurt.' She glances at him, but he's looking down so she can't see his eyes. 'After that, I could hardly argue I was a fit parent, could I? I was committed – sectioned, they call it now – that night. They thought at first that I'd deliberately tried to kill you.' He lifts his head now and looks right at her, but this time she can't bear to face him and she looks away. 'Whatever they thought, it didn't really make any difference, because I wasn't in my right mind, not by any means. And if that poor young woman hadn't followed me to the beach, well . . .' A familiar wave of horror sweeps over her at the thought of what could have happened. 'They said it was a miracle she managed to pull you out safely, especially with her head still bleeding from where I'd hit her. So you see . . .' She glances at him but looks away again immediately; she can't get the words out while he's looking at her. 'The thing is, I *could* have killed you.' She leans back with a sigh. There.

She has told him. She can hear the clock mechanism, which means it needs a new battery. It's slow, but she doesn't know how slow, because time doesn't seem relevant just now. Her son is hunched forward in his chair, hands resting on his knees, staring at a patch of carpet between his feet. His hands are nice; smooth, long fingers but not too thin. The sort of hands you'd feel safe holding if you were a child walking along a wall. A floorboard creaks in the next room as Sam moves across the floor. She pictures him hesitating as he wonders whether to come in and offer some tea or a sandwich. Not now, Sam, she says silently, hoping he'll hear. Jonathan is nodding slowly. He leans back, blows air through puffed cheeks and looks at her again. 'I think I need some fresh air,' he says.

Maggie nods dumbly. Is he disgusted with her? Does he hate her?

'A walk round the block or something; just for ten or fifteen minutes. Then I'll be back. If that's all right?'

She lets her breath out in a rush. 'Yes, yes of course.' She is weak with relief.

*

Jonathan's first instinct is to phone Fiona, but then he changes his mind and puts his phone back in his pocket. He needs to think about this on his own. He walks briskly down to the seafront, craving the salty air on his face. As he walks, he becomes conscious of the movement of his limbs beneath his clothes; he can feel the denim of his jeans moving against his legs rather than with them, as though his body is out of sync with what's around it. The wind coming off the sea isn't strong today, and yet he wants to cower from it. The pebbles are cold and damp, but he drops down onto them anyway, drawing up his legs and trying to make himself small while he allows himself to cry at last; for himself, for his mother – for both his mothers – and for his poor dead sister. Again, he's been given a sibling, and again she's been torn away. After a moment, he lifts his head and dries his eyes. Elizabeth; Mimbet. They'd played together, shared a cot until she died. His sister, the one person who'd have been like him, whose blood was the same as his blood. He can see her clearly in his mind . . . but no, he couldn't possibly remember her. And yet . . . he struggles to marshal his thoughts . . . and yet she did live; she did know him. Somehow, he feels her as a real and present connection. But then his thoughts darken as that other connection rolls in like a storm cloud.

He gets to his feet and walks down the beach until he reaches the water's edge. The tide is coming in, and he stands there for a moment, watching the rhythmic push and pull of the waves, just as he had when he was a boy. He and Alan Harper used to spend ages building dams, trying to hold back the tide, but all they could do was divert its course for a few seconds before the next powerful wave swept away their carefully constructed barrier.

Hands in pockets, he walks along the newly washed shingle and forces himself to think about his actual father:

a rapist. He breaks his step, almost as if the word has knocked him off balance. He's often wondered about people's capability for violence: *a man has broken into your house and is holding a knife to your wife's throat – you have a gun; what do you do? Or, your child is dying and the medicine that will save him costs £200 – you have no money but your neighbour does. What do you do?*

But rape? A few feet ahead, two gulls are squawking over the bloody remains of a fish. They fly off as he approaches and he kicks the fish head hard into the water. He hopes the man is dead.

It is only when he sees the pier looming ahead that he realises how far he's walked. He pauses to text Fiona: *All OK. Might be a while. U OK?* The reply comes back almost immediately: *Fine. Watching Sleepless in Seattle. Creamy pasta for lunch. Don't worry. XX*

He looks at the words. Normality.

As he heads back along the beach, a quote pops into his mind from some seventies feminist: *all men are rapists.* Do most women think that? What must his mother have felt when she first looked at him, her male child? Did she see a small replica of the man who had done that to her? He quickens his step, wondering what might have been in her subconscious when she'd walked into the sea with him.

She opens the door when he is halfway down the steps to her flat. She must have been looking out for him, he thinks as he follows her into the sitting room, and she's attempted to tidy her hair. He hangs his jacket on the back of the chair and sits down. The door opens and her husband comes in with a large tray, which he sets down on the table.

Maggie looks flustered. 'Sam ... this is my ... er, Jonathan, this is ...' She doesn't quite manage to introduce them, but Sam extends his hand and smiles.

He looks nervous, Jonathan thinks as he shakes Sam's hand; the poor man has obviously been hiding in the kitchen, probably instructed to keep out of the way until now. On the tray are two mugs, milk, buttered toast, blackcurrant jam, a slab of cheese on a board surrounded by oatcakes and another plate bearing slices of date and walnut cake. 'This looks great,' Jonathan says.

'Och, I forgot the tea.' Sam turns and heads back to the kitchen, returning seconds later with the teapot, which he carefully sets down on the table before disappearing again.

Jonathan has little appetite, but their hospitality wraps around him like a warm blanket on a cold day. A vision of tea with his parents passes through his mind. A sterile, silent affair, weak tea, cheese sandwiches, plain biscuits, never cake.

'Thank you,' he says, taking a slice of cake and noticing that it's home-made. It'll give him time to think about how to ask her; he has to know what she sees when she looks at him.

CHAPTER FORTY-NINE

Maggie sips her tea and watches her son eat the cake she made in honour of his visit.

'So,' he's saying, 'what happened after they took me to hospital?'

For a moment, she'd forgotten he was here to discover his history, not just to sit and drink tea. 'You were only in overnight, I think. Then my brother, Leonard, and his wife Sheila – she wasn't his wife then, of course – they took you home with them.'

He's looking at her keenly again.

'I haven't seen him for some years. They went to Australia not long after I came out of hospital. We . . . we didn't get on so well after my illness.' She decides not to tell him how forcefully Leonard and Sheila had persuaded her to sign the adoption papers, even though she'd probably have signed them anyway, what with Dr Carver, Dr Cranfield, the social worker, all of them telling her it was for the best. And she knew they were right. What sort of life could she have given him? Especially when she was in and out of hospital so many times before she learned to cope with life again.

'It was mainly Sheila, I think. She didn't want to be associated with me. There was a terrible stigma to mental illness back then. You'd have thought you could catch it by being in the same room. At least these days people are more . . .' But then she thinks of the clients at the unit where she and Sam worked until their retirement last year: Claire, a young mother who, after telling a neighbour where she'd been for the last few weeks, came home to find the word 'nutter' sprayed across her front door; young Dan, bullied into leaving his job then taunted by local kids until he ended up being admitted again. She sighs. 'Well, it's mostly better now, anyway.'

'Do you have any contact with him? Leonard?'

'We write, but we have different lives now.' She thinks about Leonard for a moment, wonders how happy he really is. 'They looked after you for a few weeks, Leonard and Sheila. The hospital wouldn't let me see you – Carver said it would be upsetting for us both.' She can feel tears beginning to gather, so she takes a tissue from the box next to her chair and presses it quickly to her eyes when he's not looking. 'Then two social workers came. They'd found a couple who wanted to take you straight away, and who could give you a happy family life.' She thinks she sees a shadow flit across his face at this point. Has he had a happy life? Oh, please let him have had a happy life. He's looking at her intently now. 'Go on,' he says.

'They said that even when I got better, I wouldn't be able to give you the sort of life this couple could. I knew they were right, of course, so I signed the papers.' She pauses, trying to retrieve that particular memory, but it's one that's always been elusive. 'I didn't remember any of this until much later, and I'm still not sure I remember actually signing the papers, or just the social workers telling me about it.'

She stops speaking and silence rushes in to fill the space. All she can remember clearly is feeling frustrated that nothing would stick long enough for her to think it through, and the nagging feeling that there was something she needed to do and she had thirteen weeks in which to do it. Had she asked the staff? Had they told her? *It's your baby, Maggie. You've got thirteen weeks to decide whether you're sure about giving him away.* Perhaps they had, and she'd just forgotten again. Or perhaps they'd told her not to worry, to give her brain a rest and stop trying to think too much.

Her son gets to his feet. Is this it, then? Is he leaving now? But he walks over to the window and looks out onto the railings and the pavement beyond, where all you can see is people's legs as they pass. His hair is darker than when he was a baby, almost brown now, but with flashes of gold where the light catches it. He is tall, like her, and his back is broad, like her own father's was before he became shrunken with illness. She can see the tension in Jonathan's shoulder blades. I am the cause of that, she thinks.

He turns back to face her and she drops her gaze.

*

Jonathan looks across the room at his mother. It seems odd to think of her as that: his mother. She looks pale, diminished; and she's pulled the tissue she's been holding to bits, making a heap of snow around her chair. He should go; let her rest. But first he must ask her. He has to know.

'What would have happened if my sister hadn't died?' He can hear the edge in his voice.

'Sorry? I'm not sure what you mean.'

'I mean, you had a breakdown because Elizabeth died, and I was adopted as a result. But if she'd lived, if you hadn't had the breakdown – would you have kept me?'

She turns her head slightly to the side and he wonders if she heard him properly, but then she nods.

'I'd have done my level best. As soon as you were born I knew I wanted to keep you, but it was harder than I'd thought, and they were right about me not being able to cope. It sounds silly, but I didn't realise I wouldn't be able to control everything. I thought all I had to do was feed you, change you and put you to bed. But I missed the fact that the minute you were born, you became real, live, independent beings; you were miniature people. Which meant things could happen that I couldn't control, like illness.' She pauses. 'Sorry, Jonathan, I'm going off the point.' It sounds odd when she uses his name, even though it was she who chose it. 'What I'm trying to say is, I wasn't a . . . a good mother.'

He nods. Should he just leave it at that? But he knows he hasn't made himself clear. By 'you' she means both of them; she thinks he's simply asking whether she'd considered having them both adopted. He clears his throat. 'And if it had been me who died . . .' He runs his hand through his hair; his scalp feels hot, slightly feverish. '. . . would you have kept Elizabeth?'

His words imprint on the air; he can hear them coming to definition as they hang there. He waits for her to answer.

'No, Jonathan,' she says eventually. 'I was ill. I loved you very much; both of you.' She reaches down for another tissue and immediately starts to pull it apart. 'I'm not sure I always showed it enough, but I did, I really did.'

'But what about . . .' He knows he's pushing it, but it's like worrying at a spot and he can't leave it now. 'What about my . . . the man who . . . you know; Jack?'

The name seems to paralyse her. He can see it's hurting her, but he carries on, relentless. He must know. 'It must have crossed your mind that, well, having a son . . .'

For a moment she looks as though she's going to say something, but she doesn't.

'I mean, I wouldn't blame you,' he continues. 'No one would, but you must have thought . . .' He's gabbling now. Stop, he tells himself. Shut up and let her answer.

Slowly, slowly she shakes her head, so slowly that he wonders if she's ever going to speak. 'Sometimes,' she says eventually, in a voice gone small and thin, 'sometimes, before I had you, I used to imagine a tiny baby with Jack's face. But the moment you were born it was so clear. How could I have looked at you, two of the sweetest angels God ever sent to this Earth, and connected you with . . . with that man?' She lets out a deep sigh. 'No, from the second I laid eyes on you, I never felt you were anything to do with him – not in any way that mattered. You and your sister, you were so different; so *new*. That was one of the things that shocked me – I never expected you to be quite so individual.' She looks up at him with a faint smile. 'You'll find that yourself, you know, when your baby comes.'

At the mention of the baby, Jonathan becomes aware of a sudden lightness, a casting off of some of the tension that has been almost choking him. He can feel his shoulders starting to relax. A silence opens up between them, and he allows himself to float on it for a while.

After a few moments, she clears her throat. 'Would you like some more tea?'

He can hear the worn-out clock making that strangulated sound before it ticks, as though straining to move its hands. It is a few seconds before he says yes, please, he would like some more tea.

*

Maggie feels shaky and a little light-headed as she pushes the kitchen door open. Sam is at the table reading the paper, but he stands up and comes to her immediately. As he hugs her, she can feel the tension starting to leave her body. She can hear Jonathan's voice as he talks to his wife on the phone. *I'll be a bit longer*, he's saying. *No, I'm okay; everything's okay.*

'You're doing fine, hen.' Sam kisses the top of her head. 'Just fine.'

'Sam,' she whispers, grabbing his hand. 'Should I tell him to bring her round, when she's up and about again?'

Sam shakes his head. 'You'll no' want to pressure the lad. Maybe, if . . .' He pauses, then sighs. 'Maggie, you've got to think about the possibility that . . . well . . .'

'That what?'

'Och, I don't know how to say this, but you need to be prepared for—'

'What, for heaven's sake?'

'Your boy – he might no' want to come again.'

She freezes. He's right, of course; Jonathan is only here to find out who he is. This may be the only time she sees him. She sighs and leans briefly against Sam's warm chest. In one way, she'd been dreading this meeting, but now she doesn't want it to end. It is difficult to think of how life will continue after this; how is she going to get through tomorrow, and the next day, and the next?

When she takes the tray back into the sitting room, Jonathan is looking at the cluster of photographs on the wall. 'Who's this?' He points to the school photo.

She puts the tray down, picks up her glasses and goes to stand next to him. 'Sam's sister's children – Kate and David.'

'And this?'

'That's Kate again, grown up, and that's her husband.'

He nods. 'And this one?'

'Ellie, our old next-door neighbour.' Then she realises what he's looking for, and she points to an old black and white photo in a silver frame. 'This one's of my parents – your grandparents.' Should she have said that? 'They're very young there. She was twenty, he wasn't much older.'

He lifts the picture down from the wall and studies it for a long time. 'Did you look like her?' he says. 'When you were younger?' He doesn't take his eyes from the picture.

'A bit, I think. And people said I looked like my father too. Here's one of Leonard and me just before our mother died. It's a bit blurred of me, but you can see Leonard.'

Is she imagining the similarities between Jonathan's features and her own? When he smiles, his lip seems to go up slightly at one corner, just like hers. She watches him hang the picture back in its place and carefully straighten it. Then he points to the tiny colour photo in the cracked clip-frame that she keeps meaning to replace. 'Who's this?'

'Oh, that's just me in some silly play.'

'You went back to the theatre?'

'Not properly. I'm involved with a local amateur theatre group, that's all. I still take the odd part but it's mainly stage managing – making props, like I did when I was younger.'

'I'm in an am-dram group too!' He's smiling as he turns towards her, and she cherishes this detail; this real connection.

'Do you have any other photographs I could look at? Of the family, I mean?'

Another hour passes as they go through the pictures, and when Jonathan says he needs to call his wife again, she can't resist it. 'I'd love to meet her as soon as she's up and about. You could bring her round for tea or . . . or for dinner.'

It's kind of her, he says, but Fiona's on bed rest until the baby's born, so they're not really making plans just yet.

Maggie could kick herself.

After another half-hour, he says he should be going. There is one photograph he's put aside, she notices. It is the one of him and Elizabeth, bundled up like little Michelin men and propped against the snowman she and Leonard made in the front garden. The twins weren't much more than four months old, but it was one of the few occasions when Elizabeth wasn't ill.

He picks up the photograph. 'Would you mind if I kept this one?'

She's tempted to say he can borrow it, because then he'd have to bring it back. 'Of course you can,' she says. 'I have others; you should have a picture of your sister.'

He stands to leave. 'Oh, I almost forgot.' He reaches into his jacket pocket, pulls out a piece of velvet and unwraps it to reveal seven little stones, all with a single hole through the middle. 'Do you have any idea why I have these?'

She stares at the stones; a voice is telling her that this is impossible, but there they are, the stones her own mother carefully gathered over sixty years ago. She resists the impulse to reach out and touch them. 'Wait,' she says. 'I need to check something.' She hurries along the hall into her bedroom, pulls out a small box from her wardrobe and takes off the lid. Sure enough, there are her seven stones, wrapped in faded black velvet, just like Jonathan's. As she stands there, acutely aware of her son waiting in the other room for an explanation, she is transported back to a rainy autumn day in 1947, her seventh birthday. She was snuggled on the settee in front of the fire, replete with fishpaste sandwiches, jam tarts and birthday cake, when her mother handed her the hard, knobbly parcel. She'd known what it contained; she'd wanted her own stones ever since Leonard had received his on his seventh birthday two years before.

Now, over sixty years later, Maggie feels a wave of grief wash over her, both for her long-dead mother, and for the closeness she once shared with her brother. For a moment, the desire to see Leonard again grips her so tightly she can barely breathe. She picks up her stones one by one, traces the smooth surface with her fingers, then wraps them up again and takes them through to show her son.

'It's an old Hastings myth,' she tells him. 'If you take seven single-holed stones from Hastings beach, no matter where you go in the world after that, you're destined to live in Hastings again before you die. My mother gave them to each of us on our seventh birthdays; Leonard must have given his to you.'

Jonathan looks at the two sets of stones, then rewraps his own set carefully, almost tenderly, she thinks.

'I . . . I'm glad,' he says, his voice unsteady. 'I'll keep them.'

She follows him to the door, where he shakes Sam's hand and then turns towards her. She looks at her son, standing at her front door, almost filling the frame, and she fixes the picture in her mind so that she can remember it properly later.

'Thank you,' he says. 'It's a lot to take in, and I'm not sure . . . well, I just don't know how to feel at the moment.'

There is an awkward moment when she wonders whether she too should shake his hand. He appears equally ill at ease, but then he leans forward and kisses her cheek so fleetingly that she wonders whether she imagined it. He's looking at her; she doesn't know what to say.

'One more thing,' he says. 'That man, Jack; do I look like him?'

'No,' she lies. 'Not a bit.'

As the door closes behind him, she feels tears prick her eyes. She collapses into Sam's arms like a puppet with its strings cut. 'Will he forgive me, do you think?'

'Och, shush.' He strokes her hair. 'There's no' anything to forgive. You were sick; a distraught, grieving mother. Your boy can see that, for certain.'

Maggie holds onto Sam and they stand there in the hallway for several minutes. She is so wrung out that she is half-expecting one of her episodes, but despite a sharpening of sound and colour, her breathing remains steady and her mind stays in the here and now.

'Do you think I'll ever see him again?' she asks Sam without looking up.

He kisses her forehead. 'I don't know, hen.'

CHAPTER FIFTY

Before going home, Jonathan walks down to the water's edge and stands there looking out to sea. Several minutes pass, or perhaps it's hours, he really can't tell, but by the time he becomes aware once more of the hiss and pull of the waves on the shingle, the sky has darkened and bloated rain clouds are gathering on the horizon.

*

He picks Fiona up from Lucy's, and of course she wants to know everything. Where does he start? 'Well,' he says. 'She's not hard or heartless. In fact, she's had a pretty tough time.'

Fiona nods. 'What's the story?'

'It seems I'm the result of . . .' Again the word threatens to knock him sideways. 'It turns out that . . . that she was raped.'

Fiona's hand flies up to her mouth. 'Jonno, my God!'

Then he tells her the rest, and she listens without inter-rupting, then shakes her head slowly. 'The poor woman,' she says. She looks again at the photograph of the two babies in the snow, runs her finger over it. 'So this is your sister.'

Jonathan nods. 'My twin.' He too looks at the picture for a long time.

Later, when he goes downstairs to make something to eat – Fiona fancies salty eggs and buttered toast – he notices the 'messages' button on the phone is flashing. He dials 1571: two new messages, both from his mother. She wants him to call back, but he can't face her questions now; he'll call first thing tomorrow.

'Are you going to see her again, do you think?' Fiona stifles a yawn.

'No. Maybe. Oh, I don't know.' There's a pause. 'Fi,' he says. 'I'm not sure I've done the right thing.'

'What do you mean?'

'I told her about Hutchinson, that he's looking for him – for Jack. And I gave her his number.'

Fiona props herself up on her elbow and looks at him. 'What did she say?'

'She didn't. She just looked at the piece of paper, then put it behind her clock.'

'She wasn't upset?'

He shakes his head. 'I don't think so. But was it, I don't know, *appropriate*? Considering she didn't report it at the time?'

'I don't know, but all you've done is given her the number; it's her choice now.'

'I suppose so.' He leans back on the pillow, exhausted suddenly. He tries not to think about what happened to his mother. Instead, he thinks about his lost sister, pictures her toothy smile and pudgy arms. In his imagination, she's sitting on the beach, watching the waves. He walks across the pebbles and lifts her into his arms. Now he imagines his own baby, not yet born but already loved more than he knew was possible. The baby reaches out, and as he gathers its soft little body to him, he has the sensation of stepping back into himself.

He doesn't realise at first that he's been asleep, so it takes him a moment to register that the telephone's ringing. It feels like the middle of the night, and as he hurries downstairs, he's aware of his heart thudding.

'Hello?'

'Darling, it's your mother. I—'

'Mum, what is it? What's wrong?' But as he says it, he sees that it's not as late as he thought. Not yet ten, in fact.

'Nothing's wrong, dear. Rather the reverse, in fact. Anyway, how did it go today?'

His heartbeat is slowing now. 'Fine. Well, it was . . . it went fine. It's a long story but I'll tell you all about it tomorrow.'

'Oh, I *am* glad,' she says. 'I really am, Jonathan. You know that, don't you?'

'Yes, Mum. I do know. And thanks.' He is about to say goodnight when she continues, 'Anyway, your father's solicitors telephoned yesterday. It'll take a while, of course, to get probate and so forth, but it appears your father did rather well with some of his investments. When everything's sorted out, you should receive just over forty thousand pounds.'

'What? Sorry, wha—'

'I knew you'd be surprised. I didn't mention it before because I know a lot of shares have fallen and I wasn't sure how much would be left after everything's sorted out, but as I say, Mr Windgrove rang and—'

'Sorry, Mum, I'm not quite clear. Did you say—'

'Forty thousand! Or just over. Anyway, enough for you to—'

'Hang on. Surely, I mean, doesn't it all just go to you?'

'Oh, yes, the house, the pensions, bonds and so on. But this money was specifically meant for you; he arranged it last year, just after he became ill. And Jonathan,' her voice softens, 'I think this will please you: he stipulates that you should spend the money exactly as you like.'

Again he has the strange sensation of being acutely aware of his body; he can feel his clothes – an old t-shirt and boxers – against his skin, and he can feel the air circulating around the bits that aren't covered. He's still trying to process what he's learned about his birth mother, and now Gerald ... He shivers, even though the house is warm. More revisions.

'I'll see you tomorrow, darling,' his mother says, and after a moment, there is a gentle click as she hangs up.

As he climbs the stairs again, he feels as though he can

see himself from the outside, as though he's watching the movement of every joint, the flexing and contracting of every muscle and tendon. After months of feeling 'not himself', he is now conscious of being intensely, thoroughly, and absolutely himself; more himself than he has ever been in his entire life.

*

It is well past eight when a finger of early spring sunshine slides through the curtains and wakes him. His first thought is of Gerald. Fiona was deeply asleep when he came back upstairs last night, so she doesn't know yet; he can hardly take it in himself. He turns over to look at her. She's awake and sitting up already, her shirt open to reveal her beautifully rounded belly.

'Look,' she says. 'You can see it moving.'

For half a minute or so, he stares in vain at the taut flesh. Then he sees it, a tiny hand or foot, travelling from one side to the other like a little shooting star.

CHAPTER FIFTY-ONE

Hastings, June 2009

Maggie picks up the wad of stuff that's just plopped through the letterbox and takes it into the kitchen. There's the usual collection of pizza leaflets and junk mail, a couple of bills and a postcard. 'Look.' She hands the postcard to Sam. 'From Don Hutchinson, thanking me for seeing him. What a nice thought. I'm not sure I was any help, though.'

'Och, come on. Why doubt what the fella says? What you told him tied in with what the other women said. It confirmed where that bastard was and when, so it backed up the information they already had.'

'I suppose so. But it's too late to really do any good, isn't it?' She's not sure she'll ever forgive herself for not telling the police at the time. If she had, maybe Jack wouldn't have raped those other women.

Sam puts his arms around her. 'Mr Hutchinson said it's never too late. And it means those women will know that the man who raped them is no' around any more.

You did well, hen; I'm proud of you. It's thanks to you that they're sure it was the same man.'

She sighs. 'I suppose so.'

Mr Hutchinson said they'd made the original link through Jack's brother after he was arrested with some other pensioners on a council-tax protest. His DNA showed a close match with what they had on record from the other women – the ones who'd been brave enough to report it. It turns out Jack killed himself in 1987 – stepped in front of a train after his dog was run over, apparently. He'd had a long history of depression, the brother said. Maggie is glad Jack is dead, but a little sorry that it was suicide, even after what he did to her. She has often said she wouldn't wish depression on her worst enemy, and it seems this is true, given that Jack surely must be her worst enemy. The brother was a perfectly respectable old gentleman, according to Don Hutchinson. Did he know about Jack, Maggie wondered? About what he was, what he did to women? But then she pushed those thoughts back with the memories she'd rather lose among the cobwebs.

She is about to throw the junk mail into the recycling box when a small silvery envelope slips out. It's addressed to *Maggie and Sam Kielty*. When she opens it, she feels as though a dozen fish are flipping and floundering in her stomach. She hardly dares breathe as she takes out the satiny white card. There is a single, miniature blue foot-print on the front. She opens the card and reads the silver lettering inside:

Jonathan and Fiona Robson
are delighted to announce the arrival of
George Edward
Born 4 May at 4.23 am
6lb 3oz

And written by hand underneath:

*George arrived three weeks early, which was a bit frightening,
but he and Fiona are absolutely fine now. They are home from
hospital and ready to receive visitors. I'd like very much for
you to meet them, and also George's other grandma. Please
bring Sam, too. They say George looks like me (poor little
thing!) but what do you think? He is six hours old here.*
    Jonathan

Maggie's eyes fill with tears so fast that she has to blink
several times before her vision clears. She looks inside
the envelope again, and pulls out the photograph of a
perfect newborn child, with navy blue eyes and a thatch
of golden hair.

ACKNOWLEDGEMENTS

My profound gratitude to my editor Clare Hey for her expertise and insightful feedback, especially the 'light-bulb moment', and to my agent Kate Shaw for her advice and guidance, and for her inspired suggestion regarding the structure of Maggie's story. I'd also like to thank Susan Opie, whose eye for detail helped polish the manuscript to a sheen, and everyone at Simon and Schuster for their cheerful enthusiasm and belief in this book.

I owe a great deal to the friends and fellow writers who read sections or whole drafts of the manuscript and offered constructive criticism, encouragement and moral support, not to mention coffee, cake and wine. In particular: Sue Cooper, Rachel Genn, Iona Gunning, Sue Hughes, Neil Reed, Ruby Speechley and Russell Thomas. And a very special thank you to Jane Rogers, whose generous feedback, advice and encouragement kept me going when the going got tough.

In an attempt to get my facts straight, I picked the brains of many generous and knowledgeable people on matters of DNA and police 'cold case' procedure. My thanks go to Dave Drabble, Dr Christopher Ford, K.A.C. Sara Longford, John Milne and many others. For medical advice on 'the bloody scene', my thanks to Dr Rebecca Davenport. Any remaining errors in these matters are entirely my own.

My research around Maggie's time in the mental hospital led me to a great deal of fascinating reading, but the book I returned to again was the invaluable *The Female Malady: women, madness and English culture 1830–1980*, by Elaine Showalter.

I am of course deeply grateful to my family for their continued belief in me, and especially to my daughter Emma and my son James, who I think are almost as proud of me as I am of them. But the greatest debt of all is to my husband Francis, for the laughter, the conversation, the ideas and the stories; for having more confidence in me than I had myself, and for his unwavering love and support.